BLACK HILLS

BLACK HILLS

FRANKLIN SCHNEIDER
& JENNIFER SCHNEIDER

THOMAS & MERCER

Text copyright © 2016 by Franklin Schneider
All rights reserved.

Published by Thomas & Mercer, Seattle

www.apub.com

Amazon, the Amazon logo, and Thomas & Mercer are trademarks of Amazon.com, Inc., or its affiliates.

ISBN-13: 9781503939318
ISBN-10: 1503939316

Cover design by Christian Fuenfhausen

Printed in the United States of America

CHAPTER 1

There were only a few taxicabs in the fracking town of Whitehurst, South Dakota, so Alice spent an hour watching eighteen-wheelers and dump trucks drive nose to tail in both directions of the two-lane highway, doing eighty in the moonless night. When her cabbie finally arrived, she hauled her bags into the trunk over his protestations, and they sped off toward town, not so much joining the traffic as being swept along in it. Alice thought that if they tried to slow down, they'd simply be pushed along by the truck behind them.

She sat with her head resting against the window. The vibrations from the pitted highway spread through her face and head, rendering them pleasantly numb. They were following a dump truck overfilled with sand, and grit rained down on the car, making a noise like crackling oil. Alice looked out at the rocky plains. Ironic that a place so barren had turned out to be worth, what, billions? Trillions, probably, when everything was tallied up. Ten years ago you could've had the whole state for the price of a three-bedroom townhouse. There was a lesson there about something. Progress, or relative value, or maybe something else entirely. Maybe something about surfaces, about things not always being what they seemed.

"Is the traffic always like this?" Alice said, leaning forward over the bench seat.

The cabbie nodded. "All day, every day. Even Christmas. Money never sleeps."

"Money never sleeps," she murmured. It was an expression she'd heard before, usually used admiringly, the sort of thing you saw on T-shirts. To her it seemed vampiric, further confirmation that they'd all soon be bought and sold.

Alice had researched downtown Whitehurst online, and the low brick buildings and wire-strung streetlights were just as they'd been pictured on the town's website. What the website hadn't shown were the all-male crowds, the trash, the potholes. Just another oil boomtown: ninety-nine percent men and one percent sex and retail workers. The cabbie caught her grimace in the mirror. "Welcome to Whitehurst," he said.

They turned down a narrow access road paralleling the highway, bumping over the fractured pavement toward a strip of motels with flickering neon signs. Alice leaned forward again. "Hey, when do visiting hours at the jail start?"

"Tomorrow morning. Ten, I think." The cabbie appraised her in the mirror. "You a cop?"

"Private investigator."

"Ex-cop?"

Alice laughed. "Ex-reporter. Different set of skills."

"You got one of these?" He held up a .38. "South Dakota's an open carry state. I suggest you get one tomorrow. This is an ugly town."

"I wouldn't even know how to shoot it," Alice said.

"You won't have to. Just keep it clipped to your belt where everyone can see it. No one messes with someone packing. A young woman like yourself, pretty, in this town, walking around alone, no man, no gun, well . . . that draws attention. A sort of attention you don't want."

"Thanks for the advice," Alice said, but she knew he was right. She styled herself to deflect the male gaze, with self-administered bangs, lack of makeup, and neutral clothing; in the city, men looked right past her, but here in a flyover state, she stuck out like a sore, androgynous thumb. She sat back. "Listen, you must know a lot of people."

The cabbie looked at her in the mirror for a long moment. "What kind of people?"

"Interesting people. People who know things."

"You sure you ain't a cop?"

"I'm not a cop."

"Because it sounds like you settin' me up for a bust."

"A bust? What kind of bust?"

"We got a little drug problem here in Whitehurst. Dust. You might have heard."

"No. I'm not interested in that. Have you heard anything about a working girl getting her head bashed in by a geologist, a guy who works for a fracking company?"

"You *sure* you ain't a cop?"

"I told you, I'm a PI. The geologist's wife hired me to come up here and help clear his name. He says he's innocent."

"Yeah, they all say they're innocent, though, don't they? No, I ain't heard nothing about that. Lotta bad things happen here nowadays. I can barely keep up. Don't even try anymore."

He pulled into the parking lot of the Bobcat Motel, an L-shaped roadhouse, each room opening directly onto the gravel parking lot. The neon "No Vacancy" sign was lit against the night, illuminating a faded mural of a shrieking wildcat that reminded Alice of a high school mascot. The front lot was full of trucks; in the rear she saw rows of close-set RVs.

She took out her wallet and handed the driver a twenty. "No change," she said. "I appreciate all your help. And your advice."

The driver nodded. "You go on in. I'll wait here."

"Why?"

"You're not getting a room in this place. Ever since the boom, vacancy rate is zero. This place is booked up months in advance. I knew you wouldn't take my word for it. When you come back out, I'll take you to a boarding house I know of where you can get a room."

Alice brought a room key out of her wallet and held it up for him to see. The cabbie's eyebrows climbed up his forehead.

"Well," he said. "Normally I'd offer to help you with your bags, but . . ."

She gave him a smile and then went to the back of the car and dragged her luggage out. As she rolled the suitcases down the walkway, looking at the room numbers, she was seized with a sudden conviction that the cabbie had rolled down his window and was aiming the pistol at her. She turned and looked, but he was only scribbling on a clipboard propped against the steering wheel.

That morning, Alice had been standing at her kitchen sink, lost in thought, looking at the Manhattan skyline across the river. After building up her practice for eight years, she could finally afford to move there, but now she wasn't sure she wanted to. The only thing more unsettling than the size of her bank balance, and the financial projections for her firm, was how unsatisfying it had all turned out to be. She'd thought that success would feel more, well, successful, but she was beginning to realize that it was just like failure, except with more money.

When the buzzer sounded, she'd jolted, spilling hot coffee on her hand. No one ever visited her out here in Greenpoint, certainly not unannounced. She went to the intercom and pushed the "Speak" button. "Yes?"

"Alice, it's Rachel Wilcox."

Alice froze, her finger still pressing the button. "Alice doesn't live here anymore," she said, pitching her voice low. "She moved out."

"Jesus, Alice, I can tell it's you. Buzz me in."

Alice hesitated. If she didn't buzz Rachel in, she could probably get in when someone left the building, or by pressing all the buzzers at once. Even then, Alice could just stand, safe and silent, behind her locked door until Rachel left. She seriously considered it. But in the end, she pressed the "Door" button, as she'd known she would all along.

Alice left her door cracked slightly and sat at her small breakfast bar. There was a time when she would've done anything for her former boss—not out of an abundance of affection but out of a hard-won respect. They'd been two women in a male-dominated industry; their initial friendship of necessity had, over time, become genuine and, at least until Rachel had gotten married, even profound. Hadn't it? Alice found she couldn't quite remember. As with most failed relationships, she'd blocked out the details. She didn't believe in the tyranny of one's history.

The door swung open, and there stood a woman who bore a slight resemblance to the Rachel that Alice remembered. It could've been Rachel's mother, or aunt. In her arms was a dark-haired toddler blinking placidly.

"Do I look that bad?" Rachel said. "You should see your face."

Alice forced herself to smile. "It's been so long."

She busied herself warming up coffee.

Glancing back at Rachel, she saw her looking around the apartment with an expression of intermingled alarm and disgust. That was how her face must have looked when Rachel made her entrance. She tried to see the apartment through Rachel's eyes: retro futuristic abstract paintings from chain hotel rooms, midcentury vintage furniture of outlandish ugliness, a counter full of mismatched coffee mugs, each with a half inch of red wine in the bottom. Without the lens of irony, it probably looked tacky and cheap. This was exactly why she didn't see clients at her apartment. And Rachel was a client, she was suddenly sure of that. Alice set the coffee down in front of her guest and sat. "So what do you need?"

Rachel, still clutching the toddler to her chest, gave her a bemused look, not without admiration. "It's nice to see you too."

"Is it?"

"It's not as bad as I thought it would be. I was afraid I'd come here and be humiliated by how wildly successful you'd become." All the old resentments and tensions that had defined their personal and professional relationship came surging back.

"Married with kids in Connecticut by the age of thirty-five isn't everyone's idea of success. In fact, to some people, it's the very definition of failure."

Rachel flattened her lips into a compressed line that said she didn't believe it for one second. "Okay. Look. Here's the thing—"

"You can't pay me. You're broke," Alice said.

Rachel jolted, and Alice surged with pride at breaking her smug facade. "How did you—"

"I do this for a living. This isn't a social call, because we're no longer friends. You didn't go to my office, because that's a place of business, and if you can't pay, it's not business, it's a favor. So you come to my home. Unannounced, to catch me off guard. You bring your kid along, wave him in my face to get sympathy."

"Now wait—"

Alice held up one finger. She was relishing this reversal from how it had been before, with Rachel in charge telling Alice how things were. "You're married, but you're here alone. That means it's something to do with your husband. Robert, that's his name, right? I only met him once or twice. My guess is, you broke into his e-mail, or his phone, and found something you don't like. Let me give you some free advice. If you think something's going on, something is definitely going on.

Just dump him. I'm not going to trail him across five boroughs, for no money, just so I can snap a picture of him palming some receptionist's ass, to give you the closure you need to act on something you already know in your gut is true." Alice stood. "My time's not worthless. It's not valuable, exactly, but it's not worthless either."

"Oh, Alice," Rachel said, almost in a whisper. "It's so much worse than that." Then her face crumpled, and she burst into tears.

By the time Rachel had pulled the motel room key from the diaper bag, Alice had agreed to everything. Not that she was a soft touch—she'd heard enough permutations of the hard-luck story in her eight years as a private investigator to know that they were all the same, and all lies. But seeing her former friend so wrecked, so desperate, had gotten under her skin. She would've agreed to anything just to make the tears stop, to get her out of the apartment. The sight of a strong woman brought so low suggested that it was possible for her own life to fall apart at any moment, a fear she spent a lot of time and energy suppressing.

From the look of his motel room, Robert hadn't been doing so well either. His room at the Bobcat was a diorama of middle-aged male haplessness. Dirty laundry was piled against the wall, and every surface was covered with almost-empty beers and moldering Styrofoam takeout containers, the floor carpeted with newspapers and magazines. Alice turned on all the lights, left the door open, and began sorting the garbage from evidence. The windowsill was crowded with cigarette butts and a few soot-blackened glass pipes; next to it a folding chair faced the lot. She picked up one of the butts and held it to the light; the filter was smeared a pinkish red. Lipstick.

Intermingled with the bedsheets were several pairs of women's underwear, neon colored and leopard print, and in the bottom of the closet, she found a pair of four-inch nude stilettos. She held one of them up between finger and thumb, trying to imagine who would wear them. Certainly not Rachel, who she knew had never visited anyway. In the bathroom, the sink was crowded with makeup bottles, and the wastebasket was filled with condom wrappers torn in half. Alice sighed. She'd planned on calling Rachel as soon as she got settled to give her a progress report, but she wouldn't even know where to start.

She sat on the bed, leaning back against the headboard, and thought about the handful of times she'd met Robert. He'd seemed innocuous, but then it was always the most aggressively normal who were hiding something dark.

Her memories of Robert were of a devoted but cringing man with a perpetual openmouthed grin, desperate to be liked but unaware that it was this desperation that made him unlikable. She'd known many people like this, and she knew that they had a reservoir of hurt and anger inside them that deepened as the acceptance they wanted from life receded farther and farther out of their grasp. They eventually became either bitter or hugely self-pitying, which is to say they became unpredictable. Alice had hoped, back when Rachel and Robert got married, that Rachel's love would mend whatever was wrong with him, but she knew now that this had been a naive hope.

Alice got up from the bed and continued cleaning. Underneath all the clutter was a room that belonged in a museum of midcentury Americana. Wood paneling, patterned wallpaper, avocado-colored furniture, taxidermied antlers above the bed. Alice found it weirdly comforting. The room was basically her Brooklyn apartment minus the irony.

She took her phone out; it had been buzzing every ten minutes or so with escalating texts from Rachel: there yet? what's up? tracked your flight # i know youre there. Alice held down the "Power" button on the phone until the screen went dark, then crawled into the cleanest corner of the bed and fell asleep. What was one more white lie at this point?

Alice's eyes opened in the early, gray light, and for a moment she had no idea what had awakened her. Then the noise registered. A rattling, a rumbling, coming from everywhere at once. She sat up in bed. Empty minibottles and beer cans were dancing off the edge of the bedside table, landing on the carpet with cushioned thuds. Her bags tipped over onto their sides. In the closet, Robert's clothes were swaying on their hangers, and from somewhere came a muffled crash of glass. Then it hit her.

She jumped up, fumbled with the door chain, and braced herself in the door frame. Alice had grown up in the Midwest; she'd never experienced an earthquake before. It felt like a violation—of natural law and personal security and reason.

Outside, the other occupants of the Bobcat Motel were milling in the parking lot. No one seemed very concerned. They all fell silent when Alice appeared, and she saw at a glance that she was the only woman there. Holding up one hand against the morning sun, she gave them a mollifying smile, hating herself as she did it. The tremors had already subsided. After a long moment, the men turned back to their conversations, though she saw more than a few of them watching her out of the corners of their eyes.

A portly Latino sat on a cooler next to the door to her room. He was peeling an orange and regarding her with amusement.

"First quake?" he asked.

Alice nodded. Her stomach was beginning to cramp from the aftereffects of the adrenaline. "I just got into town last night."

"Get used to it," he said. He offered her a slice of orange. She felt it would be rude to decline, so she took it. It tasted like tap water, neither sweet nor sour.

"I didn't know they had quakes up here."

"They don't, normally. The way they get the oil out is by injecting fluid into the ground, squeezing it out. Lotta pressure builds up. It's gotta go somewhere. Someday the whole town's just gonna cave in on itself. All because of greed."

Alice nodded. "Well, let's hope I get paid before that happens," she said.

The man laughed. "You and me both," he said.

He offered Alice another orange slice. She ate it, looking off past the highway to a row of bobbing oil derricks on the horizon. They looked like hammers pounding nails into the world's coffin.

CHAPTER 2

An hour later, Alice was walking along the highway's gravel shoulder, head down, hands in pockets. The first truck that had sped past sent her sprawling into a drift of urine-filled water bottles and soggy cigarette butts. Now she walked several feet away from the road, bracing herself as each caravan passed.

She'd called for a cab, but the dispatcher had told her it would be an hour at least, and she hadn't felt like waiting. A quick Internet search had revealed that there was a pawn shop only a mile away. Every couple of minutes, one of the trucks that passed blew its horn at her, the pitch rising and then falling as it sped on, a reminder that everything was relative. As if she needed reminded of that.

The pawn shop was in a strip mall, between a western wear outlet and a small Chinese buffet. Alice stopped and brushed herself off before going in, visible puffs of dust rising from her clothes as she did so. Inside, fluorescent lights glared harshly off glass cases of jewelry and guns. Sad displays of guitars, amps, juicers, and wedding gowns adorned the walls. A clerk sat behind the register, feet up, reading a newspaper. When he saw Alice, he blinked several times and then stood.

"What can I do you for?"

"I'm looking to buy a gun," she said.

"Who for?"

"For me."

"Well," the clerk said. Several seconds passed as he considered this. "I've got these in the cases, and then all those on the wall there."

Alice walked to the first display case. Lying in rows from small to large were tiny .22 derringers, snub-nosed .38 calibers, blocky .45s, comically large Magnums, and, finally, a Desert Eagle that was prominently tagged as "Israeli Manufactured." Several of the larger handguns were adorned with chrome or gold plating or had customized handgrips that had been airbrushed with likenesses of Elvis Presley, Al Pacino as Tony Montana, or Clint Eastwood as Dirty Harry. On the wall hung several racks of shotguns and rifles; near the ceiling was an oiled AK-47 with a gleaming walnut stock.

"I like to travel light," she said and tapped her finger on the glass. "How about that one?"

The clerk unlocked the case and brought up the gun Alice had pointed to. It was a single-shot .22 derringer with a pearl handle, more like a novelty lighter than an actual firearm.

"It'll fit right in your purse," he said. He brought out a milk crate filled with tiny holsters and laid out two, one made of pink leatherette, the other embroidered with flowers. "Cute," he said approvingly.

"You know," Alice said, moving back to the far end of the display case and pointing, "I think I'll take this one instead."

The clerk grimaced and brought out the .357 that had been customized with the Tony Montana handgrips. "You sure?" he asked, handing it over to her.

She gripped it in both hands and raised it to shoulder height. Its weight made her sag. "Yep."

As the clerk ran her credit card, she looked at the wall of paper practice targets. Aside from the classic generic outline and the fifties-style hoodlum, there were targets printed with headshots of Osama bin Laden, Barack Obama, and Bill and Hillary Clinton. Just over the clerk's shoulder was a target printed with a photo of a bespectacled, turtlenecked man with a gray pompadour.

"Who's that?" Alice asked.

The clerk glanced over his shoulder. "That's the head man," he said. "Steve Whitehurst. He owns pretty much the whole town. All the fracking operations are run by the Whitehurst Corporation. His family founded this town after the Indian Wars."

"You sell a lot of those targets?"

The clerk nodded. "It's our biggest seller."

Alice walked back to the motel with the Magnum in a huge leather underarm holster. She thought it would discourage the truckers from blowing their horns at her, but it drew so many salutes that halfway home she stopped, wrapped it in her jacket, and carried it over her shoulder the rest of the way.

It was midday when Alice arrived back at the motel, the sun's heat softened by a shroud of pollution. She was about to unlock her room when she heard a noise from within. She pressed her ear to the door and tried the knob; it turned easily. Alice unwrapped her gun from her jacket and unholstered it.

Pausing outside the door, she held her gun down next to her leg and took a deep breath. She was no good at this part of being a PI—the rough-and-tumble stuff. She was more of a paper-trail PI. She'd bought a box of bullets but had no idea how to, or desire to, load the gun. Besides, the reason she'd gone with the biggest gun there—really, the only reason she'd bought a gun at all—was for its deterrent value. You'd have to be insane to rush someone who was holding a hand cannon like this.

Turning the doorknob, she slowly pushed inward, raising the gun with the other hand. On the bed was a massive naked man, the white of his untanned haunches almost blinding, having sex with a woman who was hidden under his bulk. Alice cocked the hammer on the Magnum. It sounded just like it did in the movies, and it was very loud in the closed room. The man on the bed looked back over his shoulder at her.

"What?" he said. He didn't sound all that concerned.

"Get up," Alice said.

"I'm almost finished."

"I said, get up."

The man rose up on his arms and climbed off the bed. His stomach hung down enormously, and he was wearing a bright-green condom. Alice tried to keep her eyes up. On the bed lay an angular woman, dark hair, dark eyes, pink mouth. She'd pulled her denim skirt up to her waist, and she still had her flip-flops on. She lay there glaring at Alice.

"What are you doing here?" Alice asked.

"I live here," the woman said.

"Bullshit," said Alice. She shook her room key in her free hand. "This is my room."

The woman leaned over and picked up an identical key from the bedside table and shook it mockingly. "You sure about that?"

"Toss it over here."

The woman threw the key underhand across the room. Alice picked it up and held it alongside hers; it matched. "Who are you?" she said.

"I'm Bobby's girl," said the woman. She shimmied her skirt down over her hips. "Who the fuck are you?"

The fat man, who'd been following this exchange like a spectator at a tennis match, suddenly gathered his clothes and boots, grabbed a sheaf of twenties from the table, and headed toward the door. Alice tracked him with the gun.

"Leave the money," she said.

"I didn't finish!"

"Put it back."

The man pursed his lips at her but did as he was told. Just inside the door, he stripped off the condom, threw it on the carpet, pulled on his pants, and left. The woman on the bed took out a toothpick-thin Capri and lit it.

"Put that out," Alice said.

"Shoot me," the woman said, directing a jet of smoke out of the corner of her mouth. She took another drag and tapped ash onto the carpet. "You ain't Bobby's type. You a uptight bitch. But you sure ain't a cop. You ain't got that command presence, you know?"

"I'm a private investigator," Alice said. She lowered the gun and, after a moment, set it on the windowsill. "His wife hired me to come up here and establish his innocence."

The woman on the bed laughed bitterly. "Shit."

"What's that mean?" Alice said. The woman shrugged, a gesture not of ignorance but of denial. Alice had to fight the urge to raise the pistol again. "How do I know that you didn't just bribe the clerk for that key after you found out that the guy who lived here was in jail?"

The woman on the bed brought out an iPhone and swiped across it a few times before passing it over. On the screen was a blurry picture of the woman and Robert reclined on a bed. They were both naked.

"Swipe right," the woman said.

Alice did so, and the next picture in the sequence came up, depicting Robert with his face between the woman's thighs.

Alice tossed the phone back. "What would Robert say if I told him you were turning tricks in his motel room?"

The woman shook her head and made a show of ashing on the bed. "He inside. He know I gotta make a living some way. You don't know Bobby very well, do you?"

"The last time I saw him was five or six years ago. At his wedding," Alice said.

The woman nodded, savoring this small victory. Alice forced herself into a professional neutrality and extended her hand. "I'm Alice."

The woman just looked at her hand. "You gonna kick me out?"

"Well, the room's not in my name, so I don't think I could do that," Alice said. "Even if I wanted to."

"True. I'm Kim," she said. She lit another Capri off the butt of the one she'd finished and kicked off her shoes. "Course, you could always just throw my ass out at gunpoint." She massaged the balls of her feet with both thumbs. "But then I'd come back at night and spray gas under the door and throw a match in. Burn your white ass to death."

Alice fought an urge to roll her eyes. She picked up a dirty coffee mug from the windowsill and passed it to Kim. "Now that that's established, could you ash in this instead of on the duvet?"

Kim took the mug and lay back against the headboard. "So Bobby's wife is payin' you? He said she broke, can't even get him a lawyer."

Alice nodded. "We're old friends, so I gave her a deal."

"How much she know 'bout all this?"

"All she knows is what Robert told her on the phone. He's in jail, accused of beating up some girl who's now in a coma. Looking at prison time. He swore that he's innocent. Is he?"

Kim shrugged. "Yeah. But that don't really matter in this town."

"What makes you say that?"

"This used to be a nothing town, and now it's turned all the way up, all the time. Most of the cops are too scared to even get out the car. They just wanna close cases. Don't matter if they actually get the right guy, as long as they get somebody. A cop I used to fuck, he told me that they figure even if you didn't do the crime they're chargin' you with, you probably did somethin' else they charged another innocent person with, so it all kind of evens out in the end."

"Yeah, but they must have something on Robert," Alice said. "They didn't just snatch him off the street at random."

Kim tilted her head to one side in a curiously birdlike gesture, showed Alice an ebullient smile, and extended one hand, palm up. It took Alice a moment to realize what the gesture meant.

"I'm letting you stay here!" Alice protested.

"It ain't your room, bitch," Kim said. "You said so yourself." She waggled her fingers. Alice took her wallet out and withdrew two twenties and handed them over. Kim folded them in half twice and tucked them into her purse. Then she sat back and lit another cigarette. She seemed to have an infallible sense of when she had the slightest advantage. "What you wanna know?"

"Robert," Alice said. "What do they have on Robert?"

"He was the last one seen with the girl who got bashed. She got off work that night round nine, got into his truck in the parking lot. Next thing, somebody finds her on the side of the road 'bout ten, her skull crushed."

"Where were you that night?"

"Workin'. Somebody gotta bring home some money. Bobby sent most all his paycheck to wifey."

"Who was the girl?"

"Just some workin' girl like me. Nineteen years old, been out there four, five years already."

"Ah." Alice smiled ruefully. Her thoughts turned for a moment to what she was going to tell Rachel about all this. "How do you feel about that?"

"I don't feel nothing 'bout it," Kim said. "We ain't married. Not to each other anyways."

"You know the girl?"

"I grew up here. I know everybody. Who do you know?"

Alice stood up, walked to the foot of the bed, and tossed her wallet, her keys, and the box of bullets onto the long table there. The box split open, and bullets scattered across the table and rolled across the carpet. She knew what Kim was angling for, and Alice considered whether she'd make a trustworthy guide. Her gut said no, but she'd also pegged her as a bad liar, someone whose deceptions could be reliably ferreted out. "This is what I do for a living," she said. "I think I can figure it out."

"Sure, a square like you, just going around askin' questions?" In the oversized mirror on the wall, Alice saw Kim point her forefinger at her, pistol style, and pull an imaginary trigger. It was an irritatingly adolescent gesture. "Good way to get yourself shot in the face."

"Okay." Alice turned to face Kim. "What kind of arrangement are we talking about here?"

"One fifty a day," Kim said. She enumerated each point on the fingers of one hand. "Plus I get to keep crashin' here."

"A hundred a day, and the room. But no more johns," Alice said. "I have to sleep on that bed."

"Whatever." Third finger. "Plus expenses."

"Expenses? Like what?"

"Fuck you, bitch. You know what expenses are. Food and shit like that."

Alice nodded. "Is that all?"

"No." Kim put out her cigarette in the mug. "One last thing—do your fuckin' job."

"What's that supposed to mean?"

"I can tell you already decided in your head that Bobby's guilty. He cheatin' on his wife with a whore, so he must be a low-down bag of shit. Lyin', cheatin', murderin'. Somebody like you, it's all the same. Break one rule, break 'em all. You remind me of the teachers I had at Catholic school. Just lookin' down on everybody, judgin' 'em. If Bobby did it, fine, let him burn. But don't let them put him in a hole just because you don't like him."

"Wow, a hooker with a heart of gold falls for her john." She'd meant it as a joke, but when she saw Kim flinch, she knew she'd touched a nerve. "Okay, so let's get started."

"Now?"

"Yes, now. This girl that got beat up, where'd Robert pick her up from?"

"Missy? She worked out of a house on the north side."

"Then let's start there."

Kim lay back on the bed and sniffed her forearms, the left and then the right. "I smell like trucker sweat. Lemme take a shower first."

She stood and stripped off her skirt, T-shirt, and bra and walked to the bathroom. Alice realized what Robert had seen in Kim: Rachel was the sort of woman who wouldn't get undressed until the lights were off. As the shower roared, Alice retrieved her gun and holstered it. After a moment, she pocketed a handful of bullets too.

CHAPTER 3

They took Kim's car, an emerald-green hatchback. The floorboards were pristine, and the dash and upholstery were oiled and glistening. Alice popped the glove compartment. There was nothing inside except the owner's manual and a small stun gun.

"Did you steal this car?"

"It's a rental. The manager at the car rental place, he comes around now and then for a taste. None of these shitkickers will drive anything this small, so he lets me use it." Kim clicked on the radio and turned back to Alice. "Also, fuck you."

Near the edge of town, past the Walmart, Kim drove onto a frontage road that snaked behind a warehouse. Far back against a field of scrub brush was a low cinderblock building, the front of which was covered with a spray-painted mural of a naked woman. The sign in front read "El Tamarindo." Kim circled around to the back of the building, where a few other cars were scattered across the small lot. Three girls in shorts and tank tops, rags tied around the bottom halves of their faces, were pointing squeeze bottles of powder at a row of twin mattresses leaned against the building. When they saw Kim's car, they turned and glared at her, half-obscured in a fog of insecticide.

Kim drove to the far side of the building, parked, and leaned forward to rest her head against the steering wheel. She looked exhausted suddenly. "This is where I started out," she said. "I tried to unionize the girls after the house upped their cut, so management locked me in the walk-in freezer one night. I'd still be in there if Bobby hadn't bought me out."

Alice opened her mouth to say something about the mural, the dirty mattresses, the young girls, but then closed it. "Come on, let's go," she said.

Inside, the restaurant was as dark as a mine shaft; management had duct-taped trash bags over the windows, so the only light came from a few faltering neon beer signs behind the bar. A dozen tables were scattered around, overturned chairs on top of them. At the bar three or four surly men eyed Alice and Kim up and down before turning back to their beers. The only noise in the place came from a television set, mounted above the bar, that was showing a Woody Woodpecker cartoon. Kim led Alice through the dark to a blindingly lit kitchen, which looked like it had never been used. In the very back, a large, scowling bodyguard on a barstool squinted at Kim and then unlocked a reinforced steel door with his ring of keys and held it open for them.

"Welcome back," he said, his tone of voice distinctly unwelcoming.

Alice's face was almost touching the screen as she watched grainy footage of a handcuffed man. The point of a heel pressed into his bare back, dimpling his flesh, until he flopped heavily onto his side.

"Zoom out, zoom out," Alice said over her shoulder. The camera's scope widened. The woman was wearing nothing except the shoes. She walked around the man, stood just out of his reach, and said something. The man wormed his way forward until his face was resting on her feet. Then he began to tongue the very tip of one of her heels. "Damn," Alice said. She didn't care for the masochism or the foot play, but she had to admit, the voyeurism sent an illicit thrill through her.

Alice glanced over the other six monitors, each of which was split into six sections. Each section displayed a video feed from a different room of the brothel. Almost all of them were occupied. She turned to face Kim, who was seated in front of a large wooden desk with a wireless keyboard on her lap.

"That's vanilla," Kim said. "Some of the shit these guys are into would turn your hair white. They only put in these cameras after a guy strangled a girl to death just down the hall."

"Are these cameras legal?"

Kim gave Alice a look of utter contempt but said nothing. Alice walked over and sat in the chair next to Kim. Behind the desk was a deeply tanned woman in her sixties with a white crewcut. Alice and Kim patiently waited as the woman fed loose bills into a bill counter, wrapped the bundles, and stacked them crossways in a family-sized Pop-Tarts box. When she was finished counting money, she put the Pop-Tarts box in a desk drawer, locked it, and then turned to face Kim.

"Who's this?" she asked, gesturing toward Alice.

"She a PI," Kim said. "Bobby's wife sent her."

"You a cop?" the older woman asked Alice.

"No."

"An ex-cop?"

"No."

"Good. I don't like cops." She swiveled her chair to face Kim. "How's life as an independent?"

Kim shrugged. "Well, Janet, ain't nobody takin' my shit."

"Yeah, but you're making a quarter what you did here. So you're not exactly better off."

"That ain't the point."

"Of course it is," Janet said. "You clean?"

Kim glanced quickly at Alice and then downward. "More or less."

"You're a terrible liar." Janet swiveled to face Alice, who was deeply annoyed to find herself unsettled by the woman. Maybe it was the desk, with its echoes of a principal's office or a judge's chambers. "I'm only seeing you for Missy's sake," Janet said. "Whoever did that to her is still out there."

"So you don't think Robert did it," Alice said. "Do you have any videos of him from that night?"

Janet cut her eyes toward Kim but spoke to Alice. "Those feeds are on twenty-four-hour loop. They're for surveillance only. We don't make recordings. Why?"

"Well, if he was with Missy the night of her assault, the nature of their . . . encounter might shed some light on his mental state," Alice said.

"Oh, for Christ's sake," Janet said. "Robert was harmless. A misguided nice guy who tried to *save* my girls."

"Maybe he tried to *save* Missy, tried to convince her to leave the brothel," Alice said. "Then got mad when she refused?"

Janet shook her head, as much out of disappointment as disagreement. "That's just not in his character. Ask Kim. She's been fucking him for months, ever since that schmuck bought her out of this place."

Alice turned to Kim. Months. She wondered if Rachel had suspected anything. As far as Alice was concerned, living in separate parts of the country pretty much required a relaxation of monogamy, but she suspected that Rachel might hold somewhat more conservative views. "So what was he into?" Alice asked.

Kim shrugged. "Bobby's a starfish." She and Janet exchanged a quick glance.

"Fine, I'll bite," Alice said. "What's a starfish?"

"He just lays there flat. Like a starfish," Kim said. "Lotta nights he'd just get real drunk and wanna cuddle. He ain't got a mean bone in his body."

"Just because he didn't want a stiletto in his mouth doesn't mean he's a saint. I'm not sure that a man's sexual proclivities reveal anything about his fundamental character."

Janet and Kim both burst into laughter.

"Are you a virgin?" Janet asked. Kim blotted a tear from the corner of her eye, careful not to smear her makeup.

"That it?" Kim asked Alice as she rose from her seat.

"No," she said. But she realized she was out of questions. "So Robert and Missy left here together?"

Janet nodded. "Her last customer was from eight to nine. Bobby was in the bar that night, as he often is. They talked, he offered her a ride home. A few of the other girls saw her get into his truck. You can talk to them, but that's exactly what they'll tell you. There's not really much to tell."

"Where'd they find the girl?"

"On the side of the road," Kim said. "Near an abandoned refinery."

Janet pushed back from the desk and stood up. "I think you're done here," she said to Alice. "Good luck to you. I hope you're better at this than you've shown here today, or Bobby's going away for a long time. And, Kim, don't show up here again, or I'll have Lionel throw you out a window. Not a ground floor one either."

As Alice and Kim passed the bank of monitors, Alice paused and bent closer. Her eye lit on a frame showing a man lying on top of a woman. The man was pumping away with fearsome intensity, the muscles in his back knotted, the bed shaking. But the woman was staring at the ceiling with an expression of half-lidded placidity. She might have been bird-watching. Until this point, Alice hadn't made up her mind about how she felt about this place. Now she decided that she didn't like it very much.

The Whitehurst jail visiting area was in a large, sterile basement. The walls, tables, and chairs were muddy gray except one wall, painted with a lopsided mural of Mount Rushmore. Alice squinted at the blotchy presidential faces and wondered if the art was the work of schoolchildren or prisoners.

She recognized Robert before the guard even called them over, not from her memories of him—with his wild hair and cheeks hollowed out by stress, he looked like an entirely different person—but from his bearing. The other prisoners struck postures of defiance or indifference, but Robert looked slumped, defeated. He wasn't even trying to pretend otherwise. Up close she saw his upper lip was swollen and his eyes had the faded tint of week-old bruises. His crooked glasses had been repaired with tape, one lens spiderwebbed with cracks, and judging by the other prisoners in the visitation room, he was the smallest man in the jail by at least four inches and sixty pounds. Alice felt a pang of sympathy for him, despite herself. Someone had finally wiped that cringing half grin off his face, but she didn't find it satisfying at all. When Robert saw her, his lip curled back in disbelief.

"What are you doing here?" he asked.

"I'm a private investigator now," Alice said. "Rachel asked me to come take a look around."

Alice saw doubt and hope flicker in turn across his face. "Rachel must be desperate to ask you for anything."

Alice shrugged. "Maybe she doesn't really want you home."

He looked quickly over at Kim and then at the table. "Have you told her about Kim?"

"No." Alice paused. "Not yet."

"All I'll say about that is that telling her about Kim won't accomplish anything. Except causing her pain. But maybe you like that idea." Robert spoke now to Kim, who'd been examining her nails with a stony determination. "Remember how I told you that I had to come up here for work because my wife was blacklisted from journalism? This here is the woman who's responsible for that."

Kim looked at Alice. "Yeah? She ain't say nothin' about that."

"Because it's not relevant," Alice said. "And it's not exactly true either. Rachel made an informed decision, same as I did. It blew up in our faces, sure, but don't deny her the agency of her own choices. Rachel is a lot of things, but she's not a victim."

"Maybe she's not. But I am," Robert pouted, indicating his orange prison jumpsuit.

"Right," Alice said. "Let's talk about that. Kim has given me a general idea of what happened, but let's hear it from you."

Robert sighed. "There's really not much to tell. I was at El Tamarindo. Missy asked me for a ride after she got off work. I said yes. I dropped her off around nine thirty and went straight home. I had a beer and went to sleep. Next thing I know, the cops are banging on my door, and here I am."

"Did you have sex with Missy at El Tamarindo?"

"No." He seemed embarrassed by the very suggestion.

"Then what were you doing there?"

"I drink there. I'm a friend of the house. I look after the girls. If a really bad customer comes in, someone who roughs up the girls or doesn't shower, sometimes I'll buy out the girl for the night, just to save her the trouble."

Alice glanced at Kim. "Told you," Kim mouthed.

"Anyone who knows me will tell you I would never do something like this. I'm a geologist for chrissakes," Robert said.

"What exactly does that entail?" Alice asked.

"These roughnecks only know how to drill. I tell them where."

"Have many enemies at work?"

"I'd be surprised if anyone knew my name." Robert shrunk down in his chair.

"Where did you drop Missy off?"

"Down on Bighorn Road," Robert said. "South of town where it meets the highway."

"What's there?" Alice said.

"A house where you buy dust, do dust," Kim interjected. "One of the main ones. I can take you to see half a dozen dustheads who'll tell you they saw her there that night, after Robert dropped her off. Of course, they won't tell the cops."

Alice nodded. She wasn't overly convinced for or against this alibi. "I'm sure they wouldn't show up for court either. Or if they do show up, they wouldn't seem remotely credible in front of a jury. So you see my problem."

"Then come up with a fake witness. Bribe them or something. They're gonna eat me alive in here," Robert said.

A burst of resentment made Alice's stomach roil. "I don't think you understand why I'm here. I'm not here to do whatever it takes to get you out of jail. If I think you're guilty, I'm on the next plane out. I'm not a defense lawyer, and as I understand it, you and Rachel are so in debt you can't even hire one. Right now, all I see is a guy who's been leading a double life with two women in two states, a guy who's not telling me the whole story. Which doesn't inspire confidence. It makes me feel like I'm being lied to. And when people lie, it means they're guilty."

Robert leaned forward and wrung his shackled hands. His eyes began to swim. *Oh god,* Alice thought. *Not tears, anything but tears.* "Just because I cheated on my wife, that doesn't mean I'm a murderer. Why won't anyone believe me?"

"Calm down, Bobby," Kim said. She laid a hand on his arm. "I believe you."

"No touching!" the guard barked, stepping closer. Kim withdrew her hand. Robert looked at the guard out of the corner of his eye but didn't otherwise move.

"Did you tell her about the others?" Robert said to Kim. He had to bend forward to wipe his eyes with the back of one cuffed hand.

Kim glanced at Alice and crossed her arms. "Figured I'd save that for you."

Robert swallowed hard. "This sort of thing has been happening for years. Frame-ups, railroad jobs, *convenient disappearances*. They always find a way to silence the innocent."

"Who's 'they' and why would 'they' do this?"

"Nobody knows," Robert said. "You're the investigator. Investigate!"

"Thanks for the advice," Alice said. "Conspiracy theories are the last refuge of the guilty. If the facts don't favor your version of events, just reinvent the facts."

"See," Kim said to Robert. "This is why I ain't bother."

"You have to give me more than paranoid ramblings and a non-alibi if you want me to help you," Alice said.

"When Missy wakes up," Robert said, "she'll confirm everything. Then we'll see what's what."

"Maybe so. But at this rate, I'll probably be back in New York by then."

Quick as a viper, Robert shot out his cuffed hands and grabbed one of Alice's forearms. His grip was strong despite his wasted appearance. He pulled Alice so close she could smell his stale breath. In his face she saw sudden anger, but underneath that was something that frightened her much more—the wild, fluttering panic of a man clinging to the edge with both hands. "You're in on it, aren't you?"

The guard, who'd been surreptitiously drifting closer, picked Robert up by the back of his jumpsuit collar and slammed him facedown on the floor; breath wheezed out of him like a deflating balloon.

"Visit's over," the guard said. Alice and Kim retreated to the wire gate to be let out, Kim in tears and Alice rubbing the red fingermarks where Robert had clung to her arm. They watched as the guard leaned over and whispered into Robert's ear, as intimate and offhanded as a lover, then pulled him along the hallway that led to the cells.

CHAPTER 4

Alice looked at Kim sitting in the driver's seat of the hatchback. Kim was staring out at the road that led away from the jail, one small fist pressed to her mouth, tears running down her cheeks.

Alice wondered if she was in the wrong for keeping Kim a secret from Rachel. She'd found Robert's assertion ridiculous, that telling Rachel would only hurt her—as if revealing his betrayal was somehow just as bad as his actual betrayal. But he had a point, underneath his self-serving whining: the Rachel who'd come to her apartment in Brooklyn didn't seem like she could absorb another major setback from life. Looking out over the rocky flatland, Alice shook her head—that it had come to this, that she had to lie to protect the feelings of a woman she'd once considered a paragon of authority and steadfastness.

Her first, and still most vivid, memory of Rachel came from their first month working together at the *Post*. They'd only had a few wary professional conversations at that point, nothing more than watercooler chitchat. Alice was chasing a story about corrupt guards dealing drugs inside the city jail. A snitch had put her onto a disgruntled dealer who'd sold crack to one of the guards before being undercut by a competitor. The meet was at eleven at night in the unfurnished basement apartment of an old brick row house in Southeast, just Alice, the dealer—a fat man who went by the name Royal—and his three cronies, all of them sitting on new-in-box forty-nine-dollar microwaves, that ubiquitous tool of crack dealers everywhere. The first thing Royal said to her was, "How do we know you ain't a cop?"

She'd done this sort of thing often enough to know that they didn't actually think she was a cop. They were just hazing her, like high school football players hazing a freshman. How many opportunities did a guy like Royal ever get to mess with an uptight white woman with a master's degree?

"What do you want me to do?" Alice asked.

The four men chuckled, just to make her uncomfortable, and then Royal took out a joint and lit it. He dragged on it and passed it to one of his cronies, who did the same. When it came to her, Alice took two long drags under Royal's approving eye. She'd smoked plenty of weed, done plenty more than that, and it wasn't a big deal to her. But after a few minutes of idle talk, she'd felt a sinister muddling of her consciousness creeping in.

"What was that?" she heard herself ask.

"Love boat," Royal said, and everyone laughed. Alice noticed that he was sweating profusely and realized that she was burning up too. Love boat—PCP—made you burn up. That's why when you saw the police arresting some angel-dust fiend on the evening news, the guy was always naked. As she watched, Royal took his T-shirt off, exposing a glistening, doughy torso.

"Shit. I need to get home." Alice stood, wobbling. Royal quickly moved to block the door.

"No, no, no," he said. "You wreck your car or jump off a building, who you think they gonna blame it on? You just sit down. You be okay."

Alice went back to sitting on her microwave. Even today, thinking back, she wasn't sure if she'd been detained for some sinister reason or if Royal genuinely wanted to protect her and himself. At any rate, she waited a minute or two and then went to the bathroom, mumbling something about feeling sick. As soon as the door was closed, she texted Rachel the address, saying she might be in trouble and could she please come and get her.

Rachel arrived a half hour later, knocking once curtly and then walking in the unlocked basement door. By that time, Alice had forgotten she'd even texted her. All the men had taken off their shirts, a few had taken off their pants, and Alice was semidelirious, her head lolling back against the wall, her sleeves and pant legs rolled all the way up like a wader or an itinerant laborer. She'd tried to conduct her interview, but her questions kept looping off into long, nonsensical monologues, and Royal's answers were no better. Rachel took one look around the smoky room and pulled Alice up by the arm.

"We're leaving right now," she'd said.

The men all froze, and then Royal, almost casually, pulled out a .38 and pointed it at Rachel. "Who the fuck are you?"

Rachel just gave him a look of utter contempt. "What are you going to do," she said, "shoot me? Put that fucking gun away." And then she'd stared him down until he'd done just that. Back then Rachel had had what they called in the PI business "command presence."

She'd taken Alice home, put her to bed, and never said anything about it, even later when they'd become close friends. Rachel could have—should have, according to the employee code of conduct—fired Alice for that incident, but she didn't. She'd understood that sometimes you had to break the rules, a dangerous philosophy of exceptionalism that later got them both into a lot of trouble. Still, as Alice got to know Rachel better and realized how much respect, bordering on reverence, she had for the rules, she realized how hard it had probably been for her to give Alice a pass that night. It took a strong person to act against their principles, even if they knew it was the right thing to do. Whatever that meant. Maybe that was why it had been so hard for Alice to see the present-day Rachel in her Brooklyn apartment: a worn-down, desperate woman asking for charity.

Suddenly, Kim turned off the highway, fishtailing briefly before speeding down a gravel side road.

"Where are we going?"

Kim slowed the car and pulled over. "Up there," she said, pointing to a lonely, ramshackle house in the distance. "That's the dust house where Robert dropped Missy off." She took out her phone and called up a map. "See this red dot all the way on the other side of town? El Tamarindo. And this dot here is the Bobcat. Both on the north side of town, just a mile apart. And Missy was found right in between them, at this dot here. Like, if you draw a straight line between the two places Robert was that night, she was found right on that line, halfway in between, and nowhere near this place. Don't that seem a little too convenient to you?"

"Yeah, it does," Alice conceded. Admittedly, she didn't have the same instinct for men that Kim and Janet shared, but her gut told her Robert was a sniveling cheater, not a violent offender. And the facts of the case had a distinctly manipulated feel to them. "Something's not right, I agree. But to extrapolate from Robert's fishy circumstances some kind of all-encompassing conspiracy, I'm not ready for that."

"Girl, I could tell you stories."

Alice exhaled slowly through her nose. "I'm listening."

"Let's do story time at the bar," Kim said, starting the car. "I'm stressed out as shit, and I talk better with a couple in me anyway."

Before Alice could respond, Kim had floored it and accelerated the small car in a tight U-turn on the gravel road, driving so far into the ditch that Alice clutched the dashboard, thinking the car was about to roll onto its roof. She turned to scold Kim, but Kim didn't seem to even realize anything had happened. As they sped into town, past barbed-wired fields gone fallow, Alice was certain she needed a drink too.

The Cavalryman was a long, narrow wood-paneled space filled with people who took the business of getting drunk very seriously. No talk, no music, no television; nothing but the sound of glasses being lifted and then set down. Alice hadn't eaten breakfast or lunch, so all the alcohol was bombing straight into her bloodstream. If the drinks hadn't been so watered down, she'd be in real trouble. When her phone buzzed again, she turned it facedown on the bar top. She didn't even have to check to know it was Rachel, demanding an update. *She wouldn't be so eager for news,* Alice thought, *if she had any inkling of what it was.*

"You gonna answer that?" Kim said.

"Nope."

"Then turn it off."

"Nah," Alice said. "I like to know exactly when I'm ignoring someone. It gives me pleasure thinking about their frustration."

"What's got you in a evil mood all of a sudden?"

Alice swirled the dregs of her cocktail in the bottom of the glass. "One of those videos back at the brothel," she said. "It reminded me of my ex-husband. How we used to have sex. I would just lie there, bored. I'd think about work, usually. He would think about whatever he thought about. Not about me. Maybe one of the girls from his office he was fucking, maybe some girl he'd been sending pics to on the Internet."

"You were married?" Kim asked.

"Three years."

"Damn," Kim said. She chuckled.

"What's so funny?"

"Bein' married to you don't sound too fun."

"I guess that's why it didn't last."

Kim regarded her closely and then ordered two more drinks. "That was fucked up of me to say. I take it back. You still talk to your ex? You got kids?"

Alice recoiled. "What? No, no. It was never like that."

The drinks arrived, and Kim paid, withdrawing a folded bill from her wallet. Curious, Alice held Kim's wallet open with one finger and looked at her ID in its clear plastic window. "Is this real?"

Kim took a long sip of her new cocktail. "Yeah. Why?"

"This is your last name?" Alice squinted. "Holywhitemountain?"

"Yeah."

"I thought you were Mexican this whole time!"

"I'm from the res upstate."

"The Sioux reservation? I thought you guys had casinos now. Why would you leave that for this?"

Kim shook her head. "It's just like whitey to think money solves all your problems. Most of the times it's the other way round. Take this town, for example. Whitehurst used to be all right. You could at least walk down the street without some trucker trying to drag you behind a bush and get it in. Now all this oil money bein' sucked outta the ground goin' to people's minds. Still, Whitehurst is better than other boomtowns. Here at least we got Steve Whitehurst."

"I've heard that name a few times now," Alice said.

"His family founded this town way back. Oregon Trail, white-savior type shit. Every rush, they get richer. The gold rush, the coal rush, now the oil rush. But Steve Whitehurst, he ain't so bad. He hires local boys before out of towners, and he pays good. A lotta people here owe him, and they know it. You go around asking questions, those people aren't going to be too eager to bite the hand that feeds them."

"You think Robert's troubles are related to his work at the Whitehurst Corporation?"

"Not, like, directly. But Bobby worked for Whitehurst, like most everybody else in this town. Even I work for him, sort of. Every dollar I make came outta his pocket. Whitehurst is the king of this town. Any bad shit that goes down, it's gonna blow back on him. Half the shit that happens, it don't even make the news. They just sweep it under the carpet as a favor to the big man."

"If this town is so bad, why don't you leave?"

"I almost did," Kim said. She spoke almost in a monotone, her words weighed down with bitterness. "I was working on my college degree in Minneapolis. Then my mama got cancer and I had to come back to the res to look after her. Your parents still alive?"

Alice nodded. "They run a bed-and-breakfast in Florida."

"Well, watchin' your mama die of cancer is pretty much the worst thing in the world. At night I'd give her a injection and then go downstairs and try not to think. But cancer has a smell. And once you start smellin' it, you can't stop smellin' it. So I started drivin' into Whitehurst for a drink after my mama dropped off. Problem is, these bars don't close, so next thing I know, it's dawn, and I gotta be home in a hour to give Mama her next dose, but I'm way too fucked up to drive. So someone says, here's somethin' that'll sober you right up. And that's how I got started on dust."

"PCP?"

"Not sure what it is. They just call it dust. Or devil dust. Some people say it's powdered fracking injection fluid. Nice and speedy, makes you sorta numb. You just stop givin' a fuck for a while. By the time Mama kicked off, I had a three-hundred-dollar-a-day habit. Soon as I could, I sold the house, mineral rights to the family land, everything, and moved to Whitehurst. Didn't take me no more than six months to blow through all the cash. Then I took the only job you can get in Whitehurst if you a Indian dusthead."

Alice cringed at Kim's screed. "Shit," she said. "You're clean now, though, right? Why don't you just leave?"

"You ever heard the saying 'excellence is a habit'?"

"Sure."

"So is fuckin' up. It's a hard habit to break."

"Believe it or not, I know what you mean." Alice hopped off the barstool, wobbling on her feet. "You are . . . just full . . . of whore's wisdom!"

Kim laughed. "Take it easy. You puke, I ain't holdin' your hair back."

Alice's vision swam and she sat back down. "Tell me honest, no bullshit. You really think Robert's innocent?"

"Course he's innocent," Kim said. "My line of work, you learn to read men. Separate the psychos from the squares. You don't, you end up lyin' on the side of some dirt road."

"Like Missy," Alice said.

"Yeah, like Missy."

Alice felt suddenly that her comment had sounded too glib, too insensitive, but Kim didn't seem to be offended. She took another drink of her watery scotch. "Weren't you going to tell me some stories?"

Kim snapped her fingers. "That's right. Yeah, so listen. I used to be like you. When people started talkin' about conspiracies, I'd roll my eyes and be like, whatever. Until it happened to a friend of mine. He was a pastor, used to come out to the reservation when I was a kid to run a basketball program. Everybody loved this guy. Pastor Karl, they called him. Then when dust hit, right around the time the frackin' took off, he starts doing outreach, rehab, all that stuff. Got state funds for drug programs, even took a little preemie baby on *Good Morning America* and started talkin' federal money. Then one day, this young girl at the shelter he ran, maybe eleven, twelve years old, she up and says Pastor Karl touched her, and bam, he goes to jail. Where he don't last long, him being a convicted child molester."

Alice nodded. "Wouldn't be the first pedophile priest."

"He wasn't no pedo. Listen, Janet at El Tamarindo, she recruits a lot of her girls from the foster system. These girls got nothin' goin' for 'em, high school dropouts, no family. Free room and board and two hundred fifty a week in walkin'-around money sounds pretty good. Anyway, the girl who accused Pastor Karl, Nevaeh, she starts working at El Tamarindo during my last year there. We become friends, party together. She tells me Pastor Karl never touched her. Her mom's boyfriend made her say it. Raoul. Burned her with cigarettes when she refused—she showed me the scars. After Pastor Karl goes to jail, her mom suddenly got all this money. Buys a house on the lake, a car, a boat. Back then, the ones who weren't dealin' dust were spending Whitehurst money from sellin' the family farm. But Nevaeh said her mom and Raoul ain't never had nothin' to sell and were too fuckin' dumb and strung out to ever sell. Which means somebody paid them to have her put Karl away."

"Okay then," Alice said. "We go to the mom, go to Raoul, and sweat 'em. If they're as dumb as you say, it shouldn't take much."

"They both long dead," Kim said. "Ran their fuckin' speedboat into the side of the dock at high speed in the middle of the night. No lights, high as shit."

"The girl—"

"OD'd last year. Dust."

Alice threw back the dregs of her drink. She stood up again for no particular reason and swayed on her feet, wondering if Robert was the victim of a conspiracy or just the unluckiest bastard in Whitehurst. "Wait, so can you look at any guy and tell if he's a soulless sociopath?"

"It ain't failed me yet."

Alice swiped across her phone for several seconds before arriving on the Facebook page of a stocky, gel-haired man. She brought up his profile picture and turned the phone to face Kim.

"This is my ex. Tell me what you see."

Kim leaned forward. After a moment, she burst into laughter.

"Well?" Alice said. She wasn't amused.

Kim wiped her eyes with a bar napkin, shaking her head. "I think it's time to go home."

Alice passed out as soon as her head hit the pillow at the Bobcat, but she roused sometime in the inky hours of the early morning. Someone was moving about the dark motel room, someone intent on going undetected. Alice kept her eyes almost closed, her breathing regular, a habit she'd picked up from the dying days of her marriage when her husband had made a habit of sneaking out in the middle of the night to meet up with women he'd met online.

It wasn't her husband skulking about the dark room tonight, but her new roommate. She lay there listening to Kim tiptoe around the room. She wondered if Kim was going out to work, but thought this unlikely; Alice had already paid her for today's and tomorrow's work, two hundred dollars cash, as a goodwill gesture. Was she going out to buy dust? Alice had a sudden vision of Kim returning to the motel room, jittery and babbling at an unnecessary volume.

With an inrush of cool night air and then an almost inaudible latching of the door, Kim was gone. Alice sat up and checked her phone; it was half past three in the morning. She stood up and walked to the windows that faced the parking lot. Parting the blinds, she saw Kim tottering on her stilettos toward the highway, her phone pressed to her ear. When she'd almost reached the road, a man on a dirt bike pulled up in front of her. Even at this distance, he was one of the ugliest men Alice had ever seen: a massive head; bulbous red nose; greasy, thin blond hair pulled back in a frizzy ponytail; and the sort of close-set, beady eyes that Alice associated with child murderers.

As Alice watched, Kim reached into her purse and handed something to the man. She recognized it as the envelope of cash she'd given Kim earlier that night. The man counted the money without taking it out of the envelope and then slipped it into the inside pocket of his Carhartt. Then he grabbed Kim by the arm and leaned forward, speaking intensely. When he finished, they shared a brief kiss, and then he sped off on the dirt bike. As Kim walked back to the motel, Alice saw that her cheeks were wet, her mouth downturned.

Alice scurried back to the bed and lay down. Soon, the door opened and closed almost soundlessly, and Kim eased herself down onto the mattress. Alice listened to her breathing for a while and then turned to her in the dark.

"Who was that?" Her voice sounded loud and accusatory in the silence.

"Were you spyin' on me?"

"No. I woke up when you went out, so I looked out the window, that's all."

"That's spyin', stupid."

"Who was that man?"

"None of your fuckin' business."

"Looked to me like you gave him your advance. You in debt, Kim? Maybe somebody paid you to set Robert up?"

"He's my man, that's all," Kim said. "We on and off since high school. It's one of those things, you know?"

Alice nodded in the dark. "Okay." She thought about this. "Did Robert know about him?"

"Yeah. Bobby don't like him. He made me cut him off when we were together. But since Bobby went to jail, I get lonely. And a woman's got to have someone watchin' her back when she walks the streets."

"So he's your pimp?"

Kim sighed. "You don't know nothin' about it."

"Maybe he's the one who framed Robert? Wanted you back?"

Kim laughed. "Lester's sweet, but he ain't smart enough to take his hand off a hot stove."

"So what was tonight about?"

"He needed money. He don't have nobody else, so I got his back."

Alice wished she could see Kim's face in the dark. "What did he need the money for?"

"No idea. I ain't ask."

Alice considered this. "Fine," she said. She rolled back over and closed her eyes.

"That it?" Kim said.

"Yeah. Why?"

"Well," Kim said. "You just grillin' me and then broke off."

"If you say it's nothing, then it's nothing. Is there any reason I shouldn't trust you?"

"Fuck no."

"Okay then. Get some sleep. We need to go back to see Robert in the morning. I want to retrace his steps the day of Missy's assault."

Alice settled into her pillow and pulled the sheet up to just under her nose, a habit she'd had since childhood. She was just on the point of drifting off when Kim said, "Sorry I snapped at you."

Alice thought about how to respond and found herself at a loss. "Get some sleep," she said.

The next morning, Alice awoke with a dizzying hangover, which did little to slow her racing thoughts. She dry swallowed ibuprofen and tried to gather herself as Kim drove them back to the jail for visiting hours. Inside, a youthful deputy was standing at reception, writing in a ledger.

"Robert Wilcox, please," Alice said.

"No visits today," said the deputy. "Some inmates got into it. Jail's on lockdown now."

"Well, this is important," Alice said, tapping her fingers on the laminate counter. "Can I speak to your boss?"

"Sheriff Red Horse is at the hospital. He won't be back for a while."

"Oh shit," Kim muttered to Alice, pulling her out of the deputy's earshot. "Red Horse involved, somethin' wrong."

"You know him?"

"I grew up with him, up on the res. Uncle Tom motherfucker. He's whitey's bitch boy, doing their dirty work. Hauling their smallpox blankets. He'll get his someday. Driving alone on some back road at night. I know more than one dude who keeps a clip of armor-piercing in the glove compartment with his name on it."

Alice's stomach flipped. She turned back to the counter, reluctant to ask her next question. "Which prisoner was involved?"

"I can't rightly tell you that," the deputy said, looking down.

"Was it Robert Wilcox?" Alice asked.

The deputy opened his mouth to speak and then closed it. He set the ledger and the pen down on the counter and leaned forward. "Like I said, I can't say. But hypothetically, you better hustle over to the hospital," he said. "I'm not sure how much time he's got."

CHAPTER 5

Alice had been in some shabby hospitals before, but Whitehurst General was one of the worst: a boxy brick building that felt like a postwar elementary school with dropped-tiled ceilings and fluorescent-lit corridors. The ER reception area was carpeted wall-to-wall, the floor a mosaic of stains and spilled fluids. Some of the stains appeared to be fresh, and Alice wondered if they were Robert's blood.

Kim went to gather info from the nurses at the front desk, so Alice took a seat in the waiting area. During the ride from the jail, Kim had sat in the passenger seat, biting her lip and rocking in her seat. The only time she'd shown any outward emotion was when they'd hit a traffic jam and she'd punched the dashboard. The way she'd cradled her hand for the rest of the ride made Alice think she'd broken it. Quite frankly, Alice had expected an ostentatious show of wailing and crocodile tears, not an understated display of restrained feeling. She wasn't sure if she'd misjudged the sincerity of Kim's feelings for Robert or her talents as an actress.

A few chairs down from Alice, a hulking Native American man in a black Carhartt and a high-and-tight crew cut sprawled casually, his hands folded across his stomach. He turned as Alice studied him, as if he'd sensed her gaze, and gave her a big grin.

"Smile, little lady," he said. "It takes twice as many muscles to frown as it does to smile."

Alice turned away from him, her face neutral.

"Hey," he said after a moment. "I spoke to you."

Alice looked back at him. "And?"

"And I think I deserve an answer."

"Well, I guess that's where we differ." She oriented her eyes forward, not looking over even when the man slid two seats closer, so that only a single seat separated them. Out of the corner of her eye, she saw him lean over the chair, drawing so close she smelled his drugstore cologne.

"Hey," he whispered. When she didn't respond, he leaned even closer. "You better show me a fucking smile, or we're going to have a problem."

Without turning her head, Alice moved one hand to sweep back her coat to reveal the Magnum holstered under her arm. The man burst into uproarious laughter, then swept back his own coat to reveal an almost identical Magnum, clipped to his belt next to a gold badge.

"You're new in town, ain't you?" he said.

Alice hated to admit it, but she was cowed by the badge. "Yeah."

"Well, then I'll give you a pass, just this once," he said. "If you wear a jacket over that gun, it ain't open carry anymore. That makes it a concealed weapon. Which is a jailable offense in this town. Unless you got a permit for that?"

He trained his eyes on Alice's until she couldn't bear the sustained eye contact and looked away. She remembered a colleague who'd told her it was a common tactic among law-enforcement officers and dog handlers, an easy way to impose dominance. She'd tested it out on her ex-husband, to uncertain results.

"No, I don't." Knowing that any reluctance in her manner would give him pleasure, she removed her jacket and sat back casually. She was wearing only a thin tank top, no bra, and the air-conditioned hospital was very cold. The man let his eyes settle on her chest, making no effort to hide what he was doing. The dumb animal blankness that appeared on men's faces when they were overpowered by lust rendered his face a cipher, and he licked his lips.

"Much better," he said.

"So you're the sheriff, I presume?" Alice said. "I've been looking for you."

"Have you now?" With a visible effort, he moved his eyes from her chest to her face. "And why is that?"

"I've been hired by Robert Wilcox's wife to look into his case. My name's Alice. I'm a private investigator."

The sheriff extended his hand, and Alice shook it. His grip was crushing, his handshake's firmness a crude message. "Sheriff Michael Red Horse," he said. "Where you from?"

"New York."

"A private investigator, eh? Impressive. That means you google stuff, right?" He chuckled at his own joke.

Alice kept her expression neutral. "What happened to Wilcox?"

"Another inmate shanked him." The sheriff leaned in and dropped his voice to a whisper again. "He bled like a virgin on prom night."

"Wow. Great use of metaphor," Alice said. "Shouldn't a bookworm like Wilcox have been in isolation?"

"He was. Guy like that can't handle himself on the yard, so we had him confined to a single cell twenty-three hours a day. Until this morning, when he was transferred to gen pop."

"Transferred? Why?"

"I'm not rightly sure. If I was a fancy private investigator from New York, I guess I'd call it a clerical error." The sheriff shrugged extravagantly. "Right now, it's about fifty-fifty whether he pulls through." He leaned back and drew a finger diagonally across the side of his neck. "The guy nicked his artery, right across here. Lost a lotta blood, but he's alive. Best thing for you to do is get comfortable here with me, and wait and see."

Red Horse patted Alice's knee with one hand and left it resting there. When she looked at him, he raised his eyebrows and gently squeezed. Before she knew what she was doing, she'd lashed out and slapped him across the face. The utter shock in his expression was worth it, she thought, watching the reddened imprint of her hand brighten on his cheek, even if he shot her on the spot.

Alice heard a rustling behind her, and when she turned, she saw Kim standing in the doorway, taking in the scene with slit eyes.

"I'll be in the ICU, Alice," she said, and she turned on her heel and was gone.

When Alice turned back, the sheriff was looking at her, not with anger, exactly, but with appraisal. He ran his fingers over his lips and then checked them for blood.

"Maybe I deserved that," he said.

"There's no *maybe* about it," Alice said. "What if someone did that to your sister?"

"I'd chain him to the back of my truck and drag him out to the badlands."

"So why did you think it was okay to do that to me?"

"Well, any man who'd do that to my sister is a scumbag who deserves what he gets," the sheriff said in a tone that indicated he thought it was obvious. "I'm a decent guy, though. I'm the sheriff, for chrissakes. Totally different situation."

Alice opened her mouth to say something but thought better of it. She didn't want to press her luck by insisting on making this a teachable moment. Not that she was convinced he was willing or able to receive clarification on the subject.

"I see we have similar taste in guns," she said instead.

The sheriff looked down at his holster and nodded. "I don't like to take no chances," he said. "I feel like you got the same philosophy."

"I like to avoid trouble if I can." Alice rose from her seat, started to put her jacket back on, then stopped, remembering the sheriff's warning. She was unable to stop shivering. "I better go check on my friend," she said. "Robert's her boyfriend."

"That ten-dollar whore? How much was he paying her?"

"I'm not sure," Alice said carefully, grateful the cold air was at least keeping the angry flush from her cheeks. "He let her live in his room, over at the Bobcat."

"Rooms down there run three grand a month, at least," the sheriff spat. "Plus I'm sure she was getting some walkin' round money. Plus her fee for *services*." He made air quotes with his fingers when he said this. "Now she's got you paying her tab, right?"

"I'm paying her to show me around town," Alice said. "But I think she really cares about Robert."

The sheriff scoffed. "You ever develop feelings for an ATM machine? Because that's all a whore like that sees when she looks at a man. Or you. Think about the mind-set of a woman who's laid with that many men. She ain't much higher than a beast anymore."

"What's the magic number of men where a woman goes from human to beast?" Alice said. The sheriff studied her face for any trace of mockery, but she kept her expression bland. "Is it ten? Fifty? A hundred?"

The sheriff shifted in his seat, and Alice realized she'd made him uncomfortable. He straightened the corduroy collar of his coat and cleared his throat. "Four," he said.

She was tempted to tell the sheriff how many men she'd slept with—but not that tempted. She didn't see any advantage in rendering herself as less than human in his eyes, little more than a round-heeled rodent, or perhaps a petri dish, considering how large a multiple of four her number was.

"It was nice meeting you," Alice said. They shook hands again, his grip more reasonable this time.

"That's probably just something you say when you part ways in New York," he said. "But I mean it when I say it was a pleasure making your acquaintance." He drew out an ornate, gold-embossed business card from an inside pocket and handed it to her. "And I'd love to see you again. Can I take you out to dinner?"

Alice froze, and for a moment her mind went completely blank. "I don't eat dinner," she said. "But maybe coffee." She moved toward the door, and the sheriff leaped to block her.

"Well, do you have a card?"

"No. No, I don't. Not on me."

His frame blocked the door completely as he gave her a steady, solicitous look. Finally Alice took her phone out and dialed his number off his business card. When his phone lit up, he smiled slyly and saved her number to his contacts. He entered her name as "Pretty Lady." As Alice walked to find Kim, she wondered if this was going to help her break open the case or if she'd made a huge mistake.

Alice found Kim in the intensive care unit, her face pressed to the window of one of the suites. Inside, Robert lay unconscious, tethered to various monitors, his neck swaddled in bandages. He looked frail and embalmed.

"They said he's stabilized," Kim said. "Lost a lotta blood, though."

Alice nodded. "I'm going out to the car. Take as much time as you need."

Outside, she leaned against the car and dialed Rachel's number. When it went to voicemail, she hung up and redialed. This time, Rachel picked up on the third ring.

"What is it?" Rachel asked, her voice taut with fear.

"Robert was stabbed in jail." Alice thought it kinder to deliver the news right up front. "He's in stable condition now, but I thought you should know."

"Oh Jesus," Rachel said. "I've been calling."

"I know," Alice winced. "I hit the ground running."

She heard the rustle of bedclothes and the cooing of a child.

"Bring me up to speed."

"Robert gave the girl a ride home from a bar. They were acquaintances."

"Acquaintances," Rachel said. "What exactly does that mean?"

"There was nothing between them. I talked to Robert about it, and I can spot a liar." Alice turned and saw her own reflection in the car's window. *Here's one now,* she thought. "Your husband is a soft touch. He's somewhat known for it around town."

"He is that," Rachel said. "I told him to watch himself. These people can sense weakness."

Alice wondered who she meant by "these people," but thought better than to ask. "I don't know who stabbed him or why. Yet. He was supposed to be segregated, but for some reason they put him in gen pop today. The sheriff here said it was clerical error."

"Okay. So we're going to sue them for ten million dollars."

"Sure, you could probably do that. He lost a lot of blood, but I think he's stable now." She weighed how much to tell Rachel about the rest of it. "That's all I know so far. I won't know more until the girl, Missy, wakes up."

The baby had started to sob and wheeze, and Alice could hear from the undulation of its cries that Rachel was bobbing her up and down. "You know, I wouldn't do any of it again," Rachel said.

Alice closed her eyes. "What, the stuff that happened at the paper?"

"That too. But everything. Marrying Robert, having this baby. None of it has gone right."

Alice had intended to tell or at least hint at Robert's infidelity, but she saw this wasn't the time. "Well," she said. "At least you know. Better late than never."

A long moment of silence elapsed. "I better go," Rachel said. "Call me when you have something to tell me."

Alice leaned against the car, looking at her phone. She couldn't imagine anything worse than the onset of wisdom after you'd already made all your choices in life. Better to live in ignorance than with the curse of hindsight. She felt guilty, suddenly, about having judged Rachel so harshly when she'd shown up at her apartment, and about lying to her now about Kim.

From far off, she heard a coyote howl out on the prairie. *I know just how you feel,* Alice thought.

CHAPTER 6

Alice had a good instinct for momentum, a thought she repeated to herself as she walked the dusty gravel shoulder of the highway toward the police station. Kim was still sleeping back at the Bobcat, but Alice wanted to pounce on whatever small advantage she had with the local authority. The more she'd thought about the facts of the case, lying in bed and listening to Kim snore last night, and this morning over coffee, the more questions that came to mind.

The Whitehurst County police station was airy and sleek inside, more like an IKEA showroom than a hall of justice. Fracking money, Alice surmised. At the reception desk, she told the officer on duty that she was there to see the sheriff.

"You got an appointment?" he asked.

"No. I just need to talk to him very briefly."

"He don't see anyone without an appointment."

"Can you tell him Alice from New York is here?" Alice said. "We met at the hospital."

The deputy looked at her with an expression of infinite weariness and then sighed and picked up a phone.

"Yeah, there's a woman up front asking to see you," the deputy said. "I told her she had to make an appointment, but—yeah, she says her name is Alice. You met at the hospital? Uh-huh. Okay."

The deputy hung up. "Down the hall, last door on the right," he said.

This was the quietest police station she'd ever been in; she felt as if she were walking through the halls of a church. She wondered if everyone was out there on the streets policing or if the situation was so hopeless they'd all just gone home.

The sheriff's office was at the end of the hall, his name stenciled in ostentatious Wild West script on the frosted glass window of the door, which was slightly ajar. Inside she saw him sitting on the edge of his desk, having struck a casual pose. He was already watching her.

"Come on in," he said. Alice entered the quiet office. There was a strong odor of cologne in the air.

"Hello," she said. "I just had a few questions about the Wilcox incident. Do you have time to talk to me?"

The sheriff chuckled warmly, though it wasn't clear what he was laughing about. "I always got time to talk to a pretty lady." He waved a hand toward the single chair in the room, which had been placed directly in front of him. "Have a seat."

Alice stepped carefully around his ostrich boots, which he'd placed possessively on each side of the chair. When she sat down, she found that she was staring straight into his crotch. When she looked up, he was watching her.

"Who shanked Wilcox?" Alice said. "Did he have a beef with someone on the yard?"

"I said I'd talk to you," the sheriff said. "I didn't say I'd reveal details of an open case."

Alice blinked several times. She tried to push her chair backward a little, but it was too heavy to slide "Well. I don't know what else there is to discuss."

"We got everything to discuss," he said. "I don't even know where you're from." He shifted, hands folded across his lap, one leg thrown off the corner of his desk in a manner that suggested cartoon villainy. "So where are you from?"

"I grew up in Mississippi," Alice said.

"But you don't have the accent."

"I made a conscious effort my whole life to not talk like that."

"That says a lot about you."

Alice shrugged one shoulder. "I never said it didn't," she said. "Where you from?"

"I know damn well that whore you're partnered up with already told you where I'm from," the sheriff said, though not unkindly.

"Yeah. And I'm pretty sure you already knew where I grew up before I told you. Along with my criminal record, my last dozen addresses, my credit report, and whatever else you could dig up."

"Your flameout as a reporter," he said. "That didn't even take no work. That's the first thing that comes up on Google."

Alice nodded. "These days we're all defined by our worst mistakes, aren't we?"

"I don't see nothin' wrong with that. Charles Manson may bake a mean apple pie, but that don't mean he should get his own cooking show." When Alice didn't reply, the sheriff continued. "So what did she say about me?"

"Who, Kim?"

"Uh-huh."

"She said you were tough. But fair."

The sheriff just looked at her, letting his eyes go half-lidded like a basking reptile's. "Bullshit," he said.

"Okay. She said you were an Uncle Tom."

The sheriff grinned. "And what do you think?"

"I'm not really in a position to have an opinion on that."

"What's that supposed to mean?"

"How do I know if you're a traitor to your tribe if I'm not even in your tribe? I'm in no position to make that judgment."

He didn't look impressed. "Sounds like some bullshit you learned at . . . Columbia University, was it?"

"I learned that in the real world," Alice said simply. "It's important to know where you stand. In relation to other people."

This statement seemed to amuse the sheriff immensely. He stood and walked across his office and closed the door. Then he walked back and took his original position, perched on the edge of the desk in front of Alice, and paternalistically folded his hands together.

"What was it you wanted to know again?" he asked.

"Who shanked Wilcox?"

"Here's the thing." His voice had become dull, lower, as if he were speaking from underwater. It was a tone Alice knew well. The voice of a man who'd given himself over. "I'm not opposed to helping you out, but you have to help me out too."

He was staring fixedly at her now. He flicked his eyes downward and then back to her face, and when Alice looked down, she saw his hand slowly undoing his belt.

"Get on your knees," he said in a near whisper.

Alice stood up out of her chair, but instead of kneeling, she moved closer, so that their faces were an inch apart. He recoiled slightly, but before he could speak, she knocked his hand away from his belt buckle and began unfastening it herself.

"I don't kneel for anyone," she said. She unzipped the front of his pants and saw he was wearing plaid cotton boxers of a sort she associated with alcoholic uncles. She felt for the slit on the front and then snaked her hand inside his shorts. He inhaled sharply, and then his eyelids fluttered closed. "Here's the thing," Alice whispered. Her mouth was so close to his ear that she could feel her breath rebound from his skin. "I respect you. And I'm not talking about your badge. I mean you as a person. And I think I deserve that same courtesy, don't you?"

The sheriff nodded once, his features slack with an almost narcotic ease.

"I'm not something to be used by you. If we worked together, as equals, I could be so much more to you than a fuck hole. Do you understand?"

The sheriff nodded.

"It's lonely at the top, isn't it? Always having to be in charge. Making all the decisions. Wouldn't it be nice to have a partner? To not have to do it all yourself for once?"

The sheriff's breathing was shallow, and he was clutching the sides of his desk so hard his fingers had gone pink and white. "Relax," Alice whispered. "And breathe. In through your nose, out through your mouth."

The sheriff did as she told him. She stopped talking and concentrated on the task at hand. *At hand,* she thought, amusedly. She had gotten very good at hand jobs; she had a hypersensitive gag reflex, so she'd really had no choice. It was like Frisbee, or fly fishing: all in the wrist. She'd just let herself drift off into the pleasant trance state of manual labor when she felt something brush her upper thigh. She looked down and saw that the sheriff had drawn his gun and was gently sliding it up the inside of her leg.

"Don't stop," he said.

Alice didn't stop. He slid the barrel of the Magnum up her thigh until it nestled inside the fork of her legs. Then he began sliding it back and forth, slowly at first, and then faster. All Alice could think about was if the gun was cocked. No sooner had she thought this than she heard the distinct cocking of the Magnum's hammer. It sounded very loud in the quiet room.

"Sheriff," she whispered, then looked back over her shoulder at the front door, frowning as she read the name there backward. "Michael. Be careful."

"Shh," he said. His breathing had quickened, as had the pace of his gun's thrustings. Alice looked down; at the beginning of each movement, the gun was pointed more or less up into her, so that if it went off, it would blow out the entire back of her pelvis.

The sheriff inhaled sharply and kicked out one leg, striking the chair Alice had been sitting in so hard that it tumbled across the room. He let out a guttural moan and his fluid arced out, landing in long, trailing beads on the hardwood floor. His pistol dropped away from between her legs. Almost immediately, he turned away from her and shoved himself back into his shorts. He zipped up, went behind his desk, and brought out a box of tissues, which he began using to wipe the floor. Alice still hadn't moved, except to wipe her hand on her jeans.

"I'm so, so sorry," he said as he crab walked across the floor, wiping here and there. "I hope that wasn't . . . that I didn't . . . I'm sorry. That was horrible of me. I'm so sorry."

Alice's puzzlement curdled into contempt as she listened to him whine. She was familiar with the male postcoital transformation, but she'd never seen one so pronounced. "It's okay," she said flatly.

"Do you want me to . . . ?" He looked up at her from the floor, his eyebrows peaked in the middle of his forehead.

"To what?"

"To, you know." The sheriff nodded at her crotch. "There are things I can, you know, do . . ."

Alice was dying to know what, exactly, he was referring to. Did it involve his gun? His tongue? A squash? Reading aloud? But she remembered the reason she was even there.

"Just tell me what I came for," she said. "Who shanked Wilcox?"

"It was Deke Kelly. Just a small-time burnout. I don't know why he did it. Probably just don't like out-of-town eggheads."

"What's he in for?"

"Assault on a police officer."

Alice nodded. If there was a moment to push her luck, it was now. "Who put Wilcox back in gen pop?"

"I don't know," the sheriff said. "I truly don't."

Alice dragged the chair back to its spot and tipped it upright. They stood regarding each other over the top of it for a moment, and then Alice turned away.

"I've got to go meet my partner." She started to say thanks, but then stopped herself.

"Call me later," the sheriff said when Alice was halfway out the door. She turned and looked at him; something about the sag of his shoulders made him look like a little boy playing dress-up in his father's clothes. "I may have some more info for you."

Alice gave him a tight-lipped smile and pulled his door shut.

She walked all the way back to the Bobcat from the police station, though several trucks stopped to offer her a ride. Alice was tired of men, of their needs and demands and predictability. It hadn't been that long a walk, but her lungs felt itchy, her eyes stinging from the diesel exhaust.

Kim was awake, sitting at the vanity, when Alice walked in, bent so close to the mirror that a small patch of fog bloomed and ebbed at her lips. Alice unstrapped the heavy pistol from her shoulder, tossed it on the table, and threw herself down on the bed.

"Deke Kelly," she said, in the tone of general pronouncement.

"What about him?"

"That's who shanked Wilcox."

Kim didn't pause in her application of makeup, but her voice quickened. "How you know that?"

"The sheriff told me. And wait until I tell you what I had to do for it."

"You shouldn't go messin' with him. He a dope, but he still the law. He like a pet wolf, lick your hand one minute, tear your throat out the next."

"It wasn't my hand he was licking," Alice said.

Kim looked at her in the mirror and rolled her eyes. "Girl, please. That man would eat buffalo shit before he'd eat pussy. He wouldn't eat his wife's pussy on their wedding night if she was a seventeen-year-old virgin."

"Well, he offered," Alice said sullenly.

"They all offer when they know you gonna say no," Kim said. She swiveled on her stool to face Alice. Under her thick makeup, she had a badly swollen eye and one side of her lips was mashed and abraded.

"Oh my god. What happened to you?"

"I fell," Kim said.

"What do you mean, you fell?"

"Bitch, you heard of gravity, ain't you?"

Kim pivoted back to the mirror and began spraying her hair with an aerosol can. Alice stared at her back. "It was that guy on the dirt bike, wasn't it? What, did he want more money?"

"You can't lecture me about the company I keep when you out there suckin' off the sheriff for info."

"He didn't beat me up afterward," Alice said. "And I didn't suck him off. I jerked him off."

"Well, ain't that some high school shit. He have you do it in the backseat of his daddy's Corvette?" She winced as she laughed at her own joke. "Damn, inside of my mouth feels like I ate broken glass."

Alice rose from the bed and dug in her purse until she found a plastic orange pill bottle. She shook out a white oblong capsule and handed it to Kim, who immediately put it in her mouth and dry swallowed it without asking what it was.

"Deke Kelly works for Roundtree, the top dust slinger in Whitehurst," Kim said. "Deke don't even jack off without asking

Roundtree for permission first. If he shanked Bobby, it had to be on Roundtree's say-so." She smoothed her hands over the unmarred side of her face. "I don't know 'bout you, but I need a drink."

Kim and Alice had been drinking steadily by the time a hush fell over the bar. No sooner had the silence registered than Alice noticed the sound of voices had been replaced by a rising clatter of glass on glass. The bartender turned and began to scramble from side to side, arms outstretched, as all the shelved liquor bottles tottered and some fell and exploded against the cement floor. Everyone roared with laughter. The bartender caught a falling bottle of Pimm's only for two bottles of Jack to fall behind her. A cheer went up, though Alice wasn't sure exactly what everyone was cheering. Alice's stool was now vibrating beneath her, and she clutched the bar with both hands. In the mirror behind the bar, she saw the other patrons doing the same, most of them grim faced, though there were a few wild-eyed new arrivals like herself, not yet used to the tremors, holding their arms out at their sides like they were on a listing cruise ship.

By the time the quake passed, the odor of alcohol was strong enough to make her light-headed. The bartender brought out a broom and began to drag it through the puddled liquor, pushing the jagged remains of the bottles into a long-handled dustpan. Behind them, people resumed their conversations where they'd left off. Someone's pint glass had fallen over, and Kim plucked her pack of Capris off the wet bar top with a yelp. Peering inside the pack, she withdrew the cigarettes that were still dry and tossed the rest over the bar, into a puddle of glass and whiskey. The bartender shot her a glare, but Kim ignored it.

The bouncer, who'd run outside when the tremor started, came back inside, looking sheepish, and retook his stool next to the door. When Kim saw him, she stood up.

"Most of the shady shit that goes on in Whitehurst, Jerome knows about it," Kim said. "Lemme go do what I do."

Alice watched Kim pick up her drink and walk over, hips swinging. She greeted the bouncer with a hug, during which she whispered something in the man's ear. They both laughed and then settled into conversation. As the man talked, Kim rested one hand on his shoulder, stroking the fabric of his coat with her thumb.

"You with her?" a voice said on Alice's other side.

Alice turned and saw a man sitting on the stool next to Kim's vacated one. He wore a brown Carhartt jacket, and the dome of his short blond hair was matted down with dried sweat. He smiled uncertainly as Alice looked him over, and she saw he was just a kid, maybe twenty-one or so.

"Are you asking me if I'm a prostitute?" Alice said.

The kid's eyes widened. "Lord, no. I just meant, are you two, like, girlfriend and . . . girlfriend?"

"Ohhh. Are we gay, is what you're asking. Why would you think that?"

"Y'all are just real comfortable with each other. And she's kinda like the girly one, and you're the, you know . . ."

Alice couldn't help laughing. "The manly one?"

"I never said that." The kid pointed the neck of his beer bottle at her. "I never said manly."

Alice looked in the mirror behind the bar. Her greasy short hair was mussed into a sort of spiky pompadour, she didn't have any makeup on, and she was wearing an oversized gray sweatshirt. "Butch, maybe," she said. "But not manly."

"I never heard that word used like that, but okay," the kid said. He slid onto the stool Kim had vacated. "You're just butch as all get out. Lemme buy you a beer, Butch. My name's Chris."

Alice had assumed that the kid's interrogation was the prelude to a possible gay bashing, but now she realized he was hitting on her. She looked around the bar; she and Kim were the only women there. "Do you like manly women, Chris?"

Chris took a long drink of his beer. "I guess I do." Alice saw he was blushing, and she felt bad about teasing him. "My high school sweetheart won the state championship in the shotput. Each of her thighs was as big as a barrel of oil. She about crushed the life out of me when we tussled."

Alice found it amusing to hear someone talk about their high school sweetheart when they were barely out of high school. "What happened to her?"

"Well, she wanted to work for Whitehurst like me, but they won't hire no women. And she ain't really built to dance on no pole. She'd tear the damn pole out the ceiling. Her daddy's brother was a state trooper over in Minnesota, and he got her into the training program over there. We did the long-distance thing for a piece. I thought it was goin' great, I even looked into jobs over there, but then she started goin' with her training officer. Some dude old enough to be her daddy. She said he was the first man to ever make her feel like a woman, which I took to be a direct insult since I was pretty much the only other man she ever been with. Day she told me, I drove all the way over there to confront them. Tell the truth, I was gonna stomp this guy good, but he was as big as a grizzly bear. Fucker must've been seven feet tall."

"So what'd you do?"

"What could I do? I come back here and got on with my life." He took a long drink of his beer, and Alice had to admit she felt bad for him.

"When was this?"

"'Bout . . . three weeks ago."

"You'll get over it," Alice said, suppressing a laugh. "There are other women."

"Not in Whitehurst, there ain't," he said.

Alice turned on her stool to face him, her knee brushing against his. She put one elbow on the bar and rested her chin in it, cocking her head sideways. She realized she was doing an imitation of Kim. "What about me?"

They nearly drove off the road several times on the way to the Bobcat. Alice wondered, as she pawed at him, if that's what she wanted on some level, to career off the road while heavy petting with a man a decade her junior, to explode in a fireball out here in the badlands and be done with this troublesome case, these troublesome people. No, she thought, she just wanted to get laid. That was the key to getting comfortable in a new city. You never felt really at home until you bedded a local.

"Damn, girl," Chris said. He jerkily hit the brake as she snaked her hand inside his unzipped fly. "You as lathered up as a mustang, ain't you?"

She didn't answer him. She was concentrating. He was wearing fleece thermals—two pairs of them!—under his jeans and seemed to be wearing boxers underneath. "You might as well be wearing a chastity belt," she muttered.

"Just hold on till we get to the motel and we can get naked proper," Chris said, though he shifted his hips forward to make it easier for her to infiltrate his layers. "Oh shit!"

Alice was flattered for a moment, thinking his exclamation was in response to her touch, but then she saw the red-and-blue glare painting the landscape. She turned in her seat just as the sirens on the cruiser behind them started up.

"Just go," Alice said. "Cut across the badlands. There's no way a Crown Vic could keep up with this jacked-up pickup."

But the kid had already slowed down and was steering onto the shoulder. "You are a wild one, ain't you? Just a Bonnie lookin' for her

Clyde." He put the truck in park and turned off the ignition. "They already got my plates. They'd be waiting at the job site in the morning."

Alice said nothing, just crossed her arms. In the side mirror, she watched the cop get out of the car and saunter toward the truck. She recognized the silhouette immediately.

"Shit," she said.

Chris looked at her quizzically but said nothing.

There was a heavy knock on the driver's side window and then a rush of cold air as Chris cranked the window down. Alice stared straight ahead, even when the flashlight blazed in the corner of her eye.

"Evenin', Sheriff," Chris said.

A long silence elapsed. "You all been drinkin' tonight?" the sheriff said.

"I had one or two," Chris said. "But I'm stone-cold sober. I'll do backflips while saying the alphabet if you want."

The sheriff grunted. "Where you all headed?"

Alice turned to give Chris a warning look, but she was too slow. "Her motel," Chris said. He was giving the sheriff a smile of sly lasciviousness, a cat-about-to-eat-the-canary look, which the sheriff acknowledged not at all. He leaned in the window and shined his flashlight in Alice's face so she was forced to put a hand up against the glare.

"What about you, ma'am? You been drinking?"

Alice turned in her seat to face him. "Yes, Michael, I'm drunk. I haven't eaten since breakfast, and then I had about eight whiskeys. But I'm over twenty-one and an American citizen, so I figure that's legal."

The sheriff was holding the flashlight up alongside his head so Alice couldn't see his face, but she forced herself to keep looking in his direction. As she did so, she realized she was swaying in place, and that the harder she tried to stop herself, the more pronounced the swaying became. After a moment, the sheriff snapped the light off, and once her vision cleared, Alice saw he wore a grimace of fatherly disappointment that she found infuriating. She rolled her eyes and turned away.

"I'm gonna need you to get out of the vehicle, son," the sheriff said. Chris got out, and the sheriff directed him toward the front of the truck. Alice rolled down her window just in time to hear him tell Chris to put his hands on the hood.

"I'm placing you under arrest on suspicion of sexual assault." The sheriff took a pair of handcuffs off his belt and cranked one of Chris's arms behind him.

"What the fuck, Michael!" Alice shouted.

"Assaultin' who?" Chris said. He was trying to turn to address the sheriff, but the sheriff just cranked his arm up the middle of his back and pressed him facedown on the hood.

"That woman in your truck," the sheriff said. He caught Chris's other wrist, pulled it back, and snapped the cuffs closed. "She can't make no informed decisions in her state. She blows over the legal limit, the charge goes up to attempted rape."

As the sheriff walked Chris around the front of the car, Alice scooted across the bench seat and jumped out of the truck. "Were you just waiting for me outside the bar? Have you been following me?"

"Get back in the vehicle, ma'am," the sheriff said without looking back. "Interfering with official acts is a serious crime."

"You're way out of line," Alice said. "You're acting like a pissy high schooler."

The sheriff gave no sign that he'd heard her as he put Chris in the back of the police cruiser. The big rigs were giving them a wide margin, but the rush of diesel fumes made her nauseated. She tried to think what Kim would do in this situation, but she was too angry to try the purring sex kitten approach. The sheriff walked back up to her, his thumbs hooked in the front of his belt like John Wayne.

"Thought I told you to get back in the vehicle," he said flatly.

"Guess you'll just have to arrest me," Alice said. "You're not really going to charge that kid with rape, are you?"

"I could."

"Yeah, that's not much of a reason to do something. Just because you can."

"Law's the law," the sheriff said laconically. They locked gazes for a long moment before he spoke again. "You ain't called me."

"Yes, I know," Alice said. There wasn't much use lying.

"It don't take but a minute to call somebody," the sheriff said. "It's just common courtesy."

Alice nodded. "Michael," she said. "What are we really talking about here?"

The sheriff hung his head like a chastened boy. After a moment he said, "I don't like seein' you go with other men."

So he was following her. "I'm my own person. I can do what I want."

"I know."

"We're not boyfriend-girlfriend just because I—"

"I know!"

"Look, I'm sorry," Alice said. She searched for the right word, a term that wouldn't draw undue attention to his wounded male ego or presumptuously imply that he had feelings, let alone that they'd become entangled in all this. "I was . . . rude. I was a rude bitch."

The sheriff nodded. "Yeah, you were."

"And you're right. I'm too drunk to be out here. How about you let the kid go, and then give me a ride home?"

The sheriff looked off toward the kid's slumped silhouette in the back of the cruiser and rubbed his chin thoughtfully.

"I reckon I can let him off this time," the sheriff said. "But it just ain't right, him taking advantage like that."

"I think he learned his lesson," Alice said.

The sheriff brought the kid out of the backseat and unlocked his cuffs. After a short exchange, the kid nodded and walked fast to his truck. As he passed Alice, he raised his eyebrows at her, but she just stared at her feet. His truck roared to life, and then he pulled away at a conspicuously reasonable speed. She felt bad for the kid, that he'd become a pawn in the sheriff's ego drama, but that was how it was in this town. The big fish ate the little fish. And the women were bait.

The interior of the sheriff's cruiser was meticulously clean, the seats and the dash freshly oiled and gleaming in the moonlight. Four or five evergreen air fresheners hung from the rearview mirror. Alice wondered if he always kept the car like this or if he'd done it in anticipation of picking her up, and she couldn't decide which option was more discomfiting. In the center of the front seat was a shotgun resting in brackets and a bulky black Toughbook, open and oriented toward the driver. When Alice leaned over to see what the sheriff had been looking at, he slammed it shut.

"What woulda happened to you if I hadn't come along when I did?" the sheriff said. They were coasting along the shoulder; he hit the lights, and the eighteen-wheelers fell back obediently to let him in.

"I guess I would've gone home and had sex with that guy," Alice said.

"Exactly," he said, as if he'd scored a major point.

"What's that mean?"

"Regrets."

"Why do you assume I'd regret it?"

The sheriff just shook his head like she didn't get it. *No,* she thought, *you're the one who doesn't get it.* But she said nothing, only let her head rest against the cold window. Outside, the moon was half-risen on the horizon, a perfect semicircle stained a delicate lavender that she'd never seen before.

"That's bizarre," she said, sitting up. "What happened to the moon?"

"Purple moon," the sheriff grunted. "Bad omen, they say. Murders, rapes, assaults, they all spike during a purple moon. It's something in the air. Maybe it comes out of the ground. My parents thought it was evil spirits. Legend has it, there was a purple moon the night before Custer's Last Stand."

"They happen every month?"

"No. There's no rhyme or reason that I can see. They get more common in boom years. Some people think they're related to drilling." He drove with one arm thrown over the top of the steering wheel, his eyes scanning the road and the landscape with a predatory intensity. It scared Alice a little to think of herself caught in that gaze.

"And what do you think?" Alice said.

"I think you're in over your head," said the sheriff. "Your boy. You know anything about his past?"

"I just met him an hour ago. I don't even know his last name."

"I ain't talking about him. I'm talking about Wilcox."

Alice sat up straighter and cleared her throat. "What about him?"

"You do your homework on him?"

"Sure, the usual. Background, credit."

"What'd you find?"

"Nothing much. You're not talking about his bankruptcy, are you?"

"No, I ain't talkin' about his bankruptcy." The sheriff tossed a sheaf of documents onto Alice's lap. She held them close to her face, but she couldn't make out anything in the dim light.

"What's this?"

"He had his records expunged," the sheriff said. He reached up and turned on the dome light. "Years ago. Hired a pretty good lawyer to do it, from the looks of it. Thorough. But there's always something left, if you know where to look."

It was a handwritten police report from Fairfax County, Virginia, 1993. The pages were blurry photocopies, but Alice could make out the gist of things. Officers called to a residence, a battered woman, a drunken, vaguely remorseful husband named Robert Wilcox. Polaroids of the woman had been paper-clipped to the reports when they'd been photocopied; in each picture she had the same expression of sad defiance, the same stringy blond hair. She looked nothing like Rachel but more like Kim's description of Missy from El Tamarindo than Alice was comfortable admitting. In the first she had a black eye, and in the second there were finger-shaped bruises on her upper arms. In each instance, Robert had been taken to jail overnight and then released.

"These aren't admissible in court," Alice said.

"This ain't a trial," the sheriff said. "His wife didn't tell you about that, did she?"

"No," Alice said. "She might not know about it."

"Either way. It's right there in writing. Pictures even. He beats women. Maybe he gets off on it, or maybe he's just got a bad temper. Point is, he's guilty."

"Not necessarily," Alice said. "This doesn't look good, that's true. But this doesn't mean he beat Missy too. I mean, this was drunk boyfriend stuff, and it was over twenty years ago. Whoever did Missy was trying to kill her."

The sheriff shook his head. "If you'd just be reasonable, it's obvious for anyone to see. The guy's guilty as sin."

"You sure are eager to get me off this case," Alice said.

The sheriff turned in his seat to look at her. "What's that supposed to mean?"

"People in this town don't have much faith in the police. Rumor is, cops have been disappearing people in Whitehurst for years now, or at the very least, looking the other way when they're framed. And Robert's just the latest example."

"And why would we do that?"

"I don't know. Yet."

"So rumors is all you're talking about then. Jesus, Alice, you oughta know that every scumbag tells the same story when you got 'em boxed in . . ."

"Something's going on in this town, Michael, not the least of which is your distinctly prejudicial style of policing. Are you really going to tell me otherwise? Look at me."

They'd pulled into the parking lot of the Bobcat Motel by now; Alice could see the lights on in her and Kim's room. He shifted in his seat to face her, but she couldn't see his eyes, shaded as they were by the brim of his black velvet cowboy hat. "Have I let a Whitehurst man off with a warning when I shoulda run him in for DUI? Yeah, I have. Do the weigh stations fudge the numbers to keep the trucks running, and do I turn a blind eye? Yeah, I guess I do. But that's the price of doin' business. You didn't see Whitehurst before the boom. Some people'll have you believe that it was a quiet little Norman Rockwell painting, but those people are full of shit. It was nothing. Just a nothing, two-cop, run-down, empty town. You couldn't even breathe. Law's the law, but I'm also a practical man. We owe Steve Whitehurst. He singlehandedly jump-started fracking in this area, and now we got more jobs than we can fill, money flowing through. But this talk about conspiracies, that's just foolishness. And I expected better from you, Alice."

"Then why give me this?" she asked, holding up the police reports.

"I don't like seeing you waste your time."

"It's my time," Alice said. "And I think I'll waste a little more of it here in Whitehurst before I write Robert off."

"Well, I never said I wanted you to leave town," the sheriff said. "I just think there are better things to do here."

He leaned forward, and Alice could see him smile, his teeth just visible in the low light, his eyes hooded in a manner he probably thought seductive. She had to restrain herself from rolling her eyes. "You know, Michael, sometimes I think you're the most honest, upstanding Boy

Scout in this town, but then other times I remember that it's the ones who seem the most virtuous who're hiding the darkest shit."

"I'm pretty much what I seem to be," he said. "I'm just me."

Alice knew he was going to kiss her then, and she decided to let him. He wasn't a terrible kisser, though his movements had a stiffness that suggested practicing on your reflection in a mirror. His hand ran over her breasts, squeezing first one and then the other like a finicky shopper testing fruit. He reached over and ran his other hand through her hair, and she imagined him grimacing at the shortness of it back there, shaved almost to the scalp.

Alice had just given herself over to it, had started to kiss him back, drunkenly pretending he was Chris, the kid from the bar, when she felt him pushing on the back of her head. Before she knew what was happening, he'd slid his hand down to the back of her neck and was forcing her face down into his lap as he undid his belt with the other hand.

"Stop," Alice said, calmly at first and then with a growing edge of panic. "Stop! Let me up!" She pushed against his legs, but the grip he had on the back of her neck was too firm. She flailed her arms, and by chance she hit the car's horn, triggering a long, blaring report. The sheriff let go of her neck, and she sat up, scooting back against the passenger side door. "What the fuck!"

The sheriff was looking out his window at the motel. In each window, single slats in the blinds were being lifted and then dropped as the occupants noted the presence of the sheriff's cruiser. The sheriff took off his hat and then turned on the dome light, as if to forestall any suspicion of wrongdoing.

"Why did you do that?" Alice asked. Why, she thought, did she always end up talking to him like a teacher scolding a recalcitrant pupil?

The sheriff didn't look at her, just hunched forward over the steering wheel. "I don't know," he said finally. "Because I wanted to."

"I thought I was too drunk to be going home with anyone. Or do you admit that was just bullshit?"

"You would've done that for that fuckin' kid!"

"Maybe I would have, maybe I wouldn't have. Not if he forced me to."

"I don't think you understand what *force you to* means."

"That sounds like a threat."

"Just a fact," the sheriff said. "You oughta be wearing your pistol."

Alice couldn't help but laugh. "So I could shoot you when you tried to force me to give you a blow job?"

He winced at this, as if the phrase caused him physical pain. "Not me. If someone else did. Someone bad. You know me."

"Oh, so it's okay to do that, since I know you? Do you even know how fucked up you are? Someone bad. Someone bad is someone who does bad things, and what you just did was a bad thing. That makes you a bad person."

The sheriff turned on her, and she saw that she'd touched a nerve. "A bad person would've slit your throat and dumped you out in the badlands, you stupid bitch!" His eyes were wild, almost incandescent. He opened his jacket and pointed at the badge affixed to his shirt pocket. "See this? I see bad people every day. Don't you try and tell me that I'm a bad person. I know what bad is. You just better pray you don't run into any real bad men." He leaned roughly across her, and for a moment, Alice thought he was going to kiss her again, but he jerked on her door handle and threw the door open. "Now get the fuck out of my car."

Alice got out of the car. She thought of several acid rebuttals, but all she said was, "Quit following me."

The sheriff didn't say anything, just slammed the door shut and peeled out of the parking lot. Alice watched his taillights recede. He'd be texting her before he even got home, and their little dance would resume. He'd feed her information, and she'd feed his ego, each of them sure that the other had no idea they were being manipulated. Before he'd gotten to the intersection, he'd already turned on his lights and sirens, and he blew through the red light. Alice turned back to the motel just in time to see two-dozen venetian blind slats falling hastily back into place.

CHAPTER 7

Inside, Kim was lying on the bed, freshly showered and clad in a towel, swiping away on her phone. She perked up when Alice walked in. "I heard that car peelin' out, and then the sirens," she said. "He peacockin' for his new girl like a little boy with his first hard-on. You been yankin' on Johnny Law's crank again, I bet."

"What do you expect? It's a purple moon," Alice deadpanned.

Kim scowled. "Purple moon ain't a joke. You don't know nothin' about it. Did you at least get any information?"

Alice told Kim about what had happened after she'd left her at the bar: being pulled over with the kid, the sheriff's threat to charge the kid with rape, and then his clumsy assault in the parking lot. Kim didn't seem surprised by any of it.

"I told you to quit messin' with him," she said after Alice had finished. "Where you from, the big city, I'm sure you mess with all them liberated men. But it ain't like that out here. These some old-fashioned men. They want something, they take it. He the worst of all, 'cause he got the badge. He thinks he own you now. Just like a dog. You sayin' no, that's probably the first time he heard that word in a long time. He probably went home to look it up in the dictionary. Dumb motherfucker. And now he gonna come after you twice as hard. If I was you, I'd start carryin' that gun. All the time. And don't let him get you alone, ever."

"Kim, I'm not going to shoot the fucking sheriff." She kept her voice casual, though she knew Kim was right.

"If it's a choice between him and the deputies runnin' a train on you in a abandoned house or peeling his wig back, you better peel his fucking wig back. Or I'll come to your funeral just to slap the shit out of you."

"He told me something about Robert," Alice said.

"Yeah?"

"Did you know that he was charged with domestic abuse back in the nineties? When he lived in Virginia?"

"Not that shit," Kim said. "Robert told me about that after he got arrested. He said they gonna dredge up all the shit from his past to make him look bad, and he was right, wasn't he? His girl, she all fucked up on somethin'. They screamin' and shoutin', neighbors call the cops, she tells them a bunch of lies, and he has to spend the night in jail. They broke up after that. Why, you on that he's guilty shit again?"

"Well," Alice said after a moment. "It doesn't look good."

"So? It ain't admissible, is it?"

"Well, no," Alice said. "But if it comes out in the media, which it probably will if it goes to trial, the locals are going to want to see him hang."

Kim shrugged. "Don't change nothin'. Get him outta there, and we ain't gotta worry about all that. What you should be askin' yourself is why your boy keep feedin' you all this horseshit."

"Yeah, I thought of that too," Alice said.

"That sellout motherfucker. He just trying to pump up his crime stats, get him a win. Fucker's too lazy to do any real policin'."

Alice's head was pounding; the cheap liquor was clearing from her system and ushering in a hangover. She went to the bathroom, found a bottle of ibuprofen, and downed two tablets with a handful of tap water.

"Did you find anything out at the bar?" she asked Kim when she came out.

"You think these boys can keep their mouth shut?" She leaned over and turned on the bedside lamp. "Get this. So Deke, the shitkicker who shanked Bobby, he'd only been in since the day before. For assault on a police officer."

"Yeah, the sheriff told me that," said Alice.

"Uh-huh. But the way it went down is the thing. A deputy was sittin' at the counter in the diner across from the police station, just havin' coffee, and Deke walks up and outta nowhere, bam, just decks the guy off the back of his stool. By the time he got back up, Deke'd already assumed the position. Hands on his head, down on the ground. Stone-cold sober."

Alice nodded, biting her lip. "He wanted to go to jail."

"Uh-huh."

"No beef between Deke and the officer."

"Nah."

"Damn," said Alice. "And this guy worked for who?"

"Roundtree. Billy Roundtree. All the dust in this town, it kicks back to him. He ain't Whitehurst rich, but he rich enough to drop ten grand in the strip club twice a week. He a stupid motherfucker, but he on top because he got a lot of even stupider motherfuckers like Deke Kelly workin' for him. Roundtree says stomp a guy, Deke stomps him real good. Roundtree says pop a cap, Deke pops a whole clip."

"Why would Roundtree want Robert dead?" Alice asked. "Did they ever come into contact?"

"Nah. Roundtree holes up in his big house out on the prairie. He don't come into town except to sell dust. And Bobby ain't live that life."

Alice lay down on the bed. Her head was pounding. "Make room," she said to Kim, who scooted over. Alice couldn't think of any way

Robert would be connected to the top drug dealer in Whitehurst, but the possibilities weren't heartening. "Tell me honestly," she said to Kim. "Was Robert into dust?"

"He a old white dude. Strictly on that beer and whiskey."

"Maybe he was dealing on the side. Wanted to double his salary? The mortgage on his house back in Connecticut is underwater by about half a mil."

"Nah," Kim said. "You wanna deal, you got to know people. Robert ain't know nobody, and besides, he ain't have the constitution of a outlaw, you know?"

"But you do," Alice said.

"I take a little dust now and then, but I buy retail. Word gets out that a woman slingin' dust, every cowboy with a axe handle be comin' to rip me off. You got to have muscle backin' you up to sling, and Robert ain't no kind of muscle."

Alice nodded. "What then?"

Kim stretched and her towel fell away. Alice saw that she had a small Nike swoosh tattooed under her right nipple. "How do you look in a bikini?" Kim said.

Alice blinked. "I don't know. I haven't worn one since I was eight."

"Roundtree havin' a party tomorrow night, up at his house. His boys put the word out at all the houses and strip joints. He likes to party like Caligula, ten girls for every guy. Platters of dust. We could walk right in the front door. I could anyway. You'll need a little makeover."

"Okay, and then what?"

"What you mean, 'and then what'? Men like to talk when they get fucked up. They like to brag to pretty girls. And I dunno, if he too fucked up to talk, we steal his phone or some shit. I mean, you got a better idea?"

"No," Alice said. The ibuprofen had kicked in, and now that her headache had abated, she realized how tired she was. She rolled over and turned off the bedside lamp. "Can I at least wear a one-piece, though?"

"Fuck no, you can't wear no granny suit," Kim said. "I'll take you shoppin' tomorrow afternoon. I know just the place."

Alice didn't like Kim's tone of voice. She knew it well; it was the voice of someone anticipating, with glee, the imminent humiliation of someone they loved and hated in equal measure. It made Alice think of her ex-husband, and then of Rachel Wilcox, to whom she owed another progress report. "Day four: Robert seems to be entangled with local drug kingpin, I will be investigating shortly, in pasties and a G-string. Please remit payment immediately, and see enclosed receipt from Brenda's Brazilian Waxes for reimbursement." She smiled in the dark, which she considered a good sign. At least she still had her sense of humor.

Alice woke up at first light, roused from the deep slumber that follows total physical and mental exhaustion. She'd fallen asleep fully clothed, only kicking her shoes off. Careful not to disturb Kim, she slid a cigarette from Kim's pack and walked barefoot outside. This case had the markings of a paranoiac's fever dream, she thought as she smoked in the grainy dawn. She couldn't quite figure when the facts melted into speculation and delusion. Whatever was fueling Kim and Robert's conspiracy theories, Alice knew the key to it all was Missy, lying dormant with her secrets in the hospital.

She was about to head back inside when she heard the buzz of a dirt bike approaching. In the distance, she saw Kim's pimp-slash-boyfriend coming in off the highway in a cloud of dust. Alice stood in front of the door, hands on hips.

Lester sat astride the idling bike, squinting at Alice. He really was the ugliest man she'd ever seen. His sloping, enormous forehead melted into his crooked nose, and his face ended in a weak chin so recessive it looked as if his mouth rested directly on top of his Adam's apple. His face was ravaged with acne scars, and his skin was the color of fresh mozzarella. He was the polar opposite of those flawlessly symmetrical Adonises you saw in underwear ads, and in his own way, just as compelling. Alice had to admit that she could sort of see why Kim was attracted to him. He was one in a million.

"Who're you?" Lester asked. He was holding a battered manila envelope in one hand.

"I'm Alice. Kim's roommate. You're Lester, right?"

Lester smiled. His teeth were enormous and horselike. "You're the detective lady, right? I heard about you."

"I heard about you too. You come by for more money? Kim's not here."

"Ain't she? Her car's here."

"She took a walk," Alice said, more forcefully than she'd meant to.

"Awful early for a walk." Lester shut off the bike and climbed down. He looked more amused than threatening, walking bowlegged toward her with a half smile on his lips. "Maybe I did come by for a loan, maybe not. It ain't none of your business, is it?"

"People pay loans back," Alice said.

Lester chuckled. "Kimmy told me you was a do-gooder." Lester approached slowly but deliberately until his face was an inch from Alice's. He seemed to be aware of his ability to make people uncomfortable. "Me and Kimmy, we been through a lot together. Don't try to get between us."

"You're not taking her money again," Alice said quietly. It was a stupid stand to take, and she felt sheepish about it. Poor Lester. He'd just had the bad luck of crossing her path at the exact moment she'd become exhausted by the men of Whitehurst—their bullying, their bluster, their entitlement. Part of it too was that Kim was proving to be more of a help than she'd ever imagined. Kim was earning every cent of her daily fee, and it pained Alice to think of that money being pissed away in the dust houses and brothels of Whitehurst by ugly, sponging Lester.

"I thought she weren't here," Lester said.

"Just leave."

"You leave!" Lester snapped. "You don't belong here. You in the way!"

Alice reached with her right hand to her back pocket and brought out the sheriff's business card. It was conspicuously overwrought, gold-leaf letters spelling out his name in all capitals. She turned it over in her hand and brandished it at Lester like a talisman.

"That's right," Lester sneered. "I heard you're fuckin' the sheriff. You'd probably tell him I tried to rape you, get me thrown in the hole."

"I might do that," Alice said casually. "Way I hear it, he believes what he wants."

This comment seemed to chill Lester. His shoulders sagged and he took a half step backward. "Fuck you," he said, but only as an afterthought. He mounted his dirt bike, kick-started it, yawed it in a wide half circle, then zipped across the parking lot and sat idling on the shoulder, waiting for a gap so he could enter eastbound traffic.

Something occurred to Alice then. She unlocked the room, went inside, and grabbed her camera bag and gun. Then she went to Kim's bedside table and rummaged through the broken cigarettes, empty baggies, and condom wrappers until she found the keys to Kim's hatchback. Kim stayed asleep, still as a corpse.

Alice emerged from the room just in time to see Lester accelerate into traffic. She jogged to the hatchback, reversed in a wide circle and then sped across the lot toward the main road. She managed to squeeze into traffic immediately, zipping in front of a wheezing dump truck, flooring the accelerator as traffic swelled in the rearview. Lester couldn't be far ahead.

She drove along in eastbound traffic, periodically swerving to see if she could catch a glimpse of Lester ahead. She'd just started to worry she'd lost him when she spotted him off to the right, turning into the parking lot of a barracks-like apartment complex. She drove past and pulled into the adjacent gas station. She parked the car, grabbed the camera, and went inside.

The gas station was bustling with a crowd of oil workers clutching coffees and bagged doughnuts. They all looked her up and down, but Alice cut through them without taking notice. On the other side of the building, the doors opened directly onto the apartment complex's parking lot, where Lester was cajoling a tired-looking, very pregnant blond in a bathrobe. Alice raised her camera and started shooting. Lester took to caressing the woman's midsection while she regarded him with pursed lips and shook her head. He went in for a kiss, and the blond turned her head. Finally Lester stopped talking, and the two of them just looked at each other for a long moment before Lester cocked his head coquettishly. The woman broke away from him but reached into the pocket of her robe and threw a bundle of cash onto the pavement, then began to walk back to her apartment. Lester jumped off his bike and dropped to his hands and knees, clutching at the bills as they scattered and stuffing them in the manila envelope. Alice shook her head and clicked away.

As she headed back through the gas station to her car, one of the roughnecks in line said, "If you like takin' pictures, I got something you can take a picture of." Alice brushed past him without a glance.

As Alice keyed the ignition, she saw Lester heading eastbound again. Traffic had died down during shift change, and she had to wait for a truck to come by to act as a buffer between her and Lester. Alice patiently lagged behind, bobbing over to keep sight of her target. They went half a mile like this before Lester turned onto an off-ramp to a weigh station. As he passed the attendants' booth, he and the men working exchanged a friendly wave. Alice slowed so that it wasn't too obvious that she was following him, and then pulled over when she saw the flash of Lester's brake lights.

Along the on-ramp leading back to the highway stood four women. They looked cold in their baby tees and miniskirts, shifting their weight from foot to foot and hugging themselves, but each time a truck drove past, they began waving and blowing kisses and, in the case of one especially enthusiastic woman, clutching both her breasts and bobbling them up and down. Lester pulled up to them and got off his bike. Alice started shooting with the camera through her windshield, leaning forward and resting the long lens on the dashboard.

Lester held the manila envelope out like a child going trick-or-treating. No cajoling this time. Each of the women produced a wad of cash and dropped it into the envelope. Lester turned to his bike but, after looking into the envelope, walked back to the women. Without saying a word, he backhanded one of them, a young girl with blue hair and a stars-and-stripes bikini top. She fell to the ground, one hand to her mouth. Lester crouched, and through the zoom lens, Alice could see him talking to her, an amiable expression on his face. He reached into his hip pocket and brought out a small silver object, which he held up at eye level. With a deft movement of his wrist, he unfolded and extended the blade.

"Oh shit," Alice said. She continued shooting but leaned over and with her left hand brought her pistol out of her bag. Or should she floor it and run him over before he could stab the woman?

Before she could decide, the girl put one hand up slowly and brought a flattened sheaf of bills out from her bikini top. Lester took the money, put it in the manila envelope, and folded the butterfly knife. As he walked back to his bike, he looked extremely pleased with himself.

"Asshole," Alice muttered.

Lester sped off, and Alice followed. As she passed the women, she looked over; three of them ignored her, but the one who Lester had smacked gave her the finger.

Lester was headed back to town, westbound, and as Alice trailed him, hanging back, she watched him steer back and forth in wide, slaloming arcs, across both lanes of traffic. She wondered if he was drunk, but then realized no, he was just euphoric.

They entered downtown Whitehurst and slowed as the street became a jumble of double-parked trucks and wandering men, still drunk from the night before. Lester popped his dirt bike up over the curb and leaned it against a light pole. Clutching his manila envelope under one arm, he entered an unnumbered steel door at street level, and was gone.

Alice coasted down the block, executed a U-turn across traffic, and parked in front of a fire hydrant. But before she'd even turned off the car, Lester reemerged onto the sidewalk. He was no longer carrying the manila envelope. Alice snapped a few photos of him as he started his bike and then disappeared into traffic. Then she turned off the car, put her camera back in its bag, and got out.

She crossed the street and stood on the sidewalk, examining the door that Lester had entered and exited. No number, no bell, no sign. No identifying marks whatsoever, though she noticed a small surveillance camera above the door, oriented toward the street. She smiled for anyone watching, walked up the short front walk, and pulled the door open.

Just inside the door was an unoccupied barstool, with someone's iPhone sitting on it. Alice walked down the curving hallway until it opened into a dimly lit lounge. An older bald man stood behind the bar, smoothing and sorting a pile of stained and crumpled bills; next to him was Lester's manila envelope. Beyond him, men sat playing cards at round tables. There was one waitress, dressed in a cheap French maid Halloween costume. When the man behind the bar saw Alice, he stopped counting the money and looked at her, but said nothing.

"Hi!" Alice said in her sunniest voice. "I was wondering if there's a restroom I could use?"

"It's for customers only," the man behind the bar said.

"That's fine," Alice said. "I'll have a soda."

"We ain't got sodas." He'd rested both of his hands on top of the stacks of cash, as if he thought a sudden breeze might snatch it away.

There was a faint sound of a toilet flushing, and a door opened to Alice's right. A tall, barrel-chested Native American man in Timberland boots and a gray sweat suit walked out, wiping his hands on his pants. When he saw Alice, he stopped in his tracks, his eyes flicking between her and the man behind the bar, who was already glaring at him.

"I guess you think we're running a church bingo hall here," sneered the man behind the bar. "Come one, come all. Open to the public."

"I was in the bathroom," the Native American man protested.

"Are you still in the bathroom? Or can I trouble you to do your fucking job?"

The bouncer dropped his eyes and moved to stand in front of Alice. "Come on, let's go," he said.

She turned and walked back up the dark hallway. She could feel the larger man's bulk looming behind her, his steps matching hers precisely. When they reached the front door, he pressed past her and opened it.

"I'm sorry if I got you in trouble," Alice said innocently.

In response, the bouncer shoved her so hard that she stumbled and landed on her face. By the time she leaped to her feet, the door was already closed.

"Asshole!" Alice shouted. She kicked the steel door in frustration. It opened immediately. This time the bouncer was holding a stun gun alongside his leg. He said nothing, just looked at Alice with slitted eyes. Alice kept her hands out at her sides, backing up slowly until she was on the sidewalk. Only then did the door swing slowly, soundlessly closed.

CHAPTER 8

When Alice returned to the Bobcat, Kim was standing outside their room smoking a Capri, squinting in the midday sun.

"Hope you don't mind that I borrowed the car," Alice said. "Had to run a little errand."

Kim shrugged. "'S okay. You eat breakfast?"

"Nah. You want to get something?"

"Nope. We both fastin' today. If we stuntin' in bikinis later, we got to be cut up and dried out. No salt, no sugar, no coffee."

"No coffee?" Alice would've protested, but she was thinking about what she should do with the photos of Lester. She'd planned on telling Kim right away, but the moment wasn't right. It was clear from the way Kim talked about Lester that she was fiercely possessive toward him; if Alice told her about Lester's other girls now, she'd be going to the party alone while Kim systematically hunted down each of her competitors. She sat down on a cooler on the sidewalk and waggled two fingers at Kim. "If you aren't going to let me eat, at least give me a cigarette."

Kim offered her the pack and lit one of the thin cigarettes for her. "You know, you ain't got to come tonight. I can gather some info myself."

Alice took a drag on the Capri; it was surprisingly harsh considering its dainty appearance. "Why wouldn't I come?"

"You ain't seem too excited about the dress code," Kim said. "These people, they party hard. I dunno if you up to it."

Alice didn't know if she was either, but she would never give Kim the satisfaction of admitting it. "I'm from New York City!"

"A'ight then," Kim said. She plucked the car keys out of Alice's hand. "Let's go shoppin'."

Kim took her to a small shop on the outskirts of town between a pet store and an all-you-can-eat buffet. The storefront featured a neon sign spelling out "Mystique" in flamboyant cursive script. Inside, cartoonishly proportioned mannequins displayed tiny bikini tops and crotchless fishnet body stockings. The proprietor, a large matriarch wearing half-moon bifocals, greeted Kim familiarly.

"Thought you'd be in today," she said. "Lotta girls comin' in to get decked out for tonight."

"Never miss a payday," Kim said. "This my friend Alice. She need some clothes too."

The woman looked Alice up and down. "That shouldn't be a problem. What style of stuff you favor?"

Alice looked at Kim and then back at the proprietor. "I, uh, I don't know. Do you have anything like those old *Baywatch* swimsuits that go way up high on the sides?"

Kim shook her head. "Just bring two of everything you bring me, one in her size. Throw in some stripper costumes and club wear in case she don't have the heart for a bikini." Kim led her to the row of dressing rooms in the back and pulled her into the double-wide handicapped dressing room at the very end. Inside was an L-shaped bench where Kim sat and lit up a Capri. "Connie'll bring us stuff. She knows what I like."

Alice was alarmed at the prospect of stripping down in front of Kim, but was too embarrassed to say anything. Undressing in front of a man was no big deal, but then a man was generally an appreciative audience. Getting undressed with other women seemed to cultivate an atmosphere of cattiness that she found exhausting. She leaned against the wall and crossed her arms, trying to strike a diffident pose.

Kim held her pack of Capris out. "Keep smokin'," she said. "They make you not hungry."

Alice took one of the slender cigarettes, accepted a light, and watched as Kim stood and stripped down to her underwear. She was wearing a black lace bralette and cotton panties that had been turned inside out to extend their wearability. On the crotch was a large white stain that made Alice's stomach queasy when she looked at it. Kim sat back down, knees apart, hands flung indifferently between her thighs.

Alice gritted her teeth, pulled her sweatshirt up over her head, and then dropped her trousers to the floor. She looked at herself in the mirror and found that her body looked much better than she'd thought it would. She thought about what this said about her.

"I knew you had a body under there," Kim said. "You look a'ight. I dunno why you don't show that shit off a little bit."

"I don't like being looked at," Alice said.

"Bullshit," Kim said. "Everyone like bein' looked at. Just gotta get the right one lookin'."

Kim rose from the bench and stood in front of the mirror, arms lightly akimbo, her shoulders pulled back to elevate her small breasts. Alice wondered whom she was posing for, whom that defiance was aimed at. Kim's frame was petite and well proportioned, but her body had a fearsome aspect to it, an almost Goya-esque quality: her muscles starved down to sharp definition, her ribs visible as if gouged out by knifepoint. But she still had softness around her hips, and her breasts had survived the dust. It was the kind of body that would last for decades, into her fifties, at least.

Alice's own body, which she looked at now in the mirror, was of a sort that she'd thought of as lanky when she was an adolescent, but later thought of, perhaps flatteringly, as statuesque. Her thighs were long and thin, her shoulders bony, her arms willowy, her hips barely wider than her waist. It was the type of body women admired but men generally considered undesirable. Not that she cared what men considered desirable. Men had terrible taste, in everything. She just wished her body didn't make most clothes look like curtains thrown over a coat rack.

Connie came in with an armload of things for them to try on and set the two identical piles side by side on the bench. Next to them she placed a six-pack of strawberry-lime wine coolers.

"You need anything, you let me know," Connie said to Kim and then closed the door behind her.

"I buy all my work clothes here." Kim uncapped two wine coolers and handed one to Alice. "Let's slam these before we start trying stuff on. They'll go straight to our head since we ain't ate all day."

Kim was right. Before she'd even gotten the first outfit on, Alice found herself wobbling on her feet. Kim had pulled off her bralette and was now wearing a pair of thin red suspenders that she'd positioned over her nipples.

"How are you going to keep those in place?"

"Just wear pasties under. Or maybe double-sided tape, though that shit gives me a rash."

Alice sifted through her pile: there was a pink fishnet body stocking, a bra with the centers of the cups cut out, a lace corset, a pair of tiny velour boy shorts, and various sets of thigh-high stockings. At the bottom of the pile, she found a dress that had been tailored out of a black XXL throwback Minnesota Timberwolves NBA jersey. It was by far the least aesthetically offensive item in the pile. She slid it on and found that the thin polyester fabric clung to every part of her body, like a snake's skin. It only came a couple inches past her crotch, so she shimmied on a pair of fine black fishnets. When she looked in the mirror, she barely recognized herself.

"All done," she said.

Kim, who had laid all her selections side by side on the floor and stood completely nude looking down at them with an expression of utter seriousness, turned and took in Alice's outfit. "Yeah, it's okay. I do your hair and makeup, you might even pass for a real girl. Now help me pick out my outfit."

Kim seemed intent on the suspenders, so Alice picked out a pair of black short-shorts of latex-like material and, on a whim, went out into the shop to where she'd seen a display of hats and picked out a black officer's cap. She brought it back to the dressing room and set it atop Kim's head.

"You look like a sexy Nazi officer," Alice said. "I bet these Dakota white boys will love it."

"Maybe, maybe," Kim said. She reached over and cracked open two more wine coolers, handing one to Alice. Their eyes met for a moment, and then Kim looked away, as if in guilt.

"So," she said. "What's Bobby's wife like?"

"Robert never said?"

"Nah, he liked to keep that shit separated. He clammed up if I asked about her."

Alice knew what an effort it had taken for Kim, so stone-faced and seemingly invulnerable, to ask that question. It couldn't have been easy all those months, competing against a woman you had never met and knew nothing about. She made an expression of sympathy, but Kim just looked at her through slit eyes, waiting.

"Well," Alice said. "Rachel's my age, a little older. She comes from a Mormon family, but she doesn't follow the religion. She was one of eleven children, so she had to learn how to be heard or she'd have been lost in the shuffle. She's demanding, I guess. Blunt. She used to be my boss. And my friend. But mostly my boss. She's the type who tells you what she's thinking. If you're right or wrong, she'd let you know. She doesn't mince words or suffer fools. You're a lot like her actually. Like she used to be anyway. We got involved in something at work, and it went bad. That pretty much destroyed our careers and our friendship."

"Yeah, I heard a little about that," Kim said. "Robert always blamed you for him being up here in the sticks. Said you fucked up and took his wife down with you."

"That's not what happened at all," Alice snapped.

"Yeah?" Kim feigned casual interest, but Alice saw through it. She supposed that Kim still wasn't entirely sure about her character—not only with whom Alice's loyalties lay but how clean or dirty, in a general sense, she was. Normally she would've been reluctant to talk about her past—she had become a private person, having seen in the course of her work what the consequences of openness could be—but the alcohol and the atmosphere of sisterly camaraderie made her feel like unburdening herself.

"Rachel and I worked at the *Post*, in DC. She was my editor. I was a general-assignment reporter. It had taken me a long time to get there. I didn't go to a top program, but I paid my dues. I worked at weeklies for years, sitting in on zoning hearings and city council meetings and getting mothers to talk about their kids who'd been shot down in the street or who'd shot a kid down in the street. Rachel was the same. She came to the *Post* from Minneapolis, and I came from Baltimore, and I think we bonded over that. We were both workers. Climbers. The year we started, I think it was 2005, it was clear that the newspaper business was in decline. I don't think most people even thought it would survive the decade. We didn't care, though. If anything, it was motivation. Do the important work while we still could. Looking back, maybe it made us reckless too.

"A case came to our attention. A death row case in Texas. Some law students reviewing capital punishment convictions, looking for candidates for commutation. Altoona Crawley. He was in his forties and had been on death row for almost twenty-five years for the rape and murder of four women in the Houston area. No witnesses, no real physical evidence, and he'd been convicted before DNA testing became widely available. He'd been seen in the neighborhood of one of the victims, but his grandmother lived on the block. The main piece of evidence at trial was a short story he'd written in which a woman was raped and dismembered in a way that resembled one of the murder victims. The prosecutor made out like it was a confession, and the jury went right along with it. This was in Texas, where they even interpret the Bible literally.

"In Houston, if you're a young guy and you have a gold grill and neck tattoos and wear snapbacks, they get it. They may not like you, but they understand where you're coming from. But if you write horror stories and wear a trench coat and go around nappy-headed and ashy, it fucks them up. They don't have a box to put you in, so naturally, they're willing to assume the worst about you. This kid, basically, he was convicted of being different.

"So Rachel and I decided we were going to clear this man's name. Spring him from death row and get us a Pulitzer before the whole journalism establishment crashes and burns. I went down to Houston to nose around. I was good. When I worked the weeklies, I had law firms offering to triple, quadruple my salary if I came to work for them as an in-house investigator. In Baltimore there was this case where a girl got beat into a coma in a McDonald's at 3:00 a.m. on a Saturday. Surveillance cameras were down, no video. I tracked down every person who was in the place. Cops couldn't find even one.

"Crawley was tough, though. He'd dropped out of school in eighth grade, didn't have any friends. Didn't have a job—lived on a disability check for an anxiety disorder. Only person he saw with any regularity was his grandma, and she wasn't any help. I saw her my first day in town. She straight up told me that I was wasting my time, that her grandson killed all those women. I asked her why she'd say that, she comes out with all the stuff about how he'd stopped going to church, always wore black, he was listening to devil music. Those were her words! Devil music. Showed me some of the albums—Iron Maiden, that sort of thing. Tame. I went to see the detective who'd arrested Crawley, and it was the same kind of shit. Showed me some of the porn they found in Crawley's room. There was a VHS tape of a woman handcuffed and blindfolded, being fucked. Vanilla as far as kink goes. Fifty Shades type of stuff. I've looked at racier stuff on my phone in line at Whole Foods. But this detective was a Boy Scout—literally. Had his merit badges framed on the wall of his office and everything. Probably never even had sex with the lights on.

"So I was sure after a day or two that Crawley had gotten railroaded. I just couldn't prove he was innocent. First thing I looked into was finding a witness who could put him elsewhere on the night of the crimes. Problem with that was, Crawley didn't have any friends and didn't even leave the house, sometimes for days at a time. Just sat at home playing videogames until sunup and then slept all day. In a way, he was the perfect patsy. You could put him anywhere, and his only alibi was I was home, alone. Sometimes I used to wonder if the Houston PD knew about him for a while and just kept him in their back pocket for when they needed to close a high-profile case.

"The only other route to exoneration was DNA evidence. Crawley had been convicted in the mideighties, so the rape kits from the women hadn't been tested for DNA. The lawyers we were working with had been petitioning to get the evidence retested, but the county had been dragging its feet the entire way. Police departments are never eager to have their prosecutors embarrassed and proved wrong, and they'd had other problems there that made them even more defensive. Scandals involving police brutality, racial profiling, asset forfeiture abuse. The last thing they wanted was more headlines.

"So I sniffed out where evidence control was housed. Most cities, they have a modern climate-controlled facility, a staff of technicians. This place didn't even have shelves. It was just one old woman in a ramshackle little wooden building on the edge of town. Little counter in front and, in back, stacks of boxes and files about shoulder high with these tiny narrow little paths going everywhere like hamster trails or something. Total chaos. The day I went in, it was hot and rainy, and the woman who was working there had the windows open, and I can see, I can actually visibly see from the front counter, rain coming in a window and soaking a stack of files. And who knows, maybe those files weren't anything important, but maybe they were. Maybe someone's life depended on something in those files, which by the end of the day were just going to be mush. It's chilling when you think about it.

"So I ask the woman there if she has the evidence from the Crawley case, and she sort of waves her cigarette behind her and says, yeah, somewhere. Clearly she has no idea where. I asked her if there was someone I could talk to who might be able to give me a more precise answer, and she was like, nah, it's just me who works here.

"So clearly, the evidence is our best shot. I just have to get my hands on it. And look, this is real life. I'm not breaking in there in the middle of the night like a bad action movie. That just isn't how things work. But you know what does work? Blackmail. Because everyone's got something in their life that can be used against them. I don't care who you are, you have that weakness. I can see you thinking about yours right now. Don't worry, I'm not going to ask you about it. You wouldn't believe some of the work I've done, the shit I've dug up as a PI, for political campaigns, angry ex-wives, disgruntled employees.

"So I look into the woman who worked there. She was maybe fifty, worked at the DMV for twenty years, then they transferred her to evidence control. Maybe it was a promotion, maybe it was a demotion, who knows? She's just putting time in for a pension. I waited until trash day, cruised by her place late at night in my rental, and lifted her garbage. Most of it was *TV Guides*, wrappers for off-brand cookies, empty salad-for-one kits. But at the bottom of the trash, I found a little black plastic bag that was double wrapped and tied closed real tight. Bingo. I cut it open. What do you think falls out? Syringes. Couple weeks' worth. Woman's a junkie. Well, that's not any of my business. She wasn't hurting anybody, and clearly she had her life together, if sitting at home every night watching television and eating cookies while you nod off is your thing.

"I called Rachel up that night and told her I wanted to blackmail this woman to turn the evidence over to us. Sure, there'd be questions, but once we had the DNA independently tested and got a result clearing Crawley, how important would those questions really be? She said no, but I kept on, and eventually I won her over.

"So I went back to see the white-collar junkie, the one who works in evidence control. Her name was White. Regina White. I knocked on her door, and she invited me in for coffee. I'm sitting at her little kitchen table while she prepares two cups of instant. I pull out the black plastic bag of syringes and just quietly set it on the table. She turns around with a mug in each hand, and the first thing she sees is the bag. She doesn't say anything, just stands there looking at it, coffee in hand. After about ten seconds, she sets a cup of coffee in front of me and asks if I take cream or sugar. I just shook my head. I wasn't sure what she was going to do, if she was going to make a break for it or throw the other cup in my face or what.

"She sits down across from me and puts about ten packets of Splenda in her cup, one by one. Then she sits there stirring it and just looking into her cup. When she finally looks up, she's got tears in her eyes, and fuck, did I feel terrible right then. I wasn't any better than the guys who framed-up Crawley.

"The first thing Regina finally says is, 'So does this mean I'm fired?' She thought I was working for the county! I say no, this is a private matter, no one has to know about her habit. If she cooperates. I lay it all out for her then—she's going to dig up the Crawley evidence and turn it over to me, and when her superiors come asking how it got into my hands, she's going to play dumb. I thought she would argue or say she couldn't pull it off, but she just looked at me and got real quiet, and this sly, calculating look appears in her eyes, and she says, 'Okay, how much?'

"I wasn't expecting her to say that, but this is America, you know? Everyone has a right to make a buck. You get what you pay for. So I convinced Rachel to authorize a payment from the paper. We had to lie on the paperwork, but at that point, what's one more lie? Five thousand dollars. Not an insignificant sum, but not much to pay for an innocent man's life.

"Regina spent three days looking for the Crawley evidence kit, and when she finally finds it, the evidence had been completely degraded. It had been under a heavy box of legal briefs, and all the vials were crushed. The samples that weren't contaminated had evaporated long ago. But by that time, I had my blood up. I tell Regina that she's gonna go right back to the storage room, find an intact evidence kit from the same year as Crawley, and pop those in the file. She just shrugs, goes into the back room, and ten minutes later, voilà. Death row pardon in hand.

"I thought about keeping the evidence substitution secret from Rachel, but we were in it together, you know? This was our plan. We talked that night for three, four hours. She didn't want to do it. But I pulled out the big guns, the existential issues. You know, everyone gets into journalism for more or less the same reasons. They look at the world and its problems, and the cause of it all seems pretty clear—a shortage of truth in the world. If only the truth could be put out there, then it would, I don't know, dispel the ignorance and evil of the world. Sounds naive, but there it is.

"Of course, when you've become a reporter and you've had a few bylines, you realize this isn't true. There's no truth—only facts. And the last thing the world needs is more facts. The world is drowning in facts. I say *facts*, but what I really mean is *information*. I spent years checking my facts, my names and dates and places, before I realized that it didn't matter. We like to think journalism is a public service, but it's not.

It's not a trust, it's a business, and like all businesses, it's results based. Maybe you think this is cynicism—Rachel certainly did—but this isn't about cynicism as much as it's about idealism. About getting past the delusion of thinking that the truth matters. The truth doesn't set you free—freedom sets you free. How you arrive at that freedom, whether it be by truth or lies, or more likely something in between, is infinitely less important than the freedom itself. You see where this is going.

"So I bullied Rachel into going along with it. She hadn't come to the same conclusions about the irrelevance of facts, but then, she wasn't a reporter like me, out there chasing stories down. She'd been behind a desk for years. To this day it's still the only argument I've ever won with Rachel. But it wasn't all me. She had her misgivings, sure, but she could smell that Pulitzer. And it was kind of romantic for us—you know, the crusading journalists, righting wrongs, exposing corruption. And hey, if Laredo County didn't give a shit about the facts, why should we? So what if we had to become a little corrupt in the process? That's what the real world is like.

"The story ran the same day Crawley found out he was going home. It was the story of a lifetime—corruption, malfeasance, incompetence, racism, classism, all of it tied up with a nice happy ending. The public outcry was immediate. It was an election cycle that year, so half the senators in Congress made statements about it. By the afternoon of the next day, there was a crowd of fifteen thousand outside the prison, chanting, 'Free Altoona.' Rachel and I, we were golden. The *New York Times* started sniffing around both of us, and there were rumors that I would be nominated for the MacArthur. Laredo County was furious, of course, and made some noises about charging me with burglary, but they didn't have any proof. I got a lawyer, Regina dummied up, and they backed off. Didn't hurt that they were being shamed from all sides, and I was the least of their worries. The Texas state legislature introduced a bill to fast-track Crawley's release. It seemed like a done deal, which I guess is why I'd let my guard down by the time Regina called. She was fucked up, I could tell. Says she's already spent the money I paid her, and now she's having second thoughts. I should've hung up, but what can I say? I'm about to get a raise, one way or another, so I tell her sure, I'll wire her another five grand, just keep on keeping your mouth shut.

"Afterward, I thought Regina set me up, but later I found out that no, she was genuinely giving me a junkie shakedown. It was the State of Texas who'd tapped her phone. I guess they know dirty tricks when they see them. In retrospect, I should've known better, I mean, who else could've helped me get into that evidence room? They probably came in their pants when they heard us laying out our conspiracy point by point.

"Rachel, to her credit, or maybe not, didn't pin it all on me, which she could've. A rogue reporter and all that. I probably would've, in her place. She copped to her part. I guess she figured that fabricating had gotten her in that mess, so she was just gonna stick to the facts from that point forward. We were fired. Our bylines were scrubbed from the website. Even the union wouldn't stand up for us. Truth be told, we were lucky we didn't go to jail. We used our 401(k) and stock payouts to get good lawyers. Regina wasn't so lucky. She got fifteen years. I guess being a dirty player wasn't such a bad thing in some circles, and I've gotten plenty of investigative work over the years from people who've googled my name and want some of that shady magic for their child custody case. But Rachel just took to her bed. I tried to reach out to her, but she wouldn't speak to me. When she hired me to come up here, that was the first time I'd seen her since everything went down."

Alice took a deep breath and then exhaled slowly through her nose, sitting with her back against the dressing room wall, her lukewarm wine cooler still in hand. She hadn't realized how cathartic it would feel to tell the story, to get it all out in the open. She was nagged by a vague feeling that she'd somehow betrayed Rachel by telling their story to her husband's girlfriend, but she reminded herself that she owned the story too, and besides—was Rachel even her friend anymore? Had she ever really been?

Kim had smoked her way through several Capris and sat holding a small handful of the delicate butts, her legs crossed, leaning forward intently.

"Never trust a junkie," Kim said. "That's rule number one. Never ever. You think that shit makes them controllable, but nah, it's the shit that's in charge. Of them and you. Ain't no leverage you can bring that's stronger than what that shit does to a person's soul."

Alice could see that the story had had a reassuring effect on Kim, that even as she lectured Alice on the Tao of junkies, her tone was confidential and soft, not pedantic and reproachful as it usually was. Alice inwardly cursed herself for not telling the story earlier; it would've made their relationship so much smoother.

"So," Alice said, "if Robert's innocent, just know I'll do whatever it takes to get him out, up to and including putting my own neck on the line. I'm not one of those people who thinks you can get justice from a corrupt system by working through that system. I know better. So from here on out, whatever happens, whatever needs to be done, just know that you can count on me."

Kim scooted on the bench until she was right next to Alice and wrapped her arms around Alice's shoulders, pulling her close. "Thanks," she said. She drew back so she could look into Alice's eyes. "They killed that boy?"

Alice nodded once, curtly. There was more to the story, but she'd told all she could bear to tell. The rest of it she'd never told anyone, ever.

CHAPTER 9

The telling of the Crawley story cast a pall over Alice's mood, which wasn't that surprising, but it seemed to have the same effect on Kim. They drove back to the motel in a brooding silence and killed time before the party, half watching the television and taking turns smoking outside the room. Alice wondered if Kim had heard in Crawley's story a version of Robert's future, a worst-case scenario worse than the one she'd already settled on.

It was just after eight and already dark when Kim came inside after her umpteenth cigarette break. Alice was half dozing on the bed as *Jeopardy* played on television, her mouth a flat line of superiority as she listened to one of the contestants misidentify the author of *Huckleberry Finn* as Herman Melville.

"Girl, we got to break out of this funk," Kim said, her voice pitched into a high half whine. "We can't go to no party with our sad faces on. They boot our asses out."

"I agree," Alice murmured, her eyes still closed. "I was thinking, actually, that I'd just stay in tonight. I don't think I can handle a big party."

She heard Kim stomp across the room and rummage in the wooden cupboard under the television. She opened her eyes as Kim slammed a mostly full bottle of Jose Cuervo down on the top of the dresser. "This'll loosen us up," she said. Then she withdrew a rolled-up baggie of powder from her pocket and tossed it next to the liquor bottle. "And this'll get us nice and hyped."

Alice's eyes were suddenly wide open. "What's that?"

"Fuck you think?"

"I thought you said you didn't do dust anymore."

"I don't. But this is a emergency. Don't tell me you gonna granny out."

Alice sat up in bed. She wasn't against it on principle; she believed all drugs should be legal. She smoked weed a few times a month, did a line or two of coke whenever it was offered, which, in Brooklyn, was nearly every time she went to a party. She'd swallowed, snorted, and boofed untold amounts of Ritalin, Adderall, and Vyvanse in college and grad school and had relied on wine and Xanax in the jagged aftermath of her firing and then her divorce. She wasn't in any way against better living through chemistry, or even, really, shittier living through chemistry. But something about dust unnerved her. Part of it was the sheer unfamiliarity; she wasn't one of those people who bought the latest designer drugs off the dark web and took them just to see what happened. She was, at heart, a control freak.

Part of her reluctance too, she had to admit, was the cultural connotations of dust. It was a blue-collar drug, a drug of the sticks, and she had an idea of what that meant. The drugs of the city were, by and large, sensitizers, heighteners of awareness. The drugs of the country were drugs of oblivion, inducers of blackouts and fugue states. The reasons, in her mind, were obvious. And just from a practical standpoint, she didn't think it was a very good idea to pass out at a drug dealer's party in the Dakota outback.

Then again, she was curious, and aware that her wariness belied certain unsavory class-based prejudices. "Let's have a drink first," she said to Kim. "Then see how we feel."

Kim seemed to understand; she wasn't one to push anyway. She fetched two small plastic mouthwash cups from the bathroom and poured them full of the cheap copper-colored tequila. She brought one over to the bed and kept the other for herself.

"To justice," Kim said. Alice was uncomfortable with the sheer earnestness of the toast but didn't say anything. She downed the bitter liquid and exhaled a long breath through her mouth to chase away the aftertaste. She was still fighting a dry heave when Kim refilled the cup.

"To Bobby," she said. Alice nodded somberly and prepared to take the second shot. She couldn't very well refuse to toast Robert, could she? As she felt the acrid liquor slide down her throat, she knew, suddenly, exactly how the night was going to go.

It wasn't quite midnight when the hatchback accelerated out of the motel parking lot and into traffic, spraying gravel from under its rear wheels as it slid neatly between two northbound eighteen-wheelers. Anyone standing on the shoulder might have heard, from inside the small car, the muffled sound of high-pitched exclamations, though they'd be hard pressed to say if they were screams of terror or laughter.

Truth be told, Alice wasn't sure either. They were screaming just for screaming's sake, in surprise and fear and excitement, and because the air felt incredible as it flowed across her teeth and her tongue, like a chill one gets watching a singer hit a series of impossible notes. She flipped down the visor and looked in the small mirror there; she barely recognized herself. Kim had contoured her face, a process Alice had watched in amazement and which seemed to basically involve using makeup to draw a more attractive face on top of Alice's actual face. Her hair was gelled back and up into a flamboyant pompadour, and her eyes were lacquered with concentric blurred rings of eyeliner which only accentuated her pinhole-sized pupils. Normally she would've felt more self-conscious about her clearly intoxicated appearance, her dime-store stripper outfit, her inch-thick makeup, the fact that neither of them were wearing shoes and had in fact neglected to even bring any—but not tonight. Tonight she didn't care about anything at all.

She understood why people ruined their lives taking dust. Most drugs either made you more aware of your life's problems—rubbed your face in them—or just robbed you of your consciousness until you weren't capable of sustaining a coherent thought. Dust just made it so you didn't care. Alice slowly let her mind unwind, something she often did when she took drugs, and let it touch upon her usual litany of regrets, anxieties, fears, and resentments. Depending on what she'd taken, she would normally be flooded with existential dread or maudlin self-pity or a torrent of false insight, but now she felt nothing. Even as she went from minor concerns—bills she'd forgotten to pay before leaving Brooklyn, the five pounds she couldn't seem to shed, the triviality of her work—to major ones—her ruined career, her divorce, getting older, death—she felt not even a flutter of concern. It just didn't matter. None of it did.

She was suddenly aware of how much fear she carried with her every day, all day, and how freeing it was to be out from under it. Even the fact that Kim was so much higher than she was, that she was clutching the steering wheel with shaky hands, her bare feet dancing over the pedals, didn't cause her the least bit of anxiety. Maybe they'd crash, sure. They'd either die or go to the hospital and get better. Didn't really matter. She looked at her reflection in the mirror for a moment and thought to herself, *You've been searching for this feeling your entire life.*

Cars crowded the shoulder of the road a good half mile out from the party. They couldn't even see the party from where Kim parked the car, though they could hear the distant pulse of bass.

"How are you feeling?" Alice asked Kim as they got out of the car.

Kim just looked at her and let out an exultant whoop of laughter.

They walked briskly down the center of the narrow gravel road; after a minute or two, Alice realized that walking on the gravel barefoot was quite painful and veered onto the grass shoulder. "So what's the plan?" she said to Kim. As the clamor drew nearer and nearer, they walked faster and faster.

Kim looked at her, and for a moment Alice wasn't sure if Kim even recognized her. Then Kim smiled. "We find your boy Roundtree and get some answers out of him. You just stick with me. I know all these boys."

Alice silently reproached herself for asking the next question, but couldn't stop herself. "Did you bring the dust?"

"Ain't none left," Kim said. "But there won't be any shortage of it here for a couple of hotties like us."

They could see the house now, a lonesome McMansion in the middle of the prairie that looked like it had been mistakenly dropped from a plane. Every window was lit up, and from inside they heard a steady clamor of intermingled voices. The front steps were crowded with people smoking all manner of substance from all manner of paraphernalia, from cigarette to joint to glass pipe to peaked foil envelope. As Kim and Alice walked up from the driveway, the crowd subtly oriented itself to the two new arrivals, the men with lascivious interest, the women with faint, almost involuntary, resentment. Kim put her shoulders back and walked up the stairs as if she didn't even see them there, and Alice, after a moment—aware that without the dust she would've been paralyzed with social anxiety—emulated her as best she could and followed.

Inside, the house was crammed wall-to-wall with people; the windows were fogged and the air stifling from their collective body heat. They had to shuffle sideways through the packed crowd. Alice wondered where Kim was leading her but knew she wouldn't be able to make her question heard above the crowd and the music, and wasn't all that concerned besides. All around them were white men in their twenties and thirties, dressed in a style that might generously be called "urban" and ungenerously called "co-opted from black culture." Caps pulled low, Jordans, Nike jogger pants, gold chains and grills. Every man, as she and Kim passed, tried to catch their eyes, but Alice kept her gaze resolutely forward, not out of intimidation, but disinterest. Living in New York, she'd forgotten how sad and derivative life could be for people out in the sticks. Not only their style, but how they talked, how they stood, even how they quaffed from their beers and roared with laughter, jostling each other in showy camaraderie—it seemed so affected, an imitation of things they'd seen on the Internet or television.

Then again, she thought as they passed a large mirror hanging askew on the wall, she was complicit in this middlebrow spectacle too. Her very presence here, presented as a sexual object, reinforced these men's sense of entitlement, their unshakable belief, visible in every confident leer and demonstrative crotch grab, that the presence of desirable women, tanned, depilated, and perfumed for their aesthetic enjoyment, was their reward just for being a certain kind of man. There were definitely women she knew in Brooklyn who would've argued that too much makeup and cheap lingerie were a kind of brave feminist posture, but those were the type of women who, when they left the room, Alice rolled her eyes at. Context was everything, and in this part of the country, irony was nonexistent.

In front of her, Kim suddenly wheeled around and punched a kid in his midtwenties and just about her height, not slapping but actually punching him with fists. As Alice watched, the kid, momentarily too shocked to protect himself, took two quick right hooks to his nose, from which blood began to trickle.

"Keep your hands to yourself, you little shit!" Kim screamed, her fists held at the ready. The kid's friends laughed at his bloody face, and trying to play along, the kid did too. As soon as he cracked a smile, Kim punched him again, this time right in his mouth.

"Fuck's so funny?" she said.

Blood on his teeth, the kid raised both hands in a gesture of surrender. Kim walked on, glaring back at him. As Alice passed, she pointed to the kid's chest, where his white throwback Denver Nuggets jersey was rapidly becoming soaked in blood.

"You better get some club soda on that," she said; neither of them seemed to know whether she was joking or not.

Alice found Kim standing at a fireplace mantel that had been turned into a makeshift bar, splashing a jigger of Dr Pepper into what appeared to be a brimming cup of Southern Comfort.

"Little shit put his finger halfway up my pussy," Kim shouted. "I ain't no Trader Joe's. I don't give out free samples."

Alice nodded companionably. She'd have been little more than alarmed if Kim had grabbed a knife and gutted the kid on the spot. She wondered if this was how sociopaths felt all the time. She found a cup that had a half inch of warm beer in it, poured it onto the carpeted floor, and filled it with half club soda and half gin. No idea why; she hated gin. But she was already doing a number of things she hated to do; what was one more?

She and Kim, their backs to the mantel, surveyed the crowded room. Alice was surprised but also slightly comforted to note that they weren't the most provocatively dressed women at the party. Not even close. A girl across the room who was wearing a football jersey over bikini bottoms stood up from the sofa to reveal that no, she was just wearing the football jersey. Naked from the waist down. Kim saw her looking and snickered once humorlessly. "She works at El Tamarindo. Probably got paid five grand to flash it around and take all comers, that's the usual agreement for jobs like this."

Alice let this information sink in with a pleasant detachment. "Let's find some more dust."

Kim led her through the crowd to the filthy, dimly lit kitchen, where, at a large round table in a bay-windowed alcove, a group of baseball-capped men sprawled like a king and his retinue. They played cards with sullen boredom, a small fortune in fifties and hundreds piled haphazardly in the middle of the table.

"The one in the middle," Kim said into Alice's ear. "The tall one. That's Roundtree."

Roundtree was well over six feet tall but impossibly skinny, with wide-set, bulging eyes and a large, pouch-like lower lip that hung open. He had a tattoo on the side of his neck of Dopey the dwarf from Disney's *Snow White*. Alice stared at it for some seconds before getting the joke. A blond girl sitting in Roundtree's lap held a bump of dust in the recessed filter of a Parliament cigarette up to his nose; he sniffed it without looking away from his cards.

"He's the biggest dust dealer in Whitehurst. Supposedly the dude brings in half a mil in cash a week. There's a story about how last year he bought a custom Rolls-Royce Phantom—probably a two-hundred-thousand-dollar car—and took his boys on a trip to Minneapolis to party. Drives it to this club, that club, they all get fucked up, go to a hotel with some girls, pass out. Next day, nobody can remember where they left the car. Roundtree just says, fuck it, I'll just buy me another. Comes back to Whitehurst in a rented stretch limo. Nobody ever sees the Phantom again."

Alice sighed. She'd heard all these stories before. The thing that struck her about drug kingpins, third-world dictators, Silicon Valley plutocrats, was how boring they all were. It was always the same things: cars, jewelry, waste. Alice wondered if money made people boring or if it simply gravitated toward boring people. Briefly, she wondered what Steve Whitehurst was like.

"Roundtree used to come into El Tamarindo," Kim said. "I know just what he likes. What catches his eye." She brought her mouth closer to Alice's ear, until Alice could feel the warmth of her breath on the side of her head. "He likes girls with other girls."

Alice craned her neck sideways. Kim looked back at her slyly.

"Before you answer, come over here with me." She took Alice's hand and led her to the marble-topped kitchen island, which was surrounded by revelers, some of them laughing so shrilly that they might have been screaming. In the center of the island was a crystal punch bowl filled with whitish-gray dust. A girl who couldn't have been older than sixteen did a line that was at least nine inches long while her friends urged her on. When she straightened up, her eyes were electric, and a thin stream of blood began to drip from her nostril.

"Shit," she said, pinching her nose closed. She didn't seem more than mildly annoyed.

Kim produced a cheap dollar cigar and a small baggie of weed, expertly slit open the cigar, dumped the tobacco, refilled it with weed, sprinkled it generously with dust, and reclosed it. She lit it, pulled a long drag, and exhaled the bittersweet smoke in Alice's face.

"Don't wanna end up like Bloody Mary there," she said, proffering the blunt to Alice. "Plus, it's a lot smoother like this."

Alice took the blunt and drew hard on it. Smoke scalded the back of her throat, and she had to fight a coughing fit. Normally she'd be nervous about getting too high—she was prone to panic attacks—but tonight she felt perfectly assured that she would be okay. She drew in another mouthful of smoke and held it in her lungs as long as she could. She felt the dust tingling in her brain. Very soon she felt capable of anything.

Next to her, Kim hoisted herself up on the counter and sat with her legs dangling. "Come scoot over here," she said. Alice approached her, uncertain what exactly Kim was asking her to do. Kim took her by the shoulders, turned her around, and pulled her back so she was standing nestled between Kim's legs.

"You look tense," she said in Alice's ear. Gently, she slid the straps of Alice's dress so that they dangled next to her arms, her dress held up only by her breasts, and set to work massaging Alice's shoulders and neck. Alice realized they were facing Roundtree and that this performance was for his benefit. Normally she would've stiffened and become awkward and self-conscious, but she was high and drunk enough that she was able to surrender to the moment. And truth be told, the massage felt transcendent on her sensitized skin. She closed her eyes and let her head loll back, savoring the slow unwinding of her muscles, the way her skin sang at the alternating hard and soft touch of Kim's small hands. She lapsed into an almost animal state of consciousness, a warm present-tense bliss that was the opposite of her usual racing, over-reflected thoughts. Dimly, faintly, so as not to pierce this calm, she thought that this was the first time she'd relaxed since she'd come to Whitehurst, that she'd spent every moment up to now in a vigilant watchfulness, a woman in a man's town, a New Yorker in a state where that was considered an epithet. To live in Whitehurst was to choose to be either predator or prey. Before she could grapple with the implications of this, she felt Kim's breath at her ear.

"Open your eyes," Kim whispered.

Alice did, and found herself staring directly into Roundtree's dark eyes, shaded by his baseball cap but unmistakably focused on her and Kim. His face had been further slackened by the onset of lust, and right then he was the stupidest-looking man Alice had ever seen. She gave him a small, inscrutable smile, turning up just the corners of her mouth. After a moment, he tossed his head once in a summoning gesture.

CHAPTER 10

Kim hopped down off the counter and took Alice's hand, leading her over to the table. All the men at the table were watching them. They stopped next to Roundtree's chair, still holding hands, as he looked them up and down like a man shopping for furniture. Alice was struck by how short and childlike Kim seemed without heels on.

"I know you," Roundtree said after a moment.

"I used to work at El Tamarindo," Kim said. "You all came in a few times."

"Came in you, more like," Roundtree said to a round of chuckles. "You retired or what?"

"Went independent. All that fracking money on the streets, why do I gotta give up forty percent to the house?"

Roundtree nodded and rubbed his chin with one hand, a gesture that struck Alice as inauthentic, something he was parroting from a movie he'd seen. "A entrepreneur," he said. "I can respect that. I'm a entrepreneur my own self."

"We know," Alice said.

Roundtree turned his eyes to Alice. "Who are you?"

"This my girl from Minneapolis," Kim said. "She in town to party. Check out the scene."

"Fresh meat," Roundtree said, his upper lip curled lecherously. "I like that. I done run through all the pussy round here." He looked Alice up and down again, slower this time, and then turned to Kim. "She tight?"

Kim smiled. "She could pick a dime up off the floor without using her hands."

A roar of appreciation went up around the table, and Roundtree rubbed one hand over the crotch of his pants. "Why don't you two go upstairs. Master bedroom at the end of the hall. If anyone's in there, you tell them I said get the fuck out. Shower up real clean and get on the bed. I'll be up after I finish this hand."

Kim slapped Alice lightly on the ass and led her to the stairs. Just before they turned the corner, Alice looked back over her shoulder. Every man at the table was watching them go.

Upstairs it was less crowded, and most of the people loitering in the halls and bedrooms had the heavily tranquilized affect of serious junkies. At the end of the hall was a closed wooden door. Kim swept it open, Alice at her shoulder, to reveal a pimply couple having missionary sex on the bed; the man was still fully clothed and had just pulled his pants and boxers down to midthigh, and the girl had pulled her dress up to her waist. They looked like they were maybe a year or two out of high school. The man paused in his manic exertions and looked over his shoulder, his eyes ablaze.

"Get the fuck out!" he screamed, his voice cracking with rage.

Kim crossed her arms, unperturbed. "Roundtree comin' up in two minutes to put in some work," she said. "If he sees you fuckin' raw on his clean sheets, he gonna pistol-whip you both and dump you in the yard."

The man's expression fell at the mention of the bedroom's owner, and he rolled off his partner and wriggled his pants back up. The woman glared at his sudden deference but pulled her dress down and sat up, looking contemptuously at Alice and Kim. "You just a couple of hoes," she sneered.

Kim grabbed a black lacquered wooden stool that was sitting next to the door and flung it end over end at the bed. It struck the girl square in the chest, and she fell backward, wheezing, the wind knocked out of her.

"Say it again!" Kim shouted. Alice grabbed her by the upper arm and restrained her from charging at the bed.

The girl clutched her chest, tears in her eyes. Alice felt bad for her and shook Kim again. "Hey," she said. "She didn't mean it."

Kim glared murderously at the girl, who rose from the bed and hobbled over to the man. The man, his eyes downcast, clearly wanted no part of any of it. He put an arm around the woman's shoulders and led her to the door. When the door had closed behind them, Alice turned to Kim, who was smiling at her.

"What the fuck was that?" Alice said.

"Look, you got to let these bitches know," Kim said. "We sittin' up here arguin' when Roundtree comes in, his dick goes soft and there goes our chance."

"Well, what's the plan?"

"I'll jump in the shower, you search the room. We gotta make it look good, like we down to play, so we can draw him in." Kim took off her tall officer's cap and held it up to Alice's face so she could look inside. There, taped to the inside, was a small stun gun. "When all the blood's rushed to his dick and he's good and dumb, I'll hit him with this, and we ask our questions."

Kim stripped herself naked and walked into the bathroom, and shortly Alice heard two shower taps being turned on. She looked around the bedroom; it was sparsely furnished, with a bay window piled with jeans and T-shirts, a long shoe rack covered with pairs of Nike basketball shoes, and a king-sized bed with a padded headboard and a small wooden nightstand. That was it. Alice went to the nightstand first. It looked to be a solid table, but upon closer examination, the front panel didn't seem to be exactly flush with the rest of the table. Alice wiggled it; it didn't open like a drawer, but there was definitely a small amount of give. She slid the table out from the wall and looked at the back and then the sides. She felt the underside of the table with her hand and found a small depression in one corner. She pressed with her index finger and heard a click, and the front panel of the table swung open to reveal a drawer pull. Inside was a switchblade, a baggie of weed, rolling papers, a pair of handcuffs with a key inserted into one of the manacles, and a crisp stack of banded hundred-dollar bills.

Alice took the switchblade over to the shoe rack and slid it into one of the pairs of sneakers, went back to the nightstand, closed the hidden drawer, and replaced the panel. Almost as an afterthought, she patted down the headboard and then looked at the back side of it; there, fastened with a small Velcro patch, she found a loaded .38. Looking at the gun, she realized how much danger she and Kim were potentially in, but she quickly banished the thought. She started to unload the gun, but then thought better of it, reloaded the bullets she'd removed, and put the gun under the bed, close enough that she could reach it quickly if necessary.

Kim came out of the bathroom in a towel, still wet. "Find anything?"

Alice showed her the hidden drawer, the handcuffs, the switchblade she'd moved, and the pistol under the bed. "Damn," Kim said. "You good at this."

Alice nodded modestly.

"Now you better go shower before Roundtree gets here," Kim said.

Alice thought for a moment. "We aren't actually going to, you know . . . ?"

"Hell naw. I seen that motherfucker's dick, and it's got more sores than a leper. But you know, it's the carrot and the stick. We gotta dangle the carrot before we can hit him with the stick."

This plan struck Alice as half-baked at best, but she said nothing, not least because she had no alternative. She went into the steamy bathroom and stripped off her basketball jersey dress and stockings and stepped into the glass-walled shower. The shower was stocked with "for men" body washes that smelled like industrial cleansers and menthol. She rolled her eyes as she lathered herself. The insecurity of men never failed to amaze her.

When she emerged from the bathroom in a towel, Roundtree was there in the bedroom. Kim was sitting on the bed as he stood over her, talking to her in a low, implicative tone of voice. When he saw Alice, he pulled a small round tin from his pocket and shook it at her.

"That stepped-on shit downstairs, that's my giveaway shit," he said, looking from Alice to Kim. "This here is that thirteenth-floor shit."

Alice said nothing, just walked to the bed and sat down. In her experience, men like Roundtree were most intrigued by blankness, onto which they could project their desires. Roundtree opened the tin and sifted out a bump for Kim and then Alice. Some small voice in Alice's head told her that she was going too far, that a couple of lines to take the edge off was one thing, but snorting from a drug dealer's personal stash while in just a towel was the sort of thing that was likely to end badly. But the dust she'd already done made that voice, usually so commanding, little more than an annoyance, and she batted it away.

After she and Kim had taken their bumps, they watched Roundtree do one, which relieved Alice; at least she knew it wasn't cut with Rohypnol. She sat back as the dust hit her; she felt like it was turning her brain into a lattice of crystal glass, a perfectly transparent model of order and clarity. She sighed heavily and sat back against the padded headboard. When her towel came undone and fell to her waist, she didn't even care. She looked over at Kim, who was smiling like the devil herself.

"Lordy, lordy," Kim whispered. "Ain't that the sweetest little somethin'."

Roundtree fetched the stool from where it lay on its side and set it at the foot of the bed. "You know what this shit is?" he said. "Dust? It's that shit they inject into the ground to force the oil up. Fracking fluid. It's just fracking fluid, dried out and cut down."

"Bullshit," Kim said amiably.

Roundtree retreated to the stool at the foot of the bed, undid his belt, unzipped his jeans, and snaked his flaccid penis out through the slit of his plaid boxers. "Go on," he said, massaging himself. "Let's see some action."

Try as she might, Alice couldn't bring herself to feel anything about the situation, neither reluctance nor desire. She looked over at Kim and saw that she'd dropped her towel. When they made eye contact, Kim leaned over and kissed her. Alice ran one hand down to Kim's navel; it seemed she could feel the tiny invisible hairs there, individual pores. Kim rolled closer, and their legs intertwined. The feeling of skin on skin was so intense that it was nearly unbearable. Her thoughts and emotions seemed to have been transmuted by the dust into tactile sensations, which came in such waves that she could feel them compressing her consciousness down into a thin line of nothing. She let out a low moan of overstimulation and heard it echoed by Roundtree. A moment later she felt the bed shift as he climbed on, and when Kim parted from her, Roundtree, now wearing nothing but his socks, was crawling up the bed toward them, an expression of deranged lust on his face.

His hand on her calf was cold, and she involuntarily shrank back from him. He frowned but continued crawling up the bed until he was kneeling directly over her, their faces inches apart. "Don't get unfriendly now," he said.

Suddenly Alice heard a buzz, and Roundtree collapsed on top of her. He was very heavy, and as she wriggled out from under him, she felt his muscles twitching. When she looked over, Kim was holding the Taser, a baleful look in her eyes.

"Go put your dress on," she said. When Alice just blinked slowly, Kim leaned over and slapped her hard across the face. "You really can't handle your shit, can you? Sober up."

The stinging of her face seemed to reawaken something in Alice's mind, and she quickly shuffled to the bathroom and got dressed. She paused to look at herself in the mirror and was alarmed to see how half-lidded and sluggish she looked. She splashed some cold water on her face and took a few deep breaths, then went back to the bedroom, where Kim was fully dressed and looming over their prisoner.

Roundtree was still lying on his stomach, though the twitching had passed. Now he was muttering steadily. "I'm gonna kill you, you bitch. You ain't gonna get away with this," he said. His eyes fell on Alice, and she crossed her arms protectively over herself.

"Go wedge that stool under the doorknob so nobody can interrupt," Kim barked. Alice did so, amazed at Kim's transformation from sloe-eyed seductress to flinty competence. Standing next to the bed, staring down at Roundtree, she didn't seem the least bit high or drunk.

"Your boy Deke shanked an inmate in county a few days ago," she said. "A square, a civilian. I know you gave the order. Why?"

Roundtree tried to rise up on his elbows but failed. "The geologist? Fuck you care?"

"That's my heart," Kim said. She touched the stun gun to Roundtree's neck, and he convulsed. "That's my everything!" She hit

Roundtree again with the stun gun, and he began to choke, a white bile erupting from his mouth.

"Help me roll him on his side," Kim said. Together, they rolled him over and put two pillows under his head. The bile ran out one side of his lips, and he began to breathe again in ragged wheezes. When his breaths settled into regularity, he lay there, his eyes pinging between Alice and Kim, repeating the words "kill you" over and over in a low mutter.

"Shut the fuck up," Kim said, putting the stun gun close to Roundtree's face and hitting the button so current ran between the fanged contacts. "Now answer my question. I won't ask again."

"Fuck you," Roundtree gurgled.

Kim smiled humorlessly and looked at Alice. "Get the switchblade," she said.

Alice went to the shoe rack and brought the pearl-handled knife out from where she'd hidden it. When Roundtree saw the knife in her hand, all the defiance drained out of his face, and for the first time, she saw fear there. She handed the knife to Kim, who flicked it open. Even in the low light of the bedroom, it looked very sharp.

"Uh-huh," Kim said. "We found that .38 behind the headboard too. So don't even think about it. Here's how it's gonna be. If you don't answer my questions, I'm gonna take your socks off, ball one up, stuff it in your mouth, and then tie the other one around to make sure it stays in there. Then I'm gonna cut your dick off. You might die from the blood loss, or you might suffocate on the sock. Or you can talk."

Roundtree looked up at her. "What you wanna know?"

"The geologist."

"Yeah, I told Deke to take him out. So what?"

"Why? What'd he do to you?"

Roundtree spat bile onto the bed. "I was following orders."

"Orders? From who?"

"My supplier."

Kim shook Roundtree, who craned his neck to look up at her. His arms and legs were still twitching, and Alice almost felt sorry for him, lying there so vulnerable. Kim clicked the stun gun so it emitted its fearful buzz.

"His name, dumbfuck," she said. "What's his name?"

"Hicks," Roundtree said.

"That his first name or last name?"

"I don't know. I just call him Hicks."

"Who is he?" Alice said. It was the first time she'd spoken since Kim had stunned Roundtree, and they both looked at her like they'd forgotten she was even in the room.

"He claims he's a legit businessman here in town," Roundtree said. "But who fucking knows. You gotta put *legit* in front of your job title, it usually means you ain't legit. Ex-military, he says. I don't know anything else about him 'cept his phone number. I need more product, I call him up, he delivers within the hour. And if he needs something done, he lets me know. Last week, he said he needed the geologist dead, so I had my boy get inside and take care of it. That's all I know."

Kim tapped the stun gun against the side of her leg. She seemed to be deep in thought. "The side stairs in the hall, they lead outside?"

Roundtree nodded. "To the garage, and then to the driveway."

Kim stuck her chin out at Alice. "Get the handcuffs out of the drawer and cuff him." She crouched next to the bed so she could speak directly into Roundtree's ear. "Here's what's going to happen. You call up your boy, tell him you need some product. Tell him some big shots from the Twin Cities are here, wanna go in for two mil."

"He won't go for that," Roundtree said. "He always says no exports. Keep that shit in town. One of his rules."

Kim clicked the stun gun next to his ear. "Then convince him. You get him to come out here, meet up. So me and my girl can get a look at him. Then we done with you. Deal?"

Roundtree lowered his face to the bed. "Then what?"

"Between us and y'all? Nothing. We forget this ever happened."

Roundtree emitted a flat little chuckle of malice, but Kim cut him off before he could say anything. "Motherfucker, you just ratted out your supplier on a murder beef. What you think happens if that hits the street? That you a snitch? It'll be open season on your ass. Your boys'll be fighting over who gets to drive you out to the badlands and put one in the back of your head."

Roundtree seemed to consider this for a long moment. "You fucking bitch," he said, but his voice was resigned.

Kim waved a hand at Alice, who brought over a pile of his clothes. Kim rifled through his pockets until she found an iPhone with a stars-and-stripes phone case, then wrestled his jeans and T-shirt over his twitching limbs and locked the handcuffs around his wrists. Kim held Roundtree's phone up to his face.

"What's the security code?" she asked.

He glared at her. "One two three four," he said.

"Man, how did a stupid motherfucker like you ever get to be a kingpin?" Kim scrolled through his contacts until she found the one she was looking for. "You don't even use fake names. Just put the drug dealer's name right in there, didn't you? You know, I've seen your type before. You secretly want to go to jail. All this hustle is too much for you, you just want it over with. Too much stress, too many other dudes gunnin' for you. Born to lose."

Roundtree had fallen silent, his eyes oriented downward like there was something of immense interest there on the sheets.

"Here's how it's going to go," Kim said. "I'm gonna dial up Hicks and put the phone on speaker. You tell him what I told you. Be persuasive. Have him come out to pick you up. You try to tip him off, I'll taze your balls until they boil." She grabbed the short hair at the back of his head and turned him roughly so he was looking into her face. "You doubt me?"

"Nah," Roundtree said. "I don't doubt you."

Kim pressed the "Call" button and held the phone near Roundtree's mouth. It only rang once before the other end picked up.

"How's your party?" a raspy, strangled voice said. To Alice, he sounded like her grandfather who'd died of emphysema, though this man didn't sound old.

"It's dope," Roundtree said. "You need to come by. Lotta hoes, lotta dust."

"Uh-huh," said Hicks. "No offense, but management doesn't party with the workers. What do you want, Billy? I was just about to go to bed."

Roundtree smiled meekly even though the gesture wouldn't be seen by Hicks, the reaction of an employee eager to please a fickle boss. "Yo, I'm sorry 'bout that. I wouldn't call if it wasn't big. I got these two guys here from the Twin Cities. They wanna buy two million worth of product."

Hicks laughed, the sound of sandpaper on aluminum foil. "You know my policy, Billy. I don't sell across state lines. I ain't interested in a federal charge. You shouldn't be either."

Kim grabbed Roundtree's ear between thumb and forefinger and dug her nail into his earlobe. He winced but didn't emit any sound. "Thing is, they brought the cash. I seen it. Two million in a duffel bag. These dudes are serious."

There was a pause on the other end of the call and then a creaking sound, the sound, Alice thought, of someone leaning forward on a chair. "You saw the cash?"

"Yeah. Two million."

"It's just two men?"

"Yeah."

Hicks sighed. "Why the fuck haven't you already ripped them off and dumped them out on the badlands?"

"Normally I would," Roundtree said. "But my main hitter, Deke, he still inside. On account of doing that thing for you with the geologist. All these other boys, I don't trust them in, like, a pressure situation. But you—you were in the army and shit, weren't you?"

"Yeah, I was in the army and shit," Hicks said wearily. "Get two of your boys. They ain't gonna actually do anything except stand there and look tough. Window dressing. So make sure they're big and mean-looking. I get half. You all split the other half. Those are my terms."

"Fine with me," Roundtree said. "So you coming by here, yeah?"

"I'll be there in twenty minutes," Hicks said. It took Kim and Alice several seconds before they realized he'd terminated the call.

"You did good," Kim said to Roundtree. "Keep doing good and you may get out of this with all your parts attached."

CHAPTER 11

Kim cracked open the bedroom door and looked into the hallway. After a moment she waved Roundtree and Alice over. "Let's go," she said.

Kim went first, then Roundtree, then Alice, holding the gun out of sight next to her leg. The hallway was deserted, and they walked quickly down the stairs and into the dark garage. Using her phone as a flashlight, Kim found an overhead light with a pull chain. The garage was empty except for a couple of muddy four-wheel all-terrain vehicles and a motorcycle with two flat tires. It was very cold, and Alice felt goose bumps rippling across her bare arms and legs.

"Sit down," Kim said. Roundtree looked at her fearfully and then glanced at Alice as if to ask for help.

"It ain't nothing like that, you fucking pussy," Kim said. "Just sit the fuck down."

Roundtree folded his lanky frame until he was sitting with his handcuffed wrists behind him, his legs splayed out in front.

"Now draw your knees to your chest," Kim said. "Now scoot the cuffs under your ass and then around your feet so your hands are in front of you."

Roundtree did as he was told and then stood up. Kim went to one of the four-wheelers and turned the key that was in the ignition, and it chugged to life. She did the same with the other and then pushed the wall switch for the mechanical garage door. It clattered up, admitting a rush of cool night air; there were a couple of people smoking at the end of the driveway, but they barely glanced at the trio. Kim pulled Roundtree roughly over to the first four-wheeler and sat him down.

"You ride with me. Hold on tight. I ride fast." She turned to Alice and waved to the other four-wheeler. "You follow on that one. I ain't walkin' barefoot on that gravel road again, and he ain't gonna try and make a run for it if we're bumping over them rocks at thirty miles an hour. Just keep the headlight off. I don't wanna draw any more attention than we have to."

Alice gave her a thumbs-up and went to the other four-wheeler. She'd never ridden one before, but she didn't think it would be very complicated. She sat atop the machine with it thrumming under her; her dress had ridden up in the back, showing her ass and underwear, but in the darkness, she didn't really care. She also realized just then that she was still high.

Kim roared off, Roundtree clinging to the roll bar with both hands, and as Alice throttled her four-wheeler to follow, she was overcome with a childish euphoria at the sudden feeling of speed. She gave the four-wheeler more gas, and it surged forward. Soon the house was left far behind and she was traveling under an endless dome of starlight; she tried to resist but couldn't help staring straight up at the sky. If she rode into a sinkhole, well, so be it. She never saw the stars in smoggy, cramped New York, and she briefly considered whether she was living all wrong. Maybe this was the life she should be living: riding stolen four-wheelers through the starlit badlands while blackmailing drug dealers with her trusty partner in crime, the sassy, street-smart Native American call girl. At least it sounded better on paper than riding the subway and photographing cheating husbands at Starbucks.

When they reached the end of the car-choked lane, they pulled the four-wheelers around in a tight skid next to Kim's hatchback. Kim hopped from the four-wheeler and pulled Roundtree off. Alice could see he was beginning to chafe at being led around like a goat, and apparently, Kim saw it too. She took the .38 from Alice and gestured at Roundtree with it.

"Me and Alice are gonna be in one of these cars. You won't see us, but we'll be able to see and hear everything. You try and tip him off, I'll execute you. Just how you tried to do my man."

"Yeah, yeah, I get it," Roundtree said. "Listen, you don't need to be worried about me. You need to be worried about Hicks."

"I appreciate the concern," Kim said acidly. "But I think I can handle him." She reached over and uncuffed him, then pointed the pistol at his face. "Now you stand here and wait."

Kim and Alice went slinking among the cars until they found a sedan with tinted rear windows that was unlocked. From the backseat, they had a perfect, if hazy, vantage point from which to watch Roundtree and Hicks. They knelt on the tacky vinyl upholstery, their sweaty legs sticking, and watched Roundtree lean against their hatchback, arms crossed.

"It's a shame," Kim said. "He's kinda cute."

Alice turned and regarded her with open horror but said nothing. After a moment of silence, Kim spoke.

"You ever been with a woman before?"

Alice was conscious of this being a moment that would've been intolerably awkward for her, if not for the dust. "No," she said. "Have you?"

"In my line of work, you get tired of men real fast," Kim said. "Yeah?"

"Before Bobby, I was living with a woman. Tammy Jo. She was this real cute hippie girl from Oklahoma. Before she came to Whitehurst, she was a masseuse, so I got free massages every night. You ever get a chance to date a masseuse, take it."

Alice laughed. "What happened with Tammy Jo?"

"She found Jesus," Kim said. "Happens a lot around here. I mean, you look at this place, it ain't too different from the Old Testament. A desert wasteland, the prostitutes and moneychangers. We even got our version of the Romans. All these rich dudes just stealing out from under our noses. The police serve the money, just like in the Bible. You fall down in Whitehurst, they just walk right over you. I don't mean they step over you. I mean, they actually go out of their way to walk on your neck. So when these travelin' pastors show up preaching love and mercy and acceptance, that can sound real appealin' to a girl who been showerin' in gas station bathroom sinks and fuckin' for twenties. Been reduced right down to a body. That's why all the talk about the soul is so seductive. In Whitehurst, you don't get treated like a soul, you get treated like meat."

"Sounds like you had a conversion yourself," Alice said.

"Every morning," said Kim. "Then when the sun goes down, it all goes out the window."

Alice nodded; she knew all about morning-after spirituality. "Why'd you ask me if I'd ever been with a woman before?"

"Because it seems like you got a little of it in you."

Alice knew what Kim was talking about, though until that night, she'd never seriously considered it. She briefly thought about using the dust as an excuse, but she knew Kim was too savvy to buy that, and in truth, Alice herself knew it didn't work like that. If anything, the disordered consciousness was the most honest consciousness. "Well," she said finally. "Sexuality is fluid."

She knew it was a copout answer as soon as it left her mouth, and so did Kim. "I ain't proposin' anything," Kim said. "Just makin' a observation. You don't gotta get all squirmy."

Alice was going to protest, or apologize, or something, when a pair of headlights bumped up the lane. Both women fell silent and hunched down even though they were obscured by the tinted glass. It was a brown conversion van, and after flashing its lights once, it came to a stop in front of Roundtree. The driver's side door opened and a short, compact man climbed out. Alice cursed under her breath; the tinted window that hid them also made it difficult to see more than silhouettes. She couldn't even read the van's license plate. From their vantage point, she could see that Hicks was older, balding, and walked with a pronounced limp, but nothing more. His posture exuded confidence and command, and Roundtree straightened up like a boy whose father had walked into the room.

"Where's the rest of the crew?" Hicks asked; it was the same rasping voice from the phone.

"Yeah, thing is, the buyers got cold feet. I think they sniffed something out. Hightailed it back to the city."

Hicks didn't say anything, just crossed his arms and stared Roundtree down. "This all happened since we talked on the phone?"

"Yeah, man. I dunno. I guess we fucked it up. Lookin' all eager and shit. My bad. Why don't you come up to the house for a drink?"

"Why didn't you call me?" Hicks said. His voice was still casual, but there was a hint of tightness, in the lower register.

"Phone died, bro," Roundtree said. He giggled nervously once.

Something changed in Hicks's bearing then, something that Kim didn't notice but Alice recognized immediately. Many of her jobs required tailing people across the city and photographing their various transgressions—meetings with lovers, the dispensation of proprietary documents, deposits into secret bank accounts. She was very good at this part of her job, being an anxious person herself. She knew just when to conceal herself and when to present herself out in the open, casually, almost brazenly, so as to allay suspicion. But criminals are very skittish people—at least the ones who weren't caught right away—and she'd been made more than once. In these instances, her quarry never turned and glared or pointed an accusatory finger; instead, there was a subtle but unmistakable stiffening of the body, a creeping-in of self-consciousness. It was often understated enough that it could only be seen in the way they ran a hand through their hair or tapped their toe against the floor.

In Hicks, it was exceedingly subtle: the way he drew in breath, inflating his chest, and widened his stance, as if preparing for a physical assault. They were made. Alice was sure of it.

"Get down," she whispered to Kim.

"What? Why?"

"Just get the fuck down," Alice hissed.

She lowered herself on the seat until just her eyes were peering over the edge.

"Let's go for a little ride," Hicks said. His voice was light and casual, which, in Alice's mind, set off alarms.

"What for?" Roundtree said.

"I have a proposal. A business proposal."

Roundtree nodded, still leaning against the car. Alice could tell he was trying to think of a way out, an excuse to proffer. In his place, she would've too. Roundtree wasn't smart, but he had the instincts of a rodent; he knew better than to trust a cat.

"Come on, Billy," Hicks said. He was already getting back in his van. "I'll have you back here in thirty minutes."

Roundtree stood up from his slouch and made his way to the passenger side of the van. As he opened the door, he looked around the expanse of vehicles, and Alice winced. No doubt Hicks had noticed the glance too. The van roared to life and bumped down the gravel lane, the taillights glowing red in the fog.

CHAPTER 12

"We gonna follow?" Kim said.

Alice was torn. If they were caught tailing Hicks, they'd not only confirm his suspicions but also reveal who was following him. On the other hand, if they hung back, he might think he'd lost them and lead them to one of his hidey-holes. And if worse came to worse, and Hicks was planning to kill Roundtree for snitching, witnessing it would make for great leverage.

"Yeah," said Alice. "Let's go."

They climbed out of the car and crept over the gravel to the hatchback. When they opened the door, Alice leaned in and clicked off the dome light. Kim started the car and revved the small engine.

"No lights," Alice said. "Not until we hit the highway."

They bumped down the winding lane, revving in the dark, their heads brushing the ceiling as they traveled from bump to bump. If they didn't catch up to the van before it reached the highway, they would lose Hicks for good. Alice almost wished they would lose him. This was a dangerous man, and at that moment, she didn't have any desire to see blood. As they crested the last rolling berm before the highway, they could just see the van up ahead, turning right into traffic.

Kim slotted between two dump trucks, veering gently onto the shoulder now and then to make sure the van was still ahead. From behind, they looked like commonplace drunk drivers. They followed the van through the hinterlands of the fracking fields, the landscape lit pale blue by the perpetual torches of the natural gas exhaust jets, so bright you could've walked along the shoulder of the highway reading a paperback. The van was seven or eight vehicles ahead, but Alice was still nervous.

"Don't get any closer," she said.

Kim didn't say anything, but she fell back in traffic. As the trucks separating the hatchback from Hicks's van turned off at various work sites, it became harder for them to hang back, and by the time they reached downtown Whitehurst, there was only a single dusty pickup between the two vehicles.

"Do you know anything about this guy?" Alice asked as they coasted down the main strip. The streets were packed with drunk young oil workers, red faced, filthy, sullen. It looked like the unhappiest Mardi Gras ever was underway in downtown Whitehurst, with women explicitly forbidden.

"Never even heard the name," Kim said. "Definitely ain't from around here."

As they headed farther into downtown, the division between sidewalk and street became less defined with each passing block until the revelers and the traffic were freely intermingled. Most of the other drivers became timid and slowed to a crawl, but Kim drove on at normal speed, tapping the horn here and there, calmly veering around swaying drunks with inches to spare. Alice took to clutching the dashboard with both hands despite her high. Ahead of them the van was driving more or less in an identical manner; if Alice had been driving, they would've lost the van long ago.

"He think he clever," Kim muttered, to herself as much as to Alice. "He ain't half as clever as he think he is."

The center of downtown was marked by Whitehurst's main intersection, where the two primary avenues collided to produce a perpetual traffic jam. The light was red, the first vehicle in line Hicks's brown van. Kim slowed as they approached to let a hulking diesel truck insinuate itself between the two vehicles. As soon as the truck ground to a halt in front of them, the driver let his head sag forward and rest on the steering wheel.

"Do the cops even come down here?" Alice asked.

"Only if you call 'em," Kim said. "Cops around here, they more of a cleanup crew than, you know, a deterrent."

The light turned green, but the van didn't move. The diesel truck immediately laid on its horn, a resounding basso profundo air horn that sounded more like a tugboat than a pickup. Kim drummed her fingers impatiently on the steering wheel and craned her neck.

"What now?" she asked Alice.

"Hit the horn," Alice said. "Blend in."

Kim punched the hatchback's horn, which was entirely drowned out by the truck's blasts. Alice rolled her window down and stuck her head out the window to see what was going on up ahead. It briefly occurred to her that there might have been a struggle in the van and that one or both of them, Hicks and Roundtree, might be bleeding out, or worse. She couldn't think of any other explanation for the van's failure to move.

The cars behind them had joined in the protest, the air crackling with horns of all pitches and volumes, and even the crowd was shouting at the brown van, not out of any real anger but just to join in, some of the men smirking as they tossed brown-bagged empties at the van, which still didn't move. The light clicked back to yellow and then red.

"Shit," Alice said. "Should I get out and see what's going on in there?"

Before Kim could answer, the van surged forward, the rear wheels smoking as Hicks floored it. Cross traffic had just begun to creep forward, and the van had to veer wildly around the eighteen-wheelers and dump trucks that had nosed ahead.

"Shit!" Kim hissed. She laid on the hatchback's horn and cranked the wheel to the side, passing the diesel truck in front of them and surging into cross traffic.

"No, don't!" Alice shouted, but it was already too late. Kim swerved away from the looming grille of a dump truck heading east, only to be T-boned by a westbound panel truck. The panel truck was already braking when the two vehicles collided, but the hatchback was so much smaller that it was flung, skidding, a good ten feet before it jolted to rest. The last thing Alice saw before the impact was the front of the truck filling her window.

As she gingerly felt her bloodied face, she wondered if she'd been flung from the car. No, she thought a moment later, her head bleary, she was still in the car, leaning forward against her seat belt. Her nose had been bloodied by the airbag, which now threatened to suffocate her. She managed to bring her arms up to push the powdered canvas out of her face. She could hear Kim next to her, making indistinct noises of pain. The compartment of the car filled with a hissing noise as the airbags deflated, and people were now streaming toward the car, most of them more excited than concerned. Alice rolled down her window, and the first thing she saw, above the disappointed faces of the bystanders, was the brown van, idling at the other side of the intersection. Hicks was turned in his seat and watching her through his open window. He gave her a crisp salute and winked at her. Then he drove off.

CHAPTER 13

Alice and Kim arrived back at the Bobcat an hour later, dropped off by one of the deputies who'd arrived on the scene to take a report. The cops had seen right away that she and Kim were high and drunk and, with undisguised glee, had watched them fail their field sobriety tests. Halfway through her reverse mangling of the alphabet, Alice had broken off and told the deputy to call the sheriff now. Ten minutes later, his hulking truck had appeared, and all talk of charges had ceased. He'd sent Kim home with the deputies like recalcitrant pupils, mollified the truck driver who'd hit them, and taken Alice into the cab of his truck.

"Who was driving?" he asked.

Alice couldn't quite bring herself to look at him; the smugness was evident in his voice. She knew he would never let her forget that there had been a moment when she'd needed him to save her. "Kim," she said finally.

"Well, nobody's hurt, so I can make everything go away," he said.

"Thank you," Alice said. She'd almost choked on the words, and he could tell.

"You owe me," he said.

Alice nodded but said nothing. She knew she would pay for this, and then some. "Not tonight, Michael. My face hurts from the airbag, and my hangover is setting in."

He nodded magnanimously as they pulled into the parking lot of the Bobcat. "Come see me this week then. Don't make me come looking for you."

Alice scowled at him. "I pay my debts," she said, though she knew it was a lie as soon as the words left her mouth, and so, seemingly, did he.

When she opened the door to the motel room, she was almost physically staggered by the claustrophobic low-ceilinged squalor. Part of it was real, but part was the effect of her hangover and the dust comedown. She'd never taken dust before, but she knew from experience that there was a sort of Newtonian principle of drug use: an equal, opposite, and inevitable reaction to whatever you took. And sure enough, as the exhilarating disinhibition of the dust receded, she felt an oppressive flatness in its wake. She went around turning on all the lights in the room and then sat on the edge of the bed, her head held in both hands.

"Yeah," Kim said from her side of the bed. "We can do a little bump to take the edge off, but we gonna have to go through it sooner or later."

"I'll be fine," Alice said, though she wasn't at all sure, at that moment, if this was true.

"Sorry about gettin' us hit," Kim said.

"It's okay," Alice said. "He drew us out, though, so now we're on his radar."

"I'll ask around, but I can tell you right now, ain't nobody gonna know him. Guy like that walks into a bar, everybody clams up. You know who we should ask is Bobby. Maybe he crossed paths with the guy through workin' for Whitehurst?"

"Maybe," Alice said. She wasn't sure how it all fit together, only that it was liable to be more complicated than that if it involved Roundtree, Missy, Robert, Hicks, the local dust trade, and whatever else. Alice lay back on the bed. She'd look into it in the morning, but right now she needed to sleep. She'd just begun to drift off when she heard Kim's phone chirp, and then, half a minute after, she felt Kim get up from the bed.

"Where you going?" Alice asked, sitting up.

Kim was already seated at the vanity, brushing foundation onto her haggard face. "Lester's coming by in a bit," she said.

Alice scooted to the foot of the bed so that she could reach her laptop and camera bag. She took her camera out, connected it to the laptop, and started downloading the photos she'd taken the day before. "Come over here for a second," she said.

Kim paused in her makeup application and regarded Alice in the mirror. Something in Alice's voice must have struck a note of urgency because Kim rose without further comment and came over to the bed.

"Just know," Alice said as she tilted the laptop so they could both see the screen, "that I only did this out of concern for you." She started flipping through the pictures, beginning with Lester pulling off the highway by the apartment complex. "This was yesterday," she said. "You were passed out and Lester came by asking for money. I told him to get lost and then got curious."

Alice clicked through the pictures, one every two or three seconds. Lester with the pregnant woman, cajoling, begging, wheedling. Lester putting money into the manila envelope. Lester bullying the girls working the weigh station on-ramp. Lester slapping around the girl who'd held out on him. The last photo was of the unmarked storefront downtown where he'd delivered the cash.

Kim hadn't said a word through this slideshow, and when Alice finally snuck a glance at her face, she saw nothing, just a stony impassivity that frightened her. "I went inside, and it looked like an off-the-books gambling room."

"I know the place," Kim said flatly. Alice wasn't sure if Kim was angry at her, or at Lester, or not angry at all. She'd never seen anyone retreat so fully into a defensive aloofness before. It was as if Kim had seen the photos and retreated to a place where they couldn't touch her.

"Are you mad at me?" Alice asked.

"No," Kim said. "I ain't mad at you. You just doin' what you do. But damn. He said he was through with all those girls. He said he was through pimpin' and gamblin' and runnin' around. I only threw him cash because I thought he was tryin' to go straight and narrow."

"They probably all think that," Alice said, though she regretted it immediately. "All those girls."

"Playin' me for a fool," Kim said. On the very last word, her voice wavered and Alice could hear the emotion welling up under her facade of toughness. "Nah, fuck that. Fuck him."

At that very moment, Kim's phone chirped. She picked it up, looked at it, and then depressed the "Power" button until it turned all the way off. She went to the door and checked that all the locks were engaged, and then turned to Alice. "Don't answer the door no matter how many times he knocks, or what he says. Don't say nothin'. Lester's a orphan, so the worst thing for him is that feeling of just bein' abandoned."

Alice nodded. That was, she thought, maybe the cruelest thing she'd ever heard anyone say. She made a mental note never to cross Kim.

Kim went to the vanity and rummaged there among the many pill bottles. Alice noted, guiltily, that her hand was shaking. She hadn't realized Kim's bond with Lester was so strong. Kim shook several small white pills into her palm and swallowed them with the dregs of a beer. When she started to take three more, Alice stood up from the bed and grabbed Kim by the wrist.

"Slow down," Alice said. "You want to wake up sometime, don't you?"

Kim jerked her hand out of Alice's grip and, before Alice could react, dry swallowed the pills. "Fuck off me. This ain't no toy store, just because you broke it don't mean you bought it."

Kim went to her side of the bed and lay down on her back, one arm flung up over her eyes. The only way Alice was able to tell that she was crying was the stream of tears that ran from the corners of her eyes down to the pillow.

Quietly, she went around the room, turning off all the lights, and then carefully lay down on her side of the bed. She'd just fallen asleep when she was roused by Lester pounding on the door. She listened to his low wheedling patter, his mouth pressed up against the door, his voice veering from tenderness to whining to demanding, evoking long-ago nights together, promises made, debts paid and unpaid. Alice could tell from Kim's shallow breathing that she was deep in a drug-induced slumber. She'd known exactly what she was doing with the pills—she wouldn't have been able to hold out against Lester's spiel for more than a minute or two.

After about twenty minutes, Lester abruptly stopped in midsentence. He kicked the door once, so hard that it trembled in its frame, and a moment later Alice heard his dirt bike start up and recede into the distance. She crept across the dark room and pressed her eye to the peephole; he was gone. She went to the bathroom and drank cool tap water from her cupped hands and then settled back into bed.

She'd just started to drift off again when she heard a vehicle idling outside their motel room. The engine sounded more powerful than Lester's dirt bike, and the first thing Alice thought was that the sheriff was back to stalking her. She considered that she was being paranoid and then quietly got out of bed and found her Magnum in the dark. She was checking to see if it was loaded when something bumped heavily against the door. Her adrenaline surged, and she crept, bent over at the waist, to stand with her back to the wall, next to the door. When she heard nothing more, she carefully lifted a single slat of the blinds and looked out. A van was just exiting the lot; she was fairly sure that it was Hicks's van. Had he dropped someone off, Roundtree perhaps, to administer a lesson to her and Kim, someone who was at that moment lurking outside the door? Maybe he'd rigged some kind of device to the door. A makeshift bomb. If he'd really been in the military, it wasn't out of the realm of possibility.

Alice moved to look out the peephole. On the other side of the door, she could just make out an amorphous, shadowed mass on the doorstep.

"Shit," she whispered. She'd just put her hand on the knob when she heard a low moan. She cracked the door open and was alarmed when it started to push inward at once; in the dark she saw that someone was curled on the step.

Alice fumbled for the switches and clicked on the outside light. After a moment, she realized it was Roundtree lying there, his clothes torn and bloodied, his face grotesquely swollen.

"Oh god," she said and eased the door open to let him lie back. He'd been beaten so badly that his eyes were purpled and one was welded shut with blood. Above one split brow, a half-moon-shaped sliver of yellowish-white bone shone in the moonlight. When he opened his lips to moan, his mouth was a ruin.

"I'm so sorry, Billy," Alice said. He clutched her arm with one hand and made a gurgling noise, his eyes pleading. It was then she noticed that his pants were undone, his boxers torn open and soaked with blood. She tilted his body toward the light of the parking lot and saw he'd been castrated, the wound crudely cauterized, the flesh between his legs black and encrusted.

CHAPTER 14

It was noon when Kim finally roused from her benzo coma. Alice had been sitting in the folding chair by the window for two hours already, and when she heard Kim sit up on the creaky bed, she glanced back, and then took another drink from the nearly empty bottle of tequila. Kim walked across the room and stood looking down at the bloodstain by the door, the chaos of muddy boot prints from when the EMTs had come in and gathered round their patient.

"Who OD'd?" she asked, yawning convulsively.

"Nobody OD'd," Alice said, her voice hard with resentment. "Hicks knew that Roundtree gave him up, stomped him, and dumped him on our doorstep after cutting his balls off. I tried to wake you up, but you were out."

Kim didn't seem the least bit shocked or guilted by this. "Our boy ain't one for subtlety, is he?"

"I paid the EMTs to say he was just dumped in the lot. Not on our doorstep."

"Good girl. How bad was that fucker bleedin'?"

"Not as bad as you might think. Looked like he cauterized the wound."

"Yeah. That's how they do. Don't want a snitch bleedin' out and hangin' a murder beef on you. They use a blowtorch, heat a knife till it's white fucking hot, and then get to cuttin'."

Alice turned in her chair too fast, and her head spun with tequila. "What do you mean 'they'? Did you know this might happen?"

Kim shrugged, slumping back against the headboard. "Half the squeegee men you see at streetlights, they had their balls or thumbs or tongues cut off for rattin' on some slinger. Ain't nothin' new. And yeah, I figured it could happen to Roundtree if he got caught out. But fuck Roundtree. Once he tried to gut Bobby, he dead to me."

Alice took another drink of tequila, rose, walked unsteadily to the door, and toed the encrusted bloodstain on the carpet. "We have to get this cleaned off," she said. "I can't live with this here."

"Sure, we can do that. Lemme get some clothes on, and we can go shopping for cleaning stuff." Kim eyed Alice, who was swaying on her feet, staring down at the bloodstain.

They hitched a ride to the car rental office, where Kim acquired a replacement for the car they'd wrecked. The rumpled manager was clearly in love with Kim, a fact she mercilessly leveraged in getting them a loaded late-model compact. Alice hid her smirk with one hand. She'd grown used to thinking of Kim as an object of sympathy—a sex worker, an addict, a woman in a man's town—but she realized now that Kim was more predator than prey.

Alice sat in the passenger seat while Kim drove down the highway to the Walmart. Inside, it was bright and antiseptic-smelling, and they were enthusiastically greeted by a gray-haired woman. Wages were high in Whitehurst, thanks to the law of supply and demand, and the greeter probably made over twenty dollars an hour. Enthusiasm in customer service wasn't exactly rare, thought Alice—it just had its price, like everything else in life.

Kim took Alice by the arm and pointed upward. Alice looked up and saw them both on a hanging video screen meant to discourage shoplifters, in grainy black-and-white: Kim bleary and sagging like a willow tree, Alice drunk and standing aslant like a badly built shack. They laughed and then went to get a cart.

The cleaning aisle was like nothing Alice had ever seen: there were powders, gels, soaps, scrubbers, scourers, wipes, liquids, and every possible combination of each. She stood at the head of the aisle, paralyzed by so many choices.

"You ain't the first person had to get a bloodstain out their carpet," Kim said. "You ain't seen a man come back from the oilfields at night either, have you? He black from head to toe. His clothes so dirty he takes 'em off, they stand up by themselves. Every day it's like that. So Whitehurst buys a lotta cleanin' product."

They pushed the cart down the aisle, Kim selecting spray cans and powders while Alice followed like a sullen child.

"What I don't understand," she said finally, "is why Hicks would want Robert dead."

"Nah, you ain't thinkin' back far enough," Kim said. "Whoever tried to hit Bobby in the joint, that's the same person who framed him up to get him in there in the first place. Think about it. They fix it up so he goes down for bashing a little girl, but what they didn't know is that his wife is old friends with a hotshot private investigator from the city. You show up, start pokin' around, they panic and decide jailin' him ain't enough, he gotta get shut up forever."

"Damn," Alice said softly. "But why? You sure Robert wasn't trying to get in on the dust trade?"

"Nah, it ain't about that. They don't handle rivals all roundabout like that—they take them out in the badlands and dig a hole. Whatever's going on, it's bigger than territory and market share."

Alice nodded. "Well, now at least we know who's doing it. Hicks."

Kim made a skeptical noise with her lips. "I'll ask around, and you do your PI thing, but Hicks ain't the pot o' gold. He just a front man. The fact that I don't know him, fact his name ain't even on the streets—that ain't a coincidence. He's a legit citizen somebody hired to give cover to their dirty dealings. Fact that Roundtree said he's some kind of army hero just confirms it. In Whitehurst, ain't nothin' people love more than a vet. You flash them discharge papers around here, you get treated like the pope. Whoever's behind the real dirty dealin', they just buyin' themselves a smoke screen, that's all."

"Okay," Alice said. "But it's still a lead. We follow Hicks, see who he talks to, and who they talk to."

"No doubt," Kim said. "But he gonna know we comin'. And he don't play. Ask Billy Roundtree. He probably spell his name with a *i-e* at the end now."

As they waited in the checkout line with their cart full of cleaning supplies, Alice eyed the other customers. The man in front of them, an egg-shaped roughneck with a walrus-like mustache, had a cartful of Jell-O cups and a Desert Eagle strapped to his belt; the patriarch of the six-strong family in the next lane had a Colt revolver stuck in the back of his belt and a belt buckle in front that was large enough to deflect rounds from a Magnum. In his cart were disposable diapers and the largest jar of applesauce she'd ever seen. What a strange place. She wondered if shootouts ever erupted over someone trying to sneak one too many items through the express lane.

After they paid, they sat in the bustling snack bar, sipping cups of coffee. Alice was sobering up, and Kim was waking up; ideally, they'd meet in the middle.

"I'm 'bout to go see Bobby in the hospital," Kim said. "I can drop you off at the room first, or you can come with."

"Actually, the girl who Robert is accused of assaulting—what do you know about her? Maybe there's more going on there than we think."

"Missy? Her parents dead. She stayed with her grampops on the res."

Alice frowned into her empty coffee cup. "Is she Native American?"

"Nah. It's a long story, but I guess you should know it. I'll tell you on the way."

CHAPTER 15

Kim drove to the reservation along a patchwork route of dirt country lanes and oil-company access roads, all of them overshadowed by endless lines of oil derricks emblazoned with the green-and-white Whitehurst company logo. On a few of the oil roads, men tried to wave Kim to a stop, but she just steered around them. They passed a low ranch-style house with a swing set in the yard that was literally in the shadow of twin oil derricks. Alice couldn't imagine living in such proximity to heavy industry, though she imagined the royalty checks they received probably made it a bit more tolerable.

Kim slowed the car and pointed out a buckshot-speckled sign at the side of the road, reading "Welcome to Bluebottom Reservation."

"You in my country now," Kim said.

Same featureless scrubland, Alice thought, peering out the window. Except for one notable difference—the absence of oil derricks. Kim nodded when Alice asked her about it.

"Whitehurst owns most all mineral rights out here. Way it works, he can't buy no land within the reservation's border—we our own little country—but he can buy the mineral rights for whatever's underground. So let's say there's some down-and-out, no-job, hungover, dusthead

Indian sitting at home. There's a knock at the door. It's some white guy with a envelope full of cash. He says he just wants to buy the minerals in the worthless ground under you, you can keep living in the house rent-free, nothing changes, he probably won't even start digging for a decade or two—shit yes, he's taking that deal. I mean, I did. But the elders wised up once they saw that Whitehurst was fixin' to suck all the wealth out of the reservation and only give us pennies on the dollar. Barred him from the res. They can do that since we're a sovereign nation and all. Whitehurst thought they were bluffing in the beginning, got some trucks all shot up. Now it's in the courts. In the end, we just gonna get ripped off by the elders instead of by Whitehurst, but whatever."

"How much did you sell your mineral rights for?"

Kim sighed and set her jaw. "Ten thousand," she said.

"What kind of royalties?"

"No royalties. Just the ten grand."

Alice tried to hide her shock. The standard deal outside Whitehurst was closer to a hundred grand and every fifth barrel in perpetuity. "Wow."

"Yeah. They caught me in my moment of weakness, no doubt. I woulda signed for a gram of dust and a chicken sandwich."

They were driving on the main boulevard of the reservation now, a wide dirt road flanked by a few general stores and bars. A grid of ramshackle wooden bungalows stretched to the horizon, looking more like a temporary army base than a town. Some of them were half-collapsed, others brightly painted and decorated with bits of glass and colored twine. They passed a kid, maybe ten years old, wearing cutoffs and a Chicago White Sox baseball jersey. When he saw Alice looking at him, he gave her the finger and then licked it.

"What about all the casino money?" Alice said.

"It comes in, but it don't come out," Kim said. "The council of elders all drive Lexuses, but none of it trickles down. Ain't nothing we can do about it either. Downside of being a sovereign nation."

"What about the oil fields?"

"Whitehurst won't hire Indians, on account of the mineral rights lawsuit."

"Damn."

"Yeah. Ain't nothin' new, though. We been gettin' left behind for four hundred years now."

Kim steered the car through a cattle gate that led to a sort of subdivision. The smell of raw sewage wafted through Alice's open window, and the orderly grid of tract homes gave way to a chaos of broken-down RVs and medieval lean-tos. Before long, the dirt road petered out, and Kim parked in a turnaround of flattened grass.

"We'll have to walk from here," she said.

Alice got out of the car and looked around. The air smelled like burning plastic, and she had the sensation of being watched. "What is this place?"

"Rabbit Town," Kim said. "Don't worry, none of these people would dare touch an Indian."

"What's Rabbit Town?"

"It's for white people who fucked up." They were walking along a trail that cut between a bank of gas-powered generators and a refrigerator box draped with sheets of plastic. Somewhere nearby, a baby was crying. "Killers, tax cheats, drug dealers. The police can't come onto the reservation, so they hide out here. Rent's sky-high, but it beats jail."

"How many people live here?" Alice asked. They passed a girl wringing laundry in a plastic tub.

"Not sure. Two hundred, more or less. Sometimes the res sells some of them back to the police. Last winter our snowplow broke down, and we traded five murderers for new equipment."

"If this place is safe from the police, why didn't you bring Robert here?"

"God knows I wanted to. You know, knock off a liquor store or whatever to get money for the bail bondsman, bond him out, and stash him here. Last bondsman tried to come out here for a motherfucker got two barrels of rock salt in his ass. But Bobby wouldn't do it. Said the truth was on his side. He real smart, but he a stupid motherfucker too."

They came to an Airstream trailer, the top of which was covered with solar panels. Several satellite dishes and high-frequency radio antennas protruded from the side of the trailer. Kim walked up to the door and pressed the doorbell. Faintly, a voice told them to come in.

Inside the trailer, an old man was sitting in a wheelchair watching *Wheel of Fortune* on a small console television affixed to the armrest of his chair. His legs were gone from the knees down. He wore an eye patch over one eye, and that side of his face was a pinkish-red crazy quilt of scars.

"I'm Kim Holywhitemountain," Kim said. "I was a friend of Missy's. Can we talk to you?"

The man looked at them with a trembling expression. "Is she dead?"

"No, not that I know of," Kim said. She glanced at Alice. "Why?"

"When I heard the knock, I thought it was the man come to tell me my baby was dead." He clicked the television off with one hand and swiveled the chair to face them. "You said you're friends of Missy's?"

"We worked together at the . . . restaurant," Kim said.

"Missy never worked at no restaurant, to my recollection. As far as I knew, she was a whore."

Kim just looked at him. "Yeah. Okay. She and I worked at El Tamarindo together. As whores."

"Everyone does what they have to," he said. He spread his hands in a gesture that seemed to indicate his present circumstances, and then turned to Alice. "Who are you?"

"My name's Alice. I'm a private investigator. I wanted to ask you a few questions about Missy."

"Who you working for?"

"I was hired by the wife of the man who's accused of assaulting Missy." Seeing the old man set his jaw, she rushed on. "I don't think he did it, that's why I'm here. If I could find out who did do it, it would help Robert and Missy both."

"I don't see how that would help Missy. Missy's in the hospital with her head caved in."

"Well, don't you want to bring the right man to justice?"

The old man shook his head once, like a horse. "Justice," he said. "How about this. You two take me outside, and I'll talk to you while I get some sun."

Alice looked at Kim, who nodded. "Deal," she said.

Alice took the rear handles of the chair, Kim clutched the footrests, and the old man gave them instructions. He was very heavy and smelled of baby powder and urine. At one point Alice was dead certain the chair wasn't going to fit through the doorway, but the old man had them rotate and counterrotate in tiny increments until it popped through. When they finally set him down in the gravel outside the trailer, both Alice and Kim were breathing hard. Kim immediately lit a cigarette as Alice mopped the sweat from her neck. She'd forgotten to put on deodorant that morning, and a scent like onions emanated from inside her jacket.

"Did Missy have any enemies? Girls at work she had disputes with, something like that?" Alice asked after she'd caught her breath.

"Nope."

"What about boyfriends?"

"Nope."

She gave the old man a steady, half-lidded stare, what she thought of as her "cut the shit" look. He had his eyes closed and his face turned to the side like a cat on a windowsill, and he didn't look up until Alice stepped into his light and her shadow fell across him.

"What?" the old man said. When Alice didn't answer, he just pursed his lips. "I ain't hiding nothing. If you don't like the answers, maybe you should ask better questions. Missy was a good girl. I know how that sounds, but it's true. She went to work and came home. Sometimes she'd watch my shows with me, but most of the time she'd just go to sleep. She weren't into the stuff that most girls get into. All the money she earned, she put in a little shoe box under her bed, and it's still there. All of it. I never took a cent of it, and I never will."

"Last time she was seen before she turned up on the side of the road, she asked to get dropped off at the dust house south of town," Kim said.

The old man nodded. "She weren't buying it for herself. She was buying for me. It's the only thing that stops my back from hurting."

"How you feel about that?" Kim said.

"To tell the truth, I ain't beatin' myself up over it. There's a lot of bad luck out there, and sometimes you gonna run into some of it. You were saying that you thought Missy was attacked just so they could frame someone else for it?"

"Yeah," Kim said. "That man they got in jail, he ain't have nothing to do with it."

The old man nodded. "That sounds about right. Girl like Missy, she don't even get to be the main character in her own life. Just a plot device in somebody else's. Life ain't worth a shit out here, and a woman's life is worth even less than that."

Alice looked angrily from the old man to Kim, who was nodding absently, dragging on her cigarette. She knew she'd waited too long to get the background on Missy, and that guilt made her anger flare. "Bullshit," Alice spat. "That's what they say overseas too, where they stone girls for disobedience. 'It's the culture that's killing girls.' No, it's not. It's people. Men, mostly, but there are plenty of women who go along with that murderous bullshit."

The old man looked at her, his one eye bright in his ravaged face. "Do me a favor. Inside there's a cigar box in the cupboard above the sink. Bring it out here for me, will you?"

Alice checked her watch; it was already midafternoon, and she wanted to get back to town before the crush of traffic intensified.

But Kim gave her a grave nod, the seriousness of which she found compelling.

Inside, she quickly found the box, several rubber bands cinching it closed. On the way back to the door, she detoured to the small cot in the corner. There was a brown afghan crumpled on the thin mattress, and the sheets were faded pink. On the wall next to the pillow was a picture of Justin Bieber, torn out of a magazine and taped by the corners. Alice found the whole tableau so pathetic that she almost wanted to cry. On an impulse she stooped and pulled a Nike shoe box out from under the cot. Inside were neat stacks of cash, mostly fives and twenties. They reeked of cheap perfume. Alice closed the box and shoved it back under the bed.

Outside, she handed the cigar box to the old man and watched as he fumbled with the crumbling rubber bands. His hands were shaking, though it was hard to tell whether it was from infirmity or something else. Inside were a few keys on a key ring, a small military medal pinned to a purple velvet background, a bundle of foreign currency, some loose bullets, and a sheaf of faded photographs paper-clipped together. The old man brought these out and fanned them across the lapboard of his wheelchair.

"This here," he said, tapping a black-and-white photo that had faded almost to blankness. Alice and Kim bent closer. Alice could just make out the outlines of a woman in a long sack-like dress, standing against a barn. "That's Missy's great-grandmother, Eunice. She died in 1899. Indians came to the homestead, took the men and boys—one of 'em only four years old—ran green sticks through their heels, right behind the Achilles, and hung 'em upside down over a fire until their brains boiled out their noses. The women they raped and then drove their heads in with stones. Some said it was a frame job, just like you're saying. White men makin' it look like savages, to stir up support for a cleansin'. Don't really matter to Eunice, though, does it?"

"No, I guess it don't," Kim murmured. "Makes you wonder how much of them atrocities was even real."

"Well, you know who writes history. It ain't the ones trampled by it." He shuffled through the photos and brought up another, a crisper, white-bordered black-and-white snapshot of a young woman with blond curls.

"Holy shit," Kim said.

The old man smiled. "Yeah, Missy was a carbon copy. This was Tina, her mother's mother. My wife. They say everything skips a generation. She died in '58. I'd just got back from Korea. Working in the coal mines. There was a rush on then, just like today. Came home from work one day and the sheriff was waiting for me. Soon as he took his hat off, I knew what it was. The papers said she was stabbed, but that don't really tell it. I saw the body. Made 'em show me. Whoever it was, they pretty much cut off everything that stuck out. Ears, nose, lips." He waved a hand over his torso and then downward to his lap. "Everything. Everything. They arrested somebody a couple days later. A drifter. He'd touched a kiddie out in California and rode the rails out here, was the story.

"I went to court to see him brought in, and I knew right off he ain't done it. He couldn't barely look the judge in the eye. Just a worm of a man. I saw the sheriff that night in the old Cavalryman, when it was down on Spruce, and I went up to him and said, you know damn well that ain't the man who cut up my wife. To his credit, I guess, he ain't bother to try and argue the point. He just said, case's closed. Just like that. Case closed. I don't know what I woulda done if I ain't had to raise Missy's mom, Annie, on my own. Probably went on some kinda rampage.

"I started drivin' a truck, even though the money weren't very good. After what happened to my wife, I wasn't about to let my daughter outta my sight. She rode everywhere with me. I gave her school lessons at rest stops and did a pretty good job of it. She got her high school diploma at thirteen, if I recall. When we was at a motel in Fresno, while I was waiting for my next load, was when she got herself pregnant. I blame myself partly for that. Ridin' around in a truck with your dad your whole life, it leaves a girl with a certain hunger for experience. The father was just some young truck jockey staying in the room next door. He sent money for a while but then sorta faded out, as young men tend to do.

"About ten years ago was the beginning of all this fracking business. Missy and her mom was riding with me one night. Annie, Missy's mom, was lookin' to maybe get her CDL, get a rig of her own. Missy too maybe. We knew there was gonna be money to be made. We were right behind another truck that was hauling high-tensile pipe that they run under the ground. Drivers around here get paid by weight, not time, so if you're tryin' to maximize your profits, you don't drive faster, you load the truck up heavier. There're safety regs, but the weigh stations turn a blind eye. I was just thinking his load was shiftin' kinda ugly when I heard the cables snap. Pipe goes everywhere, and a length of it spears right through my windshield. Flyin' glass done my face up but the pipe . . . well, it hit Annie pretty much dead center. I guess the best thing I can say is, she ain't suffer none. I don't remember much of what happened after that, but they tell me I beat that driver to death right there by the side of the road. I guess it all just came out. If I was a real man, I woulda turned myself in after, but I didn't. I ran. I told myself it was because I wanted to raise Missy up, protect her, but that ain't true. I knowed by then that I couldn't protect her from the killin' in this place. Been out here ever since. I got to drinkin', and the diabetes took my legs a couple years back."

The old man flipped through the stack until he came to a picture of Missy, blond, smiling, dressed in black leggings, hoop earrings, and a Chicago White Sox pullover. She did bear an eerie resemblance to her grandmother.

"I knew she was marked," the old man said. "And I was right."

"She's not dead yet," Alice said.

The old man threw the photos back in the box and flipped the lid closed. "She's been dead," he said, "ever since she was born. Now take me back inside. I'm hungry."

Kim flipped her Capri to the ground and twisted a heel on top of it. Then she and Alice bent and lifted the old man in his chair, while he clutched his box of bitter memories.

CHAPTER 16

Kim and Alice drove to the hospital in silence. Alice felt more confident than ever that she would solve the case, whatever it took, however long it took. They'd been so focused on Robert that she'd forgotten there was another victim, one who needed her help even more than Robert did, and she felt that failing to get justice for Missy would be an order of magnitude more tragic than not getting justice for Robert.

The hospital was still dingy, still crowded, still depressing. Alice reflected on the fact that Missy was somewhere in the building, and that she had soon been joined by Robert, who'd been followed in by Roundtree. Not the most comforting pattern.

Robert was in a ward on the third floor; his room had to be unlocked by the deputy on guard duty, a flat-topped Aryan who greeted Kim with indifferent familiarity and openly eyed Alice and Kim from chest to knees. In the room, Robert was dozing on his back. He looked as yellowish as spoiled milk. Kim moved to his bedside and placed a hand on his upper arm.

"Bobby," she said gently. His eyelids fluttered open, and for a moment Alice saw him as Kim and, before her, Rachel had probably seen him: a benevolent, kind-faced man, eyes uncynical, face creased by thoughtfulness. He didn't, Alice admitted, look like a murderer or a woman beater, though that wasn't always a factor. Then he saw Alice standing there, and his eyes became dull with resentment.

"How you feelin'?" Kim asked. Robert looked away from Alice and up at Kim, and his face softened.

"Tired," he said. "Always tired."

"Lying is exhausting," Alice said. "Keeping your stories straight, what you told who. And the guilt. That's really the most tiring part."

Kim and Robert glared at her in unison, but Kim was the first to speak.

"Yo, I told you, Bobby ain't—"

Alice cut off Kim with a curt knifelike wave of her hand. "I know you told me. I want to hear it from him." She turned to Robert, who looked like he wanted to tear the tubes from his body and flee. "Look, I'm pretty sure that you didn't assault Missy. But I know you're mixed up in something else. Something big. And it's time to level with me. No bullshit."

"I've been nothing but level with you," Robert said. "Ask your questions."

"Were you dealing dust?"

"No."

"Were you trying to get into dealing dust?"

"No."

"Who's Hicks?"

Robert spread his hands as if his innocence could be measured literally, by the cleanliness of his palms. "Who?"

"Robert," Alice said, "I'm trying to help you. But you have to help me help you."

"I'm being one hundred percent truthful," he said.

"He'd tell you if he knew anything," Kim said. "I been comin' every day, tellin' him about how you workin' to get him out. He trusts you. We both do."

Alice believed her; she could spot a lie, but more importantly, she'd come to trust Kim too. "Robert, we think we might know who framed you. But you have to help us with why. We figure that out, we can use it to clear you." She paused and Robert nodded, all ears now. "A man named Hicks is involved. Maybe a regular citizen. Maybe ex-military. No one seems to know much about him, which, in this town, is suspicious in and of itself. Definitely involved in the dust trade. We think he framed you, then when I showed up and started poking holes in their frame job, he got rattled and arranged with a local dealer named Roundtree to have you killed in jail, to keep you quiet."

"Keep me quiet about what?" Robert said with such passion that he set off on a vicious coughing jag. One of his monitors beeped an electronic admonishment, and Kim gently pushed his shoulders back until he was reclining on his pillows. He coughed, his eyes on Alice. "I don't know these people," he said when he was able. His voice was thick with frustration, and Alice thought he might cry. "I've never heard these names. I don't know anything. I'm a geologist. I don't have any ambitions beyond that. Is it possible . . ." He trailed off, sheepish for a moment. "Is it possible they have the wrong guy?"

Alice smiled wryly. "I don't think these are the kind of people who get mixed up like that." She thought for a moment. "You mentioned your work. You work for the Whitehurst Corporation. Doing what?"

"I survey and assess. Plots they own mineral rights to. What's underneath, how much it would cost to extract. Cost-benefit analysis, that sort of thing."

Alice thought this over. Maybe. "Were you working on anything unusual before . . . before Missy was assaulted?"

Kim set her dark eyes on Alice. "You think all this shit went down over some Whitehurst shit?"

"I don't know," she said. "I'm covering all the bases."

"I don't remember anything strange," Robert said. "My work is strictly technical. I'm not involved in any of the money. I drive to a plot, assess the geology, maybe take a soil and water sample, do my analysis, and write a report."

"Who tells you which plots to analyze?"

"The company," Robert said. "I get handwritten work orders. Usually a dozen or so at a time. When I get through those, I get another batch."

"Where's the last batch of work orders they gave you?"

Robert thought for a moment. "They should be in my briefcase, in the room at the Bobcat. As I recall, I'd just finished the last of them the day I got arrested."

"I put the briefcase in the closet," Kim said. "I thought the cops might come lookin' for it, so it's under all the shoes."

Alice nodded, relieved. "Me and Kim, we'll look over those orders tomorrow and retrace your steps." She caught Kim's eye and saw the disappointment there. "Look, I know it's a long shot, but this is the job. You eliminate possibilities and move on to the next one."

"We can talk about it later," Kim said. "Right now, why don't you go off for a minute, give me and Bobby some alone time?"

"Sure," she said. "I'll meet you at the car in a few."

She went out past the blond deputy and stood by the elevators. The doors opened, and she was just about to squeeze onto a crowded car headed down when she stepped backward, letting the doors close without her. She went to the nurse's desk and smiled at the nurse on duty.

"Hello," she said. "I'm looking for a patient. Her name is Missy, and she was admitted with a serious head injury. A skull fracture, probably. She was the victim of an assault."

The nurse pursed her lips in a matronly expression of disapproval. "Mm-hmm. The asshole who did it is on this ward. Can you imagine?"

"I just visited him," Alice said. "He was framed. I don't know why, but I can tell you with pretty much total certainty that he was framed."

The nurse just glared at her. It never ceased to amaze Alice how tenaciously people clung to their initial assumptions of guilt or innocence about people they didn't even know; even in the face of definitive evidence, they resisted any reconfiguring of their inner cartography of right and wrong. Maybe they were worried they'd find themselves on the wrong side of the line.

"Missy's in the corner suite," the nurse said, pointing. "That way. You can't go in, but you can look through the window."

"Thank you," Alice said. She walked down the brightly lit curving hall until she reached the corner. Through the Plexiglas, she saw Missy lying prone, eyes closed. Just a blond wisp of a girl, grown unnaturally pale and delicate from weeks of recycled air and artificial light, tube feeding and preventative antibiotics. Her eyes were set deep in wells of purple, her whitened lips barely distinguishable from the rest of her face. Her filthy hair bundled up in a utilitarian twist. Alice took her medical chart from the plastic bin fastened to the door and flipped through it. Missy had been admitted with swelling of the brain and had been put into a medically induced coma in the hopes that the pressure would reduce itself. That hadn't, as far as Alice could tell from the chart, happened yet. She wasn't sure what the possibilities were if it never went down, but she knew they weren't good.

She put the chart back and looked in on the girl who had set all these events in motion but who, it appeared increasingly likely, had nothing to do with the actual motives and actors involved. A casualty, an accidental participant. A victim of circumstances as much as of whoever had actually fractured her skull. When Alice first became involved in the case, she'd been convinced that if Missy would only recover, would only wake up, then she would be able to give them the key to solving the case. A name, a face, something. Her initial efforts in Whitehurst had been—Alice thought shamefully—halfhearted, token, more of a stalling strategy than anything else. Just biding her time and billing hours until Missy woke up and solved the case for her. If only things could be that simple.

She thought of Missy's grandfather in exile on the reservation, and it occurred to her that he might appreciate news of his granddaughter. Proof that she was still alive, that she still existed. Alice pulled her phone out and was just about to take a picture when a voice snapped out from behind her. It was one of the nurses.

"No photos allowed!" she hissed, her voice so angry that Alice found herself at a loss for words, not that her explanation would've made very much sense or found sympathetic ears on which to fall. She simply turned and walked out of the ward, red faced and guilty, yet another victim of good intentions gone wrong.

CHAPTER 17

Traffic was backed up all the way through Whitehurst, on account of there being a house in the middle of the road. A three-bedroom prefab had slipped its ropes and fallen off the back of the truck, tumbling onto its side and coming to rest across the highway just south of town. A squeegee guy walking along the shoulder shouted that Steve Whitehurst was sending a crane to help, but it wouldn't be there for at least an hour. In the meantime, traffic proceeded at the pace of a half mile an hour.

"This shit is ridiculous," Kim said, still cranky from getting up early. She twisted around and from the backseat brought up the work orders they'd found in Robert's briefcase. "There's got to be one of these plots that don't force us to go through town."

"Who buys a house off a truck anyway?" Alice said.

"Houses in Whitehurst are crazy expensive since the fracking boom started. Little one-bedroom shacks sellin' for half a mil, rent starts at three grand a month. If you got a two-, three-year contract on a rig, you're better off buying some worthless scrubland and putting a trailer or a prefab on it." She held up one of the work orders. "This one is close by."

Alice cranked the wheel and did a screeching U-turn along the shoulder. Soon they were heading south, in light traffic.

"When shit got real bad at El Tamarindo, before Bobby bought me out, Lester gave it a shot. They were throwing up temporary housing for all the shitkickers comin' to town so fast that construction crews were walking away from jobs halfway done if they got a better offer. So pretty soon, they started paying crews up front so they couldn't walk. They did, you could get the cops, whatever. So Lester, he steals himself a truck, pays off a couple dustheads to come along and pose as his crew, and he starts bidding on these jobs. Lowballing the shit out of 'em. Framing, drywall, pouring foundations. Lester ain't much to look at, but he can talk a good piece. He got himself a half-dozen jobs, cash up front. He 'bout to come buy me out when he thinks, well shit, what if I could double this money? I could buy Kimmy out, and we can live free and easy on the other half. He goes to a card room, and you can guess the rest of it. Don't take half a day. Busted right out. By that time, some of these people who'd hired him had figured out that he was scammin' 'em, and they got the sheriff involved. Lester gets arrested and I can't make his bail. My only option was Bobby. So that's how that happened."

"That sounds like Lester," Alice said, trying to keep the malice out of her voice.

"Funny, now I ain't got either of 'em."

"Good. They're both fuckups. You don't need anybody."

Kim extended her arm across the back of the seat and tickled the back of Alice's neck. "I guess I got you now."

"Get the fuck out of here," Alice said. They both laughed. "Are we getting close yet?"

"Take the next left," Kim said. She rested her chin in her hand and gazed speculatively out the window, and Alice wondered who she was thinking about. Lester or Robert or her?

Alice turned down an unmarked gravel road, and they headed into the countryside, a wake of dust whirling behind them. Nothing in sight but barbed wire and rocks and grass.

"Stop," Kim said.

"But there's nothing here."

"Look at the GPS yourself," Kim said. Alice braked and took the phone and the work order, comparing the coordinates. They matched.

She parked, and they got out of the car. There was a steady wind blowing in off the prairie, and Alice had to slit her eyes as she looked off into the distance. The land here was utterly featureless and flat. She felt no more than a shadow of disappointment; at this point, she knew better than to expect easy answers.

"Look," Kim said. She pointed at a small wooden slat sunk into the ground with an orange plastic streamer tied to it. "I've seen those in Bobby's truck. He sets them out when he surveys."

"There's nothing here!" Alice said. Her exasperation boiled over, and she snatched the work order out of Kim's hand. On the bottom half, Bobby had scrawled a few remarks. Alkaline soil, shale formations. She didn't know what any of it meant. She began to suspect they were wasting their time.

The next plot they visited was much the same except for an old house on the land, plywood nailed over the windows, a bright "No Trespassing" sign on the front door. Alice and Kim walked along the fence line for a few minutes, but there was nothing to see except the darting of birds and the horizon.

They retraced Robert's movements all day, from plot to plot. On the older plots, the houses had already been torn down, leaving just a concrete foundation slab, and on one or two, there were fracking rigs set up, grimy towers of scaffolding surrounded by packed mud, emblazoned with the green-and-white logo of the Whitehurst Corporation. They saw nothing out of the ordinary, and by sundown, as they returned to the Bobcat, Alice felt the ticklings of despair. She parked the car, turned off the engine, and let her head lean forward against the steering wheel.

"You said yourself this was a long shot," Kim said.

"This whole case is a long shot." Absurdly, she felt a sudden urge to cry, and tamped it down. She turned her head and saw that Kim was looking at her with disapproval. She sat up abruptly and squared her shoulders.

"You just get a drink or two in you. You'll feel better," Kim said. She checked her phone. "Listen, if I leave now, I can make visiting hours, see Bobby. You mind?"

"Of course not," Alice said. "You see him every day, huh?"

"Course," Kim said. "Someone's gotta keep an eye on those slutty nurses."

Alice laughed and got out of the car while Kim scooted over into the driver's seat. Kim keyed the car to life and cranked the music up, and Alice noted that she'd undergone the transformation of a child who'd been released from study hall. She'd wasted their time and ruined Kim's day, and they were no closer to clearing Robert. She was about to apologize to Kim, but before she could speak, Kim threw the car into gear and was gone, leaving Alice alone in the parking lot with her shame.

This sensation of failure ate away at Alice as she sat on the bed, drinking bad tequila and watching the local news report about the house in the road (the crane had tipped over trying to lift it, further blocking traffic for most of the day), and before the alcohol had even hit her brain, she'd clicked off the television and gotten Robert's papers out. She was convinced something was there; she just had to find it.

Robert's notes were written in a Moleskine journal in tiny, cramped script and were so technical that they seemed to be in a foreign language. Alice googled term after term, but definitions weren't quite what she needed; she needed context, the big picture. She went on Amazon and looked at books about fracking, but none of them were what she wanted, and besides, she knew by this point in life that what you needed to know was never found in a book. That only happened in, well, books.

She put her laptop aside and lay back on the bed. Maybe her earlier gut feeling had been right and this entire detour was a dead end. But what then? She'd studied the notes, retraced his route. All she had was raw data. Formulas, jargon, figures, coordinates. Facts. She was drowning in facts. She had to think bigger. Normally she was wary of the word *conspiracy*, with its connotations of tinfoil hats and estrangement from reality—but this case, with its obscured motives, shadowy bosses, and backdrop of money and power, seemed to fit the definition. She needed to look at things from the top down. And who was at the top?

Whitehurst, she thought. Robert was just a worker ant in the scheme of things. She had to talk to the head man.

A knock on the door jolted Alice out of her train of thought, and for a moment she almost wondered if it was Whitehurst himself, that he'd heard her thoughts and transported himself instantly to her doorstep. It didn't seem completely out of character with everything she'd heard about the man, the namesake and benefactor of the entire town.

She rose and looked through the peephole, but whoever it was had covered the lens with their thumb.

"Who is it?" Alice shouted.

"It's Lester!"

Alice curled her lip in involuntary disgust. "Kim's not here," she said.

"I figured that," Lester said. "I'm here to see you."

"Me? Why?"

"Look, just lemme in for chrissakes," Lester said. "You can lock and load that Magnum of yours and keep your finger on the trigger. I ain't gonna do nothin' but talk, I promise."

Alice thought for a moment; she knew that if roles were reversed and it was one of Alice's exes at the door, Alice wouldn't want Kim talking to him or even letting him in. She was about to tell Lester to get lost when he said something else, his voice lower, muffled by the door.

"I got some information for you," he said.

"Hold on," Alice said. She went to the bedside table and withdrew her gun, checking to make sure it was loaded. She smiled, not without a twinge of sadness: she'd always be the reporter in search of a scoop. She opened the door and stepped back, holding the gun down by the side of her leg.

"Yeah, yeah, I get it, I don't blame you, I'm a real bad boy," Lester said, his words falling over themselves in a jumble. He stepped into the room, his eyes crawling over every item, every corner, in a single hyperalert sweep. He stood awkwardly in the middle of the room, his feet moving in tiny arcs over the carpet in a junkie's dance. Alice wondered if there was any dust left in town or if Lester had done it all. "Kim ain't takin' my calls," he said. He spoke as if he and Alice were old friends talking about their relationships over coffee.

"Oh yeah?" Alice said casually. He didn't seem to know who or what had caused Kim's coolness, and Alice saw no reason to tell him. "Relationships are complicated."

"Yeah, exactly," Lester said, pointing at her with a lit cigarette. "Kimmy said you were real smart. Got those city smarts."

Alice just looked at him. Clearly, he was softening her up for something.

Lester sat down, elbows on his knees, as if to confide in her. "Before we even get into it," he said. "I could get killed for tellin' you this shit. Worse than killed."

Alice started to say something patronizing—no one was more self-dramatizing than the snitch—but then she remembered the ruin of Roundtree's groin and just nodded.

"So I got to get paid for this. You got to take care of me, in consideration to the risks I'm takin'."

Alice cleared her throat noncommittally. "I understand you're taking a chance talking to me. Let's hear what you've got before we talk money."

Lester eyed her. "Damn," he said. "You all business, ain't you?" When she didn't answer, he sighed and went on. "So I got a run of cards the other night, like nothing I ever seen. The word *hot*, that don't even begin to tell it. Walked away with two large, from a twenty-dollar ante. I ain't one of them stupid gamblers who chases luck. I know better. They say luck's a lady, and that's true. And ladies, they're fickle. The more you chase 'em, the less chance you got of catchin' them. I figured, well, I done used up my luck for a while, so maybe I better take this bankroll and invest it. You know? So everybody knows the top dust slinger got retired. Roundtree. I dunno if you know him."

"I've heard the name," Alice said flatly.

"Anyway," Lester said. "Everybody tryin' to get in on the action, you know? I figure, hey, why not me? A regular Tony Montana. I could get into that. So I make some calls, get passed to this guy and then that guy. Finally I'm talking to the top man. One of 'em, at least."

"What's his name?" Alice asked.

"He ain't say."

"What did he sound like?"

Lester squinted at her. "I dunno, he sounded like nothing. He sounded like a guy on a phone. Yo, if you a DEA agent, the price for this shit just doubled. I get caught talkin' to a fed, they bury me up to my neck in the badlands and then let their dogs go to work."

"I'm no fed. Just comparing notes is all. This case I'm on might involve some high-level dust people."

"Damn, for real? Kim's new boyfriend, he ain't seem like no Scarface type."

"Appearances can be deceiving."

Lester grinned, showing his bad teeth. "City smarts," he said, pointing his cigarette at her. Alice considered whether he was putting her on, but said nothing. "Regular square becomes a drug dealer. Just like that show."

Alice had no idea what he was talking about. "Go on."

"So I tell this guy I wanna buy in. I want in on the gold rush. 'Bout time this shit trickles down to us reg'lar types. He says okay, it's gonna cost five large for a pound. Now this ain't like buyin' cold cuts at the grocery, you know, just gimme five dollars' worth. The price is the price. So I say real polite, sorry for wastin' your time, but I ain't got five large. Now here's the thing. You listenin'?"

Alice nodded.

"The guy is like, well how much you got? I tell him, I ain't even got half that. I got two. This guy says, okay, gimme two and pay me the other three after you move the pound." Lester looked at her incredulously and let out a shrill titter. "You believe that shit?"

Alice shrugged. "Go on."

His face clouded over. "Go on? Go on to what?"

It took Alice a moment to realize that Lester's story was over. "That's what you're trying to sell? Some drug dealer offered you dust on credit? Please."

"Shit," Lester said, his eyes downcast, his mouth working. He looked like he wanted to spit. "City smarts. Shit!" He winced as if speaking caused him physical pain. "Listen, this kind of shit just don't happen in the drug business. Ain't no credit, ain't no discounts, ain't no excuses, ain't shit but cash and carry. Cash in full. Somebody offers you credit, something's fucked up. You better take your roll and go home."

"Maybe your people connected you to the wrong guy. Maybe they were trying to rip you off."

"Nah. My people are legit. Dude's name was Hicks."

Alice crossed her arms and leaned back in her chair. "What else you holding out on me, Lester?"

Lester dipped his head guiltily. "Nothin'. Why his name matter?"

"Never mind. Listen, his top dealer's out of the picture. Maybe he's just eager to get the product flowing again. Special circumstances."

"Nah, don't bring that college shit in here. That ain't even how it works. Streets get dry, fiends start fiendin'—that only helps the top man. Means he can up his prices and nobody can say shit. I'm tellin' you, this shit here is a red flag. Somethin' weird is going on."

"Sorry, I just don't think the info is worth money. I believe you, it's just weak. A guy offered you credit. Big deal. It's called business," Alice said. "Why do you need money anyway? What happened to your two large?"

"I spent it," Lester said quietly. "Lost it back at the tables, and then some."

Alice felt a pang of sympathy. Lester wasn't just a pathological gambler or a pathological liar; he was a pathological loser. Fate gifts him two grand and he turns it into two grand in debt. Broke and busted, peddling bogus tips to out of towners with soft hearts. Not that soft, though, at least not where small-time pimps were concerned.

Lester looked at her from under his brows. "I bring you this shit, this golden shit, and you too stupid to recognize it."

"If you need money, go ask your baby mama. Or those girls you got working the on-ramp." As soon as the words left her mouth, Alice regretted it. But more than anything, she couldn't bear the idea of someone like Lester thinking he was getting one over on her.

Lester's eyes opened fully, exposing his yellowed, toxin-ridden sclera. "How'd you—" He broke off abruptly and frowned in thought. "Kimmy told you. She found out 'bout my side pieces, yeah? No wonder she ain't takin' my calls."

Alice gave him her most reproachful look, which only seemed to energize him. She supposed he'd been on the receiving end of those sorts of looks his whole life, from parents and teachers and then judges and parole officers, and that out of sheer necessity he'd learned to alchemize the disapproval there into a sort of contrarian glee. Otherwise he'd have been ground down long ago.

"You were against me from the minute I walked in the door," he said. "Don't matter how good my info was, you still wouldn't have paid me."

"No, Lester," Alice said, "as it happens, I genuinely think your info is shit. If I thought it was worth something, I'd pay you fair and square."

"Bull fucking shit." He stood up so fast his chair tipped backward onto the floor. He tossed his burned-out cigarette butt onto the carpet and looked at Alice as if daring her to say something. "You gonna regret this," he said. "I promise you that."

He turned and walked out, leaving the door ajar behind him. Alice waited until she heard his motorbike cough to life and recede into the distance before she walked over and closed it. She was fairly secure in her decision to not pay Lester for his weak information—she'd learned, early in her journalism days, that if you let a source pressure you into payment for subpar information, you'd be the first person they'd call every time they were twenty dollars short of a fix. But she knew she shouldn't have let Lester bait her into revealing what she knew about his other women. She hoped she wouldn't end up regretting that. She made a mental note to get her story straight with Kim.

She started to text Kim to see when she'd be home but stopped herself. It was the sort of thing she found supremely irritating when other people did it to her. She flipped on the television and lay back on the bed. On HBO, the Manhattan skyline was being incinerated yet again—the American public's version of aversion therapy via summer blockbusters—and on the local evening news, Steve Whitehurst was presiding over the opening of a community softball field he'd paid for. *Smart man,* she thought. Three minutes on the news and a wheelbarrow full of goodwill for a few thousand dollars of sod and fencing. He was surrounded by kids and beamed out at the cameras with paternal benevolence, his silver hair almost incandescent in the afternoon light. Alice wondered if the same PR people who'd recruited and vetted the kids—more than a few of them had the preternaturally poised manner of child actors—had arranged for his grays to be spray highlighted for the cameras.

Well, she thought, if he'd spent the day at the softball field, he'd probably be back in the office at the crack of dawn. She'd catch him there.

CHAPTER 18

Kim still wasn't home when Alice's alarm went off the next day. It was that hour between night and morning when the sky was the color of gunmetal. Alice didn't know whether to be worried or jealous. A little of both. She dressed herself in the most formal clothes she'd brought—a powder-blue oxford, black cigarette pants, and asexual brown flats with contrast stitching and bootlaces—and sat at the vanity, slicking back her bedraggled hair. She started to put makeup on but stopped. Her small, hard eyes, with their bags of exhaustion, looked like the eyes of a serious woman, a woman who'd been up late doing her work, ferreting out facts and names and dates, a woman to be respected and maybe even feared.

When her cab dropped her at the Whitehurst parking lot, there were only a few vehicles there: a half-dozen white security vehicles and a Prius. She'd put money on who owned the Prius. She paid and walked up the sloping concrete steps to the entrance. The building was more pyramidal than rectangular, utilitarian but subtly designed, with rounded corners and offset spaces and vaulted atriums. The central peak of the roof, which loomed over the rest of the sloping building, was made of glass and had at its center hundreds of small mirrors that reflected natural light throughout the rest of the structure. The lower roofs were covered in lush green gardens. As Alice looked on, a set of concealed sprinklers began to mist water over them.

The front door was still locked. She pressed the buzzer until a security guard came to the door and pushed it open for her.

"Can I help you?" the guard said, subtly blocking her from entering with his body.

"I'm here to see Steve Whitehurst," she said.

"You have an appointment?"

Alice thought about lying, but decided to go with the honest approach. "No. But can you tell him I'm here? My name is Alice Riley from the *Washington Post*."

The guard stepped back so the door closed and spoke into a radio strapped to his shoulder. Alice tried to look composed and expectant as she waited. After a moment, she heard the chirp of his radio and saw him incline his head toward the earpiece and then nod. He came to the door and opened it for her and then stepped aside.

"Go on up," he said. "Last elevator on the right."

"Thank you," Alice said. Her footsteps reverberated in the open space of the lobby like the clatter of rocks falling down a distant rock face. Sometimes it paid, she thought, to have a scandalous backstory. If you couldn't be powerful, you could at least be googleable.

She stepped into the elevator, and the doors closed soundlessly. There were no buttons on the wall, and she stood puzzled until a soft gender-neutral voice whispered, "Destination?" from seemingly just over her shoulder.

"Steve Whitehurst's office," she said. She caught sight of a tiny surveillance camera in the upper corner and fought an impulse to wave.

The doors opened shortly, and she found herself looking out into a bright, minimally furnished office. She hadn't felt any sensation of movement. Behind a long black-glass desk sat Steve Whitehurst; he gave her the shortest conceivable glance and then looked back at his screen. He was a gaunt man, with something slightly ferret-like about his face, his silver hair combed back, and she wondered if he was in early or at the tail end of an all-nighter. He was dressed in an ultralight running T-shirt of synthetic breathable material, loose raw-linen pants, and Birkenstocks. The uniform of the ultrawealthy, Alice thought. It was their way of showing that they had nothing more to prove.

"Come in," he said. Alice strolled forward and took in the room: all four walls were floor-to-ceiling glass, and she guessed that she'd traveled to the top of the building's central spire. The only ornamentation was a print, hanging behind his desk, of Hokusai's painting of Mount Fuji, not the well-known daytime one, with its soft blues and hazy clouds, but the more obscure dusk version, all reds and oranges, like a world aflame. Or drenched in blood.

In front of Whitehurst's desk, instead of chairs, were two air-filled rubber yoga balls. She used her foot to roll one into his sightline and then sat down on it, bouncing slightly in a manner that she thought probably undercut her efforts to appear serious and legitimate.

"Did you do it?" Whitehurst said as he typed, uninterrupted, on a soundless, paper-thin keyboard.

Alice blinked. She wasn't used to being on this end of such bluntness. "Yes," she said.

"Why?" Still no eye contact.

Alice thought this over. She'd been asked many times since she was fired if she'd done what she'd been accused of, but no one had ever asked her why she'd done it. "I guess because I believed there was a higher principle than a strict adherence to facts."

Whitehurst stopped typing and turned to her. He wasn't a man who gave his full attention right off the bat. It had to be earned. "You said 'believed.' Do you no longer believe that?"

"No," Alice said. "I still believe that facts are more or less secondary. I guess it's the higher principle that I'm undecided about."

Whitehurst leaned back in his chair and folded his hands over his abdomen and laughed. Alice wasn't sure what was so amusing and felt slightly insulted. "I imagine that sort of moral ambiguity comes in handy for a private investigator. You didn't let me down," he said. "I was afraid you'd come up here and tell me you did it for a promotion, for a Pulitzer, for your career. Something dreary and pedestrian and petty."

"Well." She had done it for all those reasons too, but she didn't say so. "I'm glad I didn't bore you."

He gave her a look that said, no, the boring part starts now. "So you're here about Robert Wilcox," he said. Alice saw that he'd phrased this statement to shock, or at least impress, though she'd assumed her presence in this town—his town—had long since been noted and investigated.

"Uh-huh," she said. "Did you ever meet him?"

"No. I employ over thirteen thousand people."

"That's okay," Alice said. "My questions have more to do with his work. I spent the last day retracing his movements around the area and going over his notes. But it's all a bit technical for me. I was hoping you'd be able to sort of contextualize it all in layman's terms for me."

Whitehurst tipped his head to one side. "You've been doing this all alone?"

"No. Robert's girlfriend is helping me."

Whitehurst nodded; none of this, she sensed, was news to him. She wondered, fleetingly, if he kept a file on every one of his employees. "But you're working for his wife, aren't you? What's that like?"

Alice shrugged. "Ambiguous."

"Have you told her about the girlfriend yet?"

"No."

Whitehurst just looked at her. He was taking her measure. "What do you want to know specifically?"

"To me, it looked like he was just driving from empty lot to empty lot. Surveying wastelands. I just don't really understand why."

"He was surveying. He's a surveyor." He spread his hands ingenuously. "I don't mean to sound glib, but do you think this has anything to do with the . . . charges against him?"

"Honestly, no." She almost pretty much meant it, and she could see that Whitehurst almost pretty much believed it. "But I don't really have any alternate theory of what happened, much less how or why. So I'm just filling in blanks while I wait for that *aha* moment. Drudge work. That's most of the job."

"Most of any job," Whitehurst said. He seemed to relax. "Do you know the history of this area? They always knew oil was here. They just couldn't get it out of the ground. In a traditional oilfield, say, in Texas, the oil is just pooled there under the surface. You just tap into it, pull it out of the ground, and get rich. Any idiot could do it. And many idiots did. Here it's spread out. Diversified among various layers of shale and sandstone. They tried everything. A Civil War veteran tried to get the oil out using a sort of mining torpedo that he patented. Made of solid nitroglycerin. Didn't really work. Not enough to make it worth the trouble anyway. They tried acid, they tried napalm. Nothing worked, really. It wasn't until recently that the technology existed to extract the oil profitably. So that's what we're doing. I won't bore you with the technical details. Wilcox was one of many surveyors we employ who evaluate recent land acquisitions for their potential oil or gas production. Some we drill now, some more difficult cases we save for when oil prices rise again."

Alice had been scribbling along as Whitehurst spoke, though she rarely if ever referred to her notes after the fact. She'd found that the act of note taking on her part made people more forthcoming, her business neutralizing her, in their view, as a listener. "So Whitehurst is acquiring land, this late in the boom? You'd think that everyone who wanted to sell would've cashed in already."

"There are still holdouts," Whitehurst said. "More than you would think, considering the money at stake. Who knows why they refuse to sell? Economics is based on the assumption that human beings are rational. I'm sure that you've found, in your lines of work, that the opposite is true. Inertia is my take. They've always lived here, so why would they leave? Good lord, there's an entire world out there, and I'm trying to pay you to go explore it! But no. More than one of my agents has been shot at showing up to make an offer on a plot of land. And then there are the people in Whitehurst who still think this boom is going to peter out, like the other booms, and that everything will go back to the way it used to be."

"Will it?" Alice asked.

Whitehurst smiled. "Life goes in one direction."

Alice had to admit she liked the man, despite the smugness of his breezy pseudo-philosophical speculations on the motives of mere citizens. She found him refreshing, which made her feel a pang of classism. Truth be told, though, she was sick of the flat, abrasive Kims and Lesters and Roundtrees. Whitehurst seemed to sense her warming to him, because he smiled and leaned forward on the desk.

"I'll have my assistant put together hard copies of Wilcox's file and his work orders for you," Whitehurst said. "Who knows, maybe they'll help jar something loose."

"Thank you so much," she said. She didn't mention that she already had the handwritten work orders, filched from Robert's briefcase; why stick a pin in his moment of magnanimity?

"Where are you staying? I'll have them messengered over." But before Alice could answer, he put up an index finger, his face suddenly alight. "Better yet—what are you doing tonight? I throw a weekly dinner party, I'm sure you'd enjoy it. We eat, drink, talk late into the night. All kinds of people. You'd be perfect. I'll have Robert's papers for you at the house."

"I'd love to," she said. "Can I bring a friend?"

"Who?"

Alice considered how to frame Kim for maximum interest. "She's a prostitute from the reservation. She tried to unionize her brothel and got put out on the street."

"A sex worker!" Whitehurst said, mock scandalized. "And a politically active one at that. Yes, bring her. The suggestion of prurience always loosens people up. Things can get a little stuffy with all these business types. At least before the wine starts to flow."

This last part was said in a low, confiding tone, hinting at debauchery. Alice had rubbed elbows with the upper classes before and knew what form that debauchery would probably take, but she didn't let on, to preserve Whitehurst's idea of her as shockable.

"What time?"

"We like to start at eight. I'll send a car for you. You're staying at . . . the Bobcat?"

So he was keeping tabs on her. She showed him a grateful smile and stood up. "I'll see you tonight. And thank you again."

Whitehurst waved a hand at her and, just like that, went back to work. It was the wave of a monarch, a wave that presupposed that everything in the world flowed from his favor.

CHAPTER 19

Kim was sleeping in the bed when Alice returned to the Bobcat, a deep, corpse-like benzo slumber. She must've gone straight from Robert's room at the hospital to the nearest dust house, a repeat of her mother's last days. Coming down, Alice thought. She was mildly surprised to find that she was jealous of Kim. She wanted to try dust again, truth be told. No, she thought acidly—not "try." Trying is for first timers. Now she wanted to use. And what was wrong with that? The word itself, on its most basic level, implied utility, usefulness. Virtues. Was this how it started, the junkie rationalizations?

She looked down at Kim sprawled on the bed as if she'd fallen from a plane, the movement of her eyes beneath her eyelids just barely visible like fish in an iced-over creek. Alice tried to imagine her dust binge, what she'd done, with whom, where she'd gone, the headlong manic energy of it, the relentless purposeless purpose, the bright eyes, the spontaneous ephemeral camaraderie. A knife of jealousy went through her. Isn't that what everyone wanted from life? Freedom, action—dispensation, however temporary, from consequences?

It would be nearly impossible to rouse Kim, and besides, what was the point, with the dinner party a good ten hours away? Alice sat down at the table by the window, opened her laptop, and brought out the stack of Robert's work orders, creased and coffee stained. She chose one at random, went to the Whitehurst County tax database, entered the GPS coordinates, and clicked over to the transfer-of-ownership tab. The plot had been purchased by Whitehurst eighteen months previous and had been owned for nearly ninety years prior by a family named Keller. It had passed at the Keller patriarch's death to Stephanie, his only child, the year before. Made sense, Alice thought—the parents held out, but the kids just wanted to cash in and get out of town. She searched for Stephanie Keller, and the first thing that came up was a funeral announcement from six weeks ago. Car accident. She found a news item about the crash: late-night collision with a utility pole, stolen car, intoxication suspected. Okay.

Alice did the same with the next work order, the next plot: same story. Whitehurst had bought the plot the previous year from a man named Menahan. Ethan Menahan. Nothing came up when Alice googled him, but when she searched for him in a law-enforcement database, he came right up. Currently residing in the care of the South Dakota Department of Corrections. She called up Menahan's record: possession, possession, possession with intent to distribute, grand larceny, burglary. Serving fifteen on the burglary. All of it starting around the time he'd sold to Whitehurst. On a whim, Alice searched for Stephanie Keller in the same database. A nearly identical story. Possession, possession, solicitation, two DUIs, wire fraud. All in the two years preceding her death, before which she'd been a model citizen. Well, booms had that effect on people. Look at lottery winners: half of them were broke or dead within five years. It appeared these two had gotten hooked on dust, sold the family plot for a quick payout, burned through the cash, and then begun a precipitous downfall. A downfall that ended one of two ways: death or incarceration.

Alice closed her laptop. Was it money that ruined and corrupted human nature, or was the worst always lying there, dormant, waiting to be awakened by whatever catalyst—money, power, desire? She supposed that whether you blamed money or human nature pretty much defined the rest of your political outlook. Either way, the good people of Whitehurst were fucked.

She stood and went over to the bed and picked up Kim's purse. She rooted through it, but there was nothing except loose cash, condom wrappers, gum, scraps of paper with numbers and names and IOUs scrawled on them. Not surprising. That was when you came down; when you ran out. Well, shit. She chugged a beer and lay down on the bed, her head buzzing, letting her limbs casually intertwine with Kim's until she fell into sleep.

When Alice woke she was the only one in bed and she had a moment of panic that Kim had set off again, leaving her to go to Whitehurst's party alone. Then she saw the outline of Kim's head and shoulders through the window, sitting outside the room and smoking.

Alice rolled over in the bed. She wondered what would happen to Kim after she left town, or after the boom died down. Best case, what, marry some oilfield jockey and start squeezing out kids? Worst case, they find her on the side of the highway some morning, head bashed in, naked from the waist down. Either way, it would be a terrible waste. Alice had to admit she'd grown to regard Kim with not just affection but admiration too, the sort of grudging but profound respect you developed for someone whose choices you found utterly confounding but who nonetheless managed to make them work. Alice had a thought that made her laugh and then, after a moment, made her lie back and think. She rose out of bed, pulled on her jeans, and went outside. Kim glanced over and gave her a curt nod and then went back to glaring out at the dusk, as if to reproach the sun for setting. Alice's stomach tightened for a moment, and she wondered if Kim had somehow found out about her meeting with Lester.

"What's up?" Alice said.

Kim looked at her with an inscrutable expression. "I'm pregnant."

"Oh . . . ," Alice said, trailing off. Her first instinct in these situations was always to express regret and sympathy, which had led to some ugly, tearful scenes. "How do you feel about it?"

Kim gave a grudging half shrug with just one shoulder and continued staring out into the distance. "It's whatever," she said.

"How far along are you?"

"Twelve, fourteen weeks. I ain't even had no morning sickness. Or maybe I just didn't notice, with the hangovers and all."

Alice nodded. She didn't know anything about the abortion laws in South Dakota, but it didn't strike her in any general sense like a very liberal place. It was just a few hours to Minnesota, though. She glanced sidelong at Kim and saw that she was almost bristling with indignation at any presumed sympathy. Never vulnerable, not Kim. The truth was, this came as a huge relief to Alice, who wasn't by nature an affectionate or sympathetic person; even the most token occasions for showing sympathy made her break out in an anxiety sweat. This, she reflected, was why, more than anything else, their partnership functioned. Kim was incapable of accepting anything, and Alice was incapable of giving anything.

"Are you . . . do you need money for . . . to have it taken care of?" Alice said. "I can loan you the money."

"I haven't decided what to do." Kim lit another Capri off the end of her last one. "Yeah, I know what you're thinkin'. I'm thinkin' it too. I been drinkin' and doin' everything else every day and night and that ain't good for the baby. But so did my mama, and I didn't come out with no third eye. People are tougher than you think."

But what if, Alice thought, but she didn't say it. She knew Kim well enough to know—to hope anyway—that if she slept on it, she'd reconsider. She was a pragmatist above all, and having a baby was about the least practical thing you could do.

"It's crazy, but I had this thought when I woke up and saw you out here," Alice said. "And I don't know, this makes me think that maybe it was, like, fate." She broke off and silently reproached herself for her lapse into sentimentality. "You should come back to New York with me, after this case. Work for me at my firm. You're good at this. You can talk to people. You're authentic. You can go places I can't."

Kim exhaled smoke out the corner of her mouth, her eyebrows raised. "You serious?"

"I'm dead serious."

"I mean, yeah, I am good at this. But—"

"But what?" Alice found herself suddenly heated. "What do you have keeping you here? Lester? Please. Robert? He's got a kid back in Connecticut, Kim. Not to mention a wife. You know he was always going back to them, right?"

"You don't know how good this pussy is," Kim said.

"Jesus Christ, Kim," Alice almost shouted. "Grow up, will you?"

Kim laughed. "Chill, it was a joke. Listen, I appreciate you gettin' all serious about my future. It's like in high school, the guidance counselors." She reached out and clasped Alice's wrist with the hand that wasn't holding the cigarette. How was it that Kim was the pregnant one, but was comforting Alice? "I'll think about your offer. I will. I got a lot on my mind, but I'll put it in the rotation."

"You could stay at my place in Brooklyn while you look for your own," Alice said. "Roommates forever!"

"Ha," Kim said, but with a tinge of melancholy. Alice decided to change the subject.

"Want to go to a party tonight? You'd have to shave your legs."

Kim perked up immediately, and Alice thought, *There's no way she's going to have this baby.*

"Definitely," Kim said. "Where?"

"Steve Whitehurst's house."

"Oh lord," Kim said. "Stories I heard about those parties, I better shave a lot higher up than my legs." She rose and bumped the door open with a jut of her hip. "Come on, you can tell me how you got invited while I call around to get us another score. We gonna need it."

CHAPTER 20

The car pulled up outside the room at exactly 7:30 p.m. As they walked from the room to the car, Alice registered the fact that Kim looked far more attractive than she did tonight. Kim was physically more attractive than she was, but Alice could usually take some psychological advantage from Kim's tacky clothes and neon makeup. But Alice had convinced Kim that a subtler aesthetic might be more appropriate to tonight's company, and Kim, made pliant and agreeable by the dust they'd been smoking and snorting since sundown, had humored her. They'd straightened her jet-black hair, applied just a touch of mascara and lipstick, and dressed her in a simple black bandage dress and knockoff nude heels. The effect wasn't exactly high society, but it was at least more sorority girl than stripper. As they'd stood regarding Kim's reflection in the mirror at the conclusion of this makeover, Alice, peaking from her last bump, for a moment hadn't recognized the imperious, angular woman there as her friend. Seeing Alice's fear-stricken expression, Kim had taken her by the upper arm and shaken her once.

"You look like you just seen a ghost," Kim had said.

Alice had made some throwaway comment about feeling dizzy, but the image had disturbed her. She felt betrayed somehow. As they settled into the backseat of the car, Alice knew that in her jeans, oxfords, and button-up, she would be invisible. That was fine; she was working, not on the make. But still.

"You better be careful," she said. "Some rich man is going to fall in love with you and want to take you in off the streets. Just like a stray cat."

"Just my fucking luck," Kim said. "I go to a billionaire's party and I'm already pregnant. Eighteen years of checks, gone."

The car took them south, out of Whitehurst proper, past the fracking towers, until they were driving in a landscape so barren that Alice wasn't sure if the car was moving or the landscape was. Of course, the dust may have contributed to this effect. She wasn't too high—nothing close to that night at Roundtree's—but her head felt nice and clean. Her best, most natural self had emerged from behind her insecurities and second-guessing. If she didn't wrap up this case and get out of Whitehurst, she was going to end up a dusthead.

Their car pulled off the highway and nosed up to a gate that had been painted to match the landscape and was nearly invisible. The driver took a card from atop the sun visor and waved it toward a scanner box, and the gate sunk into the ground to let them pass. Up they went, following a graveled road made from crushed stone taken from the surrounding landscape so that it too was subtly camouflaged. Alice felt as if they were driving into the Batcave.

"Did you know about all this?" she asked Kim.

"Sort of. Everyone knows Whitehurst lives somewhere south of town, but not many people know exactly where. We get it, though. I'd want to be left alone too if I was a billionaire."

They crested a rise in the land, and the house lay before them. It was the sort of house one saw in design magazines; maybe it was hideous, maybe it was visionary. It was bluntly rectangular, with an asymmetrical sloped roof and a base of molded leaden concrete, with small windows like portholes along the sides. The roof was covered with thousands of tiny solar panels, which, even in the moonlight, sparkled like a garden of diamonds. It was of Whitehurst himself—indifference to aesthetics as an expression of privilege. The driver stopped in a circular drive out front and hit the dome light.

"I'll wait for you here." The driver settled into what seemed a familiar pose of boredom.

The front door, which was a massive slab of concrete studded with polished stones, stood just a bit ajar, and Alice could hear the low hum of voices from inside. She braced herself to pull the door open and almost fell when it swung easily, a wonder of counterweights. Steve Whitehurst himself stood just inside, drinking from a highball glass, talking to a prim blond woman and a disheveled older man who looked like a beach bum.

"Come in," he said. "I'm so glad you came." He pecked Alice on the cheek—a bit overly familiar, she thought, but she'd been around the wealthy enough to know they weren't subject to the same expectations as normal people—and then turned his attention to Kim. He took both her hands and squeezed them in his own.

"I've heard so much about you," he said. "Good things only, of course."

"I've heard a lot about you too," Kim said. A beat of silence elapsed, and then Whitehurst laughed, taking the joke.

"You'll have to tell me what they say about me in town. No one else will. I'm glad you could join us. You're joining a long list of exceptional guests. We've had a medicine woman from the reservation, engineers, the governor of the state, touring burlesque dancers. Journalists, many journalists. We had a guest who'd won the Medal of Honor." He winked at her and then, something having caught his attention, looked closer at her and then at Alice. He gave them a flashing, secretive smile and then turned to the man he'd been talking to, waving him over. "Remy, come here."

The man shuffled over, his expression slightly sheepish at having been summoned like a pet, and stood before the three of them. "Ladies, this is Remy. He's a journalist from France, here to do a story about the fracking boom everyone's heard about," Whitehurst said. Remy inclined his shaggy blond mane at them courteously and raised his glass. "Remy, this is Alice. She's a private investigator from New York, so you two can huddle about how shitty and backward my town is compared to Paris and Manhattan. Oh, and she's also a disgraced journalist. You have to hear her story, it's very compelling." He turned to Alice, his face suddenly crestfallen. "Is it okay to tell people about that? I hope I haven't offended."

"It's fine," Alice said, and she meant it. "That was a long time ago. It's like talking about a different person."

"It's a good thing that you are out of journalism," Remy said. His English was only mildly accented, with that flat, transatlantic drawl of the type of European who was so well traveled they were essentially country-less. "Journalism is dead. It's dying."

"Well, it can only be one or the other, Remy," Whitehurst said. He looked at the women quickly to make sure they'd registered his gibe and then went on. "And this is Kim. She tried to unionize her brothel, so I'm sure you'll both have a lot to talk about."

Remy smiled politely and spoke to Alice and Kim. "Steve thinks that because I'm French, I must be a socialist and a whoremonger."

"Well, aren't you?" Whitehurst said cheerfully. Without waiting for a reply, he turned to the women. "Come on, I'll introduce you to the other guests and then give you the tour. The others have already had it."

He led them around the room, presenting them in turn to the handful of other guests. Remy's cameraman, Louie, was nearly seven feet tall and held himself so stiffly that Alice felt he might tip over and fall if she poked him. Ling-Wan and his wife, Laurel, were a Chinese couple who exuded wealth in the opposite way from Whitehurst; Laurel was young and could've been a model and was wearing, Alice thought, mid-six-figures worth of jewels, whereas her hangdog husband's suit was high-end Savile Row. They regarded Alice and Kim with cool curiosity, as if they were insects under glass. The tall blond was Whitehurst's executive assistant, Tamara—*there's certainly a story there,* Alice thought—and she greeted them with a warmth that Alice found hard to believe was genuine, though she felt bad for assuming it.

Whitehurst led them through a wide doorway and then in the hall turned to make sure they were out of earshot of the other guests.

"You're high," he said. "Both of you."

Alice felt like a child who'd been caught reading a comic nestled inside her textbook. Kim, for her part, didn't miss a beat.

"What are you, a cop?" she said, her voice offhand and teasing.

"It's bad manners to start before the rest of us," Whitehurst said. "That's all. And you shouldn't bother with that stepped-on trash from town. Who knows what they cut it with? After dinner I'll give you a taste of the stuff I get."

"Sounds like fun," Kim said, and when Whitehurst looked at Alice, she arranged her face into an expression of bemused gameness.

"Let's do a quick tour," Whitehurst said, just like that. As he led them through the house, Alice tried to figure him out. His mannerisms were those of a moneyed new-age bohemian, what she called, somewhat derisively, back in Brooklyn a "yoga bro," but in his Hefner-esque host persona, not to mention his easy initiation of them into his after-dinner dust harem—she was sure now that his assistant also served more elemental functions—he was the archetypal louche old-money sensualist. But then if it was decadence he was into, why didn't he move to New York or Los Angeles? He certainly had the money. The fact that he'd stayed in microscopic Whitehurst, a town that was named after him, no less, made her think he was a small-ponder. You saw them all the time in New York; they were the ones who moved back to Iowa or Alabama or Texas after a miserable year in the city. They just couldn't take the higher velocity, the higher density, the higher competition. When Alice walked into a bar and the bartender greeted her familiarly, that was the end for her—time to find a new place where her anonymity would be restored—but for a small-ponder, that was the beginning. They needed the comfort level of being known and knowing, of community. Whitehurst had that here—generations of it. He was the biggest possible fish in the smallest possible pond. In a way, she didn't blame him. She wondered if anyone would be able to resist that level of security, of power.

His house was an utterly bewildering mix of new and old, the spaces angular and unpredictable, cubbyholes opening into amphitheaters, hallways to nowhere, the materials a juxtaposition of luxe and industrial, obsidian and unvarnished wood, concrete and bamboo. A small bench running through the center of his office was made of ancient reclaimed stone blocks, rough-hewn and porous, and Alice stopped to run her hand over the stone. It seemed to almost radiate cold.

"That's the last remaining part of the very first house the Whitehursts built back in 1815," Whitehurst said proudly.

"Did you have it moved here, or . . . ?"

"No, that's the original site." A look of comprehension showed itself on Alice's and Kim's faces and Whitehurst grinned. "I've been waiting for you to figure it out. Or did you think my architect was just insane? Every generation expanded on the original house, but I wanted to take it to another level. I had my architects build a completely new, modern structure around the old house, enclosing it, and then we took the roof off the old house and started to strategically knock down walls. For flow and to maximize natural light. That whole outer ring of halls and galleries is the newest space, and as you move inward, you're literally traveling back through time. Like rings on a tree."

"How much did that cost you?" Kim asked.

"I have no idea," Whitehurst said matter-of-factly. "Some things are more important than money. History, for example. Come through here."

He led them through a wide wood-framed doorway and down a set of stairs, where they turned a corner into a vaulted atrium. Alice judged that they were on the side of the house facing away from the road; here the base wasn't concrete but glass, from top to bottom, and the ceilings she judged to be thirty or forty feet tall. "This space is completely new. My contribution."

The main expanse of the atrium was a large sunken seating area, but the three of them stood along a narrow observation deck fronted by a steel railing. In front of them, the badlands stretched out all the way to the horizon, so utterly desolate that Alice thought they could've been on the moon. As a spectacle, the view was of a piece with the Hokusai painting she'd seen in his office earlier: beautiful but utterly forbidding.

"The Hokusai in your office," Alice said. "Is it the original?"

Whitehurst smiled and brought his hand to his mouth, almost bashful. "It's a copy. I own the original, but I keep it in a vault. Why do you ask?"

"The view made me think of it."

"You'd never guess, but the view is worth more than the painting. Those tracts have at least a hundred million dollars' worth of oil under them, but I don't want to look out at fracking rigs every night."

Alice snuck a look at Kim and saw hate, envy, and utter incomprehension flash across her face before it settled back into her customary blasé stoicism.

"Oh, and there," Whitehurst said, pointing at a small cardboard box sitting on a nearby end table. "Those are Wilcox's papers. Everything we have on him. Tax forms, work orders, evaluations. Don't forget to take them when you leave."

"Thanks," Alice said. She knew it was technically illegal to release at least some of the papers to her, because of employee confidentiality, and she figured he probably knew that too. "I really appreciate it. I do. I'll make sure no one gets a look at them."

He waved his hand at her magnanimously. "I just hope it helps."

Kim stood by toying with her bracelet, turning her wrist clockwise and then counter as she held the metal cuff stationary. Alice realized she hadn't told Kim that Whitehurst knew about her and Robert and that she was feigning indifference at the mention of his name, something that she was fairly sure hadn't escaped Whitehurst's notice.

"I'd love a drink," Alice said suddenly. The spontaneity of her declaration seemed to surprise them all, and they all chuckled.

"Terrible manners on my part," he said. "We should rejoin the others anyway."

Alice hefted the box of papers, and they followed him through his puzzle box of a house. It occurred to her then—*oh, right, sure*—it was right there under her nose: Whitehurst was his house. Modern on the outside, old-fashioned on the inside, austere, lonely, complicated, a series of facades, perfectly executed but flawed in conception, enabled and insulated by oil and money, money and oil.

CHAPTER 21

Dinner was served Spanish-style, a series of small plates to pick at and talk over. Whitehurst was seated at the head of the table like a biblical patriarch, and he instructed them all to the seats he'd chosen for them. Alice and Kim were seated across from the French journalists, and to Alice's left was the Chinese couple, who sat across from Tamara, the assistant, who proved to be an adroit conversationalist and hostess.

When they'd settled into their seats, Remy leaned toward her. "We must touch on our host's suggested topics or he will feel insulted. And so, Whitehurst, what's the worst thing about it? For me, I think it's the coffee. There is no espresso anywhere, and the coffee they serve is not coffee. It's something else. Perhaps boiled roots they dug up in the forest."

Alice laughed. She liked the Frenchman, had liked him since their first exchange, when he'd gently chided Whitehurst. The French were immune to the charms of wealth; they thought it gauche, like fake breasts and caps worn backward.

"It's not even coffee," she said. "It's just brown water. It's like hot tap water with a dropperful of iodine in it."

"We had to buy an espresso machine for our hotel room," Remy said.

"You're welcome to come by for an espresso any time," Louie the cameraman said stiffly, and then immediately blushed.

"I may do that," Alice murmured.

Remy started to tell her and Kim about the documentary he and Louie were making for French television, about the squeegee men in all the parking lots. They'd come from all over the world to get in on the rush, but either hadn't gotten on anywhere or had busted out for drinking or dusting on the job and been blacklisted. One of the featured men in the documentary had come to town all the way from Nevada for a promised job, found that the position had been given to the foreman's son-in-law, gotten drunk, locked himself out of his car, and fell asleep in a parking lot.

"But it was in winter," Remy said. "He woke up in the hospital. His legs had been amputated from frostbite. This was his first day in town."

"Well, it can only get better from there," Kim said.

At the same time, Whitehurst was giving the Chinese the hard sell on the town's bright future, angling for them to build a hotel downtown, but they were skeptical. Alice nodded at Remy's sob stories while listening to the conversation to her left. The Chinese man was saying that he was hearing the boom was tailing off, that OPEC's efforts to drive down the price of oil, to make fracking unprofitable, were working, and that other boomtowns were drying up.

"Other towns. Not here," Whitehurst said. "OPEC's pursuing short-term goals. Like always. You know what they say about the Saudis, their grandparents lived in tents in the desert, and their grandchildren will be living in tents in the desert. They have no vision. It's money in and money out. Besides, their wells are almost dry and they know it. They're just trying to bump oil prices up for one last sell-off before it's all over. And what then? I take a longer view. I have no shortage of capital. I'm going to keep paying people, keep pulling product out of the ground, and build up reserves. And when the Saudis go dry, I'll be the only game in town, with millions of barrels of inventory."

"The Russians. The Canadians. The Finnish."

"The Arctic ice isn't melting nearly fast enough for them to compete with me. Besides, the technology for subzero underwater drilling is in its infancy. Not to mention the fact that they haven't even decided how to divvy up that virgin Arctic Ocean floor. That amount of money at stake, they'll go to war, or the brink of it at least, before drilling even gets underway."

"You never know," Ling-Wan said. Alice could see he was dug in for an argument. "If you're going to keep drilling at full capacity through the downturn, the ice could be all gone by the end of the decade."

Whitehurst shook his head. "I run a responsible company. My fleet is hybrids and will be fully electric by the end of the decade. And I'm in the process of building up infrastructure to capture the natural gas we're currently just burning off. We're actually working on a process that will bind it to a non-Newtonian fluid so we can reinject it into the ground as fracking fluid." He gestured at the glass carafe of water at the center of the table. "Even now, we use a proprietary injection fluid with zero environmental impact. That's tap water from here in Whitehurst."

"Responsible oil drilling," Ling-Wan said in a tone of disgusted irony.

"Don't pretend you have ethical concerns," Whitehurst said. "I know about the coal-fired plants you own, the slave labor in your factories in Chengdu."

"Political prisoners," he replied. "A local Chinese matter. But then Americans never have respected sovereignty, have they?"

Alice saw that their formerly civil conversation was on the cusp of turning bitter, and decided to cut in. She leaned toward the two men and raised a finger; the Chinese looked at her only reluctantly, but Whitehurst clearly welcomed the interruption.

"You know," Alice said. "The townspeople say that dust is made of your proprietary fracking fluid."

Whitehurst raised both eyebrows and leaned forward in a pantomime of surprise. "Do they?" Alice couldn't decide if he was making fun of her or was just a terrible liar. "That's hilarious. It makes sense, though. When the fracking thrives, so does the dust. They've taken that connection and made it literal. The rumor mill will always dumb things down. It's a shame, but drugs always accompany a boom."

"Not always," Kim said. Remy and Louie, who thought they'd been entertaining Kim and Alice with an anecdote about the fluctuating exchange rate at Whitehurst strip clubs looked up like they'd been ambushed. They'd been unaware of the other conversation, not to mention their nominal audience's divided attentions. "What about crack?"

"Interesting example," Whitehurst said. "And one I've thought about before. It's true, crack didn't accompany a boom. The communities where it thrived were largely impoverished before crack. But even more interesting, it prefigured a boom. Go to Brooklyn, go to LA, go to Washington, DC. All the blocks that ran with blood—literally ran with blood! Kids selling vials in broad daylight, shootouts—today, those blocks are home to million-dollar condos. Every one. That's real wealth, and where did it come from? It came out of nowhere. Out of the blue sky. You could make a case that crack created a boom."

"Just because some white people came in and bought up everything after the addicts killed each other don't mean crack is some economic miracle," Kim said. Alice could tell that Kim was on the edge of losing her temper, and part of Alice wanted her to, to pierce Whitehurst's bubble of moneyed false congeniality.

"We're not used to thinking about things in this manner. It offends our sensibilities. It offends our humanity. And it should. But facts have no humanity. Think of it like this. When I was a child," Whitehurst said, "my father took me to his father's ranch in Texas every summer. This visit I'm recalling, I was about ten. That weekend, they were burning off the fields after the close of the harvest. I remember being very frightened as his men set fire to the stubble and we watched the flames race across the field. I had never heard of someone setting a fire on purpose. The sky filled with smoke, the smell—I remember thinking, this is what hell is like. At the far end of the field, we saw a doe and two fawns rise up out of the grass, where they'd been sleeping, and run for the tree line ahead of the flames. This upset me very much. I thought the field was their home and that my grandfather was driving them out of it. My father picked me up and said, 'They burn the fields so that it'll grow back even lusher next season. And it will. And the deer will be back too. You'll see.' And the next summer, when we visited, we went to that same field, and the corn there was taller and stronger than I'd ever imagined, and when we walked in the woods around the fields, I did see deer. I saw a lot of deer. And I understood then that creating the future, creating prosperity, is messy work. Sometimes unpleasant work. But necessary work, and work that requires vision and courage."

Alice sat, chin in hand, regarding Whitehurst with studied neutrality. She wondered how many times he'd told that story at board meetings and shareholder retreats. Quite a few, judging by how concise and measured it had come out.

"But the deer you saw," Kim said. "Were they the same deer?"

Whitehurst looked down at his lap and then back at Kim with extravagant patience. "Pardon?"

"Were the deer you saw frolickin' all happy, when you went back, were those the same deer you saw runnin' from the fire?"

"I don't know," Whitehurst said. "I don't think it much matters."

"It matters to the deer."

Alice—and, she noticed, the rest of the table—perked up to see what Whitehurst would say to this. To her surprise, he smiled and chuckled sheepishly. "You know, I never thought of that."

The Chinese couple left directly after dinner in one of the SUVs that had been waiting out front. The night had been a business meeting for them, not a social occasion. Louie drifted into a car as well, begging off due to an early morning shoot. The rest of the party moved to Whitehurst's lavish observation room: Whitehurst, Remy, and the three women—Kim and Alice and the assistant, Tamara. Alice could see Remy calculating, as they all drifted to seats in the sunken living room, that the numbers were on his side. Even a billionaire could hardly claim all the women for himself, could he?

"So tell me," Whitehurst said to her after they'd all settled in. "Tell me honestly. Do you think Wilcox did it?"

"I'm sure he didn't," Alice said. "I think he's just a convenient fall guy. He's the last one seen with her, so they pick him up."

"The justice system doesn't always work the way it should," he said. "People get lazy. The system gets corrupted. I often think that if I wasn't doing what I'm doing, I'd have gone to law school."

"Well, there's still time," Alice said. It was a throwaway comment, but it seemed to flatter Whitehurst, reinforcing his conception of himself as still youngish.

"Yes, that's true," he said. "Every day is a new beginning of something. Potentially, at least."

Maybe when you're a billionaire, Alice thought. *The rest of us are pretty much subjects of our history, personal and otherwise.*

"He was framed," Kim said, not confrontationally but almost sunnily, matter-of-factly. "Then they tried to shut him up for good, in jail."

"You knew him, didn't you?" Whitehurst said. He'd been holding back that card all night, and now he laid it down, calmly. It wasn't really a question. "You were close?"

"We were in love," Kim said. She looked at each of them in turn as if daring them to say something about it.

"*Merde*," Remy said, but when Kim looked at him, he dropped his eyes right away.

"Why do you think he was framed?" Whitehurst said.

"We don't know yet," Kim said. "But we're getting closer."

Alice cleared her throat and leaned forward to cut Kim off; she didn't want her spilling all their leads at a dinner party, spreading rumor and innuendo in a town already rife with it. "Steve," she said. "You must know everyone in town. Do you know a man name of Hicks—late forties, white, about five foot six, balding, stocky? He's supposed to be a legit businessman."

"Can't say I do," Whitehurst said. Alice held his eye for a moment, to see if he'd look away—the telltale giveaway of a lie—but he didn't. "I don't actually know all that many people in town anymore. There's so much turnover, and I'm chained to my desk pretty much seven days a week. Why? Do you think this man might be involved in Wilcox's case?"

"Not sure," Alice said. "But I doubt it. Just my journalist's OCD rearing its head."

"Look, if you find something, I want you to come to me," Whitehurst said. "I know what people in town say. That the courts and the police here have become corrupt. I take that very seriously. If people feel like they can't trust the justice system to render justice, that undermines everything I'm trying to build here. The future of Whitehurst. So if there's been a wrong committed, I want to help set it right."

"Thank you," Alice said. She wondered how many press conferences he'd squeeze out of setting one single wrong right. Not less than three, she'd wager. "I'll come to you the second I find something solid."

"I'm not claiming there haven't been miscarriages of justice. There probably have. But you have to understand just how overwhelming this boom has been for the municipal institutions. Between booms, we went decades without a single homicide. Now there are two or three every weekend. Burglaries, assaults, rapes, they've all gone up a thousand percent or more. Inconceivable increases. The police we have, they're playing catch-up. They're swamped. They're good people, though, and I think that once they get a hold on things, when we staff up—a challenge in itself when the men can make four times as much in the oil fields—that things will settle down. We have the right leadership in place already, I feel very confident in that. You know the sheriff, don't you?"

"We're acquainted," Alice said. She wondered if Whitehurst knew about her and the sheriff's . . . "involvement." It didn't seem totally implausible, though the implication of surveillance, or at least information gathering, verged on sinister.

"He's a good man," Whitehurst said, in the same tone someone would use to comment on pleasant weather. His gaze wandered to the windows, and he gestured out at the slate-gray skyline. "That's the Devil's Pike." It was a tall, towerlike rock formation, wider at the top and tapered at the middle, jagged and precarious-looking. From this distance, at night, it was impossible to discern its proportions, but Alice was sure that it was very tall. "It's the last remnant of what was the primary landmass around here, when this area was all underneath a vast alkaline sea. That spire, that's all that remains of a continent. An entire geological era that was a thousand times longer than human history. There are caves at its base. I've been mapping them out for almost a decade now, and I'm still discovering new chambers."

"That sounds dangerous," Alice said. Whitehurst shrugged in a token display of modesty. Alice could see why cave exploration would appeal to a man like Whitehurst, a man who already owned everything on the surface. She doubted he was exploring so much as he was claiming new territory.

"You know what we say about those caves, don't you?" Kim said from where she'd perched on the corner of a glass coffee table.

"Of course," Whitehurst said. Seeing that the others had perked up with curiosity, he tipped his head in deference to Kim. "Why don't you tell it?"

Kim gave a little wiggle of delight and drained her glass, which Remy smoothly refilled. The night had been dominated by shoptalk about various fields, which Kim hadn't been the least bit curious about, and she was savoring her moment in the spotlight. "Them caves, that's where our braves'd go before a battle. Going way back as far back as it goes. Our story had it like this country is so bare and dead because these spirits used to roam the earth, just scourin' and burnin' and ravagin' it clean of any kinda life. I guess you could say they're spirits of death.

"Then the Great Buffalo, who lived somewhere round here with his wife, White Deer, one day, he had enough. He decided to trap the spirits inside the earth, which is hollow, as y'all know. But first he had to get 'em down in there. So he tells them, hey guys, I found this passage to the center of the earth and you won't believe this, but down in there I found all these furs and blankets and beads and arrowheads. Like, a real jackpot. But these spirits of death, they don't care about riches, so they just go on ravagin' and scourin' and burnin'. So Great Buffalo waits awhile and then goes back to them and says, hey, so I went back down there and did some more explorin' and I found a land of ten thousand virgins, all young and pink cheeked and wide hipped and hair and eyes black as night. But the spirits, they ain't care about fuckin', I guess. They just continue on doing what they were doing, not payin' Great Buffalo no mind. So Great Buffalo says to himself, well, these spirits of death don't care about no earthly anything. All they give a fuck about is pain and death and fuckin' shit up. So this is when Great Buffalo's lightbulb went on.

"He says to his wife, White Deer, baby, lemme show you this passage I found into the hollow center of the earth, you're gonna love this shit. So he takes her down there, and I dunno, I guess he's like hey what's that over there, and when she looks, he conks her in the back of the head and then ties her to the ground and cuts her liver out. Then he just leaves her like that, tied down, guts hanging out, screamin' and cryin'. And sure enough, all them spirits was like, hmm now what's this? And when they went down to check things out, Great Buffalo rolled a rock over the entrance and trapped them in there. Course, he trapped his wife too, and since she a great spirit, she can't die, so them spirits just ravagin' the shit out of her all the time and she screamin' all the time. They say that when a woman gets her monthly blood, she can hear White Deer screamin' at night if she listens real close. But once Great Buffalo cleared the earth of all them spirits, that's when human beings was born, and so we owe Great Buffalo for his sacrifice.

"Anyway, when our braves are gonna go into battle, they go down in those caves, real deep, and paint themselves up and cut themselves with pieces of flint. If they're lucky, one of them spirits of death rises out and takes up inside him. And then he's a unstoppable warrior. They say that before Little Big Horn, five hundred braves went down in them caves and every single one come out with a spirit of death inside him. There was a great-grandmother on the res who said she was there that night as a little girl and said all them braves come back with their eyeballs all black, just solid black like buckeyes, and everyone knew they had death inside 'em and stayed back. And that even after they killed Custer and all his men, they still had that death inside them. It was a bargain with the devil sort of thing. Some of them turned on each other and some of 'em turned on their families and gutted them in their sleep and had to be taken out in the country like mad dogs and put down. Some went up in the hills and became cannibals, and the rest of them just roved the country killin' and rapin' and burnin' just like them spirits used to do.

"And you know what else they say," Kim said, turning to address Whitehurst alone out of her rapt audience. "They say that that's why the killin' starts up when there's a boom. The gold boom, the gas boom, and now the oil boom. You drill down in the earth, you let some of them spirits out."

Whitehurst shifted in his seat and dropped his eyes, taking this for an accusation. When Kim saw his discomfort, she quickly went on. "I mean, that's what the old people say. I ain't sayin' it, I'm just passin' on what they say."

"No, it's fine," Whitehurst said. "It's fascinating. I'd heard the Little Big Horn story, but not the rest of it. Not the drilling part of it, and not the origin story."

"What's it like down there, in the caves?" Remy said.

"It's glorious," Whitehurst said. "There's a sacred energy you can feel, emanating from the mother earth. I'd love to take you down there some time. All of you."

As everyone agreed that they'd love to do a cave tour, speaking in the manner of people who are making an agreement they have no intention of honoring, Tamara stood and went into the next room. Shortly she came back with a hinged glass case almost like a laptop. Whitehurst caught Alice's eye and waggled his eyebrows at her. Tamara placed the case on the round coffee table at the center of the room and flipped it open; half of it was a flat mirrored surface and the other half had tiny glass vials of powder strapped in. Whitehurst looked over the various vials and then selected one, which Tamara carefully poured out and divided into lines. Alice watched them work with an almost childish delight swelling in her chest.

Kim went first. She did her line with a short, expert snort, and then sat back in her chair with her eyes closed.

"Oh, wow," she said. "Oh, fuck."

Remy went next, then Alice. Alice bent over the glass and pulled the powder into her nostril in one neat inhale. She felt it burn her sinuses, and then it hit her. It was much better than any other dust she'd had, even Roundtree's. Not only did inhibition, fear, and anxiety fall way, but so did thought, consciousness, and personality. As the drug took hold, she felt as if she'd been reduced down to animal consciousness, breathlessly soaring from present moment to present moment. When she looked up and locked eyes with Remy, she saw her pure exhilaration mirrored there.

For an instant she thought they would high-five. Instead, he leaned forward and kissed her. They kissed for a while. She wasn't sure how long. She seemed to have lost her capacity for reflective thought. Next thing she knew, she was lying back, her shirt off, and Remy was sucking her breasts, first one and then the other, careful not to neglect either. She let her head fall to the side.

Across from them, Whitehurst had reclined into Tamara's embrace; the blond assistant was nuzzling his neck from behind as he kissed Kim with a hunger Alice found startling. Kim was curled on his lap, her dress pulled up and down so that it lay bunched across her abdomen. She either hadn't worn underwear or had taken it off already. Remy had noticed them too. He stood, stripped his clothes off, and went over to the three of them. Kim didn't stop kissing Whitehurst or seem to even open her eyes, but she sensed Remy's approach and reached behind her to take his erection in hand. He moaned softly and said something in French.

Alice watched them with a feeling of detachment. She began to stir, to join in, when she was suddenly stopped in her tracks by a thought. What if she was not made use of? She had a sudden image of herself perched on the far end of the couch, like some sad nude gargoyle, diddling herself while the others lay intertwined and heaving. She realized that she'd gone past feeling high and was beginning to accelerate into paranoia. Her mind tightened like a vise. This was a familiar experience for her; very often when she smoked pot or took hallucinogens, her anxiety took over. These speculative worst-case scenarios cropped up like poisonous mushrooms, becoming self-fulfilling prophecies. There was nothing to do but lock herself in a room alone and get drunk until she passed out.

She stood up and buttoned her shirt. "I'm, uh, I think I'm going to leave," she said.

She turned and walked away before she saw if anyone acknowledged her, pausing only to grab the box of Wilcox documents and put on her shoes. Outside, she collapsed into the backseat of the car that had brought them. The driver, silent and unsurprised, quietly started the car and drove. By the time the car turned onto the highway, a high-pitched tone like a dog whistle had come to dominate her consciousness. She had never been this high before, on anything. Fucking Whitehurst, trying to show off with his pure powder. He was too sheltered to know that regular people didn't cut their powder down to make it last; they cut it down so they wouldn't overdose.

The wall-to-wall traffic that had always seemed so claustrophobic was what saved her. She concentrated on the trucks around them, to the exclusion of all else, and their proximity became comforting, almost womb-like. When they finally pulled into the Bobcat parking lot, Alice had lost all sense of time and place. The driver, still bored, said nothing as she grabbed the box of papers and stumbled to the door.

The room looked almost unbearably squalid to her, a diorama of slow-motion failure. The crumpled piles of clothes, the empties lining the windowsills and end tables, the overflowing trash cans, all seemed to pose the same rhetorical questions: What do you think you're doing here? You don't really think you have any hope of solving this case, do you?

Alice turned all the lights on and then, after a moment, turned them all off. She found an unopened bottle of cheap tequila and sat on the bed drinking from it. It was warm, and her stomach tried to send it back up, but she closed herself to the possibility. It was her body that had ruined her night, and now she would punish it. She took several more swigs of tequila, trying her hardest not to think. She felt a sudden vibration in her pocket and withdrew her phone. It was the sheriff calling. She declined the call and, as she did so, saw he'd called six times already and left several messages. She dialed voicemail, and his voice filled her ear.

"Missy stroked out about ten this evening. Aneurysm. Waiting on the death certificate, but my guess is, before noon, we're gonna be chargin' your boy Wilcox with murder. This is just a courtesy call."

Alice lay there in the dark trying to feel something, but she just felt faded. She took one more drink and silently dedicated it to Missy. No, she decided after a moment. Missy was beyond help now. Robert, though, needed all the help he could get.

CHAPTER 22

Robert didn't look so good when they brought him into the visiting area. The guards directed the three of them to sit at a table by the window. In the morning light, Robert's skin looked translucent, like the merest touch would leave a bruise. He'd limped as they brought him out, and when he sat he winced and grasped the bandage on his throat. They'd transported him back to the jail as soon as he'd stabilized, no doubt, with biweekly checkups from a prison nurse barely qualified to be a vet tech. Alice had seen a lot of oozing stitches in county, a lot of indifferently set bones. Jail was a throwback to a Darwinian time in more ways than one: heal thyself or die.

"So you heard," Robert said. "I guess I better get a lawyer."

Alice nodded. She didn't have to mention the late-night call from the sheriff; Missy's death had been all over the morning paper. "I'm sorry, Robert."

"Missy didn't deserve that," he said. "I wish that if someone had a problem with me, they would've just come at me. Instead of involving an innocent girl."

"We're makin' progress on your case, though," Kim said. "We gonna get you out soon enough."

Robert turned to look at Kim for the first time since they'd sat down. Alice had been having her morning coffee when a car dropped Kim off at the room, and they'd come directly over. Kim was still in her dress from the night before, her hair tousled, makeup smeared, virtually exuding morning-after musk.

"It doesn't look like you're going lonely in the meantime, though," Robert said. "I didn't ask you to wait for me, but you could at least have showered."

"I came as soon as I heard," Kim said. "People are saying they gonna try and give you the needle, baby. Make you a example."

Robert's jealousy disappeared in an instant, as if it had all been a show he was happy to abandon. "That's what the guards said. They said I was gonna be charged with aggravated kidnapping on top of murder."

"They shouldn't be saying shit like that," Alice said. "I'll talk to the sheriff about it."

"Have you told my wife yet?" Robert said.

"Wouldn't you rather she hear it from you?"

"Honestly, no. She's not going to take it very well. I don't think I can handle a scene like that right now. Can you do it?"

"I'll call her as soon as we're done here," Alice said.

Robert cleared his throat. "Could you do it now? I don't want her finding out from the Internet. She'll freak out."

Alice sighed almost imperceptibly. This wasn't, by any stretch, part of her job description. But she hadn't done very well by Robert so far, and she felt obligated to help him out in the matter. She stood up. "I'll let you two have a minute alone. I'll call Rachel from outside."

The lot was beginning to fill up with visitors, harried single moms herding their kids into the jail while clutching cartons of Marlboro reds and family-sized plastic bottles of instant coffee. Alice wondered if she'd be selfless enough to keep buying her man smokes and coffee if he was behind bars. She decided she'd probably outsource it to the kids' chores list. "Make your bed, rake leaves, mail Daddy razor blades."

She walked to a distant corner of the lot and stood under a flowering dogwood tree. She took out her phone and stared at it. The longer she thought about what to say, the harder it would be to call. She closed her eyes and took a deep breath. She would never forgive Robert for making her do this.

Rachel picked up on the first ring; in the background, her child was screaming. "What's the latest?" she asked.

"The girl died," Alice said. "They're going to charge Robert with murder."

"Okay," Rachel said, her voice no more troubled than if Alice had told her she'd dinged up her car. "How are you progressing on clearing him?"

"I'm not quite there yet. But I have some leads."

"Tell me."

Alice told her about the party at Roundtree's, Hicks, retracing Robert's week of work orders, visiting Whitehurst. It sounded muddled and desperate when she laid it all out, and Alice could tell from Rachel's silence that she thought the same.

"Well, you're covering all the bases," Rachel said finally. "You always were a base coverer."

Alice couldn't tell if this was an insult or a compliment, so she said nothing.

"Don't tell me you think Robert was involved in drug dealing," Rachel said.

"No, he's not the type."

"No shit. Look, what if . . ." The child's wailing swelled as Rachel comforted it. "Alice, I didn't send you up there to solve a crime. You know that, right? I sent you up there to free my husband. You see the difference?"

"That's what I'm doing."

Rachel sighed, the familiar condescending heave of breath Alice remembered from their days at the paper. "No. It's not. Remember when we were working on that story about lead water mains and I came into your office after a couple weeks and you had all those index cards on the wall, laying out some conspiracy all the way back to Lord Baltimore and, I don't know, King fucking George? Remember what I said to you?"

Alice did remember, of course, but she didn't want to give Rachel the satisfaction of saying so, so she said nothing. Like most conversations she had with Rachel, this one was turning out to be decidedly one-sided.

"I said, 'Just write the fucking story.' And you did, and it was good. So here's what I want you to do. I want you to find out who assaulted the girl, and then I want you to produce a witness to this crime."

"Produce?" Alice felt a familiar flutter of dismay in her stomach, a sensation from dreams she had of reenacting childhood humiliations. "Rachel, I don't really . . ."

"Oh, for fuck's sake. You'll do it for an award, but you won't do it to save my family?"

"It's just not that simple."

"Of course it is. Find a fucking junkie, coach them up, and pay them off." Rachel's kid wailed. "Shit. Okay. Don't do a fucking thing. You still have Robert's room?"

"Yeah. Why?"

"Just sit tight. I'm coming up there. I'll be in late tonight."

"Rachel, wait. Your kid—"

"I'll leave her with my mom. All right, I have to go book a flight and a car. Probably should've done this from the beginning. You were always a great reporter, but you needed someone standing over your shoulder all the time, making sure you didn't fuck up."

"Wait, there's something that—" Alice began, but Rachel had already ended the call. She glared at the phone as if it had somehow betrayed her. She had a sudden vision of Rachel and Kim meeting face-to-face, with her, Alice, caught in the middle. That this was not just a possibility, but now a near certainty, was clearly a monumental failure on her part.

By the time Kim returned to the car, Alice had more or less gotten over her panic. She had a plan: she would appeal to Whitehurst to come up with a hotel room for his employee's grief-stricken wife—if anyone could come up with a room in the booked-up town, it was him—and would sit Rachel down, first thing, and tell her about Robert's . . . dalliance. Rachel wasn't sheltered, nor naive. She knew what men were like. How prone to boredom, how needy, how weak. What was infidelity next to Robert's life? That would be her rationale if Rachel asked why she hadn't told her right away about Robert's girlfriend, that it seemed trivial and Victorian to care about such things when there were weightier—literally existential—concerns to be confronted. She wondered if Rachel would buy it. Probably not.

Kim had walked across the lot toward the car with her head down, and it wasn't until she was opening the passenger side door that Alice realized why. She'd been crying. She sat in the passenger seat with her fingers and thumbs knit together, sniffling.

"He wants to keep the baby," Kim said.

"You told him?"

"I had to. I owe him that much."

But is it even his? Alice thought, but didn't say it. "He's just having a moment of panic. Looking at lethal injection. He thinks the baby is his shot at living on."

"Yeah. I guess."

"Kim," Alice said. She'd told herself as soon as Kim had begun speaking that she wouldn't take sides, wouldn't advise, would just listen, but she couldn't stop herself. "He's not going to be around for this baby. If he's not dead, or in prison, he's going back to his wife and his other kid. You're going to be stuck raising this baby alone."

"Yeah, so? My mama raised me alone."

Yes, exactly, Alice thought, and immediately felt lacerating guilt. "His wife is coming to Whitehurst."

"Yeah? When?"

"Right now. She thinks I'm fucking up, so she's flying in to take charge. She'll be here tonight."

Kim had taken off her shoes, but now she wriggled her feet back into them. "Message received. I'll get my shit and clear out before sundown."

"No, no, no," Alice said. "Nobody wants that. Nobody's saying that. I'm going to get Whitehurst to put her up somewhere. If he can't get a room for her, he has plenty of room in that house."

Kim scoffed, but visibly relaxed. "Yeah, I'm sure he be happy to have her. Look at this." She opened her small purse and withdrew a sleek diamond tennis bracelet. "This morning, Whitehurst pulls this strongbox out, keys in the code, and takes out this bracelet. Gives it to me. He don't say nothin', but it's clear it's a shut-the-fuck-up payment. Dude had fifty more in the box, I saw 'em myself. I mean, how many orgies you have to have during a average week if you got a ready-made box of shut-the-fuck-up bracelets for your hoes?"

Alice took the bracelet and ran it through one hand. If it was real—and why would a billionaire pay off women with fake diamonds?—it was worth as much as a high-end sedan. "What are you going to do with it?"

"Cherish it forever," said Kim. "Fuck you think? I'm gonna sell it. Use the money to get Bobby the best lawyer in the state."

Alice wondered if Robert had any idea how lucky he was that he had two women like Kim and Rachel working on his behalf, two fearless, uncompromising steamrollers. And herself, of course. Probably he didn't appreciate it. Then she wondered if it would all be enough.

While Kim showered, Alice leafed through the box of papers she'd gotten from Whitehurst. Everything he had concerning Robert was there: tax forms, employee evaluations, expense reports. There was a printed-out spreadsheet, dozens of pages long, of Whitehurst's assignments, which, Alice assumed, some functionary had used to fill out the handwritten work orders they'd retrieved from Robert's briefcase. To be honest, she couldn't even remember why she'd wanted the papers in the first place. Her completist impulses, probably. Maybe Rachel was right; she was too caught up in the background, the interconnections and minutiae. Missing the forest for the trees.

Thinking of Rachel, she dialed Whitehurst's office. The receptionist put her right through.

"Morning," Whitehurst said, sounding far too energetic for a man who'd been up all night doing dust and fucking. "How you feeling?"

"Hung over," Alice said. "I came home and drank almost an entire bottle of tequila and then passed out."

Whitehurst laughed. "I'm sorry. I should've warned you that it was the strong stuff."

"It's not your fault. That happens to me when I get too high. But look, I'm calling to ask you a favor."

"Go on," Whitehurst said in the equivocal voice of a man who's used to being asked for favors.

"Robert Wilcox's wife is coming to town. She'll be here tonight. You heard that the girl who got assaulted died overnight?"

"Yes, I read it in the paper. Tragic."

"So Robert's getting charged with murder, and his wife thinks I'm dragging my feet on the investigation."

"Are you?"

"No. I'm being thorough. That takes time."

"But she wants results."

"Uh-huh. I haven't told her about the girlfriend yet. Who still lives, along with me, in Robert's room here at the Bobcat. So you see my problem."

"I can get you a room, easy," Whitehurst said. "Most of the rooms are just rented out in blocks by the month, by big companies, for out of towners. Just sitting empty most of the time. I'll have Tamara make a few calls, but it won't be a problem. You know, it's funny you called. I was just thinking about you."

"Were you?" Alice said.

"You have a very analytical mind," Whitehurst said. "I was impressed by our talk. And as you said, you're thorough. You get it right, no matter how long it takes. I want you to write my memoirs for me. I've been searching for someone I can trust with the project. It'll take years, but trust me when I say that money is no object."

What's the catch? Alice thought, and then she said it out loud. "What's the catch?"

"No catch. You could even work from New York if that's more comfortable for you. If there's a catch, it's that you have to start immediately. And I do mean immediately."

"Why the rush?"

"If you spread this around, I will absolutely take legal action against you," Whitehurst said in the amiable tone of voice of a man merely stating a fact. "But I'm sick. No, I'm not sick. I'm dying. So I don't have a lot of time to waste."

Alice's first thought, though she felt guilty letting herself think it, was that he was lying. That he wasn't sick and he just wanted her off Robert's case. She hadn't let herself acknowledge it until just that moment, but while she liked Whitehurst, she didn't trust him. She suspected he was involved in Robert's frame job; she just wasn't sure if he'd lent an active hand in planning it or if he'd just had foreknowledge of it, as he had foreknowledge of everything that happened in his town. Or maybe she was just too cynical and too vulnerable to the reflexive middle-class distrust of rich people.

"Let me think about it," Alice said. "Not for long. I appreciate your need for urgency. Just let me get Rachel Wilcox settled, bring her up to speed, and then I'll have an answer for you. No later than tomorrow night."

"Fine," Whitehurst said, a touch of petulance in his voice. "Call back this afternoon and Tamara will tell you where the room for Wilcox's wife is."

Kim came out of the bathroom in a huge outrush of perfumed steam and stood at her suitcase naked, nudging the crumpled clothes there with one foot before selecting a pair of ripped blue jeans and a pink tank top. When she saw Alice sitting on the bed absorbed in thought, she kicked the corner of the bed.

"What's on your mind, boo?"

"Whitehurst just offered me a job," Alice said. "The only catch is that I have to start immediately."

Kim blinked once, slowly. "Uh-huh." She pulled a chair over and sat down. "So he's in on it."

"I'm not just being paranoid?"

"Fuck no. Ain't no coincidences. He tryin' to mothball you. You think he and Robert had some kind of run-in?"

"I doubt it's personal," Alice said. "I don't think he'd allow himself to enter into a personal conflict with a regular person. I think he sees himself as above all that."

"You got to be extra careful here on out," Kim said. "Whitehurst got eyes everywhere. He owns this town, literally."

"I think I'm going to go see the sheriff. See if I can get any new info out of him. There's still something missing, something we don't know. You want to come along?"

"Nah, you know I don't fuck with that Uncle Tom motherfucker," Kim said. "I'm gonna go pawn this bracelet and then they havin' a memorial service for Missy out at El Tamarindo. So I won't be back till late. I figure you need some time to set things straight with Bobby's missus anyway."

"You sure that big doorman's going to let you in?"

"He'll let me in the second that folded-up fifty hits his palm."

CHAPTER 23

Kim took the car, so Alice walked the mile down the highway to the police station. The ground shuddered under her feet, the perpetual tremor of traffic. She was wearing her Magnum on her hip, and its weight made her stride loopy and off balance. She thought about Rachel as she walked; despite all the time that had passed, on some level she was still the eager reporter wanting to impress her editor. If there was anything more she could uncover about Robert's case, she wanted to do it now, today. Even though that required her to endure more of the sheriff's ham-handed advances. She knew that using him like this was dangerous, but she didn't see any other option.

A truck ground to a halt on the gravel shoulder, and the driver leaned out and told her to hop in. Alice just waved him away without breaking stride. She was getting used to this town, the bad air and the bad food and the bad men. She couldn't decide if that was something to be proud of or worried about. She wondered if Kim would take her up on her offer to come to New York and work for her, and if she did, how she'd adapt. South Dakota to New York wasn't the same as New York to South Dakota; scaling up was harder than scaling down. And if she had a baby in tow, that would make it even harder. She thought back to her first year in New York: the crushing loneliness, the implacable sense of alienation. Kim was tougher than she'd been, but toughness could be a liability if you had to bend but could only break.

At the police station, two deputies were wrestling a drunk roughneck out of a patrol car and toward the building entrance. The drunk resisted with all his considerable strength, and they could only proceed in fits and starts as the deputies swept his legs out from under him, dragged him a few feet, and then stopped to repeat when he regained his footing. The deputies were looking at Alice out of the corners of their eyes, and she wondered what methods they'd have resorted to if there hadn't been a witness.

Inside, the same deputy was working the front desk as the last time she'd visited. Before Alice could speak, he just waved her through. "He's in his office," he said.

Alice frowned, then set off down the hallway. She passed another deputy, and instead of staring coldly straight ahead, the man tipped his hat toward her and smiled. "Mornin'," he said.

The sheriff was sitting behind his desk, signing papers, when she walked in. She half suspected from the vacant look on his face that he was signing them with Xs.

"Have you been telling everyone about me?" Alice asked. The sheriff looked up from his papers with a start and blinked several times.

"What do you mean?" he said.

She closed the door and sat down in the chair in front of his desk and then watched as the sheriff shot out of his seat, fast walked across the office, reopened the door wide, and crammed a doorstop under it to keep it open. He glanced up and down the hallway and then retook his seat behind the desk.

"I wondered where you'd been," he said. His hair was cut so close on the sides of his head that she could see his pinkish scalp, and his uniform was pressed to military precision. "Thought maybe you'd skipped town."

"No," Alice said. "Actually, I may be sticking around for a while. Steve Whitehurst asked me to help him write his memoirs."

The sheriff raised his eyebrows in surprise. "Wow. You must have made quite an impression on him." His face darkened for a moment as he considered what form that impression-making might have taken. Alice would've chided him, but she liked the idea of him being uncomfortable. "Well, that'll be good for you. For your career. And this little town here might grow on you. Among other things." His confidence visibly flowed back into him, expanding his torso and contorting his mouth into an expansive grin.

Alice kept her face pleasant and noncommittal. "Life is full of surprises."

The sheriff frowned. "You sound like Forrest Gump," he said. "I guess that's how you think we all talk around here."

"No," Alice said patiently. "I just don't know how you expect me to respond to your constant attempts at . . . I don't even know what it is. Courting, I guess?"

The sheriff wasn't put off by this at all; if anything, he seemed to have been perversely encouraged. He straightened his tie and folded his hands in front of him benevolently. "How about with some honesty? How about a simple yes or no?"

Alice tipped her head sideways and smiled, as if she were taking his measure, though this was just a stalling tactic. The thought of being in a relationship with a man like the sheriff was abhorrent to her. She could just imagine it: opening doors for her like she was disabled, ordering for her at restaurants—bad restaurants, surely, none of that "foreign" food nonsense—abbreviated missionary sex with the lights turned off. Talking baby names on the second date. No oral, ever. Well, not for her. Going to the strip club with his boys, because that's just what men do, but if she so much as laughed at another man's jokes, she'd be a whore. She had zero interest in any of it. But she was here to get information from him, so she couldn't turn him down flat, at least not yet.

"Michael," she said. "That's just not how things are done where I'm from."

He exhaled harshly, like a child who'd been denied a second dessert. "You talk like you're from another planet. You're from New York! That's still America!"

"Not really."

The sheriff held both hands out in front of him as if cradling an invisible sphere, as if literally shaping his argument. "Look. I know how you all do things out there. You screw around and put everything in every hole and do whatever you want whenever you want, and then, eventually, if the fancy strikes you, maybe then you pair off and play house together. But hear me out. What if you all are doing things exactly backward?"

Alice tried hard to keep her face neutral. "What do you mean?"

"What I mean is, my parents, they were real simple people. Grew up on the reservation. Dropped out of school in eighth grade. Worked the land. My father's father, Elijah Red Horse, got together with my mother's father, John Tall Trees, and they agreed that their children were going to get married. My parents were no more than twelve, thirteen at this point. No one ever asked them what they thought or what they wanted to do. Which probably strikes you as unfair. And I don't doubt that when they were married off at fifteen, there were some awkward moments, and maybe even some tears. But let me tell you something. My parents were together for sixty-four years, and they were the most loving, devoted, passionate couple I ever saw. Nowadays, people think the passion and love has to come first, and then you lock it in with the commitment. But what if the opposite is true? What if the love and passion is a result of the commitment?"

Throughout this monologue, Alice had become increasingly uncomfortable. She often had this kind of empathetic experience; when her friends dragged her to open-mic night at comedy clubs and some amateur bombed, she sat squirming and flop sweating in her chair as if it were she herself bombing. And now she felt all the humiliation and embarrassment that the sheriff was too oblivious or ignorant to notice; she could feel her face burning up, her body shifting uncontrollably, her spirit actually withering from pure mortification. She wasn't sure she could've taken one more second of it without screaming. And now the sheriff was staring at her solicitously, waiting for a response.

"Wow," she said. A moment passed. "Did you just ask me to marry you?"

The sheriff shrugged in faux nonchalance. "It depends. What's your answer if I did?"

Jesus motherfucking Christ. Was this really happening? She thought about the night she'd gone home with that kid from the bar, when the sheriff had pulled them over and threatened the kid with rape charges. How he had tried to force her face into his lap in his cruiser afterward.

"Okay," she said. "You've made your case that I've got things all backward, so now let me make mine. What you really want is, excuse me for being blunt, to fuck. But before you can do that, you have to neutralize my power to threaten or hurt you. You don't want to marry me so much as control me. Not that there's any difference at all between the two. Because if you don't own me, if you don't control me, if I have my own desires and my own agency, then I might fuck other men, which you see as a threat to your masculinity. Your ego. Which, as large and characteristically brittle as all men's are, can't handle any perceived threat without going into full crisis mode. But here's the thing—if you want to fuck, we could just fuck. It doesn't have to be a big deal. We don't have to enter into a sacred compact first. We could fuck right now." She'd said it rhetorically, but she had to admit she found the prospect somewhat exciting. Not that she suddenly found the sheriff any less repulsive, but the idea of destroying his pretensions toward virtue, of revealing himself to himself, was undeniably appealing. She supposed that she had a touch of the sadist in her.

Something of this arousal must have made itself visible in her demeanor, because the sheriff's anger quickly turned into alarm, and he looked out into the hallway. "Lower your voice," he growled at her.

"What I don't understand," Alice said, "is how you could find courtship so appealing, but fucking so shameful. It's the same thing. Courtship is just a means toward fucking. Your parents, Jimmy Red Horse and Janey Tall Trees, or whatever the fuck they were called—you do realize they fucked, right? That's where you came from. They fucked in the kitchen, in the car—did you have, like, a sofa you sat on, as a kid, and watched cartoons from? In the living room maybe? When you were at school, your parents fucked on that sofa. Or when you were asleep. Silent sweaty fucking. Your dad probably put his hand over your mom's mouth to keep her from crying out and waking you up. I bet your dad had huge hands. You probably sat and watched *Looney Tunes* while, unbeknownst to you, you were touching the invisible stain of your father's emissions. Imagine, if you will, the sound of your father's potbelly slapping against your mother's lower back as he fucked her from behind—"

"Shut your fucking mouth!" the sheriff said, bringing his hand down on the desk. All sound in the hall and entryway ceased immediately.

"Or maybe it's just because I'm a woman," Alice said, looking steadily back at him. "I'm sure you talk about worse things with the boys."

"Never you mind what I talk about with anybody else." He examined the palm of the hand he'd brought down. It was reddening and looked like it probably stung. "I don't want to hear no more dirty talk from you. It don't amuse me, and it sure as hell don't excite me, if that was your goal."

Even now, Alice thought, he was sure that her intentions were directed toward his pleasure, to entertain or titillate him. She almost had to admire the depth of his self-absorption.

"If you've got some business here, let's just take care of that," the sheriff said. He sat back in his chair as if to put distance between them.

"Okay," Alice said. "So this guy Hicks."

The sheriff leaned forward in his chair again. "You know Hicks?"

His sudden intensity took Alice by surprise. She hadn't intended to mislead him, but now that the opening was presenting itself, she'd be a fool to let it pass. "Well, yeah," she said casually.

"You've met him?"

Alice nodded. It wasn't, technically, a lie. "Yeah. White guy, fifties, about my height, balding. Ex-military, which is obvious before he even tells you."

The sheriff seemed to relax, though Alice got the impression it was just for show, and that he was still watching her closely. "Well, you don't win the Medal of Honor without having your shit squared away."

Alice concealed her surprise; Red Horse knew Hicks? "What does he do? I mean, in Whitehurst."

"I thought you met him."

"I did. Kim and I met him at a party. We didn't really talk about work."

He seemed to find this plausible. "Why you so interested in Hicks?" He blinked several times. "Wait, you're not, you know, interested in him, are you?"

Alice chuckled and waved a hand at him. "Come on, Michael." She pursed her lips in mock reluctance. "Okay. Truth is, he's interested in Kim. You know these military types. All those years going to off-base cathouses, they get addicted to paying for it. Can't get it up off the clock. I just wanna make sure he can pay his bill. So I'd appreciate it if you didn't tell him about this little sit-down."

The sheriff looked off out the window and grunted. "I thought he was a faggot. Way he looks at you, straight on like that, it's too intense. Seems questionable." He looked back at Alice. "I wouldn't worry about his bankroll. He's the man behind Greenworld Fluid Dynamics."

"What's that?" Alice said.

"You know that environmentally friendly fracking fluid Whitehurst is always bragging about? They're the contractor that makes it. With all the oil Whitehurst is pulling out of the ground, Greenworld has got to be a cash cow."

Alice wondered if her pulse was audible in the room or just to her own ears. This was, she thought ironically, what was known in the business as a "break." If Hicks was the main supplier of fracking fluid, that meant that the rumors that dust was just dried fluid were either literally true or had grown out of the fact that it was being manufactured by the same person and possibly in the same facility as fracking fluid. And come to think of it, what better cover for a drug manufacturing plant than the production of a proprietary industrial fracking fluid? On the heels of this thought, she realized that Whitehurst had been lying that night at his house when he said he didn't know Hicks. There was just no way for them not to be, at the very least, acquainted. And the fact that he'd lied meant he was involved in something. That he was hiding something. But what?

She couldn't understand, no matter how she figured, how Robert tied into all this. She'd seen the fear in Robert's eyes the last time they'd visited him in jail, after he'd been charged with murder. He was facing lethal injection, and he knew it. If he'd been holding something back, he would've told it then. So logically, he had nothing to tell. Whatever he'd done, however he'd run afoul of Hicks and maybe Whitehurst, he didn't know about it. He didn't know what he'd done. This, Alice thought exultantly. This is it!

The very next moment she looked up to see the sheriff regarding her with suspicion and hostility. He could see her thoughts pinballing, the connections being made, and he clearly didn't like it. He was in on it too. Not all the way in—she didn't think he believed that Robert had been framed; his simplistic law-and-order worldview wouldn't allow it—but he knew the game was rigged, and he had a good idea of who was pulling the levers. She cleared her throat.

"I found a witness," she said. "They saw Robert and Missy the night of her assault."

The sheriff looked back at her with an expression of mild confusion; now it was his thoughts that were pinballing. "Who?"

"They don't want to come forward just yet. You know how people are in Whitehurst. They don't trust the system."

The sheriff scoffed. "Guilty people never do. But go on."

"They saw them parked out by the dust house. Here's the thing. Missy pulled a gun on Robert," Alice said. She was just improvising now, letting it all come off her tongue like a trumpet solo. It scared her, how good she was at lying. "Tried to rob him. They were both high. He was just defending himself, and she ended up with her skull bashed in. It was self-defense."

"So why hasn't he told us this version?"

"He's banking that the case will fall apart in court. In the meantime, the guy has a wife and child. A wife who has no idea he's been leading a double life. He wants to go back to them, get clean, go back to work. Resume his life. That will be hard to do if he admits he was getting high on the side of the road with a teenage prostitute."

The sheriff nodded, thinking it over, weighing its plausibility. Alice hoped dearly that he'd be thrown off the scent; she sensed that things could get very dangerous if anyone knew she was onto the truth.

"So what do you want from me?"

"Just tell me that there's a possibility of justice here." The best lies have a germ of truth, she thought.

The sheriff let a ghost of a smirk flatten his lips. She could almost hear him thinking it: *Guess she ain't as smart as she thinks she is.* "I can't give you no guarantees. But you bring this witness forward, the process'll do what it does. You just got to trust the process." He looked toward the open door and leaned forward over his desk. "Tell me, who is this witness?"

Alice shook her head. "I can't tell you that yet. Soon. But not now." She wondered how it would happen if she gave him a name. Who would he call, who would he pass it up to? Would he know the particulars of what would happen, or would he just think of it as doing his job? How long would it be before the witness had an "accident"? Even just this talk, she realized, would be passed on.

She thought about what the head men—Whitehurst? Hicks? Some third as-yet unknown figure?—would say when they heard. *Well, she's turned fabricating witnesses into a cottage industry, hasn't she?* It was a perversely believable lie. Maybe she should've done that from the beginning. She could have left this sordid little town weeks ago.

"I get it," the sheriff said as he stood up to signal the end of their interview. "They're out at the dust house that time of night, they probably got their own dirty deeds to hide. Look, you're always welcome here, but call first next time, okay?"

Alice allowed him to escort her out of his office with a proprietary hand on her lower back; his deputies looked at him with a congratulatory glint in their eyes.

"Tanner!" he bellowed, gesturing at an officer at a nearby desk. "Give this young lady a ride back to her motel, will you?"

"Yes, sir," the deputy said, his voice crisp but his eyes sliding over Alice's body, from torso to knees and back up again. He looked at the sheriff with a crafty implication, and the sheriff smiled and half shrugged as if to say, I can't help it, they all want me. Alice pretended not to notice.

CHAPTER 24

Night had just fallen when Alice finally returned to the Bobcat, shuffling across the gravel lot from the highway to her room. From inside the RVs in the parking lot, she could hear the labored cadences and laugh tracks of network television. Everything about her visit to the sheriff had depressed her, and she desperately wanted a drink and some dust. But Kim's car wasn't in the lot, and their room was dark. Alice considered that someone in the motel probably sold, but she doubted they'd sell to her; she didn't look like a cop, exactly, but she didn't not look like a cop either. She would ask Kim to go on a run when she returned from Missy's memorial service.

Missy. So who'd done it? In a way, she was here in Whitehurst on Missy's behalf, not Robert's. The wrongs done to Robert could still be reversed. Missy was the one who needed justice. Though what was justice for the dead?

She was deep in this course of thought as she took her keys out to unlock the door of the motel room. When a hand shot out of the darkness and knocked them from her grip, she almost screamed from sheer surprise.

It was Lester. He'd been standing in the shadow of the overhanging eave, still as a statue.

"Kim's not here," Alice said sharply.

Lester didn't say anything, just came toward her, and in the light he looked like he hadn't eaten or slept or bathed in several days; he also looked very high. When she stooped to pick up the keys, he put one foot on top of them.

"I just come from the whorehouse," Lester said, his voice tight with venom. "Kimmy wouldn't talk to me, but some of the other girls would. She told them all about your pictures. You been stalkin' me. Interferin' in my business."

"I thought Kim should know the truth."

"I had everythin' arranged just perfect!" Lester wrung his hands in agony. "You come along and ruined it. It ain't your concern how I keep my affairs. What about that don't you understand?"

"Everything isn't about you!" Alice said angrily. Slowly, slowly, she brought her right hand up and rested it on the butt of her Magnum. "That's what you don't understand. People aren't resources to be exploited. Kim isn't." Alice felt like she'd been spending her whole time in Whitehurst arguing some variation of this theme, this deconstruction of male narcissism; the sheriff and his conception of her as a prize to be won and kept, Steve Whitehurst and his patronizing white benevolence over his town, Lester's cynical pimping. She was tired of it. "Just get the fuck out of here, Lester. I don't have anything more to say to you."

Lester showed his teeth. "Or what? You'll shoot me?"

His eyes had remained fixed on hers as she'd brought her hand to rest on the Magnum, and she'd taken this to mean that he hadn't noticed the movement. She inhaled and slid the gun out, holding it next to her thigh.

"I'm only going to do whatever you force me to do," Alice said. "It's all up to you, Lester."

"Bullshit," he said. He edged one foot in front of the other, and she realized he meant to advance on her. "You don't got it in you. You gonna bluff me, I'm gonna call you on it."

Alice brought the gun up and held it steady in both hands. "Lester—"

Lester put both hands on the gun, quick as a flash; Alice thought he meant to take it from her, but he didn't pull or wrench. On the contrary, he was running his hands down the pistol, almost tenderly, until he found her finger crooked in the trigger guard. Then he insinuated his own finger in front of hers and began pressing on her finger and, by proxy, on the trigger.

"Go ahead," he whispered. He had the barrel pressed against his sternum. She found herself fighting against his grip, trying desperately not to fire the gun. In an instant, she realized that the feeling of security the gun had given her all this time had been nothing more than a delusion. Lester was right about her—she didn't have it in her.

When he abruptly spread his hands wide, the gun dropped from Alice's hands onto the pavement. They stood looking down at it, Lester with contempt and Alice with surprise, as if one of her limbs had detached itself suddenly, a limb she hadn't even realized was prosthetic the whole time.

"Lester—" Alice said, but then his hands were around her throat, squeezing, his thumbs pinching into the flesh on each side of her voice box. His face was an inch from hers now. He smelled like he was already dead in his center and that the rest of him just hadn't gotten the message yet.

"This is what happens to nosy bitches," he said, his voice husky. She wondered in a flash if he had an erection. Her feet moved in a half jig of panic, and she felt her foot bump against the pistol. It might as well have been a mile away. Faintly she could hear the sounds of television from the RVs. What could be worse than dying with a laugh track in your ears? She could feel her pulse now in her eyes, the blood backing up into the veins and arteries and throughways of her head. She was going to black out soon if she didn't do something. She brought her hands up around Lester's arms and fumbled at his head. She grabbed a lock of his greasy hair but let it drop. No. Hair pulling was for stupid girls, catfighting in the clubs. She reoriented, found his ears, and dug her nail into one lobe. When he tossed his head, as she knew he would, she cradled it with her other hand and then, with a vicious circular motion, corkscrewed her thumbnail into his left eye socket. She felt his lid slide up over her nail and felt the surprisingly firm jelly of his eyeball under her thumb. He let out a bloodcurdling shriek and released her.

Alice leaned against the wall, gasping for breath, light headed as her blood rushed back. Lester bent at the waist, hands clapped over his eye. He seemed to be simultaneously crying and dry heaving. Alice's gaze fell all at once on the gun. She picked it up by its barrel and brought the butt down across the base of Lester's skull. He went down onto his side, muttering confusedly. She might have left him there, but she heard him still making threats, calling her a bitch, dead bitch, meddler, fucking whore.

Alice felt a swell of anger, but also a strange sense of responsibility; it was necessary for Lester to be taught a lesson, and if she didn't do it, who would? She stood over Lester and clubbed him in the kidneys with the gun; when he uncurled his body, she stomped her foot into his groin with all her strength. He yelped and curled protectively around his wounded parts, and she repeated the process, pistol-whipping his lower back and then stomping his balls. Her neck had begun to hurt, badly, and she'd suddenly become very resentful. After a while she beat him with the gun anywhere she could, on his knees, his shoulders, his arms, his ankles, his ribs. He was letting out a high-pitched, continuous wail now, the shrill blubber of a child.

She laced the fingers of one hand through his greasy hair, close to his scalp, and then, crouching low, began to drag him across the parking lot. She didn't have any specific plan; she just wanted him away from her home, as if he were a contaminated object, though later, after her rage had subsided, she wondered if she might have dragged him to the highway and left him to be run over by the trucks.

When they were halfway across the lot, a pickup turned off the highway and skidded in the gravel, stopping just short of them. Alice had the gun in one hand and the other wrapped in Lester's hair as he struggled weakly and bled from the mouth and nose. The driver of the truck leaned out the window and looked at them, spotlighted there in his lights. Alice raised the pistol and pointed it at him. Immediately, the truck reversed away from them, fishtailing in the gravel, and sped around the corner of the motel, leaving them in darkness. The spell, though, had been broken. Alice let Lester's head fall to the ground and wiped her hand on her pants. Jesus.

She hadn't thought she was capable of losing her composure like that. She supposed she was lucky that she was too—what, scared? moral?—to use the gun, or Lester would be dead.

"Get up," she said. He was still curled on the ground, and when she spoke he peeked at her from between his hands, which were clapped over his face. "Get up!"

He did so. His entire manner had changed, like a dog who'd been whipped. He stood slouched in front of her, one hand covering his wounded eye, as if waiting for permission to do otherwise.

"Don't ever come back here," she said. "To see Kim or for any other reason. Ever."

Lester just nodded once and then, giving her a wide berth, made for his dirt bike in a limping, bent-over lurch. Alice watched him go and then went back to her room. She turned the light on and looked at her neck in the mirror. Already the red marks on her neck were turning into a bouquet of bruises. She felt a perverse sense of pride at them.

She hefted her Magnum, grimacing. She supposed she'd always known, on some level, that she couldn't ever use it on another person, but she'd thought it would keep her safe, as a prop, or a talisman. Not so. Not if the sense of false confidence it gave her led her into situations where she would need it but would be unable to use it.

This realization just affirmed her belief in the essential importance of authenticity in all things. The lapse into falsity was the beginning of the fall. She went to her bedside table, unloaded the pistol, and put it and the loose bullets in the top drawer. She would pawn it or give it to Kim. She wouldn't wear it ever again, though. She felt a strange sense of relief at this resolution.

Alice checked her phone; nothing from either Kim or Rachel. Rachel would be getting into town soon, in the next hour or two, and she wondered what Rachel would say when she saw the bruises around her neck, when she heard the story. You should have shot him—that's what she'd say.

CHAPTER 25

Alice was wide awake when Kim arrived back at the motel. She'd drank a pot and a half of the terrible motel coffee, intent on staying up until Rachel arrived in town. But she hadn't heard anything since Rachel's terse message that her flight had landed in Minneapolis. That had been seven hours ago, and Alice had spent the evening checking her phone every five minutes while watching syndicated television and pressing ice cubes against her aching neck.

Kim clacked up the sidewalk in her heels and then burst through the door, preceded by the sour odor of cheap champagne.

"Smells like you got some on you," Alice said.

Kim let out a strangled squeal. "Why you sittin' in the dark?" She sat on the desk and kicked off her stilettos. "Yeah, you give these hoes a bottle of bub, and they gonna spray it all over."

"How was the memorial?"

"Sad. Most of them didn't even know Missy, they were just there for the free drinks. Half of 'em were shitkickers just wandered in off the street, didn't even know they were at a funeral." Kim flicked on the lights and sat at the vanity. She'd just begun to wipe her makeup off when she caught sight of Alice in the mirror.

"What the fuck happened to you?" She turned in her chair to look at the garland of bruises on Alice's neck.

"It was all my fault," Alice said. She'd been rehearsing her lie all evening. She'd decided not to tell Kim about Lester's involvement, the beating he'd taken. Kim and Lester's separation seemed to be taking, but the quickest way to reestablish their bond was to rekindle Kim's sympathy for him. She knew Kim's hard carapace was only to protect a soft, near-defenseless heart. "I walked down the road for a soda, forgot to take my gun. Cut across that vacant lot over behind the car wash and came across some dusthead bitches getting high in a burned-out car. They tried to take my phone and money, but I got away. It's no big deal."

Kim walked over to the bed and bent close to Alice, squinting at her neck. "What'd they look like? I bet I know 'em. We find 'em and stomp the shit out of 'em."

"They jumped me from behind," Alice said. "And it's pitch-black out there anyway."

Kim gave her a flat, knowing look. Alice stared back, inwardly reproaching herself for concocting such a pat, airtight story—an obvious lie. Kim recognized a lie when she heard it, but luckily for Alice, she also respected the need for discretion.

"Okay then," she said breezily. Then she furrowed her brow. "Just tell me this—it wasn't the sheriff, was it?"

"No," Alice said. "I'd tell you if it was." She remembered then everything she'd learned at the sheriff's office about Hicks and his connections to Whitehurst. She told Kim about Greenworld and how familiar the sheriff had been with Hicks. Kim took it in with an increasingly disgusted expression.

"So this Hicks, he the one behind all this evil shit," she said.

"Uh-huh. And while you were out, I did some research. The sheriff mentioned the Medal of Honor. Thing is, there haven't been that many Medal of Honor recipients. I looked at the list, and Hicks wasn't on it."

"Damn," Kim said. "He made it up?"

"That's what I thought too. But that's not the type of thing you just make up. It's too easily disproven. It's like lying about winning an Oscar. All it takes is ten seconds on Wikipedia and your story is blown. So I did some research. Most militaries in the world have a Medal of Honor they give out. But Hicks struck me as thoroughly American, and it's not easy for an American to enlist abroad. One of the few forces that takes Americans is the French Foreign Legion. And wouldn't you know it, they have a Medal of Honor. It's called the *Legion d'Honneur*. An American named Dwayne Hicks received it in 1988."

Kim made a dismissive sound. "So Hicks was a French soldier?"

"Not even. The Foreign Legion is more of a mercenary force than anything else. They take anyone, literally. Murderers, rapists, psychopaths. You think the American military is an imperialist occupying force—they got nothing on the Foreign Legion. Back in the eighties, they were providing security for corporations in the Amazon. Logging operations, gold mines, oil companies. Raping the rain forests, basically. The indigenous peoples protested, so the Foreign Legion was brought in to eradicate them. As far as I could tell—the translation was a little wonky—Hicks's regiment was guarding a gold mine in Brazil that had been using the locals as slave labor there. The Foreign Legion claimed they were attacked by leftist rebels—this was the Sandinista era—but it was actually a slave uprising. Middle of the night, the slaves bomb the corporate quarters, the barracks, kill all the overseers, and most of the legionnaires. Except Hicks. He gets away and does a reverse *Die Hard*. One bad guy against overwhelming numbers. Keeps them from destroying the mining equipment, blocks the mountain passes so they can't escape, terrorizes them at night with his guerilla-style tactics. When reinforcements arrived a week later, he'd racked up a three-figure body count. The mining company was so grateful that they made a huge donation to the legion. And the legion gave Hicks their highest honor, the Legion d'Honneur."

"Motherfucker's the ultimate company man," Kim said.

"Uh-huh. He spent some time in the Middle East as a hired gun, and now he's in Whitehurst. Our problem."

"We got to be careful. I'll ask around, see what I can find out about Greenworld, but I ain't never heard the name." Kim sat down on the bed and ran her index finger gently over the bruises on Alice's neck, her face pained. "You sure you don't need anything?"

"Actually, you could give me a ride to the corporate housing complex north of town. Robert's wife was supposed to text me when she got into town, but I think her phone may have died. I'm hoping that Whitehurst had a car meet her at the airport and take her to her quarters. She was due hours ago."

"Sure, I'll run you over there," Kim said. She drummed her fingers on the vanity and bit her lip and then managed to blurt out, "Will I see you again?"

"Kim. I told you. Rachel is not your replacement. I'm not Robert. I'm not fucking either of you. Rachel is a client and you're my friend. Those two facts aren't mutually exclusive."

"Well, if you wanna be technical about it, we did kinda fuck." Her tone was lighter, though. She turned to the side and looked at herself in the mirror, pulling her dress taut. "Am I showing yet?"

No, it's still too early, she started to say, then reconsidered, then said anyway, "There's still plenty of time."

Kim patted her stomach and looked at Alice. "You ever had it done?"

Alice nodded. "Twice."

"Damn. You got any regrets?"

Did she? The first time had been with her college boyfriend, when she'd still been a child herself. The second time, the result of a one-night stand, unplanned and unwanted and unrealistic. "No. None."

"You always sayin' I'm the cold one, but you a straight baby murderer. I had it done once, and I ain't gonna lie, I think about her every day." Kim sat heavily in the chair and looked off into the corner of the room as if she might see the ghost of her lost child there. "She'd be five next June. Course, I don't know if it woulda been a girl or a boy, but I like to think she'd be a girl. Named Marie after my mama. She was Lester's, I think, so she'd be a little dark-eyed blondie, cute as all hell. I don't know why I did it. Lester pressured me. Not like you're doing, real subtle-like, but, like, full-on pressing me."

"Kim," Alice said. "I'm not pressuring you." Though as soon as she said it, she knew it was a lie. "I just want you to keep your options open."

"Yeah. What you don't understand is your options ain't the same as mine. You got a career in the big city and a whole life. What do I got? My life is only goin' in one direction, and it's a lonely one. I dunno, havin' a baby, I think it'd be good for me. Make me get my life together. Stop doin' dust, fuckin' around. Some people need that outside pressure, some kinda responsibility, to make 'em stop fuckin' up. We ain't all like you with your willpower."

Alice pursed her lips; she couldn't think how to react. She didn't agree with Kim's conception of a child as a medium of self-improvement, but as Kim had said, her life didn't necessarily contain the same advantages and options as Alice's did. Maybe she shouldn't judge. "Well, whatever you want to do. But you should be going to a doctor at least. They have special vitamins for pregnant women to take."

"Yeah, yeah. I know. I'll go. You wanna go with?"

"Me? Why, are you afraid of doctors?"

"Yo, doctors around here were sterilizing native women for decades without even telling them. So I got plenty reason to be scared."

"Sure, I'll go. Make an appointment tomorrow. If you really don't trust the doctors around here, call over to Minneapolis and I'll drive over with you."

Kim popped out of her chair and jingled the car keys in one hand. Her mood seemed much improved. "Let's get going," she said. "I gotta get to bed early now that I'm bein' a responsible mom."

Alice rose and wiggled her feet into her shoes next to the door. She jumped when Kim came from behind and wrapped her arms around her shoulders. Alice waited for Kim to say something, but she didn't speak, just clasped her shoulders for a moment, squeezed, and then released her.

When they set out on the road, Alice realized why Rachel was late. Traffic was worse than usual; after twenty minutes they were maybe half a mile from the motel. There'd been an accident somewhere, or a truck had tipped over while turning onto the shoulder from one of the water stations. Alice was about to suggest going back to the motel when Kim spoke.

"I had a dream the other night," she said. "About my babies."

"Babies?"

"Yep. They came to me in the dream. They twins. A boy and a girl. They said they comin'. They said everything's gonna be all right."

Alice wasn't sure how to respond to this. "Next time you talk to them, ask about lottery numbers."

Up ahead they could see the red-and-blue glare of emergency lights painting the night on each side of the road. As they drew closer, Alice could see a caravan of law-enforcement vehicles on the right side of the road, the sheriff's hulking truck among them, and on the other side, a pair of fire trucks bookending a steaming wreck that had been melted to a warped skeleton. As they passed, Kim stared at the wreckage, but Alice looked at the men on the other side of the road and caught the sheriff's eye. She recognized the look of something like terror in his face; it told her, instantly, what had happened there.

"Oh shit," she said. "Pull over!"

Kim looked at her, startled, but pulled over. Before the car had come to a full stop, Alice had flung the door open and was running back toward the sheriff. The highway patrolmen and the deputies bristled at her approach, but the sheriff said something to them, and they parted for her.

"It's her car, isn't it?" Alice said.

The sheriff took her by the arm and guided her away from the road and the other officers. "I can't talk to you about the details of our investigation," he said, more over his shoulder than to Alice. When they were out of earshot, he leaned close and whispered harshly in her ear.

"God damn it, you know I'm not supposed to be feeding you any information," he said. "You're making me look bad here."

"I don't care about any of that," Alice said, tearing her arm free from his grip. "That's Rachel Wilcox's car, isn't it?"

The sheriff regarded her with resignation. "All we know so far, for sure, is that it's a rental out of Minnesota. Out of the airport. We're checking with the rental agencies now on any cars of this make and model, and who it was rented out to."

"Was there a crash? What happened?"

"Don't know. Someone called it in, nine one. By the time we got here, it was burnin' white hot, so there was probably an accelerant involved. Wasn't much left by the time the fire trucks got here."

"Was there anyone inside?"

"We don't think so. Forensics might tell a different story, but we doubt it."

"Did anything survive the fire?"

"Not up front. We're about to pop the trunk, though."

Alice stood by the dripping wreck while the sheriff fetched a pry bar from one of the cars. The patrolmen and deputies glared at her; normally she would've been cowed by them, but at the moment she was seized with guilt. If this was Rachel's car—and she was sure it was—it was her fault that she'd convinced Rachel to walk, defenseless, into—what?

Alice thought back to an expression from her journalism days—*cui prodest*, which was Latin for "who benefits." Inevitably, whenever you deconstructed a crime or conspiracy or scandal, the actors could be sussed out by using this formula. In this situation, Rachel had probably been intercepted by whomever had framed Robert; with one private investigator already closing in on them, adding a famously dogged ex-journalist to the pursuit was the last thing they wanted. Rachel's abrupt decision to come to Whitehurst hadn't given them any time to set up one of their preferred frame jobs, so they'd just snatched her, which explained the fire. Couldn't risk leaving any DNA behind. This was another reason she felt Rachel was probably still alive: Why go to the trouble of a snatch and grab for someone you were just going to kill? There were a lot of risks in disappearing an out of towner—an upper-class white woman, no less—and these people clearly weren't rash. They were meticulous. They were planners. Which meant they were probably, at that moment, coming up with a plan regarding what to do with Rachel.

The sheriff returned with a crowbar, pulling on a pair of latex gloves. "Don't touch anything," he said to her.

He swung the crowbar and struck the trunk directly on the lip of the door; inserting the prying end of the bar into the resultant dimple, he broke the latch with a quick downward motion. The spring mechanism had been melted, so he had to lift it open. The trunk compartment held three or four inches of black water. A melted spare tire lay partially submerged alongside what remained of a wheeled carry-on suitcase. When the sheriff shined his flashlight across the items, Alice almost darted her hand inside, but remembered at the last moment that he'd told her not to touch anything.

"There," she said. "On the suitcase handle."

Hanging from the handle of the carry-on was a plastic-sleeved tag, of the sort that held the handwritten name and address of the owner, in case the luggage was lost in transit. The plastic had melted, but the tag inside had survived. The sheriff lifted it with one gloved hand, but Alice knew before she even looked what name she would see there. Rachel Wilcox.

CHAPTER 26

Alice felt bleary and enervated the next morning. She'd had a nightmare of burning alive, a child crying from somewhere in the smoke, and woke up in a pool of sweat. She wished she could go back to sleep, not because she was tired, but because everything about the day ahead filled her with dread and anxiety.

Kim wasn't in the room, and Alice was seized with a panic that she'd be left to hitchhike around town as she tried to track down Rachel. Stupid, she thought, to let herself be so dependent on another person. When Kim walked in a minute later with two large coffees, Alice knew she should've been relieved, but instead she felt a flash of irrational anger.

"Where've you been?" she snapped.

Kim just looked at her, wide-eyed, and held up the coffees. She set one in front of Alice and then retreated to the other side of the room.

"I'm sorry," Alice said after a moment. "I didn't mean that. I didn't sleep well. I had nightmares about burning alive."

"I know," Kim said. "You were screaming in your sleep. I figured you'd be feelin' about as bad as you can feel today."

Alice took a tentative sip of the coffee, burned the roof of her mouth, and took another sip anyway. The pain seemed to focus her mind as much as the caffeine did. She went online and checked the local news. There was a short article about the car fire the night before, but no mention of a body, as Alice expected. That meant Rachel was alive, being held as leverage. She wondered if someone would call her with a rock under his tongue to disguise his voice, tell her to get out of town by noon tomorrow or her friend would face the consequences. Probably not. This wasn't some Hollywood movie; the threat here was wholly implied. Back off or Rachel Wilcox will pay the price. She considered calling some of her old contacts in the news industry, but she didn't have anything solid yet, just rumors. No reporter with any kind of juice would stick their neck out for a story this heavy on speculation.

If there was an upside, it was that murders, especially murders of upper-class white people, drew a lot of heat. Rachel's captors wouldn't kill her unless they were forced to. She'd just have to make them feel safe then. Her efforts from here on out would have to be muted, and she knew she should probably put on a pantomime of preparing to get out of town. Start backing toward the door, so to speak.

"You think they'll kill Rachel Wilcox?" Alice asked Kim.

"They ain't showed much taste for murder so far," Kim said. "They more about getting the system to do their dirty work, rather than getting blood on their hands. But you got 'em cornered. Hard to say what they'll do."

Her thoughts ran back to Robert, to whatever it was he'd seen or heard or discovered to get him framed in the first place. This was the key to everything. She rubbed her eyes as if to clear them. What wasn't she seeing? All he did was work and come home and drink, right? So it was probably something at work.

Her eyes fell on the box of papers she'd gotten from Whitehurst, sitting on the desk next to the notes and work orders they'd recovered from Robert's briefcase. They'd taken on a presence of their own in the room, and Alice realized it was because they represented unfinished business: work she was avoiding, like tax filing or sending invoices or paying bills that piled up on the counter. And besides, this was what she always did when she hit a wall: she immersed herself in the facts. She supposed that made her a hypocrite, considering she trumpeted the irrelevance of fact at every opportunity. But there it was. Maybe it was the English major in her that believed everything was there in the text. If you didn't see it, you just weren't reading closely enough.

"You holding any dust?" she asked Kim.

Kim shifted in her seat and looked over her shoulder, as if Alice might have been speaking to someone else. "Might be. Why?"

"I'm going to work through Robert's papers. Maybe there's something in there that will help us. And if there's not, at least we'll know. Some dust would help speed things along."

Kim grimaced. "Man, you wanna use this shit to study?" But she pulled a rolled-up baggie out of her purse and threw it on the desk. "We need to be out there, talkin' to people, choppin' it up."

"Why don't you do that while I do this?" Alice said. She cleared off a corner of the desk and carefully portioned out a line of the dust. "See if you can find out anything about Hicks or Greenworld. I'll concentrate better with you out of the room anyway."

Kim rose from her chair. "Sure, boss," she said sarcastically.

As soon as Kim closed the door behind her, Alice did the first line and chased it with a cup of coffee. Almost immediately she felt it hit her bloodstream. Crystalline, she thought to herself. Normally she'd have to perform an hour-long ritual of procrastination before getting down to work, but now she found herself laying out the papers until they covered the surface of the desk and then working her way through them systematically. Up and down the rows and then across and then diagonally, looking for patterns or correlations or connections. Deciphering Robert's cramped penmanship took a lot of time, many false starts and trying out multiple variations, almost as if she were translating the text. Usually she'd have found the effort unbearably tedious, but now it was almost pleasurable. When the motel room door opened again, she whirled in her seat.

"Back already?" The irritation was evident in her voice.

Kim, standing in the doorway, looked at her phone. "It's been almost three hours."

Alice checked her watch and found it was true; she'd had no sensation of time passing, no sensation of anything at all, actually. It was as if she'd been temporarily transformed into pure thought, a weightless phantom flitting over the papers like a butterfly. "Did you find anything?"

"Nah. Ain't nobody heard of Greenworld. But—" Kim held up an index finger to make sure Alice was paying special attention. "I did think of something. Remember when we were at Whitehurst's party, and he was givin' us the tour? Braggin' about all the guests he'd had at his house?"

"I remember."

"Didn't he brag about hostin' some war hero? Medal of Honor for killin' some brown people?"

"Shit," Alice said. "Shit!"

"Sounds like our boy Hicks, right?"

"Shit," Alice said. She was almost jealous she hadn't made the connection. "I told you were good at this."

"I never said I ain't. How about you, you find anythin' yet?"

"No. I'm not done yet, though."

Kim picked up on the implication and backed over the threshold. "I'll go have some coffee in the diner next door," she said. "Text me when I'm allowed back in."

Alice went back to it. Her eyes slid over the text as her mind moved lightly over other topics. Whitehurst. Hicks. Whitehurst and Hicks. The lineup of suspects was being winnowed down, the floor lights dimming,

dimming, until the last two stood spotlighted. She didn't know why yet, and in the waning clarity of her high, she realized she might never know.

Now that they knew she was closing in, it was likely they'd start covering their tracks with even more care than usual. They'd probably spent the last few days erasing hard drives and shredding documents. Most cases didn't end; they just sort of petered out. Missing persons who stayed missing, suspected affairs that remained suspicions, nagging maybe for years. Answers were rare, and she knew better than to expect them. If anything, her investigative work had reinforced the lessons of her journalism years: a confirmation of ambiguity as the default state of existence. She might never know why Robert had been framed, never know who exactly had done it, might never—her mind shrank from this train of thought, but she forced it ahead like a recalcitrant child—find Rachel, alive or dead. She wondered if starting to prepare herself for this eventuality was the same as conceding it. As with so many things in life, there was a fine line between resignation and—

Wait. Something made her pause. Her eyes flicked back over the work order she'd just read. She recognized it as one of the plots that she and Kim had driven past—a big nothing, just rocks and scrub and prairie grass. She held it next to the master list of Wilcox's assignments that Whitehurst had printed out for her until she'd matched the dates. The GPS coordinates didn't match. Whoever had filled out Wilcox's work order had transposed two digits and sent him to the wrong plot. And Whitehurst had handed her the original work orders because he didn't realize what had happened. For a moment, Alice couldn't breathe.

She quickly gathered her phone, keys, and wallet and went to fetch Kim. When she turned to walk across the lot, she saw Kim herself running toward her. For a moment she wondered if Kim had somehow read her mind, had picked up her epiphany through a telepathic bond forged between two dustheads.

But as Kim drew close, Alice saw that she was crazed, terrified.

"Kim, what—"

But Kim ran straight past her. Alice turned and gave chase.

"What is it? What's wrong?" She was running too now, shoulder to shoulder with Kim. She tried to slow Kim by grabbing her arm, but Kim wrenched herself free and ran on. When they reached the rental car, Kim took out her keys, dropped them, picked them up, and jabbed them at the keyhole, missing each time by a greater distance.

"I gotta go," she said, as if to herself. "I gotta go."

"Kim, talk to me." Alice had never seen Kim this affected by anything. "What is it?"

"Lester," she said. She thrust her phone into Alice's hand and went back to unlocking her car. Alice read the text on the screen.

```
Just know that whatever I did, I did
because I aint had no other choice,
and that I always loved you before
anyone else. I won't tell you to be
good after I'm gone cuz you a bad
girl to the core but at least be good
to yourself. Thanks for everything
and dont forget me.
```

"Kim, this is just a ploy for attention," Alice said shakily, though she wasn't sure if she believed that. She thrust the phone back at Kim. "You're doing exactly what he wants you to do."

But Kim had succeeded in letting herself into her car and keyed it to life. She threw it into reverse, sped backward out of the space, and floored it, kicking gravel against the sides of the assembled RVs as she skidded onto the highway and then disappeared into traffic. Alice was left standing next to the empty space.

"But I solved the case," she said out loud, and then, realizing there was no one there to hear her, turned and went back into the room.

CHAPTER 27

The taxi that pulled up was a weather-beaten Crown Victoria, and when Alice got in the back, she saw that towels had been spread over the seats. The driver, a portly middle-aged man with graying muttonchops, looked at her in the rearview and then turned and gave her a closer examination.

"You ain't pregnant," he said.

Alice had told the dispatcher that she'd gone into labor alone in her hotel room, with no friends or family in Whitehurst to help her, and that it was an emergency situation, the baby's skull partially breached, fluids and tissue spurting, et cetera, and the sympathetic woman had cancelled a series of appointments to send a car to Alice. Before the driver could tell her to get out, she held up a hundred-dollar bill.

"Okay," he said after a moment. "Nothing illegal, though. And that hundred is on top of the regular fare."

"Fine," Alice said. "All we're doing is driving a couple miles out of town, to an empty field. I'm going to get out of the car and take a quick look around. That's all. There won't be anyone else there."

"Sounds like a pickup," the cabbie said. "We get pulled over, I get charged for possession too."

"It's not a pickup. I'm not going to bring anything back to the car. I'm just going to take a look around. That's it."

"Why?"

"I'm paying you a hundred dollars to not worry about it." She tore the hundred in half and handed one half over the front of the bench seat. The driver took it and looked at it mournfully.

"You ain't have to do that," he said. "I woulda trusted you for it."

As they drove through town, Alice slumped low in her seat. The chaos and disorder seemed to have taken on a sinister aspect, a sort of unity. At red lights it seemed entirely plausible to her that the window of the adjacent vehicle might roll down to reveal the barrels of a shotgun. She wasn't sure if this was a natural consequence of what she'd discovered about the town or if she was experiencing side effects from the dust. The driver kept glancing at her in the rearview like he expected her to bail out of the car at any moment.

After they left town, she directed him using the maps app on her phone. They turned down a dusty county road and continued on for five miles, passing nothing, not even a dead ranch or a fracking rig. Alice understood why some people defended the boom: this land wasn't good for anything. You couldn't farm it; you couldn't even live on it. Well, white people couldn't. Kim's people had done okay, until they'd been wiped out.

It occurred to Alice that maybe this whole mess was just karma, dividends of that original sin. Colonialists getting their comeuppance for genocide. There was truth in rumor, Alice thought. Dust wasn't fracking fluid, but that rumor sidled right up to the truth. And maybe the same was true with the old wives' tales about drilling and underground spirits. Bad things did happen when the drilling started; maybe the evil spirits were just a crude surrogate for the ghastliness of human nature, of capitalism.

A half mile from their destination, they reached a cattle gate barring them from further progress. Alice was sure it hadn't been there the first time she and Kim had driven past. It was fastened shut with a large steel padlock, and the ditches on each side of the road were too sloping for the Crown Vic to navigate.

"If I pried that lock off, would you drive me down the road?" Alice asked.

The driver just looked at her in the mirror.

"Okay," she said. "I'm gonna walk down the road a piece. I should be back in fifteen minutes." She leaned forward. "Hand me the car keys. I don't want to come back and find that you've ditched me."

"Why would I do that?"

"You look like you have a vivid imagination," Alice said dryly. She gestured at the meter, which had ticked up to nearly eighty dollars. "Look, you can make well over two hundred dollars for doing nothing. Or you can be a dick and make nothing. Work with me here."

The cabbie sighed and turned the car off and handed the keys to her. "Am I gonna regret this?" His tone made it clear that he considered it a rhetorical question.

Alice walked around the cattle gate and headed down the road. After a couple of minutes, the road ended in a small packed-dirt cul-de-sac. This, she figured, had to be where Robert had parked his truck. She checked her GPS position; the coordinates on his faulty work order were just ahead. She left the road and walked through an area of low carpet-like scrub that clung to her ankles.

The land began to slope upward. She wasn't sure what she was looking for, and the problem was that there was nothing here. Just an endless rocky plain punctuated by patches of coarse yellow brush and the occasional gnarled dwarf tree, bent and scoured by the wind sweeping over the badlands.

She came to a level clearing and examined the land before her. Well, if it was obvious, then someone else would've found it already. She walked back and forth in semicircles of increasing radius, her eyes at her feet. It was rough ground, and with the slope, she soon broke a sweat. The shadows of clouds moved over the prairie ahead of her.

She walked for several minutes, her mind wandering as her eyes did their work. What, she wondered, if it was something in, say, the soil sample he'd taken? What if it was something in the geology, something she didn't have the experience to recognize?

A movement caught Alice's eye, and she stopped and scanned the horizon, but it had ceased, if it had even been there in the first place. A chill went down her spine. She'd just commenced walking when she saw it again. She whipped her head around. About thirty yards out, a patch of grass was moving. Alice dropped to her knees, watching intently. The grass was undulating wildly but regularly, as if it were being shaken. She wondered if it was two animals fucking. Deer, or maybe wolves? She wished she'd brought her gun, talisman or not. She kept her eyes on the movement and crab walked forward, staying low.

As she drew closer to the movement, she noticed that the grass had started to thin out, that what greenery remained was sickly and dying. It would've been impossible, from a distance, to spot the area in the sea of prairie grass. There was a slight ammoniac odor in the air too, and the soil under her feet was dry and cracked. Tiny crystals sparkled in the parched ground. She pinched up a couple of them between two fingers and examined them. They looked like sea salt but had a strong chemical odor.

Ten feet from the movement, she heard a low roar and realized what it was: a vent. The grass was being whipped back and forth by outrushing air. Just as she had this thought, the roar ceased and the grass fell still. Alice straightened and walked until she was standing over the vent, a corroded rectangle of steel mesh set directly into the ground. She got on her knees and tried to peer into the shaft, but she could see nothing. Was there an underground facility of some kind here? She couldn't imagine there was, unless even the entrance was hidden. More likely the vent was connected by a series of airshafts to a facility somewhere nearby.

She turned and looked back at the taxi, which was now a half mile distant. She doubted she'd be able to find the vent again if she returned. Below her, she heard a distant slam and then the crank of a compressor. The air around her began to rise, and then she found herself engulfed in the warm outrush from the vent. Immediately, her eyes began to burn. She stumbled away from the vent, pressing her fists into her eyes, which were already tearing profusely. Her throat constricted, and she began to gag. Behind her, the outrush intensified, and she could feel the gas rising around her, suffocating her. She began to stumble forward, blind. Her foot went into a hole in the dirt, and she screamed and fell to one knee. Bracing her hands on the ground, she turned her hips and pulled, trying to free her foot. With each breath she took, the burning in her lungs sharpened, and she began to dry heave. It occurred to her that she might die out here on the prairie, all alone.

This thought flooded her with adrenaline and self-pity, and she surged forward, wrenching her ankle free but slamming her face into the ground. She pushed herself up and limped forward as fast as she could, trying not to inhale, her head swimming now. The pain in her eyes and throat and ankle had merged into one tremendous pang that hammered at her brain. When she was on the point of passing out, she took in a breath and found that the air around her was clear. She collapsed to the earth.

A minute passed as she lay there breathing. She turned over and sat up and felt her injured ankle with both hands. To her relief, there was no bone poking through. Her vision had come back, though her eyes still burned. The outrush of gas had stopped; Alice looked around, but she had no idea where the vent was. So this was what Robert had discovered. Or not discovered.

She was sure that he would've mentioned it to her, or Kim, if he'd found a mysterious vent in the middle of an empty plot of land. More likely, someone had seen him surveying and decided it was easier to dispose of him than to take the chance that he might have stumbled upon their . . . what? There was only one thing that sensitive, for which they'd put a man in jail to avoid the minuscule chance he'd discovered it. Dust.

Somewhere around here, all the dust was being made. Alice realized that in her panic, she'd stumbled uphill, away from the vent and the taxi. Ahead, the land rose sharply and then dropped away. She rose to her feet and limped along until she could see over the rise. On the plain below her was an unmarked concrete building surrounded by cracked pavement and a few smaller Quonset huts, the entire installation circled by chain-link fencing topped with coils of razor wire. Alice dropped to her stomach so that only her head protruded above the grass.

This was Greenworld Fluid Dynamics—she felt no doubt. This was where Hicks was, and Rachel. She made a note of the GPS coordinates in her phone. She thought about Robert, innocently setting up his surveying gear on this ridge, looking through his scope at the distant compound as someone there leaned closer to a bank of surveillance camera feeds and picked up a phone. Poor fool. She backed away from the lip of the ridge, still on her stomach, and started the long walk back to the taxi. Halfway there she came upon a rattlesnake sunning itself on a flat shelf of sandstone. The snake rose up and hissed at her, but she didn't even slow down, just veered around it and kept limping on. She had more dangerous things to worry about.

The taxi driver had dozed off behind the wheel but jolted awake when Alice opened the door and got in.

"What happened to you?" he asked. He put a hand over his nose and quickly rolled all the windows down.

Alice leaned forward and looked at herself in the rearview. Her eyes were bloodshot and red rimmed, and she had a small cut above her eyebrow, which had oozed blood down her face. She had no memory of cutting her head. Along with the bruises from her fight with Lester, this made her look like she'd been in a bad car crash. She licked two fingers and tried to clean the blood from her face. Well, she wouldn't be getting laid any time soon.

"A skunk," she said. "I was just walking through the grass, and I came across this . . . skunk with her babies. She rose up and sprayed me down. Can't blame her, I guess. I took off running and stepped in a gopher hole, and that's when I hit my head."

The driver just stared, his hand still over his nose. He turned and looked out at the prairie where she'd gone, but there was nothing there except grass, rippling now in the breeze. Alice felt in her pockets, found the keys, and handed them to him without further comment.

As he maneuvered the car though a five-point U-turn on the narrow gravel road, something occurred to Alice, and she thought, *Why not. Why not press my luck?* She took her phone out, consulted the map, and leaned forward to speak to the driver. "Let's take a scenic route back," she said. "Circle around that ridge and take the first left."

"I ain't makin' no more stops," the driver said vehemently.

"No stops. You won't even have to slow down."

He sighed but took the turn when they came to it. Alice didn't know what she hoped to see—a placard at the front door with the company name and logo emblazoned on it? Rachel's sad face at a barred window?

Before they were even in sight of the compound she'd seen from the rise, they came to another cattle gate barring the road, chained shut, the ditches on each side all but impassable, a bright laminated "No Trespassing" sign fixed to the top rail of the gate. The driver didn't even ask her what she wanted to do, just cranked the car into a U-turn and headed back to town.

CHAPTER 28

The first thing Alice did when the taxi dropped her off at the Bobcat was to get in the shower. She lathered up head to toe and held her eyes open with her fingers to let the brackish Whitehurst water run through them. Still they burned. It also became increasingly clear to her that she was having trouble breathing. When she tried to take a deep breath, her lungs refused to fill more than halfway. Once she realized this, anxiety seized her, and her breathing became even more labored, and soon she was light headed and queasy. She rested her forehead against the shower wall, the water flowing over her.

"Easy does it," she said to herself. She stood there until her breathing slowed.

She dried off, dressed, and sat on the bed, taking slow breaths. There was definitely something wrong with her lungs. Alice took out her phone and texted Kim. `Need to go to ER, can you pick me up?` She stared at her phone for an indeterminate amount of time. No reply. Finally she went to the sink, unfolded one of the white hand towels there, and wet it under the faucet. If her lungs were damaged, it wouldn't help if she walked all the way to the hospital in the smog and exhaust of Whitehurst. She tied the wet towel around the bottom half of her face and went out.

It took her half an hour to walk to the emergency room. No one stopped to offer her a ride, with the towel wrapped around her face. She weaved through the parked cars toward the lighted archway of the entrance, and as she put the now-grayish towel in a trash can, she noticed a familiar sight: Kim's car. It was parked aslant in one of the handicapped spaces. A feeling of dread crept over Alice's skin.

Inside, the ER was only half-full. Alice found it surprising that the hospital had any empty beds in a town so anarchic. She remarked on this to the intake nurse, who nodded while scrawling Alice's information down on a clipboard.

"Whitehurst employees have access to the Whitehurst private clinic, which is quite nice," the nurse said. "And free. Only the truly indigent come here."

Alice realized, as the nurse said this, that she was including her in this group—the indigent. She saw her reflection in the window behind the nurse and had to admit that, with her gashed brow, black eye, mashed lip, bruises, and scrapes, she certainly looked unfortunate.

She took an empty chair and texted Kim. `Saw your car in the hospital lot; are you here? I'm in ER.` This time, a reply came instantly. `I'm here but stay away.`

Alice frowned at this reply, and then winced; frowning sent a stab of pain through her lacerated brow. She considered the possible interpretations of "stay away." Was Kim blaming her for Lester's suicide attempt, or was it something darker? Was she in trouble?

The intake nurse called Alice's name and led her to a small ward of beds separated by paper curtains. A white-haired male doctor was waiting for her, reading her intake form. He looked at her, and then his face hardened into a mask of cold professional objectivity. Alice wasn't usually one to care what other people thought about her, but for some reason she felt compelled to justify herself to this doctor.

"It's not what it looks like," she said.

The doctor folded his hands in front of him and set his feet, as if to prepare himself to be physically buffeted by the lies to come. "No?"

"I'm a private investigator from New York. I'm here on a murder case. In the course of running down a lead, I think I was exposed to exhaust fumes from a drug lab."

His expression didn't change. No doubt he'd heard more outlandish stories, perhaps every day. He looked back at her form. "It says you're having trouble breathing?"

Alice nodded. "My lungs only fill halfway. The gas also burned my eyes, if that helps."

"We see this now and then," the doctor said. "Your lung capacity will return over the next few days, as long as you aren't exposed to any more gas. I can give you a saline wash for your eyes, if they have any residual irritation. What about the rest of your injuries? Your eyebrow needs stitches."

"When the gas hit me, I took off running and fell," Alice said sheepishly. She wondered if the doctor was buying any of this; she tried to gauge his face, but he'd turned away to bring disinfectant and a needle out of the supply cabinet. "The older bruises on my neck are from a fight. I got jumped by a man—a pimp—who was angry that I told his girlfriend he was cheating on her."

The doctor took her by the shoulders and moved her closer. "Don't move," he said. He squirted a stinging alcohol solution onto her split eyebrow, soaking up the runoff with a pad of gauze before it trickled into her eye. "Have you considered going into a less dangerous line of work?"

"I used to be a journalist," Alice said. She took a deep breath as the needle went in. "But I got caught fabricating. You can google my name, the whole story comes up."

The doctor's face was inches from hers, and he was rigid with concentration as he wound the silk thread in and out of her flesh. "You know, I'm supposed to report any cases like yours to the sheriff's office," he said.

"Why?"

"Most of the time, people with your symptoms are involved in the manufacture of drugs. Surely you know about our town's little problem. I say *little problem*, but there's nothing little about it."

"I know about it," Alice said. She wondered what he'd think if she told him how many times she'd taken dust herself. She considered several different phrasings of her next question before she asked it. "Are you going to report me?"

"Don't see the point." He tied off her stitches, snipped off the ends, and stood back. "This town could use a little competition. Dust doesn't cause crime, dust prices cause crime. And prices are too high. That's what happens in a monopoly. I'm a pragmatist. If you're starting a rival operation, good for you. Just stay under the radar as long as you can."

So he hadn't believed a word she'd said. "Thanks for the advice, Doc."

"I reported dozens of cooks," the doctor said. "And they all got busted. But the dust problem, it just got worse. And then I realized one day—the police weren't arresting criminals, they were taking out the competition. Now I take a more laissez-faire approach to it all."

Alice couldn't hide her surprise. "You think the sheriff is in on it?"

The doctor waved a hand dismissively and began to write her a prescription. "I don't know the details. I don't think about it. But the scale of what's happening in this town, it couldn't go on without the blessing of the overriding power structures."

She took the prescription slip from him and looked at it: Percocet. She'd rather have dust, she thought. When she looked up at the doctor to thank him—for the painkillers and everything else—she saw that he knew exactly what she'd been thinking.

Alice walked up and down the hallways of the first floor of the hospital, looking into each door she passed. It was mostly offices and waiting areas. She walked purposefully, with her prescription held in her hand like a hall pass, and no one stopped her. She took a stairwell to the second floor and did the same; she passed patients being wheeled to scans or surgery, some of them in obvious pain, some shaven and resigned, some unconscious. She smiled and waved at a frail child she passed in the hall; the child just looked away. On the third floor, she passed through maternity, looked in briefly on the numbered bassinets of the nursery. Alice thought of Kim, calculated the weeks. Finally, she reached the general patients' area. She began to stop at the nurses' desk, but then she realized she didn't know Lester's last name to ask after him. She turned down the main hallway and walked on slowly, her head swiveling to look into each room she passed. She passed a dozen rooms before she found Kim.

She was sitting at Lester's bedside, her back to the doorway. Lester was reclining in bed, clad in a paper gown, his eyes bloodshot and his neck bruised and abraded. Rope burn. Lester saw Alice in the hall, and his face hardened, which prompted Kim to turn. When she saw Alice there, she stood up and marched into the hallway.

"I told you to stay away," Kim said. She stood very close to Alice, in a manner that Alice had at first taken for offhand intimacy but now realized was meant to be confrontational.

"I came to get my lungs looked at, and thought I'd drop by. You haven't been answering my texts, and then when you did, finally, I couldn't tell if you were angry with me or if you were being held hostage."

"No one's holdin' me hostage," Kim said. Her voice was low but uneven with constrained emotion.

"Okay," Alice said. She paused for a moment. "Do you want to know what happened to me? I think I've figured out what's been going on."

"I don't care," Kim said. "Just get the fuck outta here."

Alice blinked. She tried to look into Kim's eyes, but Kim kept her gaze averted and studiously blank. "Why are you so angry at me?" Alice asked.

"Lester tried to off himself!" Kim hissed. "Because of you! You ain't have to stomp him like that. And you kept it a secret, because you know it was wrong."

"Kim, he attacked me," Alice said. Now her voice too was trembling with anger. "He would've killed me."

"Bullshit. Lester's harmless. Besides, he only mad because you fuckin' with him and me. And the way he tells it, he got every right to be mad. I don't know why I wasn't. You had my mind all fucked up." Kim's voice escalated as her hands flew up in accusation. "Why you even followin' him, takin' pictures, drivin' a wedge between us? Yeah, he in the wrong, but he just doin' what comes natural. You can't blame a person for that. But why you meddlin' in our shit? I'll tell you why. You pretend you wanna help me, but really, you jealous of Lester. You in love with me."

Alice couldn't help but smile at this. "Wait, what?"

"You heard me. The way you look at me. That night at Roundtree's. How you been creepin' closer and closer in bed since you moved in. First time I saw you, with that short hair and men's clothes, I had you pegged. I just didn't see how you were blockin' me off. Invite me to New York so you could have me all for yourself. You even tried to murder my babies."

"Holy shit," Alice said quietly. She almost had to tip her hat to Lester; he hadn't missed a single detail. "Kim, I'm your friend. I'm not in love with you. I don't want anything from you. I just want what's best for you. Lester's playing on your sympathies for him, jerking you around. He didn't really try to kill himself, it's just his way of getting your attention."

Kim stared at her with such disgust that Alice thought she might spit on the floor. A passing nurse gave them a curious look. "You think you smarter than everybody. Smarter than Lester, smarter than me, smarter than this town. But guess what? You ain't so smart at all. Lester told me 'bout how he came to the room after you convinced me to cut him off. Something else you kept a secret because you know you in the wrong. Tried to sell you some info, and you ain't interested."

Alice frowned. She wasn't sure what Kim was getting at. "Yeah, I remember. It was trash."

Kim shook her head in a pantomime of sympathy. "See? You ain't half as smart as you think you are."

"I'm not trying to be the soft touch for every dusthead pimp in Whitehurst." Kim bristled with anger at this description of Lester, and Alice had to admit that it gave her a swell of satisfaction. "Listen, I figured out where they're keeping Rachel Wilcox."

Kim crossed her arms and cocked one shoulder. "Fuck do I care? I hope she dies."

Okay, Alice thought, *I sort of walked into that one.* She supposed she'd been trying to show off, to rebut Kim's accusation that she wasn't as smart as she thought she was. She leaned closer and examined Kim's pupils. "Are you high right now?"

"Oh, fuck you," Kim said. She turned back to Lester's room and then stopped. "I'll come by the room later tonight to get my shit. Try not to be there."

Alice reached out and grabbed her by the upper arm. "Kim, wait—"

Kim wheeled on her, simultaneously wrenching her arm free and whipping the back of her hand across Alice's face. "Fuck off!"

Kim's knuckles caught her across her bruised cheekbone, and the pain was immediate and immense. That was what she responded to—the pain, she later told herself, though even later she would wonder and then, eventually, acknowledge that she'd reacted out of emotional pain as much as physical pain, that Kim's rejection had wounded her deeply. Before she knew quite what she was doing, she'd slapped Kim with her open hand.

Kim stared back at her for an instant—the first time she'd made eye contact with her for their entire conversation—and then pounced. Kim grabbed her by the hair and wrenched her viciously sideways, making a steady growling noise like a wounded animal. They careened into a metal cart and crashed to the floor in a tremendous clatter. Someone nearby was screaming, "Stop, stop!" Kim banged Alice's head into the floor and then began to punch her in the face, using her hair to jerk her head into her oncoming fist. Alice ate two or three punches and then caught Kim's wrist in midair. She surged forward and drove her free hand into Kim's nose. Kim recoiled, her eyes curiously blank. Alice turned her hips and was able to get on top of Kim. Kim still had her by the hair, though, and pulled her head close so that Alice couldn't get any proper distance to throw a punch. Blindly, Alice pounded away at Kim's ribcage, each of her chopping blows punctuated by a grunt from Kim.

Suddenly, someone pulled her off of Kim, and as she watched, a burly male nurse picked Kim up from the floor and held her in a bear hug. Someone was screaming, and Alice realized it was her. As she slowly regained her senses, she heard Kim, squirming in her restrainer's arms, screaming, "Kill you, kill you, kill you," like a ritual incantation. Alice's face hurt badly, and something dripped down into her eye; she'd popped her stitches.

"I'm all right now," she said over her shoulder. "You can let me go."

The arms loosened, and Alice straightened. The man who'd held her back was a young red-haired kid in white scrubs, more wide than tall, who cut his eyes away in embarrassment when she looked over at him. Her anger had passed like a summer squall, but Kim was still in full lather. If anything, being restrained seemed to intensify her rage, and as she struggled against her captor, her threats expanded to encompass him, the hospital, and the town of Whitehurst itself. A small crowd of nurses and paper-smocked patients had gathered in the hall to take in the spectacle.

"Kim," Alice said, moving closer. "Calm down or they're going to call the police."

Kim spit in Alice's face. As Alice wiped the saliva from her check, the hall was completely silent, except for one sound: a low, dry, humorless rasp of a laugh. Alice turned and saw that it was coming from Lester. He'd seen the whole thing from his bed, and now he was looking at Alice with the patronizing faux benevolence of someone who'd not just won, but who'd outmaneuvered an opponent who'd insulted and underestimated him, an opponent who now stood completely defeated. Alice did the only thing she could. She turned and walked away.

CHAPTER 29

Alice maintained her composure through the restitching of her wound, but as soon as she reached the darkness of the parking lot, she leaned against a car and sobbed, as much from shock as grief. She felt much better afterward. She hoped this wasn't the end of her and Kim's friendship, but deep down she knew it probably was. Already, she sensed an expanding void in herself: the feeling of loss after a breakup, the self cleaved back into singularity.

She wiped her face dry and then walked to the circular drive at the front of the hospital, where she entered an idling taxi. When the driver asked where she was going, she almost said the Bobcat Motel, and then reconsidered.

"Take me to a car rental office," she said. She should have done it long ago.

The taxi dropped her at the airport. Alice walked through the quaint terminal, feeling a thrum of nostalgia even though it had barely been a week since she'd flown into Whitehurst. Looking back, it seemed much longer than that. She thought about her stay in Whitehurst; the more progress she'd made unraveling the case, the worse things had gotten for the people involved. Missy, Robert, Rachel, Kim. Herself.

Sometimes it went like that. People thought the truth set you free, but it could just as easily kill you. Especially when it had been buried, its exposure required the demolition of the structures of lies that had been erected over it. That demolition usually had casualties. She had a sudden impulse to buy a one-way ticket to New York and leave, now, abandoning her belongings at the motel, changing her phone number so none of these people could ever bother her again. Ten years earlier, she might have done it. Back then she still thought you could run from your troubles. Now she knew you just carried them with you.

At the car rental counter, she looked over the laminated menu of rates and vehicles, and did something uncharacteristic. She picked out the biggest vehicle, a towering Expedition that was the size of a van, with the engine of two hot rods. Alice was paying for the rental out of her own pocket, so why not rent something that made her feel secure? Environmental responsibility was one thing, but she felt that she could suspend that if the environment itself was hostile toward her.

She drove back to the motel in the towering vehicle, looking down, literally, on the traffic around her. It was like steering from a crow's nest. Fifty feet from the turnoff into the Bobcat's lot, traffic was at a standstill. After a moment, Alice cranked the wheel and steered the Expedition over the median and across the opposing lanes of traffic and popped the curb in front of the Bobcat.

Back in the room, she sat on the bed and thought about what to do with the rest of the night. She knew she should work on the case, but she felt an overwhelming urge to go out and get drunk. This, she recognized, was how she always felt after a breakup. An irresistible desire to assert her reclaimed freedom, primarily by fucking up. She thought about Kim, about the ugly scene at the hospital. Fucking Lester. She should've shot him when he'd attacked her. With the bruises around her neck, Lester's reputation, and her relationship with the sheriff, she would've walked. She wouldn't make that mistake again.

Oh, who am I fooling, she thought. *I'm no killer.*

She took her phone out and texted Kim. I'm sorry; can we talk? She didn't wait for an answer; she could just imagine Kim looking at the text and then curling her lip and putting the phone away. Well, she'd just wear her down.

In the bathroom, on the sink, she found a bottle with an inch of cheap rum left in it and took it to the bed. As its burn spread through her gut, she remembered something and brought out her computer. She checked her phone to get the GPS coordinates of the vent and the compound beyond it, found them on Google Maps, and then searched for the plot in the Whitehurst County records. For a moment, as the search loaded, she had a surge of hope that maybe they'd been sloppy, that it would be owned by one Dwayne Hicks—but no. As she'd figured, it was registered to a shell company—LDH LLC. The *D* for Dwayne and the *H* for Hicks, maybe, but then what was the *L*? She ticked off the possibilities: Whitehurst, dust, Red Horse. Nope. Alice was good at word puzzles, standardized tests, crosswords, and she let her mind flit lightly over the problem, free associating. L—D—H. And then it hit her: *Legion d'Honneur.*

It wouldn't stand up in court, but it was good enough for her. She clicked back to the tab with the satellite map image of the compound and zoomed in as far as she could. That was where Rachel was; she'd bet on it. And it was Hicks who had her. No one had called her or sent any notes, but they didn't have to. The message was clear: any move Alice made against them would have consequences for Rachel. Alice wondered how long they would hold her before paranoia got the better of them and they took her out in the badlands and shot her. If she backed them into a corner, she knew they were capable of murder.

The sheriff wouldn't want to raid Hicks's compound. But like all domineering men, he was easily manipulated. And she knew the perfect way to ensnare him. She sat back, smiling in the dark. Tomorrow, the sheriff would learn a lesson about power and the burdens of authority.

In twenty-four hours, Hicks would be in jail and Rachel would be free. She toasted this thought with a swig from the bottle of rum and then, because it had been a very hard day, passed out almost immediately.

Alice awoke at dawn with a hangover. She felt not rested at all, and her mind began racing immediately with thoughts of the day to come. She sat up and looked around the room. Kim hadn't come in the night to take her things. Maybe that meant she wasn't moving out? Or, she thought, maybe she had moved on so completely that she wouldn't even bother coming back for her junk. Alice found her phone on the bed: no texts, no calls. She sent a text to Kim: I just want to talk, we can work this out. I need your help.

As she showered, she thought about the puzzle before her. It wasn't that the pieces didn't fit; it was that she had a nagging feeling that she didn't have them all. Hicks made dust in his compound, where he also made fracking fluid for Whitehurst. Robert, due to the bad luck of a clerical error, had stumbled onto the Hicks compound and possibly the vent, which, with his scientific background, he'd have reasonably been able to deduce was associated with the manufacture of dust. Hicks, calculating that an outright murder would be too suspicious, had schemed to frame Robert to keep him quiet. The sheriff probably didn't know the particulars, but he seemed, at the very least, to be allowing this framing to go on, as long as it seemed legit on its face. But she remembered the sheriff's distaste when they'd discussed Hicks; "faggot" was how he'd so crudely described the man. Why would he go along with Hicks's machinations? For what purpose? She knew the sheriff well enough to know he wasn't in it for the money. What then? There was still the vague specter of Whitehurst's involvement—at the very least, he'd lied about knowing Hicks. Maybe he was more directly tied in? The sheriff wouldn't take orders from Hicks, but he would from Whitehurst. But she couldn't imagine why Whitehurst would be involved in what was, relatively, a petty drug-peddling operation. Even if it took in millions, it didn't compare to the billions Whitehurst was sucking out of the ground. Not to mention the generations of wealth he'd inherited from previous booms. Whitehurst wasn't a stupid man. He'd never endanger all that to sling dust.

Alice could only think of one person, other than Hicks, who had substantial insight into the dust business. Roundtree. He was probably out of the hospital, and she doubted he was very busy these days. She checked the time; it was a quarter to eight in the morning. The sheriff didn't come in until after ten, so she had a couple of hours to kill. She would go pay Roundtree a visit.

She applied heavy makeup—*If only Kim were here to help*, she caught herself thinking, and felt a stab of melancholy—and dressed herself in one of Kim's outfits, a lace tank top and tight skirt. She planned on going directly from Roundtree's to the sheriff's. In the mirror, she looked like a girl you might see in the mall, like a porn actress, like a sexual object tailored and presented for the male gaze. She looked perfect.

By the time she headed south in the shattering morning sunlight, the traffic was already heavy, the air smelling of ozone. She felt indestructible, riding high in her tank, with her war paint on. The first turn she took was a wrong one, and she had to backtrack to the highway; but two hundred feet down the second one, she saw something next to the road that piqued memory and alarm in equal measure. Two four-wheelers left to molder in the elements. They were the ones she and Kim had ridden out the night of Roundtree's party so they could observe Roundtree's meeting with Hicks. She remembered the euphoria she'd felt on that ride, high as a kite, under the stars, and smiled.

Roundtree's house looked even lonelier in the daytime, sitting out in the middle of the rocky prairie like the last remnant of a destroyed civilization. The balding lawn was speckled with red Solo cups and crushed beer cans, and Alice realized that the house hadn't been cleaned since the party. She wondered if anyone even lived here anymore. She parked the vehicle and got out, checking her phone to see if Kim had texted back. She hadn't. When Alice looked up, the front door to Roundtree's house was open, and there was Roundtree, coming down the steps in a bathrobe, a gun pointed straight at her face.

"What you want?" he asked. His voice was reedy and high-pitched, and Alice thought, with faint horror, that this was what happened when you castrated a man.

She put her hands up. "I just want to talk."

He stopped ten feet from her but kept the pistol trained. "Open all the doors and pop the back."

She did so, as he shadowed her cautiously. When she swung the back open, he waved the gun at the floor mats. "Slide that off real slow so I can see the spare tire compartment."

"Come on," Alice said. "Do you think some assassin's curled up down there, waiting to jump out, guns blazing?"

"We gonna find out," Roundtree said. He waved the gun at her. She pulled the mat aside and raised the plastic lid of the spare tire compartment. Inside was a tire and a folding iron. Roundtree nodded and lowered the pistol.

"When the man decides to take you out, he send somebody you don't expect," he said. "So when I saw you pull up, I figured this was it."

"Look," Alice said. "I don't know if you blame me for . . . for what happened to you. But I never ever thought anything like that would happen."

To her surprise, Roundtree just shrugged and looked at her blandly. "You in the game, you know it only ends one way. I been waitin' for this since I was just a young un. Besides, even if I did blame y'all for everything, I ain't really feel anger no more. Doctors said that's what happens when they take your balls. Hormones. I ain't thought about a woman neither. It's crazy. All I used to care about was fuckin' and flexin', and now that's all just gone. Tell the truth, it's sort of a relief. That shit was exhausting." He turned toward the house and cinched his robe tighter. "You wanna talk, why don't you come in for a cup of coffee?"

The interior of the house was in even worse shape than the yard, with plastic cups of flat beer clustered on every surface, cigarette butts ground into the carpet where they'd been dropped, the sink overflowing with takeout containers. It reminded Alice of one of those houses you'd find on the slopes of a volcano, abandoned in a moment.

"Don't you have any friends who'll clean this place?" Alice said.

"They all gone," Roundtree said. He rinsed a pair of mugs and spooned a tablespoon of instant coffee into each one. As he did so, Alice noticed that he was still wearing his hospital bracelet. "Feedin' off whoever's the new top man." She knew what it meant—the resignation in his voice, the fact that he'd been so utterly drained of his bravado, that he spent his days in a bathrobe, gun in hand, in an empty house he didn't bother cleaning. His comment about the man sending someone. He was just waiting to die. Alice went over to the sink, opened the cabinet underneath, and brought out a trash bag. Then she began emptying cups of beer and bagging them up. Roundtree watched her.

"So what you wanna know?" he asked.

"Hicks," Alice said. "Tell me what you know about his business. There's something there that I still can't figure."

Roundtree squirmed and scratched his head absently with the barrel of the Magnum. "Yo, I know I already snitched on the man, but that don't mean I'll do it again. At least right now I'm alive. That could change real quick."

Alice nodded. "I could help you," she said.

Roundtree sat in silence for a long moment. "So you are a cop," he said finally.

Alice let the statement go unaddressed, not quite a lie but not the truth either. "I have pull with the sheriff."

"What's that mean exactly?" Roundtree asked. He leaned forward, elbows on knees, and Alice caught a glimpse of the bandages around his groin, the bloodstains there.

She had hoped to navigate this part of the conversation without any outright lies, but she saw now that that wouldn't be possible. She also saw that Roundtree had something good for her; why else would he be so eager to strike terms? "Witness protection," she said. "You get a new name, relocated somewhere warm. Arizona, maybe. Florida. Hormone treatments maybe. You know, they have testosterone replacement therapy now. It'll make you how you were before, balls or no balls."

"You think I wanna be like I was before?" Roundtree said. "Fuck that. I'll take that one-way ticket, though."

Alice had already filled the trash bag, and now she tied it off and tossed it in the corner. "Okay. So here's what I know so far. Hicks is making the dust, and I know where. I know he's also making the fracking fluid for Whitehurst. Wilcox, the guy your boy shanked in jail, found Hicks's dust factory, so they had to get rid of him. What I don't know is how Whitehurst fits into it."

"You found the elephant, but you just got it by the tail," Roundtree said.

"What's that supposed to mean?"

"Hicks ain't tell me nothin' about his business. He treated me like his errand boy. But I know how much money he got comin' in and how much he got goin' out. He had me and my boys going to Canada once a month to bring back a truckload of chemicals for his dust cook, and I know for a fact that that buy alone cost him more than he brought in from a month of dust sales. A lot more. He always runnin' in the red, but he always got cash on hand for whatever. I mean, he was payin' me bonuses for slingin' an extra lot even though he ain't even makin' money on that shit. So somebody's gotta be payin' him for his trouble. And only one man in town got that kinda money."

Alice leaned back against the counter. "If he was losing money on dust, maybe his contract with Whitehurst is just a payoff, to make up the difference. But then what's the point of selling dust if not for profit?" She remembered then what Lester had told her the night he'd come trying to sell her information and she'd turned him away. "Somebody told me that after you got . . . after you retired, he tried to buy a pound of dust, get in on the rush. When he didn't have the money, Hicks offered to give it to him on credit, and he came to me saying that that was how he knew something fishy was going on."

"That's what I'm sayin'!" Roundtree pointed at her animatedly. "Hicks was always doing shit like that. Drugs on credit. To down-low fiends! Then when they ain't pay him back, and they never fuckin' paid him back, and me and my boys got ready to go collect, Hicks'd say, don't worry about it. We thought maybe he was just gettin' everybody hooked on that giveaway dust and then up the prices to make a killin', but he ain't never raise the price up even after we got damn near everybody hooked. Whatever his game is, it wasn't money, because he ain't really make none. You just got to figure out what his game is."

Alice's well-honed cynicism rejected this last sentiment outright; everyone's game was, when you got right down to it, about money. Some just had a cleverer angle than most. (Most weren't clever at all.) *Cui prodest,* she thought. Who benefits? Who benefits from the slow disintegration of the town? And then it hit her, literally staggered her with the sudden intensity of the epiphany.

She put both hands on the kitchen counter to support herself. Oh god, she thought. He'd even been arrogant enough to rub their faces in it that night at the party, with his well-worn allegorical anecdote about burning off the fields, about the crack years setting the stage for a resurgence of wealth. When most people heard the conspiracy theories about the CIA pushing crack in the inner city, they rolled their eyes, but Whitehurst must have admired the ingenuity, the sheer simplicity of it. All those properties Wilcox had been so busy assessing, the steady stream of new acquisitions, all the holdouts suddenly eager to sell—Alice thought about the plots she'd looked into, dumped for pennies on the dollar by desperate addicts. Even Kim had succumbed, Alice remembered, signing away generational wealth for a handful of coppers. What was it she'd said? Whenever you hit rock bottom, there's a Whitehurst agent there with an envelope of cash.

It was a brilliant plot, in a sociopathic sort of way. So brazen and up-front that no one would ever suspect. The big lies, as they said, were the ones that stuck. She looked up to find Roundtree staring at her.

"You look like a rat just ran up your back," he said. "You gonna tell me?"

Alice opened her mouth and then closed it again. "I don't know if I should. I don't know if you'd believe me. I don't know if I believe it myself."

That was a lie, though. She did believe it. It also occurred to her that she was in a precarious position, and that if Roundtree knew she had figured out the whole conspiracy, he might well be able to barter this information with Hicks for a pardon.

But Roundtree didn't press her, just sat back with an expression almost of relief. "Yo, you ain't got to tell me twice. I ain't barely know nothin', and that almost got me killed."

Alice nodded absently. He was right, of course. Nothing more dangerous than the truth. A sensation of weariness but also exhilaration had descended upon her. It was the feeling of the elimination of all unknowns, of pure airtight determinism, falling as finally and decisively as a guillotine.

CHAPTER 30

The sheriff's parking spot was still empty when Alice arrived at the station, so she pulled her rented Expedition into it. She sat in the driver's seat, her hands drumming on the steering wheel. She was anxious to get things started. She felt good about her plan, and if she couldn't induce the sheriff into helping her, she would drive straight from here to the FBI office in Minneapolis. What Whitehurst was doing here was unprecedented; every law-enforcement agency in the federal government would be fighting to get a piece of this case. But first, she had to free Rachel Wilcox.

Alice checked her phone for the time: five minutes to ten. She thought, *Why not?* and sent a text to Kim. Please call me. She'd just hit "Send" when the blast of a car horn sounded from behind her. She turned in the seat to see the sheriff's truck nosed up to her bumper. She opened her door and hopped down, walking with a wide smile back to his driver's side window. Her chin barely came up to the glass.

"You can't park there," the sheriff said, looking down her shirt.

"Let's go for a ride," Alice said. "I need to talk to you about something sensitive. I'll move my car when we get back."

The sheriff heaved a sigh and stared straight ahead, the muscles in his jaw fluttering as he ground his teeth. Then he looked back down at her and gave a single nod. "Fine. We can't be gone for long, though."

Alice made a show of relief, though she'd been sure that he'd agree. She tottered on her heels around the front of his truck and climbed into the passenger side. The truck's cab smelled strongly of cologne and the sickly sweet odor of chewing tobacco. The sheriff looked over at her without warmth, but with great interest.

"Where should we go?" he asked.

"Someplace private," she said.

He nodded and pulled out of the lot. They headed south through town, past the Walmart, past the strip clubs, past the Bobcat. Alice craned her neck to see if Kim's car was in the lot, but it wasn't. They passed one of the big gas stations on the edge of town, where several strung-out panhandlers stood on the shoulder, proffering various hand-lettered placards of woe.

"You think those stories on their signs are true?" Alice asked the sheriff.

He didn't even look over. "No. I think they're dustheads trying to get their next fix."

"Probably right," said Alice. "Do you ever feel sorry for them?"

Now the sheriff snorted with laughter, an ugly, contemptuous sound. "Why would I feel sorry for them?"

"What if it wasn't their fault? What if, you know, they were forced, by circumstances, to become addicts?"

"What kind of stupid shit is that?" he asked, squirming in his seat as if the idea caused him physical pain. "Did someone come into their house and hold a gun to their head and say, snort this dust or you die? No? Then they don't get a pass and they damn sure don't get my sympathy."

"Maybe you're right," Alice mumbled, though she didn't in any way think he was right. She wasn't sure if his stridency on this subject meant he knew about Whitehurst's plan and condoned it, or considered the state of the town to be the reflection of some kind of natural order based on moral fallibility.

The sheriff turned off the highway and took a gravel road that wound between two tremendous hills of crushed rock, then opened onto a massive pan in the earth. The ground had been gouged out by heavy machinery, which lay, rusted, here and there, and around the main mineshaft, the striations of millions of years of geological tumult lay exposed. The sight of it struck Alice as somehow obscene. The sheriff pulled the truck over, put it into park, and turned off the engine.

"This here's the old Whitehurst silver mine," the sheriff said. "Not even many locals know about it. It's about as private as it gets, here in town."

Alice mimed a little shiver of admiration. "I bet you brought a cheerleader or two back here when you were in high school."

"Might have," the sheriff said, his pride evident. He stared out at the land, remembering, and then came back to Alice. "So. What's this you need to talk to me about?"

Alice had had an entire monologue thought out, which she'd rehearsed as she'd driven from Roundtree's to the police station: how it was too bad that things between them had gotten so screwed up, that it had been all her fault for forcing her foolish ideas of equality onto the relationship and not respecting his views, which, now that she'd had some time to consider them, seemed downright commonsensical, and to which she would now like to humbly submit herself, if he could find it in his heart to allow her the favor of a clean slate. But instead of saying all this, she just slid over and kissed him, with an abandon that surprised them both. She thought he'd resist, but he accepted her kiss with a grace that she realized sprung from anticipation. He'd expected this all along.

She slid one hand down his chest and undid his seatbelt and then his actual belt. He angled his hips to help her run the zipper down on his pants, and when she worked his erection out through the slit of his boxers, it quivered with eagerness. This was going to be easy, she thought. She kissed him and bit his lower lip, and when she felt his hand going to the back of her head, she pivoted smoothly on the seat to straddle him. Her skirt rode up onto her waist, and she wasn't wearing underwear.

"No, don't," he whispered. "I've got a condom in the—"

But she'd already lowered herself onto him, and now she began to rock her hips. He brought his hands up to the front of her chest and pushed her back, but the steering wheel boxed them in.

"Stop a minute," he said, his voice hoarse. "Stop!"

Alice just put her arms around his neck, holding tight, and pumped her hips as fast as she could. She felt his entire body go rigid, and he let out a strangled cry. She felt a warmth spread inside her, and she slowed and then stopped her movements. Underneath her, the sheriff relaxed by degrees until he was so limp, his head lolling against the headrest, that he might have been asleep. Alice leaned forward until her mouth was right next to his ear.

"And now," she said. "You're going to get all the troops together and raid Hicks's compound and free Rachel Wilcox. Or I'm going to go to the hospital, tell them you raped me, and get a swab or ten of your DNA for the rape kit."

Alice climbed off him and sat back in the passenger seat, working her skirt down and straightening her hair in the side mirror. The sheriff didn't move, but she saw that his eyes were wide open and staring at the ceiling.

"What?" he said hoarsely.

"You heard me. What's it going to be?"

He slowly brought his hands down and buttoned his pants. There was something almost childlike in the way he looked down, carefully fastening his belt and securing its end in his belt loops. For a moment Alice felt bad for what she was doing. She'd never had any affection for the sheriff—and as a collection of values, attitudes, and beliefs, she had a savage contempt for him that bordered on hate—but still. Even if a dog bit you, you felt bad after you kicked it. He rested both his arms atop the steering wheel and let out a long, gentle sigh.

"I can't do that. Hicks gets a pass in this town."

"Says who?"

The sheriff looked at her sidelong. "You know who."

"Yeah, I do," Alice said. "You know why? You know what Hicks and Whitehurst are doing in this town?"

"I don't know, and I don't want to know!" For a moment Alice thought he might clap his hands over his ears. "I got my ideas, but it don't matter what I think. It's above my pay grade, and I'm happy to leave those decisions to my betters."

A sadistic joy welled up in Alice's chest. "Hicks is making and selling dust at a loss, funded by Whitehurst. And as people get hooked and hit rock bottom, Whitehurst is right there, cash in hand, to buy their land. And now that these people are junkies, the money just sends them into a downward spiral. Right into prison, or an early grave. He's literally killing this town, and all for real estate. What would've taken decades and cost him hundreds of millions has taken a handful of years and probably only cost him six figures."

The sheriff nodded slowly, mulling this over. "To tell the truth, that don't really change my thinkin' on the matter."

"And here you are," Alice said. "Their guard dog. Busting the competition, slapping bullshit possession charges on dustheads, getting them nice and desperate for when the Whitehurst agent comes calling with an offer for the family farm."

Alice saw that her approach was having the opposite effect from the one she'd intended, that all the sheriff's unearned righteousness and smug machismo was flowing back into him. "Call it what you want. I'm enforcing the law. That's my job. Someone's cookin' dust, I bust 'em. Period. Someone's doin' dust, I bust 'em. Ain't no excuses."

"Fine. Bust Hicks. He's making it all."

"I ain't heard nothin' about that." He set his jaw and turned in his seat to face her.

"I just told you."

"I ain't heard nothin' about it," the sheriff repeated, as if he hadn't even heard her.

"Jesus, Michael," Alice spat. "Do you know what a fucking hypocrite you are? You pretend you're all about law and order, but that's not really true at all, is it?" But the sheriff had fallen into a posture that Alice remembered from her ex-husband: the patient resignation of a man being nagged, someone who wasn't listening, merely enduring. It infuriated her beyond all logic. "I will do whatever it takes to make sure you go to prison for rape if you try to shrug this off."

He winced at this but quickly pivoted into smugness. "I'll beat the charge."

"Maybe, maybe not. Even if you do, your time as sheriff would be over. Then what? You gonna be a security guard at a mall in Minneapolis?"

"Listen," the sheriff said. "These people, these dustheads, these dealers and dust cooks—you say I'm bein' used or whatever. Well, what if that's true? But not by Whitehurst. What if I'm just part of a larger system? Like, a natural order. Survival of the fittest, say. They use drugs because they're weak. They commit crimes because they're weak. Because they can't hack it in the real world. What if man's law, which I'm charged with enforcing, is based on a higher law? A natural law? Like, Darwin and that sort of thing? You ever considered that?"

High school, Alice thought. *It's like arguing with a high school student, and not even a particularly precocious one.* "There is no higher law. Drug addicts are no more in defiance of evolution than people who've taken antibiotics. And how does Rachel Wilcox fit in with your little fascist-Darwinist philosophy? She's innocent."

The sheriff rubbed his chin and idly blew air out through his teeth. "Okay. What if I said I could get Rachel Wilcox released, unharmed, if you would just drop all this?"

"So Hicks does have her? Where, at his little dust factory?"

"I ain't answerin' no questions," he said, chopping his hand down as if to literally cut this exchange short. "Will you drop it?"

"What about Robert Wilcox?"

"I can't make no promises. But I might be able to work somethin' out. Get him a deal, time served plus probation."

Alice was actually on the point of saying yes when she was stopped by the sudden recollection of what Robert was charged with. Missy's murder. Even if Robert walked, there was still that crime to be answered for, so senseless, so brutal. She thought about the pages torn from magazines taped up on the wall of that dreadful trailer, the shoe box under her bunk, filled with small bills. When Missy's grandfather died—which would happen very soon—all that remained of Missy would go into a burn barrel or a donation bin. And then who'd remember her? The inconsequentiality of her short life didn't serve to make this erasure more palatable—if anything, it made it unbearably tragic.

And as always with Alice, her motives were equal parts altruism and selfishness. The other side of it was that she didn't know if she could live with herself if she let Whitehurst, that smug turtlenecked trust funder, win. Knowing he was still up here, doing his tin-pot CIA psychopath impression, pulling strings and treating the town like his personal Monopoly board. The investigative reporter in her—the upsetter of applecarts and stirrer of shit pots—couldn't resist this opportunity to press her advantage. It wasn't every day that you got one of the fat cats by the balls, after all.

"No," Alice said. "I want you to raid Hicks's compound, arrest that murderous piece of shit, and then I want you to get ready to arrest Whitehurst. Say no, and it's rape charges for you, and I take this case to the FBI in the Twin Cities. Personally, I don't give a shit what you do."

The sheriff's mouth fell open, working mutely as he tried out one response and then another and then another. He truly hadn't expected her to stick to her guns, Alice realized.

"Well," he said. With one hand he swept back his jacket and unsnapped the strap of his holster. Then he slowly withdrew his Magnum, cocked it, and pointed it at Alice. The end of the barrel was close enough to her face that she could see its interior, the smooth-bored, burnished steel, clean and oiled.

"Go ahead," Alice said. Her voice was low, but in the hushed compartment of the truck, it sounded very loud. She looked into the sheriff's face and tried to figure out if she wasn't scared because she didn't think he'd do it or because she didn't care if he did or not.

His lips were quivering like a child puckering his mouth against the onset of tears, and she could see from the bobbing of the gun that his hand was shaking. "You won't do it," she said. Her voice was firm, without the slightest quaver. "You're a fucking coward. You're a spineless, dickless little bitch." She winced inwardly at this, but she was determined to say whatever would wound him, no matter how vile.

The sheriff made an almost inaudible grunting noise. She doubted anyone had spoken to him in this fashion since he was a child. They were in uncertain territory, both of them. Finally, he spoke.

"Get the fuck outta my truck," he said.

Alice allowed herself the satisfaction of a smile. Having won, she had no doubt that she could've ordered him to drive her to her very doorstep. She could've told him to get out of his own truck, and he'd have obeyed. But she found she had no more stomach for him. Her disgust had mounted to a degree that was almost tactile. She reached over and opened her door.

"Good-bye, Michael," she said. She didn't expect him to answer, and he didn't. She stepped out of the truck without looking at him and slammed the door behind her. Instantly, the engine roared to life, and the truck accelerated away. She watched its taillights recede until they disappeared, then she bent down, used one finger to wipe the trickle of fluid from the inside of her leg, flicked it away, and started walking.

It took her an hour to get back to the Bobcat on foot. She could've walked to the road and hitched a ride, but she felt the need for solitude, and by the map on her phone, it was a straight line from the mine to the rear of the motel. Nothing but flat prairie, as of yet unbroken by fracking rigs, and she followed a low ridge of shale north. As she walked she thought about what she would do now. She had reached a point at which all options had been winnowed down to one, which she found equally a relief and a source of anxiety. She would pack her things at the Bobcat, walk or hitch to the police station, fetch her rental, and drive straight through to Minneapolis. Once there she would present her findings to the FBI, the Minnesota state troopers, the local police, whomever it took to get a group together to go and free Rachel. After that, she would figure out the rest of it. Hicks, Whitehurst, Robert's exoneration, justice for Missy. Justice for Whitehurst, the town. That would take years, if not decades, considering the lawyers Whitehurst was liable to hire. She realized that this case was likely to take up most of the rest of her professional life, that it would come to define her as her dishonesty had defined her for so long.

The wind rustled across the prairie, and Alice looked uneasily over her shoulder. She suddenly felt the peril of her situation, how exposed she was, how problematic to all the wrong people. She thought about her gun back in its bedside drawer. She'd feel much better if she had it clipped to her belt. Then again, maybe she deserved whatever she got. She'd certainly done plenty of bad things these past couple of days. Her false promise to Roundtree, entrapping the sheriff. She made a mental note to pick up some Plan B at the drugstore. She had no intention of going to the hospital to have a rape kit done; it had only been a threat, an attempt at leverage. Actually following through wouldn't get her any closer to what she wanted.

The land was so flat that she saw the motel when she was still a mile out. In the lot, a dozen RVs were parked, and on the rear bumper of one, she could just make out a boy, maybe ten or eleven, his parents probably at work in the oilfields. He sat with one hand shading his eyes, watching her approach. She had tired, and the last half mile took her quite some time. When she finally made it to the lot, he was gawping at her in utter puzzlement, a woman sprung apparently from the earth itself, walking out of the empty horizon.

"Hello," she said to him as she passed. Coming around the side of the motel, she saw Kim's car in the lot. Perfect timing. Whatever pettiness had come between them would surely recede into irrelevance once Alice told her all that she'd discovered, all that was at stake. She quickened her step, but as she went to insert her key into the door, she found it was already ajar.

She pushed it open with one hand. Kim lay on her back, on the floor, a gaping wound in her upper chest. Alice started to step forward, but the carpet was soaked with blood. Kim's eyes stared unseeing at the ceiling, the blankness there an order of magnitude greater than the deliberate blankness that Kim had so often retreated to in real life.

Alice stood in the doorway, looking at Kim's body for a long moment, then stepped inside the room and gently closed the door behind her. She walked to her friend's body, the pressure of her steps forcing Kim's blood to well up from the disgusting, matted carpet, coating the edges of her shoes. Alice stooped down and held two fingers against Kim's lifeless neck. She pressed her palms against her friend's blank face, then touched her arms, her belly, and finally, she held her hands. They were so heavy. She felt the impossible weight of life lost, life ruined, life wasted. Alice didn't care about the crime scene. She sat down in Kim's blood and held her hands until she could stop crying, then she got up and started to work.

CHAPTER 31

Alice's Magnum was on the bed, the bedside drawer thrown open. The shooter had left the weapon almost as a taunt; even if she disposed of it, a dozen locals could put her with the gun, and a dozen more had seen her and Kim fighting at the hospital just the previous day. Alice knew from experience that this had all the hallmarks of a story that would dominate headlines for weeks. The lesbian angle, the drugs, the city girl and the country girl. She'd be pilloried in the court of public opinion. It was a great frame job, some part of her thought. She almost had to give them credit.

The other part of her thought that here, finally, was what it felt like to hit rock bottom, to have no options and no hope. She'd flirted with failure all her life, driven by some contrary, self-destructive part of her personality, some remnant of an unhappy childhood perhaps, or a sense of guilt at the station in life she'd been born into. Sometimes she'd even let herself think that she'd tasted it. When she'd lost her job, when she'd gotten divorced. But she saw now that those were trivial mistakes. Here was true and utter failure, not something stumbled or backslid into but orchestrated by enemies as smart or smarter than oneself, as ruthless or more ruthless, with unlimited resources, material and moral.

But she also realized that she only sought these situations out to prove to herself that she could escape them. She despised unconditional self-confidence. She believed it was something that had to be continually proven. And it was this part of her that took charge now. She went to the window, lifted a slat in the blinds, and looked out at the parking lot. Deserted. No one had heard the shot, or at least no one had thought it worth calling in. They would be coming soon, though. Or maybe, she thought, they were sitting on her rental at the station, ready to pounce when she showed up for it.

Her eyes swept the room, assiduously avoiding Kim's corpse. She saw Kim's bag sitting on the bathroom sink; her keys would be in her bag. She would take the gun too, murder weapon or not. Alice gathered what she needed as a plan began to form in her mind.

The camera's viewfinder was flipped around so Alice could see herself. She scooted her chair closer to the camera until just her head and shoulders were framed in the video. She saw that her eyes were ghoulishly red and bloodshot.

"Do you have any eyedrops?" Alice asked Gerald, turning in her chair to where the lawyer sat behind his desk, regarding her with flat disinterest.

"Nope," Gerald said. He didn't bother checking his desk drawers. "It's a nice touch anyway, the bloodshot eyes. They see you've been crying, it shows you're remorseful, that you've got a heart."

Alice considered this. It also distracted from her dilated pupils, from the fact that she was high as hell. She'd found a fresh quarter of dust in Kim's bag, and she'd been running on nothing more than dust and adrenaline the past few hours. Even with the dust making her feel remote and hollowed out, she'd broken down again after she'd buried Kim's body out in the badlands. She'd have preferred to give Kim a proper funeral, but the calculating part of her knew that the frame job against her would be much more difficult if there was no body. So she'd driven out into the prairie, her phone powered down, the battery taken out, until she'd become lost. Then she'd dug a hole and buried her friend in the middle of nowhere. She'd read somewhere that Kim's tribe burned all the deceased's belongings on their funeral pyre, so she'd put Kim's bag and her cigarettes and her phone and all the clothes littering the floorboards of her car in a pile on top of the grave and set fire to them. Then she'd sat on the front bumper, doing bumps of dust and sobbing. By the time the flames died out, she knew what she had to do.

In the next town over from Whitehurst, a charmless little desert hamlet named Dry Rapids, she'd gone to a sporting-goods store for supplies, and then found a lawyer's office in a decrepit strip mall, nestled between a gym and a car stereo emporium. Gerald Rogers, Esquire, a balding good ol' boy in a thirty-year-old suit. If he'd been surprised by the conspiracy Alice described, he didn't show it. At the conclusion of her story, he just scratched his head and said, "And you want me to do what now?"

"I'm going to leave a video deposition of everything, and all the supporting documents, with you," Alice said. "If I get arrested, or turn up dead, or just disappear off the face of the earth, I want you to make sure it all gets put out there. Law enforcement, the media. I've got a list for you."

"I can do that," he'd said, nodding. The lawyer didn't strike her as trustworthy so much as he seemed too lazy to betray her.

So Alice turned to the camera and began reciting her story, starting from the very beginning, looking strangely martial in the desert camo fatigues she'd bought and changed into. It took almost forty-five minutes to tell it all. When she was done, she leaned over, turned the camera off, and did another bump of dust.

"What you gonna do now?" Gerald asked her.

"I'm going to go to Hicks's compound and free Rachel Wilcox," she said. She jutted her chin at the canvas duffel bag she'd brought in with her, from which protruded the stock of a shotgun.

"I admire that can-do spirit," Gerald said. He leaned back in his chair, producing a ghoulish creak. "But don't you think that's better left to a SWAT team?"

"I don't trust anyone at this point," Alice said. Which wasn't the entire truth. She didn't want to see Hicks get a slick lawyer and cut a deal for probation. She wanted revenge. "Plus, I walk into the police station, they're probably going to arrest me on the spot for Kim's murder."

Alice expected him to keep trying to dissuade her, but he just sat back and folded his hands across his belly. "I guess you thought this out already," he said. "So good luck. How long should I sit on all this before I send it out?"

"Not long," Alice said. "Two days." She took out the cash she'd withdrawn from the bank, nearly all her savings, and counted out five one-hundred-dollar bills onto his desk. "Is that enough?"

Gerald nodded without even looking at the money. "That'll be just fine," he said. He cleared his throat awkwardly and twiddled his fingers. "If this guy Hicks is really some kinda military hotshot, you better be careful. Shoot first, ask questions later."

"I don't need to ask any questions at all," Alice said. "I already got all the answers I need. He shot my friend in the back. I intend to return the favor."

CHAPTER 32

Alice drove to within a mile of Hicks's compound, parked in the ditch, unscrewed the license plates, threw them into the tall grass, and went the rest of the way on foot. She would've preferred to wait until the sun started going down, but time was of the essence.

She lay on her stomach on the overlooking ridge, the stippling of grass and shadow perfectly mirroring the camo pattern of her fatigues, and examined the distant compound through a pair of binoculars. Only two vehicles there: a white pickup and Hicks's van. No movement anywhere. The vehicles were parked next to what, through the magnification of the binoculars, looked like a small mobile office, set fifty feet off from the main building, a blocky industrial structure of concrete and steel.

Alice tried to determine if she was out of her mind. As she mulled this over, she took out the baggie of dust and did another bump. Hicks was dangerous, and he wasn't alone. His men were likely armed, but then so was she. And she had the element of surprise. Her main concern was whether or not she was engaged in, well, utter folly. This all struck her as hopelessly adolescent and foolish, derivative of comic books and bad movies. Storming the bad guy's fortress, guns blazing. She thought of the contempt she'd had for the people at Roundtree's party, the inauthenticity of their every gesture and word, their lives as pop culture pantomime. She wondered if she'd fallen into the same trap.

But then, try as she might, she couldn't think of any alternative. Not one, at least, that would so perfectly address her various needs for revenge, redress, confrontation, and victory. She desperately wanted to win out over these philistines, these vulgar schemers, these capitalists. These men. Maybe she was no better than they were, when it came right down to it. *Okay. I can live with that,* she thought.

A movement caught her eye, and she swung the binoculars around. Smoke had begun to rise from the smokestack of the main building. Alice watched it billow and dissipate. Something about it seemed sinister to her, although maybe, she thought, she had just done too much dust. The smoke could only be produced by two things: either they were back to business as usual, in which case they would be distracted, or they were disposing of evidence. She couldn't wait any longer.

Alice stood and began trotting toward the compound, her duffel slung over her shoulder. As she jogged, she repeated in her mind the names Missy, Kim, and Rachel. That was why she was here. Missy, Kim, Rachel. Halfway to the fence, she became violently afraid and had to stop and do several more bumps of dust.

At the fence she scanned the compound with her binoculars to make sure there were no cameras mounted up high and checked the ground perimeter for anything resembling motion sensors. Then she withdrew a pair of bolt cutters from the duffel. In thirty seconds she'd clipped herself a hole big enough to duck through. She'd come in so that the mobile office blocked her from the view of anyone in the main building, and she walked over and chinned up to one of the windows of the trailer. Inside was a small desk and many file cabinets, the drawers of which had been thrown open and emptied. A few stray papers lay on the floor, but that was all.

"Shit," Alice muttered.

She peered around the side of the trailer. Across from her, a windowless metal door was set into the side of the main building. Shading her eyes with one hand, she checked the eaves and corners of the building for surveillance cameras, but there were none she could see. She walked across the pavement, her heart pounding, and tried the door. It was locked. Well, she thought, it couldn't be that easy.

She walked the perimeter of the building. There were no windows on the ground floor, and only one other roll-up door, which was also locked. When she'd gone all the way around, back to the first door, she stood there for a moment, thinking. Why hadn't she brought lock picks? Well, because she didn't know how to pick locks, for one. With great trepidation, she withdrew the shotgun, a double-barreled twelve-gauge she'd bought earlier that day. She broke it open as the sullen clerk had shown her, confirmed that it was loaded, and closed it. She raised it to her waist and trained it at the lock of the door. It was a solid steel door; she didn't really know if the shotgun would be powerful enough to destroy the lock. She didn't know much about shotguns, or steel, or locks. At this distance, who's to say the shot wouldn't rebound and hit her? She lowered the gun.

After a moment, she raised one fist, hesitated, and then rapped twice on the door. From inside she heard a rustling, and then someone pushed the door open. It was a gangly blond kid with a goiter-like Adam's apple, wearing a bright-yellow rubber biohazard suit and carrying two large document boxes. He looked at her with hostile curiosity.

"Can I help you?" he said.

Alice swung the shotgun up from behind the door and set the ends of the barrels under his chin. "Step back," she said.

He did so, and she stepped inside, letting the door close quietly behind her. They were in a small fluorescent-lit anteroom with a linoleum floor and a tin ceiling. The kid was looking at her with a sort of pity now.

"You're too late," he said.

A tremble went through Alice. "What's that supposed to mean?"

"If you're here to rip us off. All the product is burning up right now. All the precursors, everything." He started to put the boxes down, but Alice gave him a tap on the chin with the shotgun.

"You're fine just like that," she said. "Where's Hicks?"

"In the rubbish room."

"How many of you are here?"

"Just me, Hicks, and Kev."

"Who's Kev?"

"My little brother," the kid said. He looked about nineteen, so she couldn't imagine how young his little brother might be. The kid looked right down the barrels of her shotgun and swallowed. "You gonna kill us?"

"Don't be stupid," Alice said. The kid relaxed visibly. "You have a woman here too, don't you? Name of Rachel?"

"Yeah," the kid said. "She's with Kev and Hicks."

Alice felt a thrill of relief. "Okay, good. What's with the suit?"

"The smoke from the burning product. It'll kill you quick, you breathe it in."

Alice considered this. This could work. "Here's what you're gonna do," she said. "I want you to put those boxes down, real slow, and then take that suit off. Don't try anything, or I'll give you a barrel in the kneecap."

As the kid followed her directions, she stooped and, with one hand, withdrew a zip tie from her duffel. Once the kid had taken off his biohazard suit, she waved the shotgun at him. "Turn around and cross your wrists behind your back."

He did so, and as she tightened the zip tie around his wrists, she saw that he was trembling. Without the bulk of the suit, he was just a string bean of a kid, maybe a hundred pounds soaking wet. Probably just a couple years out of high school. She put her mouth next to his ear. "Don't worry, I'm not going to hurt you or your brother. I'm here for Hicks and the woman, that's all."

He cocked his head to talk back over his shoulder. "You know, he's some kinda military badass. You best be careful."

"I know," Alice said. "I'm not here to talk to him. He killed my friend. I'm here to kill him. Minute I see his face, he's getting both barrels."

. The kid didn't say anything, just nodded. Then he said, "Good luck," and sat on the floor, his bound arms protruding awkwardly to the side. She couldn't tell if he'd meant it as a sincere wish or a warning.

Alice walked down the winding corridors of the building, the bulky latex suit swishing audibly as she went, and the visor already fogged half over from her breath, narrowing down an already-narrow field of vision. She had the shotgun held down along the side of her body. Before she'd left the kid, she'd done the rest of the dust she'd brought, and she felt supercharged and profoundly restless, ready to jump out of her own skin.

She rounded a corner and saw, through the small Plexiglas portholes set into a pair of double doors, flashes of orange: men in biohazard suits. She backed up to gather herself. Missy, Kim, Rachel. Then she came around the corner again and walked calmly toward the doors.

As she drew closer, she saw that the two men inside worked frantically, tossing plastic-bagged bricks of powder and boxes of papers into a massive smoldering pile of trash that was burning in a sunken concrete dock. High above, a row of ventilation fans whirred, but the room was still thick with smoke. Even from the hall, the joined roar of the flames and the fans was deafening.

The problem was that in their identical suits, Alice couldn't tell which one was Hicks. She hadn't been acting tough when she told the kid that she was here to kill Hicks, not talk to him. She had every intention of shooting first, and from behind. If she had any lingering questions about the conspiracy, she'd ask them while he bled out. But now she couldn't tell who was who. She thought back to the night of Roundtree's party, when she'd first seen Hicks. His limp, his rasping voice. Neither of which helped her now. And the longer she just stood there dumbly in the window, the greater the chance that one of them would turn and see her, and poof, there would go her element of surprise.

Alice checked to make sure the hood of her suit was securely fastened, and then reversed the shotgun so she was holding it by the barrel, and pushed through the double doors. Neither man heard her over the roar of the fire. One of the men was closer to her, and praying that she would get lucky, Alice swung the wooden butt of the shotgun down across the back of his head as hard as she could. He fell bonelessly to the ground. The other man turned to look at her, and she saw that she'd chosen wrong. Hicks backed up, his hands held out, his face showing a complete lack of fear. Alice reversed the shotgun to put the trigger under her finger.

"You're too late!" Hicks shouted in his sandpaper rasp.

"I'm not here to rip you off," Alice said. "Where's Rachel?"

"I know what you're here for," he said. He gestured at the burn pile with one hand. Alice backed away until they were separated by six or seven feet and then looked in the direction he'd pointed. She didn't see it at first, among the blackened papers and drifts of charred powder. Then, in an instant, it resolved itself within the clutter. A rolled-up blue tarp, already curling at the edges with small orange flames. Two pale feet protruded from one end, one foot still wearing a white rhinestone-encrusted flat. At the other end, she saw a tuft of blond hair, smeared with red.

"That's on you," Hicks said. "You should've taken the sheriff's advice. We don't make empty threats."

Alice felt her face contort, with rage or grief or pain or just pure unadulterated feeling. Just before she pulled the trigger, Hicks darted into a crouch; the shot missed him entirely. He covered the distance between them with a speed she wouldn't have thought possible, and in her surprise, she blindly fired off the second barrel. Another miss. Then he was on her. She brought the shotgun up between them, holding it with both hands, but he twisted it viciously so that the butt struck her across the face, rotating the hood of her suit and blinding her. Then he began raining blows down on her face and head. She tried to turn the hood back so that she would be able to see, but he grabbed her by a wrist and popped her elbow. Pain shot up to her shoulder, and she couldn't move her hand or wrist. He was on top of her now, riding her hips, and he struck a huge blow directly on the point of her nose that drove her head back against the concrete floor. Her vision fizzled and sparked. She could hear herself screaming now, but she had no sensation of actually screaming.

Desperate, she took in a breath and snatched her hood off with her good hand. From atop her, Hicks regarded her calmly and then punched her in the ribs. She wheezed and then drew in an involuntary breath. Her lungs burned, and at that first breath, she was higher than she'd ever been in her life. At the second, she felt her heart flutter and hitch, and she knew that in another few breaths, it would stop entirely. But she also felt the dust in every part of her body: her brain, her muscles, her hair and teeth. *I didn't know your teeth could get high,* she thought idly. But they could, and hers were. She bucked her hips, and Hicks lost his balance, and she squirmed out from under him, moving now with a manic energy that surprised even him, and as he put his hands on the ground to steady himself, she dived forward and began striking him wildly, using her incapacitated arm like a club. She saw fear in his eyes, and his fear seemed to transmute and flow into her as strength. When she surged toward him, he struck her in the chest with the flat of his hand and was able to bring one leg up to kick her in the face. But she barely felt it. She caught his leg in both arms and clung to it, refusing to let him get away. He scooted backward, and his leg came off in Alice's arms.

They both froze. Alice regarded the leg with mute horror. Then she saw Hicks's empty pant leg and looked at the bulk in her hands:

its smooth carbon-fiber contours, the steel ball joint at the knee, the elastic harness. *The military,* she thought. *He used to be in the military.* She took the prosthetic by the ankle and swung it with all her strength at Hicks's head. He'd tried to move backward, out of range, but hadn't been able to push off with just one leg, and the heavy steel knee joint caught him across the temple. He sat back, dazed, and Alice found her discarded hood and pulled it on, pressing the air filters to her mouth as she breathed.

Revitalized, she hefted the leg in her good hand and hit him again, harder. Then she hit him again, and again, and again. She wasn't sure how many times she hit him or how much time had passed, but when she stopped, the inside of his hood's visor was smeared with blood and tissue. He wasn't moving except for an occasional muscle tremor.

With her foot, she worked off Hicks's hood. His face was a ruin, his nose caved in, his eyes swollen shut. He'd bitten through his lower lip, and as Alice looked on, a bubble of bloody saliva swelled over his mouth and then popped. She knelt next to his head and slapped him once, roughly. He moaned.

"Kim, the woman in the Bobcat," Alice said. Her throat had been burned by the smoke, and her voice sounded much like Hicks's. "The one you killed with my gun. Did you kill her yourself?"

Hicks coughed and then nodded. "Orders. From Whitehurst."

"She was pregnant, you son of a bitch."

Hicks coughed again, and she saw inside the ruin of his mouth. "I know," he whispered.

Alice thought about going back to her duffel and getting more shells for the shotgun, but instead she dragged his body to the lip of the concrete dock and kicked him over into the burning waste. He landed without a sound. With her eyes, she found the tarp wrapping Rachel's body, but it was burning in earnest now and had shriveled to slag. She sagged with a sudden light-headedness, threw Hicks's prosthetic leg into the fire, picked up her shotgun, and went out.

CHAPTER 33

Halfway to Whitehurst's house, Alice had to stop because she thought she might be dying. Not in the overarching existential sense in which we're all dying, second by second, but in the sense that she was pretty sure her heart was stopping. She braked the truck to a halt in the middle of a desolate prairie—she'd taken a pickup from Hicks's compound; no sense traveling by road and risking arrest if she could go overland—and rested her head on the steering wheel, massaging her upper chest with her good hand. Too much dust.

She could feel the muscle of her heart seizing and spasming. The pain was huge, overwhelming—and for a moment she seemed to leave her body. Then she came back. She bent to the floorboards and rummaged through the trash there. She found a half package of crackers, stale and filthy, and ate them with furtive rodent-like movements.

As she ate she thought about what she'd done. She was still very high, and everything that had happened at Hicks's compound seemed like something someone else had done, something Alice had heard about or watched on television, reenacted badly on a true-crime show. When her mind tried to touch on anything outside the present moment, her thoughts became mired and befogged, and she wondered if that fog would ever clear or if her brain had been permanently scarred by the dust she'd breathed in at Hicks's compound.

Night fell as Alice drove on. She had to make a wide detour around a fracking operation, but she knew from her phone that she was getting closer to Whitehurst's home. Rocks hammered the undercarriage of the truck as she sped over the uneven ground, and as she picked up speed, the space around the truck seemed to bend and warp until it enclosed the vehicle in a tunnel of light. Alice had the distinct feeling that if she took her hands off the wheel, the truck would continue along this predetermined path by itself. She felt like a bullet in the barrel of a gun, which was appropriate, considering her intentions. She looked at herself in the rearview, and a bruised, bloody, wild-eyed harridan looked back at her. A tooth knocked out—when had that happened?—hair matted with blood, some hers, some not hers. Barely human.

As she floored it, her eyes drifted upward to the rising moon, and she saw that it was rendered there in a delicate lavender tone. Watercolor moon, purple moon. She wasn't surprised.

Whitehurst's Prius was parked in the drive when Alice skidded to a halt there, blocking him in. She leaped from the cab of the truck, shotgun in hand, and went right through the front door. The first person she encountered was a maid, an elderly white-haired woman wiping down one of the floor-length mirrors in the entryway, who took one look at Alice and then screamed. She turned to flee, but Alice caught her by the hair and pulled her to the marble floor.

"Where's Whitehurst?" Alice asked, her voice low and abraded.

"He doesn't keep any money in the house!" the maid said. She'd gone completely limp in Alice's grip. A prey response.

"I'm not here for money," Alice said. "Where is he?"

The maid pointed to one of the picture windows. "The caves," she said. "He's mapping the caves under the Devil's Pike."

Alice looked out at the distant rock formation looming against the horizon. She quickly zip-tied the maid's hands to a wrought-iron railing and jogged back to the pickup.

A rutted dirt track led from Whitehurst's manse to Devil's Pike. The country here was pure badland, where not even the tough prairie grass could survive, and as Alice sped across the emptiness, lit up eerily in purple, she felt she'd traveled to another world. She was still extremely high. Her heart tremors had lessened, but her body was afire with a manic energy so intense it almost read as pain, and as she drove, her hands hammered out a rhythm on the steering wheel and her feet danced over the pedals.

At the base of the rock formation was a panel truck, the rear door open to reveal a computer workstation. Whitehurst's executive assistant, Tamara, the blond from the party, was sitting at the workstation talking into a headset. When she heard Alice's truck approaching, she stopped talking and turned to look. Alice drove right up behind the truck and leaped from the driver's side, shotgun in hand.

"Take that headset off right now," she said.

The assistant began to talk in a high-pitched patter; Alice could make out the words *gun, killer, PI*. She leaped up into the truck and struck Tamara across the face with the butt of the shotgun, cutting her off in midsentence. The headset flew off her head, and she fell to the floor of the truck, unconscious. Alice could see that her jaw was broken, and a trickle of blood was coming from her ear. She hadn't meant to strike her that hard, and she felt a sensation that she knew would later be guilt. She picked up the headset from where it had landed and put it on, hearing nothing but a muted hiss, like the run of water through pipes.

"Whitehurst," she said.

Silence, and then the sound of a man clearing his throat. "What do you want?"

"You know what I want."

"I don't have any idea," Whitehurst said with a breeziness Alice found unconvincing. "Money? I have ten thousand in a safe back at the house. But how do I know you'll let me go after I pay you off?"

"Fuck your money," Alice said. "You know exactly why I'm here. I'm here because you had Kim Holywhitemountain killed, to frame me. Just like you had Missy killed to get Robert Wilcox out of the way. Not to mention all the other lives you ruined. Saturating the town with dust so you could buy up all the land for pennies on the dollar."

"You're not making any sense," Whitehurst said.

"I just came from Hicks's compound."

A long silence. "You saw Hicks?"

"I beat him within an inch of his life with his own fake leg. Then we had an enlightening little talk. He was still breathing when I dumped him into the incinerator." Alice let out a ghoulish little chuckle that was part sob. "You ordered Rachel Wilcox's execution too, didn't you?"

The line abruptly went dead. Alice took off the headset and set it on the desk. On three mounted computer screens was a 3-D rendering of the winding subterranean caverns below her. A blue glowing beacon marked Whitehurst's location, deep in the earth, at the end of a long, tapering passage. Alice bent close and studied the map; as far as she could tell, there were no other ways in or out. She photographed the map with her phone. Then she took two headlamps, a canteen, a handful of flares, and a coil of rope from a box of caving supplies on the floor of the truck, jumped down, and made her way, under the purple moon, to the yawning black maw that was the cave entrance.

The air in the cave was musty and thin, utterly neutral; Alice wondered if this was how the earth had smelled before man. The floor of the tunnel she descended had been cleared and swept, and Whitehurst had affixed a strip of soft white LED lighting to the wall. It was almost like she was on a spelunking tour.

She descended for close to an hour, walking fast, carrying her shotgun in her good arm, sipping now and then from the canteen of water she'd taken from the truck. She thought about her old life, back in New York, and realized that, come what may, she would never return to that. A maudlin self-pity, only partially the result of the dust, swept over her. She should never have taken this job, she thought bitterly. She shouldn't have done a lot of things, but it was too late for all that now. It occurred to her once again that there was an inverse relationship between how close she'd gotten to the truth and the welfare of the people involved, herself included. In a way, it was as if they'd been sacrificed on the altar of truth, justice, and various other bullshit ideals. It was up to her now to make sure something came of it all.

The tunnel widened, and Alice emerged into a yawning cavern. When she looked upward, her headlamp was just able to illuminate the far reaches, filled with hundreds of tiny furred forms hanging upside down. A chill went through her. The walls were covered with a sprawling mural, hunters and deer and wolves and bison, each rendered in a few impressionistic finger strokes, the charcoal and ocher and red clay faded to grays and browns. The walls had a uniform dimpled texture, and she realized they had been knapped down by hand, that the entire cavern was likely man-made, the work of years. She swept the light over the figures until she came to one that caught her eye. Antler headed, rendered in a chalk white, much larger than the other figures, with shapely hips and breasts. This figure was lying on its back, bound at the wrists and ankles, its head thrown back in apparent agony, and several amorphous, fanged shapes swirled around it. Alice remembered the Native American legend Kim had told them at Whitehurst's party, about the goddess-wife White Deer, sacrificed to entice the spirits of destruction to their doom, and she wondered if this could all be blamed on evil spirits, instead of on her—she hadn't really let Hicks burn alive, had she?

Get ahold of yourself, Alice thought suddenly. Her dust high had settled from a generalized mania into delirium, which worried her. This wasn't a forgiving place in which to lose your wits.

She went on, through galleries festooned with stalactites and amphitheaters of flowstone. In one of these rooms, she saw a pool of water glinting in the far recesses, and out of curiosity she went over to see what lived in it, if anything. But when she touched the surface of the pool, her fingers came away covered with black and viscous oil.

And then, something utterly unexpected: the LED lighting ended. Ahead was a darkness more profound than she'd thought possible. This, Alice supposed, was as far as Whitehurst had explored. She checked her crude map and saw that she'd already passed his last GPS position. He was somewhere ahead, waiting, or perhaps just fleeing headlong into the unknown. In other circumstances, in another mental state, one in which she wasn't already in a state of psychological flight from what she'd seen and done these past days, one less narrowed by dust to the twin imperatives of revenge and murder, she might have hesitated. But as it was, she plunged ahead without a second thought.

CHAPTER 34

It was different in the dark. Her already-frayed nerves became jagged and raw. Sounds—the trickle of water, or perhaps oil, the occasional far-off concussions of fracking operations—took on outsized significance. She became acutely aware of the mass of earth above her, pressing down like the weight of history, just a hair away from crushing her. She was sorely tempted to pop one of the flares from her supplies bag, but she didn't know how far she had to go and couldn't risk waste. It occurred to her that she might have to turn back.

A familiar smell floated toward her, so out of place that at first she thought it was a trick of the brain. Sweet, singed. Whitehurst, somewhere ahead of her, his flight fueled by dust. Well, it was only fair. She was high too.

"Whitehurst!" Alice shouted. Echoes whanged off the rock walls. "I'm coming for you!"

She didn't know why she'd shouted it. Just the whim of a moment. It was more to prop up her flagging courage than to scare him. She wished she had some dust to smoke, but she hadn't thought to save any.

After a while, the tunnel began to widen and then, suddenly, came to a plunging drop-off. Alice leaned carefully out over the edge to look, but the light of her headlamp petered out in the void. Had she missed some turnoff in the dark? Had Whitehurst somehow gotten around her and back to the surface?

She took a flare out of her bag of supplies, broke it open, and tossed it over the edge. It floated down, painting the cavern bloodred. A hundred yards down, Alice caught a flash of a figure braced against the sheer wall, looking upward, before the flare passed and returned the figure to darkness. The sight of Whitehurst reawakened an anger that had been dulled by her long walk in the dark, and her blood leaped. She walked quickly along the rim of the drop-off, her headlamp trained downward, until she found his rope. It was nearly the same color as the rock floor, lashed to an outcropping and pulled tight through the scree. She briefly wondered if she'd be satisfied by cutting his rope, letting him fall to his death, and returning to the surface. No, she quickly decided. She wouldn't find that satisfying at all.

She'd never rappelled, but how hard could it be? She watched the rope shimmy against the rock as Whitehurst slid downward by increments. Finally it fell still. She looked over the edge and saw the flare dying far below, the circle of light it cast no bigger than her thumbnail.

Alice used the coil of rope she'd brought with her to lash the shotgun to her body, crouched, took the dangling rope in both hands, and gingerly lowered herself over the drop. There was no way to descend without letting the rope slide through her hands, and soon her palms were blistered and red, but she didn't feel it. She was thinking of Whitehurst, cowering below, and the thought gave her immense pleasure. Let him see what it was like.

She found the sensation of being suspended in open air far preferable to being in the claustrophobic tunnels, and she was disappointed when her feet touched the pebbly ground. She clicked her headlamp on and looked at her hands. They were slick with blood. She swept the headlamp around her, but the light was too weak to reach any of the walls. After a moment, she rummaged through her bag and brought out another flare and broke it in half. The chamber lit up red, and she saw three tunnels before her, one of them quite large, and another as tall as a man, and the third as small as a burrow. She considered these three options for a moment and then, on an impulse, looked behind her.

Whitehurst was crouched against the cliff face, arms clutching his knees, looking at her from the corner of his eye.

"Ah," he said softly. "I almost had you there."

Alice wondered why he hadn't attacked her while her back was turned, crushed her skull with one of the large rocks lying around, but then she realized that he'd meant to wait until she passed, climb back up, and cut the rope. He stood but stayed where he was against the cliff wall. How frail he looked. Cut off from his wealth, his estate, his adulators and enviers and hangers-on, his traditions, and the town itself, he was just a man. She wondered if he knew that.

"Well," he said uncertainly. He started to smile at her, but the smile died when he saw Alice's face. "I suppose you want an explanation."

"Nope," Alice said. "I figured it all out myself."

"Fine," he said. "Kill me. You'll be killing this town too. You're here to punish me for what I've done, but you should recognize the greater good. The big picture. You can surely see that I'm doing necessary work. You of all people."

Alice flinched. "What's that supposed to mean?"

"Don't be a fucking hypocrite." She saw a flash of the Whitehurst she knew was there, impatient, demanding. "You know the ends justify the means. Or you used to. Maybe you've forgotten."

Ah. The Altoona Crawley affair. "No," Alice said. "That was a mistake."

"Why, because you failed? No. You were absolutely right to do what you did."

"I don't subscribe to ideas like *absolutely right* anymore."

Whitehurst scoffed. "There's a higher authority than *the rules*." He made vicious air quotes when he said these last two words.

"I don't disagree," Alice said. "But it's not you."

She thought she'd scored a conclusive point, but Whitehurst was ready with an immediate riposte. "The higher authority belongs to anyone with the guts to seize it. You had it once. Then you lost your nerve."

Alice started to tell him the rest of the Crawley story, the part she'd never told anyone, but then stopped. *Let him die in ignorance,* she thought.

"I buried my friend today," she said. "We had an argument, and we hadn't made up yet. You killed her before we could. I'm going to have to live with that."

Whitehurst spread his hands in a gesture of mollification. "I'm sorry about that. I truly am. But there's a price to pay for everything. That's what all the stories are about, the spirits under the earth, the purple moon, dust being fracking fluid. The Indian warriors possessed by death. People always turn everything into a fucking fairy tale, but you boil it down, they're all about the same thing. Consequences. Did those warriors have demons from the center of the earth inside them? Of course not. But they'd seen and done some horrible shit. Split open a soldier's head with a stone axe. That'll give anyone PTSD. Is dust fracking fluid? No. It's an analgesic amphetamine. A second-year chemistry major could make it. But people know, they sense, that it's connected to the fracking rush. Great Buffalo wants to clean up the neighborhood, he had to sacrifice his wife. Nothing good happens without a sacrifice."

"It's always the women that suffer, isn't it?"

"No. Not just women. Everyone suffers. There's a human cost is all I'm saying."

"A human cost." Alice nearly spat the words out. "What about the purple moon? You forgot to explain the purple moon."

"I don't know about that. Maybe it's true what they say, something comes up out of the earth. Or maybe it's just a trick of the light and people think that they have license, when they see it, to give in to their basest impulses."

"There's a purple moon tonight," Alice said. "I saw it before I came down here."

The implication wasn't lost on Whitehurst. "I'll say this. If a man committed murder during a purple moon, I wouldn't think that man should be absolved of consequences."

"What about a woman?" Alice said.

Whitehurst straightened his shoulders and shook his head. "You're no murderer. I think that's clear. I'm going to climb back up this rope and go home. You come out when you've cooled off. I give you my word that you won't be in any trouble, legal or otherwise. And my word is good."

Whitehurst turned and, grasping the rope in both hands, braced himself with one foot and then leaped upward, already beginning to climb. Alice leveled the shotgun and fired off one barrel just to his left. The blast was very loud in the cavern, and a backfire of rock shards stung the side of her face. She went to one knee, trying to blink away the blood that had begun to flow into her eyes. She was dimly aware of Whitehurst abandoning the rope and running past her. She turned just in time to see him go through the middle tunnel.

The pain from the shards was overpowering, and after a few steps, Alice had to stop. She touched her face and pulled a piece of rock the size and shape of a shark's tooth from her forehead, looked at it, and then cast it aside. She splashed water from the canteen into her eyes until her vision cleared, and then she went on.

The middle tunnel widened into another large gallery, but the ground beneath narrowed until it was a ledge barely two feet wide, a flat wall to the left and nothing to the right but a yawning chasm. Up ahead, Alice could see Whitehurst's headlamp bobbing along. She quickened her pace. The pain of her wounds and Whitehurst's pompous posturing had awakened her bloodlust, and she was thinking now of Kim's unseeing eyes, dead, in the motel room.

Whitehurst had stopped moving, and as Alice drew close, she saw why: the ledge had narrowed further and then disappeared, leaving him standing on the edge of a sheer drop-off. When Alice came upon him, shotgun at the ready, he was staring down, and when he heard her approach, he looked at her over his shoulder. She had to give him credit: there was no fear in his eyes.

"Whitehurst," Alice said. "You motherfu—"

He leaped out into darkness. Alice half expected him to land on the other side, on some unseen ledge, but when she reached the drop-off, she saw his headlamp spinning down, down, down, farther than she would've thought possible, and then, after what seemed like a full half minute, she heard the far-off but unmistakable sound of impact.

CHAPTER 35

Alice had thought of herself as a lucky person for most of her life. When she'd met Brandon, her ex-husband, all her friends had told her how lucky she was, and she'd believed them. He was handsome and personable and had a great job. But after she'd discovered his cheating, and they'd gone through a messy divorce, she often thought back to those early salutations of good fortune. What could, at first, seem like good luck might later reveal itself to be, in fact, quite bad luck. You could never be sure; life had a way of turning everything on its head. This relativity of luck is what Alice now thought of.

After Whitehurst had leaped to his death, Alice had trudged back to the cliff face, found the rope, and started to climb. She hadn't even gone four feet up when the rope snapped. She'd almost laughed as she sat there in the dark, the slack rope falling down around her like confetti. Maybe the sawing action of two people rappelling down it had rubbed it against a sharp outcropping, or maybe it was just a flawed rope. Ropes failed. Regardless of the reason, Alice was lucky it hadn't snapped when she was a hundred feet up the wall, sending her to plummet to a certain death. Then, almost immediately, she thought, no, it was actually quite bad luck, as she was now left to starve to death, alone in the dark.

She sat on the stone floor and cried. Her tears were hot and slick on her face, and she was ashamed of them, but she couldn't stop. When she'd gotten it all out of her system, she wiped her face and then took stock of her supplies. She had her headlamp, which would last, she figured, up to ten, twelve hours, and one spare. She had her own phone and the phone she'd taken from Tamara, Whitehurst's assistant. They could be used as flashlights when her other options failed. She had one more flare, a coil of rope, and half a canteen of water. Oh, and she still had one barrel of the shotgun. There would be no slow death for her; if she couldn't find a way out, she would end it herself. She thought, with bleak irony, that she hoped she would be able to do it with as much resolve as Whitehurst had. The thought of suicide buoyed her spirits, and she stood and went on, taking the large tunnel first.

This tunnel went steadily down, but what choice did she have? At times she had to scoot on her butt down a steep slope, the rattle of loose rocks preceding her into the dark, and she braced for a sudden drop-off. This went on for hours. She marked the time by the gradual dimming of her headlamp. After a while she came to another chamber, half of which was covered in a pool of water, utterly still on the surface but filled with darting shapes. Alice knelt at the edge of the pool and drank the cool, coppery water. Her headlamp illuminated dozens of tiny translucent fish, eyeless from untold years underground and utterly without fear of man. She was able to catch handfuls at a time, and she lay eating them alive until her stomach was full.

The dust had worn off, and she could feel herself becoming hazy and irritable with sleep deprivation. Occasionally she heard distant concussions, fracking perhaps, or the sound of tectonic plates deep in the earth.

The ground had long since leveled off, and now—at first she was convinced it was just wishful thinking, but no, it was undeniable—she was walking uphill. Hope, that contemptible worm, squirmed its way into her heart. She was breathing hard, and she drank from the canteen more often than she liked, but her hangover had left her delirious with thirst.

She'd been walking nearly half a day when she came to—something. She saw it ahead, just a ghost in the far reaches of her dimmed headlamp—what it was, she couldn't tell, but definitely not stone. It was a form that looked almost human, and in her diminished state, Alice was convinced it was the body of White Deer, bound, poisoned with centuries of hate and suffering, still somehow clinging to life. She had a sudden vision of herself crouched over the goddess and feeding on her flesh, choking it down as the deer woman struggled, helpless.

But it was just Whitehurst's body. Alice's spell of delirium passed as understanding dawned, and she glanced up, in the direction from which he'd come. His shoes had been flung off, but somehow he was still wearing his glasses. His limbs were twisted, and the top of his head had burst open, but his face was intact, his eyes oriented slightly upward in a vaguely quizzical expression. Alice settled on the cold stone beside him and slept.

She may have woken in the night, but the darkness was so absolute when she opened her eyes that it was hard to say if she was conscious or still asleep, and because of this, she wasn't sure, at first, if what happened in her mind was a dream or a memory.

But no, Rachel was there with her, and Alice recognized where they were: the Texas State Penitentiary. The day of Altoona Crawley's execution by lethal injection. This was memory, locked away, shameful, untold, and, some part of Alice thought, never to be told.

They had flown from Washington to Houston and driven an hour north to the prison in Huntsville where condemned men were executed. This was after they'd both lost their jobs; they had nothing better to do. She and Rachel both felt partly responsible for Crawley's situation. Not wholly responsible—they weren't the ones putting the needle in.

But partly. They'd had a chance, a good chance, to free him, and they'd failed.

Inmates weren't supposed to receive visitors from anyone except the chaplain and their attorney on the day of execution, but by this time, even the kid's attorney had abandoned him, and Rachel had been able to convince the guards that they were his pro bono lawyers. It wasn't so much her argument that won them admittance as it was the guards' indifference. There was a distinct feeling of festivity among them that day, which Alice found repugnant.

She and Rachel sat in folding chairs on one side of a hazy Plexiglas window. After a minute, two guards brought Crawley in, manacled at the wrists and ankles. He sat across from them and looked from Rachel to Alice and then, as if it was a tremendous annoyance, picked up the telephone receiver on his side. Alice did the same, tilting toward Rachel so they could both listen at the earpiece.

"Altoona," Alice said. She stopped, her voice choked with emotion, and under the counter she felt Rachel give her leg a supportive squeeze. "I'm sorry. We did all we could. We almost got you out, but it went bad there at the very last."

Crawley looked at them both, the telephone clutched awkwardly in his manacled hands. In his eyes there was a twinkle of bemusement, but mostly there was hate, a hate that stunned her in its intensity. He shook his head. "I killed them women. All of 'em. And if you'd got me out, I woulda killed more."

Then he hung up the phone and rose to be escorted back to his cell. By the time the State of Texas carried out his death sentence, six hours later, Alice and Rachel were already on a plane back to DC. They hadn't spoken on the car ride back to Houston, and they hadn't spoken on the plane, and in fact, they didn't speak again at all until the day Rachel had showed up, unannounced, at Alice's apartment in Brooklyn to beg her to save her husband's life.

CHAPTER 36

When Alice awoke from her half slumber in the dark, she was deathly thirsty. Remembering that she would pass the pool with the blind fish again as she backtracked, she drank her entire canteen. Whitehurst's body had begun to smell even in the chill of the cave, and Alice was glad to be leaving it. She shined her headlamp down at him before she set out, whether out of sentiment or just to see another human face again before she died, but mice or insects had been at his eyes, and there was nothing in his face that she could draw comfort from.

She walked all day, checking the time on her phones. She was weak now and made bad time. At the pool, she drank and ate the small, cold, raw fish and then napped and did it again. She should've felt revived, but it had the opposite effect, and by the time she reached the pile of rope at the base of the cliff from which she'd started out, she was just about exhausted: of energy, of hope, of the will to live. She pondered the shotgun for a long while, slumped against the wall, thinking of her life and all that it might amount to. Finally, she went to the third and smallest tunnel.

This tunnel was so small that she had to crouch just to enter, and she could see that it became smaller farther on. For all she knew, it ended just beyond the reach of her headlamp. It was this thought more than any other, certainly more than courage, which enabled her to crawl into the tiny claustrophobic tunnel: *What's ten more feet, it'll probably end completely in another twenty.*

Soon she was scooting along on her stomach. She did this for a very long time. At moments she could feel the rock against her back as she squirmed through a gap of mere inches. She came to a puddle and lay there with her face in it, drinking the muddy water until it was gone. In the depression left behind was a single pearlescent stone, and she picked it up and marveled at its perfection, that she was the only human being who'd ever laid eyes on it.

Her headlamp failed completely soon after that. She scooted forward in the dark, holding up a phone ahead of her each time she rested. When she turned it on, she caught a glimpse of her face in it, bloody, smeared with mud, gaunt. She looked crazed. She was, she realized, crazed. With fear, and hunger, and desperation. She crawled on.

After a while she heard something—something new. A far-off rattling that grew and grew, and Alice was sure there was something rushing toward her in the small tunnel. She braced. In an instant she was buffeted against the lobed rock walls by a tremor that passed through the earth all around her, shaking her as she wept and cursed, at what she didn't know.

After the tremor, Alice spoke, just to hear the sound of her own voice. The words came out: "Rachel, Missy, Kim." She crawled on. Hours passed without thought. Finally, the tunnel widened until she could go along at a stooped stagger, her stiff legs shaking in the cold. And then it widened still more, until Alice was walking along just a wall, with no ceiling or opposite wall visible, moving through a huge unseen cavern. She felt no hope, no relief, only a grim resignation, a desire to get it over with already. Whatever it might be.

And then, up ahead. A gem, or a coin—no, a spot of light, no bigger than a dime, unmistakable in that darkness. Alice let it fall upon her palm and sat like that for a long time, feeling the warmth of it. Then she searched until she found the light's source. It was slanting through a tiny channel in the wall, and when she pressed her ear to it, she heard a distant roar. It could've been waves, or traffic, or just the wind. It was the world, it was everything.

She ran her hands over the wall and felt something moist and crumbly between the stones. Soil. She began to scrape it out of its channels with her fingernails until she could wiggle the stone in front of her. Eventually, with a supreme effort, she was able to pry the stone out of its nook. She went at this for hours, scraping and digging and prying. She'd gone two or three feet toward the light when she absolutely couldn't go on anymore. She lay down and slept again. She awoke once and, not seeing the spot of light, panicked, thinking she'd wandered in her sleep, but then she realized it was nighttime. She found the hollow she'd dug out in the wall and went back to digging.

She couldn't see the sun itself, of course, but as she dug, she watched that pinpoint of light emerge from the dark, first gray and then blue and then yellow and then white. It was the most beautiful sunrise she'd ever seen. After half a day of digging and resting, she was so close to the light that she could see her hands as they picked away at the earth, bloodied, the fingernails torn and bent backward. The distant roar had sharpened into the unmistakable sound of traffic. And then, a sudden inward collapse of earth and rocks as something gave way, and with one more desperate scrabble, Alice emerged, wide-eyed and unbelieving, into daylight.

She was behind a gas station, painted gaily in red and green and yellow, and beyond that was the familiar sight of the highway. Already, the squeegee boys in the parking lot had seen her emerge from the earth, and some ran for the gas station while the rest came over the trash-strewn grass toward her. Alice fell to her knees and then onto her stomach. She heard them talking around her as she lay there, and then she felt many hands on her as they lifted her up and carried her. She let herself be taken along, and when she opened her eyes, she saw, inverted, a legless man on a wheeled board, her ankle propped in one of his hands as he helped carry her along. He saw her looking at him and gave her an uncertain smile, and she let herself cry then, not tears of joy, but of grief, because she'd survived.

EPILOGUE

Three Years Later

Alice sat in the visitation room of the South Dakota State Penitentiary, waiting to see Robert Wilcox. He was late, but Alice wasn't impatient. She'd gotten much better at waiting.

"There he is," said Gail from where she stood leaning against the wall. She jutted her chin at the metal table, her thumbs hooked over her gun belt. "You go 'head. I'll hang back in case he tries something."

The guards were supposed to stand tableside for every visit, to prevent the passing of contraband, but Alice was known as a good inmate and had arranged, with many bribes and extra shifts on her work detail, for her visit with Robert to be private. She figured they had a lot of things to say to each other, and some of them could be damaging for her if they reached the wrong ears.

"He's harmless, Gail," Alice said. "Look at him."

And he did look utterly harmless; he'd put on weight since the business in Whitehurst, and his hair had started to go, giving his face a comical, oblong shape. When he saw Alice and the guard looking at him, he blushed, and Alice thought he looked just like an eggplant. She waved at Robert and then stood up.

"You never know," Gail said.

Alice rolled her eyes and then went over and sat at the table. Robert stood uncertainly until Alice gestured at his chair.

"I brought these for you," he said as he sat down. He put a carton of Marlboro reds on the table, then a pack of Oreos. "Can I slide them over to you or . . . ?"

"Just leave them there," Alice said. "I'll take them when I go."

He folded his hands on the table in front of him, heaved a sigh, and then cleared his throat. "I'm sorry I haven't visited before," he said finally.

"It's okay," Alice said. "You don't owe me anything."

Robert showed a pained grimace. "That's the thing, though. I do."

"What I did, I did of my own free will. If some good came from that, well, I'm happy about that. But you don't owe me anything."

Robert looked at her sidelong, and she realized, after a moment, that he couldn't tell if she was serious or if she was making fun of him. "Jesus," he said. "Prison's made you philosophical." When she didn't reply, he hurried on. "You been keeping up with all that stuff that's been happening in Whitehurst?"

"No," Alice said.

"Yeah, well, I still get work up there. Now that Whitehurst is gone and his company's broken up, all the other corporations have come in. Wow, you thought that town was bad back then? You should see it now. They've widened the highway to four lanes, and it's still packed around the clock. But the new workers they've brought in, they stay in these big old camps they've built outside town. Man camps, they call them. Got mess halls and bunks and leisure centers right inside the fence so they never have to go outside the wire except to the airport when their stint is up. All the bars and motels and restaurants have gone out of business. That sheriff, he lost his job thanks to those papers you had your lawyer send out, but I still see him around up there. I guess he started a private security company, guard all them man camps from the locals or the terrorists or environmentalists or whoever he's selling as the latest menace. Doing pretty well for himself, by the look of it."

Alice nodded. She actually had been keeping up with the developments in Whitehurst; she just hadn't wanted to discuss them with Robert. "What do you want to talk about with me?" she asked.

Robert leaned forward and started to whisper, but Alice quickly cut him off. "Relax," she said. "Acting like you're telling secrets draws attention. Just speak normally."

He cleared his throat and sat up. "They never found Rachel's body," he said. "I know it's not possible, but sometimes I catch myself thinking she might still be out there somewhere. Did you ever see . . . ?" He trailed off, looking at Alice with pleading eyes.

"I saw her, right after they killed her. In the factory that burned to the ground. I don't think she suffered."

Robert nodded. "The man that did it . . ."

"He suffered," Alice said flatly. "He got what he deserved, and then some."

Robert looked at her in open fear. "Christ," he said. "They never found any bodies in that factory. Burned too hot."

"I know."

"What about Kim?"

"They shot her in the back. I doubt she saw it coming, or felt a thing." Alice fought an urge to look over her shoulder to make sure none of the guards had crept into earshot. "I buried her on the prairie."

Robert looked at the ceiling and released a long, hissing breath. "I figured it was something like that. They found all that blood in the motel room, but that was it. You ever think about her?"

"Every day."

"Me too." A baby wailed at the next table, and they both turned to look at it for a moment, grateful for the distraction. "You know, they still send search parties down in them caves, looking for big shot Whitehurst. But they say that some tremors collapsed the tunnels, buried him down there. Now there's rumors that he faked his own death and he's living high on the hog somewhere. South America, somewhere."

"He's dead," Alice said. "I saw his body." She thought about how, in her delirium, she'd taken his body for the dead goddess and had seen herself surging ahead to eat it. "He jumped off a cliff rather than accept what was coming to him. He died a clean death. But what the fuck does that really mean? He's dead. The official story about how I lost him down there after a long chase, that was just something my lawyer told me to say."

Robert rubbed his chin and narrowed his eyes at her. "Wait, so if all these bodies are disappeared, what do they have you in here for?"

"The woman outside the caves," Alice said. Her therapist had told her that she must say the victim's name when she talked about her crime, to put a human face on the incident, so she closed her eyes and did. "Tamara Burke. Whitehurst's assistant. She's paralyzed now, because of me. Aggravated assault. That's five years in this state. Might be four with good behavior."

She watched Robert's face as he did the calculation; his eyes widened slightly. "You know, the thing that keeps me up at night is how pointless it all was. I didn't even see their dust factory. Sure, I drove out there, but I barely got out of the car. Between constant phone check-ins with my wife, the late nights with Kim, and the drinking, I didn't have anything left for the job. I was just rubber-stamping those work orders."

"They didn't know that," Alice said. "And they couldn't take the risk. Besides, it wasn't pointless at all. We stopped Whitehurst from ruining more lives. And we got you out of jail, got your life back."

Robert looked pained. "Not much of a life," he said.

Alice had to count to three before she spoke, to tamp down her irritation. "Then join a book club, Robert. Try online dating. Make some friends. I'm in prison, what's your excuse?"

"That's not what I meant." He suddenly looked apologetic, almost sheepish. "I have liver cancer. The doctors say I have eighteen months, maybe two years."

Alice was struck with a pang of remorse so sharp it took her breath away. "I'm so sorry," she said. "I didn't know."

"You don't have to apologize. That's one of the main reasons I came today. I'm starting chemo next week and I might be bedridden for a while. A lot of people who spent time in Whitehurst are coming down with rare cancers, you know. After the company dissolved and all their cronies cycled out of the local government, they started doing real testing on the soil and water. Turns out that environmentally friendly fracking fluid they were always talking about might not have been so safe after all. You should get screened."

Another thing to worry about. She suddenly had the distinct feeling that Robert was a contagion, that he'd brought in with him all the problems and worries of her past, of the outside world, and transmitted them to her. She wondered if this was what it felt like when addicts relapsed.

Robert took his phone out, swiped it to life, and rotated it to show her a photo of a curly-haired girl on a pink bicycle. "That's Lydia." He turned the phone and looked at the photo himself, beaming. "She's the other reason I came up here. When she's older, she's going to have a lot of questions about her mom and everything that happened. And if I don't beat this cancer, she's going to need—not a mom, I wouldn't put that on you—but some adults in her life. I don't mean financially, I put the life insurance money from Rachel in a trust for Lydia, but just . . . there for her. So she has someone to talk to, to go to when she has questions about life stuff. And you know, Rachel's parents are gone, and she was an only child, so when I'm gone, you'll be her only connection to her mom. I know this is a lot to put on you all at once. You can think about it and get back to me."

Alice surprised herself. "I'll do it," she said. She opened her mouth to say more, then closed it. She'd almost said, "That would be good for me," but she didn't like the way it sounded, what it implied. "I'd like that," she said simply.

Robert looked furtive suddenly, and she wondered if she'd been deceived. "Here's the thing," he said. "I thought—I hoped—that you might say that. But I didn't want to ambush you. Lydia's in the waiting room with the nanny. Would it be all right if I brought her in?"

Her first instinct was to say no, that she wasn't prepared for that conversation. Then she asked herself what she had to fear from a five-year-old girl. Her fear, she realized, was a fear of disappointing Lydia, and the most crushing disappointment for the girl would be if Alice sent her home without seeing her. Alice felt a tiny flare of resentment toward Robert, but quickly calmed herself.

"Sure, bring her in," she said.

Robert rose from his chair, walked out of the visitation room. Alice heard Gail walk up behind.

"All done?" Gail asked.

"Not yet, actually. He's bringing in his daughter to see me. Her mother is dead now. She was my friend."

Gail sighed. "You know all guests are supposed to be cleared twenty-four hours before the visit."

"I know. I'll understand if you veto."

Gail looked at her for a long moment. "I can backdate the log. You owe me, though."

Alice gave her a wan smile. "I know." She waved a hand at the carton of cigarettes Robert had brought her. "You want a pack of reds?"

"You know I don't smoke them cancer sticks," Gail said. She returned to her spot against the wall. Alice looked toward the door and saw Robert coming back in; behind him followed the girl from the photo. Alice sat up straighter and forced herself to smile. Robert stopped ten feet from the table, turned, and spoke to the girl. She looked up at him and then walked forward alone. As she climbed into the chair, Alice marveled at her resemblance to Rachel. She had the same unruly hair, the same determined set to her mouth, the same long eyelashes.

"Hello," Lydia said. "I'm Lydia."

"I know," Alice said. "Pleased to meet you. I'm Alice."

"I know," Lydia said. She looked around the visitation room and smoothed her hair back with one small hand. "Do you live here?"

"Yes," Alice said. "Sort of, yes."

"Is it like day camp?"

"Yeah. Except they won't let me leave."

"I went to a day camp like that. They wouldn't let me leave, so I pretended to be sick and they called my dad to come get me."

Alice laughed and then noticed Lydia looking her over closely.

"Why are you crying?" Lydia asked.

Alice brought one hand up to her face, and it came away wet. She hadn't even realized she was crying. "It's not because I'm sad," she said. "You just look so much like a friend of mine."

"My mom?" Lydia asked.

"Yes, your mom." Alice swallowed. "What do you know about your mom?"

"She's dead," Lydia said. She stated it as a fact that had no connection to her, like the weather or a state capital. Alice realized the girl probably had no memories of her mother at all, and she understood for the first time what Robert meant by Alice being one of Lydia's only connections to her mother.

"That's right," Alice said. She noticed, with her investigator's eye, that the little girl's navy-blue sweater had fine white hairs clinging to it. "What's your cat's name?"

Lydia brightened. "How'd you know I have a cat?"

"I can always spot a cat person. Your mom was a cat person too. Did you know that?"

Lydia shook her head, her hair swirling.

"Would you like to hear a story about your mom and a cat?"

"Yeah." Lydia leaned forward and propped her chin in both hands.

"Well, this was when we both lived in Washington, DC. I had a cat named Bandit who would go outside during the day. One day I came home from work and Bandit was way up in this tree in my backyard and couldn't get down. I called the fire department, but their ladder didn't go high enough. I tried climbing up there to rescue Bandit myself, but where he was, the branches were too small to support me. By this time, it was dark out, and it had started raining. Thunder and lightning and wind. You could hear Bandit meowing up on his perch. He was really scared, and so was I. I didn't know what to do, so I called your mom, and she came right over.

"She went out there into the rain and stood at the bottom of the tree, looking up. I had to watch from inside because I'd been out there so long and gotten so wet that I couldn't stop shivering. But from the window I could see she was talking to Bandit, and over the wind I could just barely hear her tone. It was calm and warm and totally unguarded. She talked like that for almost half an hour, and then Bandit jumped down one branch, and then another, and pretty soon he was in your mom's arms, and she brought him inside and we all sat by the heater with blankets wrapped around us. I always wondered what your mom said to Bandit out there that gave him the courage to come down, but I never asked. It seemed wrong to ask, like maybe it would ruin the magic, you know?"

Lydia nodded. She was completely absorbed in the story, so Alice went on talking even though there wasn't much more to tell. "Your mom was my boss. She was my friend too, but she was my boss before that. She was kind of like—you have a principal at school? She was kind of like a principal. She had to enforce the rules, be in charge. And she was really good at that. It was just her job at first, but I think that became who she was after a while. Like she could never turn that part of her off. Even after we became good friends, I almost never saw that side of her from the night when she talked Bandit out of the tree. That's why I was happy when I heard she had you, because I knew that you'd help her let that part of herself back out. I was even kind of jealous of you for that, though now I see that was dumb."

Alice broke off; she'd been talking to herself as much as to Lydia. Lydia still had her chin in her hands, but now she was looking at the tabletop, and for a moment Alice thought she'd made the girl sad. Then she realized she was just bored.

"Sorry about that," Alice said.

"It's okay," Lydia said. "You want to come meet my cat sometime?"

"Sure, I'd like that."

"When?"

"As soon as they let me leave here."

Lydia seemed to consider this. "Okay," she said.

Robert approached them then, and it took Alice a moment to realize that he and Lydia were leaving. From his awkwardness so far, she'd assumed their good-bye would be awkward and prolonged, but no, here he was, hitching his pants and reaching for Lydia's hand. Well, she thought, he was after all a man, and men generally didn't stay interested very long after they got what they came for.

"You need anything, you write or call," Robert said. Then he turned on his heel and left, a tottering middle-aged father, Lydia trailing after him.

At the door, Lydia turned and waved at Alice, and Alice waved back. As she did, she felt a tremendous burden of rage melt away. Through her court-mandated therapy sessions, the anger-management classes, the long, dark hours in her bunk, staring at the ceiling, the one thing she hadn't been able to resolve in her own mind was the fact that, in the end, she'd ruined her life for Robert. A man she'd never liked, never respected, a cheater, a coward. For a while, she'd tried to see it through the lens of a sort of noble self-abnegation, but she couldn't maintain the necessary perspective. In the end she was more heart than head, and her heart brimmed with fury at the waste of it all, of the life she had tossed away. But now she knew that she hadn't done it for Robert. She'd done it for Lydia. And that made all the difference.

Alice stood and turned to let Gail escort her back to her cell. When Gail saw her face, she reached into her back pocket and handed Alice a tissue. Alice wiped her face with it and gave Gail a smile of gratitude.

"Don't worry about it," Gail said. "You gonna be okay."

Alice laughed then with such force that several nearby tables looked over. "I was just thinking the exact same thing," Alice said.

About the Authors

Photo © 2016 Anya Ferring

Franklin Schneider studied writing at the University of Iowa. He is the author of the acclaimed memoir *Canned: How I Lost Ten Jobs in Ten Years and Learned to Love Unemployment.*

Jennifer Schneider lives and works in New York City. She has an MFA from the University of Wyoming. She writes with her brother often; this is their first published project together.